Pra
bes

Bait and Switch

"In *Bait and Switch*, Larry Brooks takes you on a smart, funny, sexy, scary ride through a minefield of betrayals in the glamorous, surreal world of the super-rich. It's a wild trip that will have you trusting no one and watching your back till the final page. Strap yourself in and enjoy!"
—Michael Prescott, author of *Next Victim*

Serpent's Dance

"AN INVIGORATING DARK TALE. . . .
Few writers of passionate suspense thrillers can provide the complexities of plot that Larry Brooks achieves. *Serpent's Dance* is an exciting tale of seductive vengeance." —Harriet Klausner

continued . . .

Pressure Points

"[AN] ADDICTIVE THRILLER. . . .
Performance seminars have long been the bane of the corporate world, yet few authors have explored them in fiction to the candid degree that Brooks does here. [He] crafts his characters with care, lending them opaque dimensions that make them appear both sympathetic and loathsome." —*Publishers Weekly*

"LARRY BROOKS HAS DONE IT AGAIN!
Pressure Points is a clever, twisted, bone-chilling tale that grabs hold and doesn't let go. Everyone's a suspect and the twists and turns keep coming until the final moment." —Danielle Girard

"LARRY BROOKS HAS WRITTEN AN EXCITING THRILLER. . . .
In *Pressure Points*, ignoring reality could mean death. . . . Mr. Brooks keeps it fresh because reality is so blurred." —*Midwest Book Review*

Darkness Bound

"Grabs you by the throat and doesn't let go. . . . It's as scary as hell." —*New York Times* bestselling author Lisa Jackson

"Teasingly erotic, [*Darkness Bound*] is that rarest of sexual thrillers, in which sex isn't gratuitous but a convincing means to an end. . . . A high-stakes game of strategy and deceit, in which the prize is life. The novel's final scenes burst with the intensity of a first-rate horror film, and it's difficult to detect a loophole in the intricate plot." —*Publishers Weekly*

"Dangerous, diabolical . . . and absolutely delicious in the creepiest way! The twists and turns gave me whiplash. A wild, thrilling ride!"
—Thom Racina, author of *Secret Weekend* and *The Madman's Diary*

"Full of surprises, *Darkness Bound* is one sneaky read." —Leslie Glass, *New York Times* bestselling author of *The Silent Bride*

"Erotic obsession, sexual betrayal and murder . . . fast-paced." —*The Oregonian*

"So believable and very frightening."
—*Midwest Book Review*

"I found myself enjoying *Darkness Bound* in the same way I'd enjoy . . . Hitchcock thrillers two generations ago." —Norm Harris, author of *Fruit of a Poisonous Tree*

BAIT AND
≫ SWITCH ≪

Larry Brooks

A SIGNET BOOK

SIGNET
Published by New American Library, a division of
Penguin Group (USA) Inc., 375 Hudson Street,
New York, New York 10014, U.S.A.
Penguin Books Ltd, 80 Strand,
London WC2R 0RL, England
Penguin Books Australia Ltd, 250 Camberwell Road,
Camberwell, Victoria 3124, Australia
Penguin Books Canada Ltd, 10 Alcorn Avenue,
Toronto, Ontario, Canada M4V 3B2
Penguin Books (NZ), cnr Airborne and Rosedale Roads,
Albany, Auckland 1310, New Zealand

Penguin Books Ltd, Registered Offices:
80 Strand, London WC2R 0RL, England

First published by Signet, an imprint of New American Library,
a division of Penguin Group (USA) Inc.

First Printing, July 2004
10 9 8 7 6 5 4 3 2 1

Copyright © Larry Brooks, 2004
All rights reserved

 REGISTERED TRADEMARK—MARCA REGISTRADA

Printed in the United States of America

Without limiting the rights under copyright reserved above, no part of this publication may be reproduced, stored in or introduced into a retrieval system, or transmitted, in any form, or by any means (electronic, mechanical, photocopying, recording, or otherwise), without the prior written permission of both the copyright owner and the above publisher of this book.

PUBLISHER'S NOTE
This is a work of fiction. Names, characters, places, and incidents either are the product of the author's imagination or are used fictitiously, and any resemblance to actual persons, living or dead, business establishments, events, or locales is entirely coincidental.

BOOKS ARE AVAILABLE AT QUANTITY DISCOUNTS WHEN USED TO PROMOTE PRODUCTS OR SERVICES. FOR INFORMATION PLEASE WRITE TO PREMIUM MARKETING DIVISION, PENGUIN GROUP (USA) INC., 375 HUDSON STREET, NEW YORK, NEW YORK 10014.

If you purchased this book without a cover you should be aware that this book is stolen property. It was reported as "unsold and destroyed" to the publisher and neither the author nor the publisher has received any payment for this "stripped book."

The scanning, uploading and distribution of this book via the Internet or via any other means without the permission of the publisher is illegal and punishable by law. Please purchase only authorized electronic editions, and do not participate in or encourage electronic piracy of copyrighted materials. Your support of the author's rights is appreciated.

To Laura and Nelson
With love and gratitude, for all of it

To my sister, Bev, our angel
God broke the mold after you

To my family
Richard, Tracy, Eric, Scott, Lynn, Kelly, Paul
and the seven munchkins
for your love and support

To Mary Alice and Anna at Cine/Lit
for your wisdom, skill and friendship

> Prologue <

All things considered, it was a great night to die. The requisite literary elements were in place—horizontal rain in the headlight beams, a deserted and utterly dark winding road, an impossibly late hour for a business meeting. And of course, motive. Without motive there would be no story. Without motive, all you had was an accident.

Funny, how four billion dollars splashes a dollop of paranoia onto the lens of one's worldview. Which was why, like a fly repeatedly slamming against the window of his otherwise quiet accountant's existence, his boss's words buzzed in his mind as he drove his Mustang through the storm to meet with the man.

Willing to bet the farm here, son? Your entire career? Mine?

Four days, and the words still echoed. The more he listened to them, the harder he thought about it, the more he suspected the fly was him.

Here's the four-billion-dollar question—other than you and me, who knows about this?

On any other night, on any other road, he would be surfing his collection of CDs, which ranged from alt-rock to rap metal. His new girlfriend abhorred both—she preferred light jazz with a glass of chardonnay—but tonight his mind was filled with weightier issues, such as the end of life as he knew it.

Don't show this to anyone, don't mention it, don't even hint at it. Code your files, shred any copies. A leak could kill us, not to mention our client. You tell me which is worse.

The serpentine highway leading west into the hills out of San Jose had claimed dozens of lives over the past two decades. Sure, there had been blown tires and alcohol and other pieces of morbid statistical trivia, but everyone knew it was the road. It had been said that the architects of California State Highway 17 had graduated from the University of Six Flags, such were the pitch and frequency of the hairpin turns. If you didn't lose your lunch, odds were you'd lose your cool, or worse, if you were careless enough to glance down to change radio stations.

His boss—the asshole otherwise known as Boyd Gavin—had called that afternoon with instructions to meet him in Santa Cruz for a meeting with representatives of Arielle Systems, their largest client. A few suits from the state district attorney's office would be there, which told him all he needed to know: it was come-to-Jesus time. No explanation was offered regarding the strange hour—the meeting was scheduled for eleven—so he assumed they were tacking it onto an existing agenda that included dinner and pretentious cigars to get their stories straight. Strange he wasn't invited for *that*, since he was the linchpin of the entire conversation.

Give me a few days. We play our cards right, we might get out of this with our asses and our resumes intact.

The time had come to toss the entire mess at the fan. The market would crash on the news, outraged anchors would wax eloquent on corporate greed, a remote truck from CNN would commandeer the parking lot, and he would be the guy they wanted to talk to. Unless—and this was more likely—Gavin assumed the role of come-clean spokesperson for the firm, keeping him in the background for what Gavin would assure him was in the best interests of his career. What a guy, that Gavin.

He was halfway to Santa Cruz, cresting the hills with a series of turns that made Watkins Glen look like a Malibu track, when he noticed headlights coming up fast behind. Within moments they were right on his ass, where, despite having plenty of room to pass, they remained for nearly a mile. On any other night he'd write it off to the preponderance of type-A high-tech marketing pukes who inhabited the area like deciduous trees. Maybe flip a finger, just for grins. But this was not any other night.

When was the last time, he asked himself, that the fly got out alive?

They were approaching a steep uphill grade when the SUV made its move. Odd, because of all the places one didn't want to pass on Highway 17, this was it. Signs with flashing yellow lights warned of an impending curve while recommending a speed of thirty-five miles per hour, which local commuters knew was twenty too many.

Work with me here, okay? Haven't shot a messenger yet, don't plan to now.

Paranoia, my ass. Suddenly, motive had headlights.

The young man instinctively let up on the accelerator as the SUV pulled alongside. He glanced over in anger, his racing heart skipping a beat when he saw that the tinted passenger window was lowering. A man leaned out with what appeared to be a gun in his hands.

He hit the brakes, but the SUV matched the move, closely enough for the gun to hold its mark. Strangely, it wasn't pointing at his head, but toward the rear window. In the microsecond that followed, a part of his brain that wasn't engaged in survival noted that the barrel looked odd, a bad prop from the Sci-Fi Channel after midnight.

Amazing, how time slows in the moment of reckoning.

The gun fired, shattering the glass. The car filled instantly with an untraceable polypropylene vapor that would burn cleanly away in the aftermath. A second after that, the car's interior erupted in flames.

The SUV braked and swung in behind the Mustang, which was now an inferno. Then the SUV accelerated so its aftermarket front-impact guards were kissing the Mustang's rear bumper, pushing it into the guardrail ahead.

Within milliseconds his throat had involuntarily closed and the skin over his corneas had burned away—as had his eardrums—so he didn't see or hear a thing as he crashed through the barrier precisely in the middle of the curve. The car tumbled through blackness for six hundred feet before impacting upside down upon a jagged outcropping of rock in an explosion no one would see.

In the fragment of spinning darkness before the quiet came, the young man in the Mustang retained two thoughts. One, he hadn't shredded his copy of the file, as he'd been instructed. And two, someone else knew. Someone he trusted. Someone he might have even loved.

There wasn't a body part or a shard of metal left that couldn't be stuffed into a sandwich bag.

No one would recall seeing an SUV or any other vehicle in the area at the approximate time of the crash. Investigators would accurately conclude that the fuel tank had erupted on impact, though they would never discover that the bolts on the guardrail had been loosened earlier in the day. Without suspicion of foul play the cause of the accident would remain undetermined and quickly written off as just another victim of Highway 17.

The annual fiscal audit of Arielle Systems would be finalized and published without a hitch, signed on behalf of the firm by Senior Partner Boyd Gavin, who, along with the deceased's mother and girlfriend, wept at the memorial service the following week.

PART ONE
>> <<

> 1 <

The two men looked at each other with what the street called "hard eyes," though neither was familiar with the term. Both hailed from neighborhoods that had SUVs in the driveways and nets on the playground baskets.

"You look nervous, Mr. . . ."—the man in charge here glanced at a pad in front him—"Schmitt."

"That's good. Lucky guess, or should I call you Sherlock?"

Neither broke eye contact, though the man in the necktie squinted, as if he'd never met a wiseass before.

"I don't get it," said the man. "You come in here—your idea, by the way—cut a sweet deal for yourself, then go all Bruce Willis on us. What's up with that?"

"Color me paranoid."

"Really. Why don't you tell me about it."

"I'd rather you tell me about my deal."

"I made some calls, everybody's signed up. At some point you gotta trust."

"I'm not too keen in the trust department. Especially lately."

"That's unfortunate. Try to work around it."

The man named Schmitt was sitting at a well-worn table with a hideous green surface, something the DMV might have cast off when the new budget popped. The man in the bad necktie, who had been sitting on the edge of the table to gain some sort of psychobabble height advantage, took a chair across from him, producing an envelope from a folder. From it he withdrew two photographs, candid mug shots, which he plopped onto the table in front of his guest. The lighting in the room was dull, but not enough to mask the surprise in Wolfgang Schmitt's eyes.

"Friends of yours?"

Schmitt's mouth was gaping open slightly. Sherlock studied his face intently, never once looking at the pictures.

After a few moments he added, "I take it you know these people."

Schmitt nodded slowly. His head twitched, a quick snap or two, as if to emerge from some dizzy reverie that had fogged his ability to think. As if he couldn't believe his eyes.

"You guys are good, despite the rumors. I come here to cut a deal, and you show me pictures of people I haven't even described yet. That's a nice trick."

"We try," said the man.

"Remind me not to piss you fellas off."

For the first time, the man now known as Sherlock demonstrated he was capable of smiling. "Maybe we should take this from the top," he said. "If you're ready."

Schmitt glanced down at the photographs. And again, he shook his head, this time in resignation.

"Ready or not," he said.

And so it began.

> 2 <

ENTRY #11: ADVERTISING—the career hipper-than-thou twentysomethings can't wait to crack, and burned-out fortysomethings can't wait to leave. After a few decades schlepping chips, shoes, booze, soap, hope, and the all-important corporate image, you wake up one hungover morning and realize you've contributed absolutely nothing to the universe.
—from *Bullshit in America*, by Wolfgang Schmitt

Six Weeks Earlier

Funny how things turn out. There I was, sitting in what was easily the most ridiculous business meeting in the history of the Windsor knot, when it suddenly dawned on me that my advertising career was history. That I had broken through the lowest possible threshold of professional humiliation and self-flagellation, which in this business is something south of subterranean. Quitting wasn't something I had been pondering; the idea just descended upon me like a heavenly truckload of fertilizer. Upon the meeting's conclusion I would slither back through a maze of mauve Herman Miller cubicles to my little eight-by-eight—trust me, the ad agency digs you see in the movies are pure bullshit—cast off my pretentious artsy-fartsy tie, and write a scathing letter of resignation. Then—free at last, thank God, I'm free at last—I'd go to lunch.

That's what I *intended* to do. Except, out of sheer habit bordering on addiction, I happened to check my email before heading out. One of the messages would change my life.

Hey, shit happens. But I digress.

The meeting was about gum. Chewing gum. Chiclets, to be precise. I hadn't seen a Chiclet since I was a kid in the car going to church, when my mom would pop them by the handful in an attempt to camouflage the smell of Salems on her breath. The gum—they actually had a flavor called chlorophyll in those days—made her smell like a science experiment, but then again, my mother reeked of an entire science *fair* most of the time. Now, nearly three decades later, with my dear mother languishing in a home for the intellectually departed, Chiclets had returned to my world in the form of a sales conference gimmick. My client was a marketing clone from one of our largest high-tech accounts, whose current mission on earth was to arrange for a box of Chiclets to be on each conference attendee's pillow when they checked into their room at the Bonaventure Resort in Florida. A fine idea indeed. That and the T-shirts with the meeting's theme emblazoned across the back—*"Chew 'Em Up, Spit 'Em Out"*—would have them panting to get back out there and sell sell sell. No matter that the vast majority of invitees would be falling-down drunk from the flight in.

Chiclets on the pillow were easy enough to arrange (career tip: make the client think you *live* for shit like this), but the kicker was that the company logo was to be imprinted on each piece. Today's meeting was convened to present samples to the client and, God willing, move on to more pressing issues, like the seating chart for the awards banquet.

What a valuable service to mankind I was performing.

The client was a twenty-six-year-old Berkeley MBA named Becky who had missed her true calling in the funeral industry. I'd worked with her before, and from the gravitas of her demeanor, not to mention her I-wish-I-had-a-penis wardrobe, you'd think tchotchkes and cute little promotional videos about print cartridges were the precursors to the return of Jesus Christ. Or in her religion of choice, the resurrection of David Packard.

After holding a piece of the gum up to the light and considering it solemnly, Becky announced, "This is the wrong PMS."

Time and space froze. The angels trembled.

"Is not," shot back our lead graphic artist, Stacy, an attractive enough woman in an Ellen Degeneres sort of way, which gave her and Becky some common ground. She was also a known ball-buster who tended to storm out of meetings when someone had the audacity to challenge her "art," which actually happened rather frequently. In her spare time she did calligraphy on antique toilet fixtures, so go figure.

"No," said the client in a firm tone, "it's wrong."

To appreciate the moment, you need to know that Little Miss Pants-in-a-Wad here didn't know what the term "PMS" even meant until the previous meeting. At least in the graphic design sense. She was most certainly an authority when it came to the more common interpretation of the acronym.

Following my client's lead, I held a piece of the lime-tinted gum toward the heavens and analyzed the color with all the heartfelt concern of a diamond cutter. Everyone in the room was doing the same, the fate of the world at stake.

"Awfully close," I offered.

Becky turned to face me with an expression of outrage no less extraordinary than that of the courtroom audience at the reading of the O.J. verdict.

"Excuse me?" she practically yelled. "Did you say *close*?"

"As in," I responded, "nobody will notice."

"Nobody will notice? Are you, like, shitting me? You obviously haven't met the executive vice president of marketing—which someone in your position ought to know means *branding*—who will quickly and happily fire the ass of anyone who fucks with the corporate design standard! Which means me, which in turn means you. Are we perfectly clear here?"

It was now okay to curse and rant, my client having set both precedents in one sentence. Such are the rules of engagement in meetings like these.

The room began to tilt. Maybe it was the fact that my old man used to ask if we were perfectly clear right before he'd pop one upside my head, but Becky was beginning to really piss me off. In another time I would have answered with the word "Crystal," but one of my trademark shit-eating grins wasn't the best strategy at the moment, a moment in which I realized I wanted to be anywhere on the planet except in this business in this room with this woman. Instead I waited for the silence to become poetically awkward before I pulled out my best I-won't-sink-to-your-level tone.

"Becky. Chill. It's *gum*, for shit's sake."

I didn't think her previous facial expression could be surpassed, but that little masterpiece of contortion was a distant runner-up now. You'd think I'd just announced my intention to masturbate on her shoes.

Little did I know that one of the junior designers attending this meeting—a kid who shaved his head to better show off the tattoo of a vine creeping up the back of his neck—had taken the liberty of popping one of the samples into his mouth. Chewing gleefully, it was he who broke the silence and, in some small way, helped change the course of my life.

He said, "Dude, it tastes like chlorophyll!"

"*Excuse* me?" said Becky the client. "Since when did anyone ask for *your* opinion?"

It was in that instant that I decided I was out of there. Not that Ink Boy here was a friend of mine or anything, or even that I was the selfless defender of the nonexempt employee. But Becky had just crossed the line.

Her eyes were menacing slits as she leaned across the conference table in my direction. "Just fix it," she said, sounding exactly like you'd expect a rattlesnake to sound if one were suddenly graced with the ability to speak in our equally forked tongue. With that, she snatched up her purse and an oversized tote bag sporting her company logo, and stormed posthaste toward the door.

"Becky," I said loudly—okay, I *barked* it—not recognizing my own voice.

She turned back, also not recognizing this tone from me. Her eyes dared me to cross the line.

I said, "One of us needs to get a life."

Her jaw dropped open. Normally, having delivered such a coup de grace, I'd have grinned like Jack Nicholson ordering egg salad. But not today.

She remained motionless for many seconds. Then her head began to shake as she slowly turned and completed her imminent departure.

The creative team remained both motionless and silent for nearly a minute. Then, still chomping on the gum, his teeth a pale shade of green, the tattooed designer finally said, "I love this freaking job," which made everyone laugh.

Everyone, that is, except me. I didn't love this freaking job at all. And thank God, based on what was waiting for me in my office, I no longer had to.

> 3 <

ENTRY #38: STARBUCKS—inexplicably long lines, preposterous pricing for a mediocre product, bad music, pretentious interior design, self-important employees, and a founder who owns an NBA team and is laughing all the way to the bank—at us.
—from *Bullshit in America*, by Wolfgang Schmitt

The email read:

Wolf, meet me for coffee on the corner at ten thirty to discuss your future. This is a one-time offer.

In addition to its fortunate timing, several things about this crisp little communiqué commanded my immediate attention. First, it was unsigned. The sender remained somehow unidentified in the header, meaning she or he knew her or his way around Outlook Express better than I. I instinctively knew this wasn't a joke. I get plenty of them on a daily basis—I belong to a secret global cult in which improper sexist humor is freely exchanged over the web. Besides, no one at the agency would invite me to coffee in this fashion, or perhaps at all. My social standing among my peers, like my love life, was in the shitter.

It was also personalized to me by name and location, thus eliminating the possibility that this was some form of dreaded email spam, which some people find as distasteful as the clap.

No, this was something else entirely. This was for *me*.

My name is Wolfgang Schmitt. People who know me call me Wolf, something an unknown purveyor of spam would never presume to know. Not *The* Wolf, as an adjective or a nickname more apropos to the WWE, and certainly not because of any interesting behavioral aberrations, though I've been told I have my share. Nor is it because of anything to do with my hairline—which at the age of thirty-nine is solidly in place for now—or any other part of my anatomy, for that matter.

Actually, I had a gut feeling about this. It was a time in my life, a *season* so to speak, when something had to give. There I was, staring forty in the face, four months into a shattered heart that wasn't responding to therapy, the camel's back of my career having been broken that very morning not by a straw but by a piece of chlorophyll gum, and now this. Fate would not be so cruel as to dangle this before me in my time of need, were it not utterly sincere.

So at 10:25 I found myself sitting at a little round table with a ridiculously overpriced cup of hot chocolate in front of me, surrounded by black-clad urbanites too young to realize they couldn't afford to do this each and every morning, waiting for someone to walk through the door and change my life.

Her name was Marni. And she was the last person I expected to see, if for no other reason than the fact that she already worked for me, and that in the four weeks of her employment we'd barely exchanged a word.

* * *

Marni was my assistant. Not that this was her title, or that she would admit to such a thing. I would never speak it aloud for fear of drastic repercussions, but that was the reality of our working relationship. Despite her looks, straight off a WB prime-time hit— a killer all-black wardrobe that was much too hip for Portland, Oregon, and an all-black attitude to match—I was too immersed in self-pity to be hormonally distracted. Her business card said she was a "Client Services Administrator," which meant she did the grunt work on my accounts, of which there was a continual preponderance. She'd been with the agency for only a month, not long enough for her to fully comprehend my pending meltdown or the fact that my sex life was in a coma.

All of this contributed to my confusion when she marched straight to my table without so much as ordering a latte and, sitting down, uttered the words, "You smell like chlorophyll."

There are no secrets in advertising.

I winced as I tried to make sense of the moment, noticing that she held my stare with a combination of humor and patience, which is known in ladies' rooms around the world as *watching the bastard squirm.*

I finally said, "*You* sent the email?"

"I did."

"Your idea of a joke?"

"Do I seem like someone who'd pull a joke like this?"

"You seem like someone who wouldn't recognize a joke if it came with an instructional video."

She was settling in, parking her expensive designer bag on the table, taking off her very L.A. black leather jacket and then draping it over the back of her chair, moving with the smug grace of a woman who enjoyed being watched. She continued to keep her eyes fixed on mine, as if searching for a tic she might utilize as we commenced sparring. In another time she would have been my worst nightmare—I have an admitted weakness for tall women who use wardrobe as weaponry, women with long, blond, Breck-ad hair, puffy lips that look good wrapped around the straw of a tropical cocktail, and a demeanor that screams gender superiority—but I had bigger problems at the moment than the resurrection of my mojo.

"I'm a bit confused," I confessed.

"Can't say I blame you there."

"I think we're getting close to lawsuit territory, so here's the bottom line: if this is an invitation, the answer is, you're very good at your job and I appreciate all your hard work, but no thank you."

A rash of sexual harassment lawsuits at the firm and the training workshops they had precipitated had sensitized me to this carefully scripted response to such unspoken propositions. The fact that I was known to be single and newly available, enhanced by overblown rumors of my prolific nocturnal presence around town over the years (this being among the things I was intending to change about my life) and certain assumptions regarding my character born of the fact that I used to do a little local modeling on the side—I quit when they wanted me to model Jockey shorts in the Sunday supplement—all made me a juicy candidate for the next accusation.

"You work hard at earning that reputation, don't you."

"Excuse me?"

"As a cynic."

"Could be worse. You want a latte? Cappuccino?"

"No thanks. I don't drink coffee. Just like you."

Both of our eyes beheld the venti vessel before me for a moment—somewhere in the course of modern evolution the term "extra large" had been rendered obsolete—which had a betraying smudge of chocolate on the lid, thus validating my status as something less than a real Starbucks kind of guy.

She looked back at me with a bitter confidence I had never noticed in our time together at work.

"Unlike you," she continued, "I do enjoy the occasional cocktail and the much more infrequent cigarette, and, again like you, I am somewhat addicted to endorphin highs resulting from thirty minutes on a Stairmaster. Color me complex. Short of that and a love of Chinese food, we don't have much in common. So no, we're not remotely in lawsuit territory here. Quite the contrary, actually, so I won't flatter myself if you won't."

"I almost forgot, we're here to discuss my future."

"You catch on."

"Are you, like, selling Herbalife by any chance?"

Her smile returned and, I had to admit, helped to illuminate the room on what was otherwise a typically steel-gray Portland day. Perhaps it was because she had just told me in no uncertain terms that I was not her type, but for a moment I almost wished things were different, that she didn't work for me or for the agency at all, that I wasn't still in love with someone who had betrayed me and all that was sacred, that hope hadn't crashed and burned, even that I was remotely in her league, which I wasn't. The fact was, she reminded me of Tracy. Both were women who always belonged to someone else, and you found yourself wondering just who the hell he was.

"You don't know me," she said. Before I could

respond with something that might get me sued, she added, "And you think I don't know you. But that's where you're wrong."

"I sense a corner being turned," I said, sipping from my drink.

"I've been watching you. Evaluating, actually."

In a flash, I inventoried the past few weeks, scanning for moments in which I had noticed her attention fixed on me in ways that, in retrospect, seemed conspicuously intense. It was a blank screen, but then again, with my head up my ass as it had been since the Big Breakup, I wouldn't have noticed a team of IRS auditors waiting for me in the john.

"Buzz around the watercooler," she said, "is you're the shit, and I have to say, though my tastes run a little more Al Pacino than Ricky Martin, I wasn't disappointed when I saw you."

"That usually comes later," I interjected.

"You're modest yet confident, quiet yet quick to say the right thing, the strong silent type, the deep, brooding, slightly dangerous type, and very good at what you do for a living, which, if I had to guess, you hate doing."

"Ricky Martin?"

"I calls 'em as I sees 'em."

"Are we talking about a dating service or a job?"

"You're perfect for what we have in mind."

"We? Now *that's* interesting."

She smiled, that comfortable smugness back in place.

I said, "Okay, this is where I say the right thing—enough with the witty bullshit. The point is?"

"I have the feeling you might be open to making a change. Am I right? If I'm not, I'll leave you to your hot chocolate."

I squinted through my confusion. "For the sake of

argument, let's say you *are* right about my lack of fondness for my job description."

"In that case, please allow me to continue."

I kept nodding as I put my elbows on the table and rested my oh-so-square chin on my palms. She, in turn, shifted her oh-so-perfect ass in her seat.

"I'm not exactly who you think I am. Or more accurately, *what* you think I am. I'm actually here on a recruiting assignment, and while I do indeed work for the agency—at least, until a few minutes ago—I'm really in the employ of another company which has, shall we say, an interest in you. I took this job for the sole purpose of getting close to you, to see who you are, how you react to stress, how you work with others. And, as I just said, you appear to be perfect for what we have in mind."

I already had my hand up, not to ask a question, but to halt the approaching train wreck.

"Time out. In mind for what? Work for who? And how do *they* even know who I am . . . and what the hell does the buzz at the watercooler have to do with *anything*? In any order would be fine."

She squirmed, uncomfortable for the first time.

"Sorry about the interruption," I added.

"If I'm right about you—and I'm always right about men—my guess is your rampant cynicism won't stop you from checking this out."

"At the risk of asking the obvious . . . checking *what* out?"

"My employer is interested in discussing an opportunity with you. I can tell you that the money will be significantly more than you're making now, and I think you'll find the benefits to be even more, how shall I say, *appealing*."

"Doing, how shall I say, *what*?"

"I'm not at liberty to say."

"Of course you're not. It's either Herbalife or the CIA."

She smiled and looked away sort of shyly—unusual for her. Everything about her was different with the tables turned, she with the power, me with the question mark.

Her eyes suddenly snapped back from whatever moment of reverie had distracted her.

"Will you agree to an interview?"

"Based on . . . what, nothing? This is insane."

"That it is."

I could feel her reading my mind, something I'd apparently missed over the past few weeks. I also recognized a sort of dare here, an invitation to step into the unknown. The man they were looking for—whoever *they* were—would have the balls to take that step. Even if it was insane.

"When?" I asked.

"Now," she shot back, expecting the question. Then her eyes flicked toward the door. Actually, to the curb just outside, where a black Town Car was waiting, the driver holding the rear passenger door open.

"You'll be back here in less than three hours. Think of it as a long lunch. Which will be provided, by the way."

I exhaled, half-whistle, half-sigh. "Well, now you're talkin'," I said half-heartedly.

"No guts, no glory," she said. It wasn't just the recitation of a locker room cliché. It was something posted on the monitor on my desk, among many quotes I kept there. Something to challenge myself in these trying times. She *had* been watching, and closely, too.

My eyes remained fixed on the car as I said, "What we have here is a certifiable defining moment."

"That it is."

With that, Marni got up and left the coffee shop without so much as a parting glance, putting on her coat as she went. As she passed the car, she exchanged a subtle nod with the driver and jaywalked toward our building across the street. The driver watched her go, as any man with a vivid imagination and a modicum of testosterone would, then turned and looked back in through the window, directly at me.

Defining moment, indeed. Sometimes you ask, as I had done that very morning, and sometimes it is given. It is what we do with these opportunities that charts the course of destiny: *It's my life, it's now or never* . . . so sayeth the great sage, Jon Bon Jovi. Most of us are one of two things: blind or chickenshit. We wouldn't know a crossroads in our lives if it had a set of stoplights and a Denny's.

I wondered: What's the worst that could happen? Given my situation, with one foot out the door and the other tap-dancing around a resignation letter, and with my heart pounding in my chest like a drum solo, what was there to lose, anyhow?

Little did I know.

> 4 <

ENTRY #44: HMOs—from the folks who believe bypass surgery is an outpatient procedure, and who incent your doctor to deliver the absolute minimum possible care without killing you. And then, because they can, they raise their rates thirty percent annually. It is a little-known fact that the concept was pioneered by Saddam Hussein.
— from *Bullshit in America*, by Wolfgang Schmitt

A little context. Mine were the actions of a desperate man. Present a defining moment to one and he'll bite every time.

The prior week I'd paid a visit to one of those body-scanning places that are popping up in malls next to Gap stores. Who would have thought it would come to this: Do a little shopping, while you're there see if you have any tumors. Just what we need: the McDonald's of diagnostic medicine. I'd been having some minor chest pains lately—since my girlfriend bolted, in fact—which my doctor, after a fruitless EKG, said were most likely due to gas and a keen awareness that the big four-oh was just around the corner. I'd seen an ad for a weekend special on heart scans—a hundred bucks, regularly four-fifty, such a deal—so I thought I'd prove her wrong. Actually, I don't know what I was thinking. The scan showed the calcium content in my heart tissue to be off the charts, literally: a score of 503 on a scale that ended at 500. Which, they told me, translated to a ninety-six percent probability that I would experience a major cardiac event in the near future. They suggested that I see a cardiologist immediately, and that I have a nice day.

My doctor—who, like most doctors, was not used to being second-guessed—told me to get my money back. She refused to authorize any further testing—I once used the word "gatekeeper" in her presence and she nearly threw me out of her office—but nonetheless gave me the number of her favorite cardiologist in case I wanted to waste my own money. Which I did, to the tune of twenty-two hundred bucks for a thallium stress test that came up with nothing. Heart like a racehorse, they said. Where, I wondered, was all that calcium hiding? And when, I wondered, would my cardiac event arrive? The cardiologist told me to relax, to get on with my life, that everybody had calcium in their heart to some degree, and to have a nice day.

Since then, at least once or twice daily, a little twinge in my chest kept reminding me that forty years of clean living didn't mean shit, and ten grand a year in HMO premiums meant even less. At least my doctor put me on Lipitor to lower my cholesterol, saying with a smug little grin that it would fry my liver long before my calcium-infested heart seized up.

Gets a fella thinking. Gets a fella hearing a subtle tick, tick, ticking in the background of his life.

My father, the longshoreman, died at sixty-nine of a massive coronary, eight years after his obligatory bypass following a lifetime of bacon, Swiss steak, Camels (he did the fashionable thing and quit in the early eighties), and the occasional round of golf, which, God bless him, he sincerely thought was exercise. In my formative years he'd told me that real men don't wear suits to work, only to weddings and funerals—an intellectual giant, my old man—and my brief foray into baseball's minor leagues was the only time in my life when I sensed any hint of approval from the guy. Looking back, and being honest with myself in a way that becomes apparent only after some trauma awakens you to the truth, I realized some of my choices—the downtown career, the modeling, the womanizing and, because real men drink Budweiser, my status as a nondrinker—were made just to piss the sonofabitch off. I'd be damned if I would turn out to be *him*.

I did, however, wear a kickin' double-breasted Hugo Boss to his funeral.

My mother, on the other hand, saw me as perfect— her opportunity to shine, albeit via a reflection. For too long I believed her, which, again in retrospect, was the cause of much childhood grief. As in, I got beat up a lot. She refused to fly, which meant her window to the world was a television, in front of which she planted herself every evening beneath a down comforter turned the color of old newsprint from years of nicotine wafting in our living room. Every morning she'd study the listings and circle her viewing choices for that evening, and if nothing good was on she'd drink Early Times and 7-Up until she passed out. Of late, while my love life was disintegrating, my career was self-embalming and my heart was hardening into an abstract coffee table ornament, my mother was in a rocking chair in a state-funded retirement home fifty miles away, watching *Hollywood Squares* and wondering why Charo and Charles Nelson Reilly weren't there, with absolutely no clue who I was when I visited, which I did every Saturday.

I don't play golf, either. I like a little perspiration with my exercise. Over the long run, this, along with the nondrinking thing, was both career and social suicide. I do play serious basketball at my club against former Pac-10 players, I lift significant weights regularly, and I haven't lost much off my 4.5 tennis game, yet men seem to shrink back in homophobic horror when it becomes known that I don't play *the great game of golf*, or that I refuse to sit around analyzing college football. Or that I don't fish or, God forbid, hunt. As for the drinking thing, I am judged for my choice far more than I judge others for theirs, though I have to admit I've never met a drunk woman I found attractive, or a blitzed man who made me sit up and say, yeah, I want to hang with *that* guy. I'm the one Kenny Loggins was singing about—*Never got high, oh I was a sorry guy . . .*

I spend a lot of time alone.

For years, my only real earthly vice has been hamburgers—something I had to quickly reconsider—yet I refused to touch anything that has seen the inside of a deep fryer. The CD player in my car has stuff from Faith Hill, Josh Groban, Saliva, and the original cast recording from *Phantom of the Opera*, much to the utter confusion of my passengers. I spend enough on non-FDA-approved nutritional supplements to finance my unborn child's private school tuition, yet I refuse to consider Rogaine, liposuction, or Viagra, now or in the future as the need may, shall we say, arise.

Actually, I'm a little confused about it all myself.

About the "looks" thing: I don't see it. In my mirror is a guy with lucky hair, pale, droopy-lidded eyes and a woman's eyelashes, and a nose you wouldn't wish on a collie. I'm in good shape, but frankly that's because I work at it. Not for vanity—okay, a *little* for vanity—but because of a sincere desire to outlive my father. Talk about your social prejudices: because of the way you look, some folks stay as clear as if you had just returned from an emergency room in Ethiopia. Women are certain you're stuck up—hoping that you are, in fact, because they love the "bad boys" and like to fix things. Men want to kick your ass, but if they can't they just serve you attitude, and if they can you have another problem altogether. If you carry yourself with a modicum of confidence, just be yourself and don't care what others think—isn't that what Dad said?—you do nothing but exacerbate these perceptions. You know it's their problem, a blatant manifestation of insecurity, but the consequences are very much yours. And on the list of things for which to feel sorry for someone, being too good-looking for your own good—again I stress, not remotely my assessment—doesn't get you much in the way of sympathy.

Frankly, most of the time it sucks.

About a year ago I started writing it all down, recording the bullshit when and where I saw it. *Bullshit in America*, I called it. At first it was just therapy, but then the entrepreneur in me took over and I saw dollar signs. There was a lot to be pissed off about, and I felt the public might relate. The more I wrote, the more unloading I discovered was necessary. About the world in which I live, and especially about my relationship with women. I fear, for all my bitching and moaning, that I can fix neither.

Fact was, in those quiet moments of truth that were occurring more and more often in my life, and based on the evidence, at the age of almost forty I didn't really know who I was.

But I was about to find out.

> 5 <

ENTRY #184: THE BOARDING PROCEDURE USED BY SOUTHWEST AIRLINES—one of the great ironies of the modern world is the fact that Southwest Airlines is the most consistently profitable airline in the industry. That's like saying Willie Nelson is the sexiest man alive.
—from *Bullshit in America*, by Wolfgang Schmitt

Context is everything. It's one of my favorite words, actually, though I don't usually toss it off in conversation for effect. My old boss liked to use words like *verisimilitude* and *milieu*, two of several reasons everyone thought he was an asshole, so I try to watch it where vocabulary is concerned. Never hire anyone who starts a sentence with the word "Dude!" and never work for a guy who doesn't know the difference between *mute* and *moot*, I always say.

The context of this particular limo ride was that of going through a sort of celestial door. There's life before the door and life after, and there I was with my hand on the big brass knob. Behind me was a career that had grown as stale as the *Star Wars* franchise and a girlfriend who, despite her absence, refused to lift her spiked heel from my throat. My best friend was in the midst of a divorce from a woman who recently whispered in my ear at a cocktail party that she'd like to suck brie from between my toes, and my other best fortysomething friend, the guy who showed me the ropes back when, was still hitting the bars every night looking for a reasonable facsimile of Morgan Fairchild. Thus, married or single, especially with my career in a morgue drawer, I believed this much to be true: Life sucks, your heart gets shredded—if not completely calcified—then you die. Unless, of course, someone offers you a new start at the precise moment at which the darkness threatens to make you rethink your moral code. Without that context I'd never be sitting in that Town Car, wondering more about where we were going than why.

I was simply ready for a change, the bigger the better.

The driver's name was Joe. He had greeted me with a handshake and the announcement that he would be my driver today. And I thought the hat was a Village People thing.

"So, Joe," I said as we got in, "where to?"

"Can't say," he said. "They told me you'd ask, and that I shouldn't answer."

"They?"

I could see him shrug his shoulders as we pulled away from the curb. He looked like an extra from *NYPD Blue*, with the puffy nose of an ex-alcoholic, and for a moment I flashed on the possibility that something slippery was afoot. We were heading west over the moneyed hills, which was the logical route toward an interview since this was where the chip crowd and the athletic-shoe boys staked their turf— the two best games in town. The only dangerous things on the east side of Portland were the food and the Trailblazers.

was fishing for. I don't like getting dissed, and when it happens I tend to reverse the heat. Hence the irregularities of my nose—thanks to a barroom incident back in college—which rendered my profile what the local modeling agents called "interesting in an Owen Wilson sort of way."

Then he smiled, completely ruining the moment.

"Not since I quit drinkin'." He went on to explain his journey through AA, which was more than I wanted to know about Joe the limo driver. I smiled, trying to be polite.

"You must be some important guy," he said. His eyes sparkled, no dis intended.

"Oh yeah," I replied. "That's me. One important guy."

"You nervous? You seem nervous."

"Terrified."

He turned back with a little smirk, his gaze again scanning the horizon. "It's all good," he said. "Relax and enjoy the ride."

All good. Right. I couldn't think of anything to say to that, so I turned my own attention to the horizon, waiting for whatever it was that was coming for me.

> 6 <

ENTRY #201: THE PRICE OF MOVIE POP-CORN—the time for rebellion is now. Take a big purse and stop at your local convenience store on the way. Then leave the candy wrappers on the floor so they'll know. It's what Rosa Parks would have done.
—from *Bullshit in America*, by Wolfgang Schmitt

What happened next I found to be eerily metaphoric. What began as a dot on the colorless horizon grew into a speck of hope, then an incomprehensible blur of a moving target, then a clear and enticing vision still far beyond my reach. Sort of like love. At least, right before it goes spiraling out of control on its journey toward an inevitable crash and burn.

Such was my frame of reference these days.

It was an airplane. Not just any airplane, but the Ferrari of civil aviation, the Dom Perignon of private jets, the elusive holy grail of economic status. It was a Gulfstream V business jet—we're talking L.A. to London nonstop—and you had to have more than forty million before your name went onto the pink slip.

"Know who it is?" I asked as we watched the jet land.

"No clue."

"You get me out of here if I flash a few twenties right about now?"

"Didn't take you for a coward, Mr. Schmitt."

"Me neither," I replied, conscious of an uneasy stomach that reminded me of standing at the bus stop on the morning of my first day of high school. I took solace in a vague recollection of that day turning out okay, and the subsequent realization that ninety-five percent of what you worry about turns out okay, too.

Then again, this wasn't exactly just another day at school. And this was certainly no bus.

The Gulfstream taxied back from the far end of the runway and turned off onto the tarmac, coming straight for us at an alarming rate of speed. There were no markings on the fuselage, though it was painted a metallic silver with maroon accents that reminded me of a can of Coors Light. Thirty yards in front of us it executed a sudden pivot before stopping. The hatch lowered immediately, the turbines at idle.

Nothing happened for a few moments. Then Joe turned to me, extended his hand, and yelled, "Good luck." A moment later I was very alone, standing in the rain, facing a forty-million-dollar celestial door.

Across the street from the Hillsboro Airport was a strip mall, the parking lot of which provided a clear line of sight to the tarmac while you enjoyed a sandwich. That was precisely what was happening inside a rented Ford Taurus as the Gulfstream pulled to a stop in front of the car in which Wolfgang Schmitt waited, a woman behind the Taurus's wheel, a man next to her.

"Think he'll do it?" asked the man, chewing as he spoke, peering through binoculars.

"Like he has a choice?" asked the woman.

Her companion just nodded, as if his question was indeed a silly one. There was a comfortable honesty between them, the kind that is unique to professional partnerships that have weathered a few years of covering each other's backs. The man was married and had two sons at home who wished he was around more, and the woman was in a committed relationship with an artist named Kristen, so the pressure was off. Both needed the money to keep their lives on track, and toward that end they needed each other.

"Seems like a nice kid," said the man.

"Kid? He's only two years younger than you are."

"Yeah, but he seems, I don't know . . . lost."

"People who look like that are usually a little lost. They're looking for something. Fucks them up, if you ask me."

"Yeah, aren't we the lucky ones," said the man.

"Welcome to mid-life," said the woman. "He'll get over it. So will you, by the way."

Now it was the man who offered a look of sad disapproval, to which she immediately responded with a sheepish shrug.

"Not fair, is it," she added after a moment, still squinting through the weather. How anyone could live in this shit was beyond her. A quarter-mile away the Gulfstream's hatch was open, and the Town Car was just now pulling away.

"Long as I get paid," said the man, his voice tired.

>7<

ENTRY #77: EXECUTIVE COMPENSATION—
multimillion-dollar signing bonuses, golden parachutes,
fantasy island perks, all without the slightest relationship to profitability. All that brainpower, and nobody
can spell *accountability*.
    —from *Bullshit in America*, by Wolfgang Schmitt

Few moments in the human experience invoke the degree of unmitigated, primal terror as does walking into a room full of strangers who are certain to turn and look at you. You can cling to your type-A Dale Carnegie swagger all you want, you can do it a million times as you ascend toward your candidacy for President of the United States, but if you have a pulse, it still scares the living shit out of you.

For a real thrill, try it in a luxury private jet sometime, especially—as I was about to find out—one that's owned and occupied by one of the richest men on the planet.

I was greeted by a woman of robust stature standing just inside the hatch. With a convincing smile and a Black & Decker handshake, she said, "Thanks for coming today, Mr. Schmitt."

Before I could answer, her other hand had pushed a button that commenced the raising of the hatch behind me, which nearly hit me on the ass as it snapped securely in place.

"I'm Monica," she said quietly, eager to set me at ease. She was one of those souls gifted with what Tracy would call *good energy*, immediately likable, pushing sixty. Chances were she knew where all the bodies were buried. Either that or she was the company lawyer, an even more chilling thought since it meant she was the one who had buried them.

Her eyes flicked toward the back of the cabin, where a man I immediately recognized was sitting in a bench seat that stretched the entire width of the airplane. He was speaking into a headset microphone and gesturing with his hands, with no apparent awareness that I was there.

In another seat, looking at me with all the warmth of a demolition-yard car crusher, sat a man wearing a black turtleneck sweater, a fact I found ironic because he had no neck. He looked like Odd Job from that old James Bond flick, though he had a face more like a pissed-off noseguard and, no doubt, a serious lack of interpersonal skills. I could see a coiled cord that extended from an earpiece disappearing under the collar of his Armani jacket.

"Mr. Scott will be with you in a moment," said Monica, motioning toward an aft-facing seat directly in Odd Job's eyeline, still speaking as if we were in a library at naptime. "Please, make yourself comfortable. Can I get you anything? Coffee? Soft drink?"

"No thanks," I said. I was tempted to ask for an air sickness bag, but conquered the urge. Now that I knew who my host was, and who would break my kneecaps if I happened to make a sudden movement, I was genuinely in need of one.

Matching her conspiratorial lack of volume, I said, "Any chance you could tell me where we're going?"

She smiled. Then she turned the tables on my keen sense of perception as she opened the cockpit door and, with the dexterity of a ballerina, climbed over the console, and assumed the left seat—she was, it turns out, the pilot—quickly closing the door behind her without looking back. I decided then and there to do as my good friend Joe had recently suggested and simply enjoy the ride.

As I settled into the seat, my gaze met that of the bodyguard. I ventured a meek little nod, somehow resisting the urge to utter *How's it hangin', Sparky?* He almost nodded back—his chin dipped slowly and then slowly returned to neutral—and you could almost hear the gnashing of cables and gears.

Enjoy the ride. Right. Sixty minutes ago I was debating the cost-benefit analysis of chlorophyll gum with a client who frankly needed a good shagging, and here I was taxiing for an imminent takeoff with none other than Nelson Scott, a Silicon Valley legend of Ellisonian if not Machiavellian proportions, who had spent five of the last six years among the top fifty players on Malcolm Forbes's little list.

We are used to airplane interiors with all the personality of a dental waiting room, but this was pure Hefner with a touch of Buckingham Palace. The cabin was done in a sort of old-money law office motif, like the cigar lounge in a stuffy downtown club. Even the lighting fixtures looked as if they came from Renovation Hardware. There were twelve seats, each with its own flat-screen LCD and DVD player.

The close proximity of the ridiculously famous is a strange sensation. Looking at Scott sitting at the rear of the cabin, I felt as if I'd known him for years. The face was familiar from a thousand magazine articles and a hundred sound bites, the persona as much myth as legend. And yet, here in the flesh, there was a vulnerability that didn't translate through the media, his skin pale and translucent like a child's, his hands frail and feminine as he conducted his telephone conversation, completely unaware of my presence. He was smaller than I would have guessed—we mistakenly assign mass to our titans of industry—and I wondered if some of what the press had painted as a notorious attitude was the result of the realization that he was a disappointment in the flesh. He was nearing fifty, and as with his peers, all his money and all the king's doctors could not keep the decades at bay, the ravages of living at the speed of sound, each takeover and every market swing having carved a piece of his soul away.

He appeared not to notice when Monica hit the gas and the airplane bolted down the runway with astounding power, the world tilting at a grotesque angle seconds later. The ground fell quickly away, followed immediately by our being swallowed whole into the clouds. A Gulfstream is capable of nearly vertical flight—you won't find that one in the manual—and it felt like we were close to it now.

I chanced a glance at Odd Job, who, having decided I was not an assassination threat, had turned his attention to a magazine called *Flex*. Just another day at forty thousand feet with the boss.

Without pausing from his headset conversation—he was waxing strategic on the potential PR spin that could be imparted to an impending round of layoffs—Nelson Scott stood, met my eyes, and offered a firm handshake. He was wearing a crisp white shirt that had his initials embroidered on the French cuffs and sported diamond links the size of dimes. (Note to self: Humble understatement would not be the hallmark of this man.) He held up one finger to indicate that he'd be with me momentarily, then went back to his seat and resumed the body language of the spin conversation, all without missing a dictatorial beat.

My rusty pilot's sensibilities told me we were banking north. In fact we were already well into the state of Washington—not to mention my state of confusion, which shares a border with my state of panic—before Scott pulled off the headset and, as promised, turned his full attention to me. It was not without significance that I noticed Odd Job gently setting aside his magazine at the precise moment this occurred.

> 8 <

ENTRY #129: "I DID NOT HAVE SEXUAL RELATIONS WITH THAT WOMAN"—arguably the most humiliating, self-effacing, bald-faced lie ever perpetrated upon the American public by an elected official. Two guys in Arkansas actually believed him.
    —from *Bullshit in America*, by Wolfgang Schmitt

Suddenly I was the most important thing in Nelson Scott's universe. It was a skill set that served the fiscally charmed well, and it was working now. He approached me with an extended hand and actually introduced himself by name, seeming not to assume that I knew but well aware that I did. Everyone knew who Nelson Scott was. A nice touch, that, and a tough line to walk. The word "natty" popped into my head because it looked as if someone had ironed his shirt with refrigerator enamel. His hair was short and, thanks to a handful of artfully applied pomade, he was ready for his close-up.

"You fly, right?" he said, plopping into the seat in front of me, his bodyguard across the aisle to his left within arm's reach. I wondered how he knew this—I'd done ground school back in eleventh grade and had flown a few hundred hours in small props, though not in years—since it wasn't part of my known oeuvre at work.

"Used to. How'd you know that, by the way?" I

added a smile to soften my edge, which I'm told is sharper than I realize. More fodder for Schmitt's Big Change.

He ignored the question, using the moment to buckle in. The agenda, and the obligatory social stops along the way, would be of his design. His grin was childlike as he put up his hands and looked around the opulent cabin. "You like?"

I nodded and said, "Very cool," hoping to impress him with just how very at ease I was.

"Monica lets me sit right seat sometimes, fly the approaches, do the radio. Doesn't like it, but hey, what are you gonna do, right?"

Right. The three of us shared the humor at this acknowledgment of Scott's power, and the bodyguard's face looked as if it might crack wide open from the effort. From what I'd read, Nelson Scott was the Saddam Hussein of software: you vote wrong, your head gets mailed home in a sack. Rumor held that there was a box on the company employment application that was to be checked if you could spell *sycophant*.

I was determined not to check that box today.

"Marni says good things," he offered, the humor suddenly gone. My Marni and Nelson Scott on a first-name basis. Who'd a thunk it?

"I have a lot of questions," I said, "beginning with her."

"I assume you know why you're here," he said.

"She said something about a job," I replied.

His expression shifted toward mock surprise. "Marni said that?"

"I thought so. No wait, she said, *Hey Wolf, wanna take a ride in a cool jet?* I said *Sure*, and here I am."

His expression held fast. Perhaps *I* was the surprise now.

"She said you were a bit of a wiseass. I like that. I believe the word she used with you this morning was 'opportunity.' Am I right?"

"Man like you says you're right, you must be right." I tried to recall the exact text of my time with Marni, but it was useless. "Opportunity" and "job" are synonymous when you're miserable.

In the awkward pause that followed, I looked over at Señor Odd Job and asked, "How am I doin' here?"

The big fellow said, "Guess we know how that nose got busted."

Scott, who seemed delighted by this little testosterone moment, said, "We have a lot in common, you and me."

I nodded while looking around the cabin again. "Yeah, I can see that."

"We're both smart and we're both smartasses, and it gets us in trouble more often than not. We strive to show how unimpressed we are when we should be legitimately humbled, and that gets us nowhere, too. Tough to let go of the little games that have gotten us by over the years, isn't it? We're suddenly interested in growth in our impending old age, both personal and financial. We don't have all that many friends, and we rationalize it away by labeling others losers while they label us judgmental and selfish. Or in my case, megalomaniacal. Still bugs us, though, in the quiet of our own guilt. And, lest I forget, we're both pretty much zeros in the love department. All the sex we want, but love, for all our obvious charms and assets, continues to elude us. How am *I* doin' so far?"

I tried to match his smug expression, admiring the way he'd handled that little oratory. We were now brothers in pain and suffering, men with souls. Only difference was, his had many more accountants than mine.

"I can see how a woman would have trouble with all this."

"More relevant, we're both suckers for an interesting opportunity."

"There's that word again."

"One of my personal favorites."

"I still have questions."

"Shoot."

"Marni came to the agency to observe and evaluate me. Which implies I was identified as a candidate for this so-called opportunity before she arrived. How did that happen?"

"If I tell you, he'll have to kill you."

I refused to look over at Odd Job, though I could sense his hopeful glare.

I raised my eyebrows in patient anticipation of his answer.

He thought a moment, a menu of options flickering behind his eyes. Then, the cursor having stopped on one, he smiled.

"A man in my position has resources. Let's leave it at that. You're here, the opportunity is at hand; what happens next defines the character of the individual. Marni says she believes the timing is perfect, and because I already know the money will be satisfactory, I see no reason we cannot consummate a deal today."

"One of *my* favorite words," I said.

"Money?"

"Consummate."

It took a moment for Scott to nod an approval, and I wondered if my attitude had just wandered over the line. It was a line I knew well, having doused many a fleeting hope in the past with my irritating tendency to floss with it.

The pitch of the Gulfstream's engines decreased subtly as we leveled off at cruising altitude, still, I sensed, bearing due north.

"Well," I said, slapping my knee for emphasis, "since this isn't a *job* interview and I'm told I suck at idle chitchat, I guess I don't know where to take it next. So it's your move, Mr. Scott, and I have to say, I'm all ears."

"Call me Nelson. We're about to become personal friends, you and me."

"Of which we have precious few."

He grinned again—gee, he really *did* like me—and I knew I was supposed to sense a shadow of sincerity lingering somewhere among the gears that comprised the steel trap of his mind. A lesser cynic might have bought it.

"I know far more about you than you'd think possible."

"Why do I not have trouble believing that?"

"I didn't get where I am without doing my homework. I choose my team well, and I treat them even better."

I chanced another glance over at Dr. No-Neck, who had been staring a hole through me the entire time, no doubt wondering how he'd kill me when the time came. I'd better learn to watch my back if, perchance, I ended up making more money than this guy.

"I appreciate your confidence," I said, though I doubted I sold the line well.

"This is going to sound odd."

I waited, keeping my eyebrows arched. I wasn't exactly enjoying his discomfort, but I had to admit, it was somewhat fascinating watching a billionaire squirm in his forty-thousand-dollar leather seat.

BAIT AND SWITCH

"I assure you, this is all very legal, though of debatable moral verisimilitude. You'll get over it. I know I have."

I bit my lip. Hard.

"What?"

"Nothing," I said. "Please continue."

"You'll think I'm crazy, but I'd ask that you seriously consider my offer. I'm prepared to pay you a ridiculous sum of money."

"Why don't you just say it, Nelson."

He drew a deep breath, closing his eyes for a moment, as if reconsidering everything one final time.

His eyes snapped back to me, once again those of a billionaire.

He said, "I want you to seduce my wife."

> 9 <

At the moment Nelson Scott's Gulfstream lifted off from the airstrip in Hillsboro, Oregon, his wife, Kelly, was straddling her lover in what used to be Scott's bed, but was now part of an impending property settlement, the likes of which would make national news once finalized. The home—all nineteen thousand square feet of it, not counting the tennis clubhouse and gym—was a castlelike fortress situated atop a small mountain overlooking the Santa Clara Valley, with a helipad that was more functional than the garage. On the advice of her lawyer she'd moved out when she and her husband separated, taking residence in a downtown San Jose penthouse Nelson had purchased to house out-of-town guests who preferred to fly under the radar of common hotels.

Now, just to piss him off, Kelly liked to bring her new lover up to the mountain villa when Nelson was away on business. No one on the domestic staff, even the security personnel, dared challenge her presence, and once the bedroom door closed behind them, she and her lover were as alone as if everyone had gone home for the holidays.

The bedroom was actually an entire wing, with its own fitness center including a lap pool, massage room, and his-and-hers closets the size of small apartments. Inside each was a computer-controlled "garment management system," which was, in fact, an elaborate conveyor belt affair that fetched whatever article of clothing had been summoned via keyboard command. That one had made the cover of *Popular Mechanics* in the mid-nineties, when the house was constructed. The bed itself was a canopy affair imported from Spain that weighed in at more than two thousand pounds, with sculpted arches of brushed bronze that could support a suspended human being should one be so inclined, though that particular carnal nuance never materialized in the course of the Scotts' eighteen years together. The kinkiest thing ever attempted here was the duplication of a few moves from a porno flick directed by Gerard Damiano, best known for his classics, *Deep Throat* and *Splendor in the Ass*, who on a lark had once been a dinner guest.

Kelly Scott made love with her eyes closed, which was odd because she liked to tell stories when she had sex. Her lover wondered whom she was casting in these fantasies, confident he wasn't part of the script. You make love virtually alone for eighteen years, you tend to close your eyes and populate your movie with actors of your own choosing. Either that, or you learn to hate the act. Both eventually land you in divorce court.

Nonetheless, her lover thought she was a beautiful sight. Her hair was blond, straight and slightly beyond shoulder-length, very Michelle Pfeiffer, to whom she had been told she bore a resemblance. Her thirty-nine-year-old body had been maintained by the best money could buy—the Scotts used to travel with their own trainer, at least until Nelson pulled the plug, fearing Kelly was getting a bit too enthusiastic about her sessions—and her face, while childlike, had taken on a regal grace with age. Her eyes were a pale blue, a distant ice that people claimed made her hard to know.

"Nelson never let me be on top," she said, suddenly breaking precedent as her eyes popped open. It was her preferred position now, and this comment spoke volumes about her estranged husband.

"Didn't know what he was missing," said her lover, who, after three months of visits here, still kept an eye on the bedroom door. He wasn't particularly fond of the frequency with which Kelly spoke of her husband—Nelson Scott was not an easy man to extricate from your life—but he was even less fond of Scott's reputation as a control freak with a violent temper and lots of steroidal bodyguards on the payroll. But he knew when to pick his battles—his profession had taught him that, and quite well—and now was definitely not the time.

Besides, he was untouchable these days. Even here, lying in the man's bed, beneath his wife.

When it was over and she had collapsed onto his chest, he quietly said, "God, I love it when you do shit like that."

She had talked through the entire thing, a story about some guy in France who was offering a hundred grand to any woman who could kill him with sex. The gist of Kelly's narrative was her interest in the job, and how she would make it happen.

Kelly, he had recently learned, loved to talk in bed.

She said nothing now, though she did snuggle her face tighter into the nape of his neck. They remained utterly quiet for several minutes.

"I have to get back," he finally said, gently pushing her away. Unlike her, he had a job to tend to, and for the time being everything depended on his keeping it intact. Kelly remained on the bed, watching him dress, twirling into the mauve satin sheets. The maids would clear the room of all evidence of their presence, but it still made her smile to be here, fucking someone in her husband's bed.

"You know what I like best about you?" she asked.

"I'm a good listener," he said with a wink. Little did he know she would rather it was he who did the talking.

"That too. I like it that you're making my husband suffer."

He smiled, appreciating that she was still trying to spin him up. To be blackmailing the bastard and balling his wife in his bed while he was at it—this was indeed a rare privilege.

"A woman scorned," he said. "I pity the man."

"That's right. Don't fuck with us."

"Maybe you should have practiced your little death-by-sex number on him. Skip all the lawyer horseshit."

Her eyes were suddenly distant.

"Death is too kind for Nelson."

Kelly's attention had drifted to the expanse of glass that overlooked the valley. In the distance, an Alaska MD-80 was on final approach to the San Jose airport, where her husband had departed several hours earlier in his forty-two-million-dollar private airplane. Make that *their* airplane.

"All I wanted was a picket fence and a few babies. I gave him eighteen years to figure it out."

"There are a few hundred million women who don't feel sorry for you."

The distant gaze quickly focused back on her lover.

"Do you feel sorry for me?"

He stopped dressing, taking care with his answer. He sat on the side of the bed and stroked her hair as he said, "I'm sorry he hurt you. I'm glad you're in my life. I don't feel sorry for you because I know how much *I* care for you."

She smiled. "You're sweet." Then the smile vanished. "Besides, I have other plans for my husband."

He rose, again addressing the buttons on his dress shirt. "It's him I feel sorry for."

She looked up with a nasty little grin on her face, one she knew he liked. "Pretty compassionate, considering you've got his balls in the palm of your hand, too."

"Man's gotta make a living. What can I say."

Kelly Scott flopped back on the bed and stretched. Life was good. And it was about to get better.

"I'm going to watch him bleed," she said, "and I'm going to make it last as long as the law allows."

Boyd Gavin, general partner for the accounting firm that audited Arielle Systems' books, leaned down and kissed her, his suit coat slung over his shoulder, very Sinatra.

"And guess what?" she called after him as he walked from the room. "The color of his blood is green."

> 10 <

ENTRY #75: HOLLYWOOD—they complain there are no good scripts out there, then they invest a hundred million in bombs like *Battlefield Earth* and *3000 Miles to Graceland*. They should give an Academy Award for best comedy by a studio executive.
—from *Bullshit in America*, by Wolfgang Schmitt

So there it was. Nelson Scott wanted me to seduce his wife. I should have known.

Now, I'd seen *Indecent Proposal* more than once, and at the time had engaged in many a lively debate with friends over whether I'd let my wife earn a million bucks in that fashion, or if I was Demi Moore whether I'd go for it or not, or if Robert Redford was an asshole for even asking. In each case, I'd leaned far to the right—not a chance in hell. Even as a guy who'd never been married, or even been close for that matter—this being years before Tracy ruined my reputation as a player—I knew it was a positively Faustian deal, with no possible upside for anyone involved. Only the studios make out on a deal like that.

Then again, Nelson Scott hadn't yet mentioned how much money he was talking here, so after all these years my mind remained open, as did my options.

"Excuse me?" was all that I could say. I waited an obligatory moment to see if his face betrayed a trace of humor, however black, but his eyes were as sincere as a United Way billboard. An organization, by the way, he once chaired.

Scott turned to his bodyguard and said, "He doesn't believe me."

The bodyguard offered no expression.

"Is this, like, some billionaire kink thing?" I asked.

"You mean, do I want to watch? The answer is *no*. It's a billionaire business thing."

"You want me to seduce your wife . . . for business."

The bodyguard broke in with, "Maybe you shut up long enough for him to finish, you'll understand."

"Have I done something to offend you?" I asked, suddenly realizing that I hadn't, and thus was being once again unduly dissed. I turned back to Scott and added, "Speaking as a former marketing genius, I don't think he's the guy for your next recruiting poster."

Scott smiled. At me or at the Hulk, I wasn't sure.

"I apologize," he said. "Bruce's edge comes with the territory."

"Bruce?" I said, unable to resist. Ever notice how, when someone wants to throttle you, a little vein tends to pop up on his temple? That was Bruce right then.

Scott shot a little nod to the beast, who turned his beady eyes away, his version of leaving us alone.

"Business," I reminded my host.

"My wife and I are separated."

"Sounds expensive."

"How perceptive of you. And precisely at the heart of my proposition."

I shifted into a more comfortable position to indicate my readiness to listen.

"We've been married for eighteen years, since she was twenty-one years old. In Cali-fucking-fornia. Do you have any idea what this divorce is going to cost me?"

"Yeah, those lawyers can be real leeches," I said, which made him chuckle out loud for the first time. Anyone else and I'd have been *sure* he liked me, but this was Nelson Scott, the billion-fucking-aire. Every smile, every chuckle, was a calculated manipulation.

"I'll cut right to it," he said, checking his watch. I hadn't noticed until now, but the Gulfstream was descending rapidly. "Upon a final decree of divorce I'll owe my lovely wife assets totaling over fifty million dollars. And that doesn't count paying for her fleet of lawyers. But frankly, it's not the fifty I'm worried about."

"Chump change," I chimed in with a shrug.

"Fifty doesn't get her boot out of my ass. We had a prenuptial agreement that defined a monthly maintenance obligation, to be computed according to my current financial status."

"Down here in the twenty-five percent tax bracket we call that *alimony*."

His smile returned but was distant. It remained fixed for several seconds before he said, "She's gonna love you."

"Wait till she sees my ten-forty."

"The alimony is three million a month. For life."

I opened my mouth to offer a witty bon mot, but the well was dry. He raised his eyebrows, claiming the moment.

"Either that," he went on, "or I sign over half my company to the little bitch, and that's not an option. Over my cold, dead, cryogenically preserved corpse."

"Hope you fired the bastard who did *that* contract for you."

"That was eighteen years ago. And I was the bastard who insisted on the terms, very generous terms. At the time I was young and stupid and, I thought, quite in love. At the time I had sixteen employees, a five-million-dollar loan, and a wife with the body of a fucking goddess. You'd have signed it, too."

I whistled softly as I nodded.

"You can afford the fifty," I said, "but the three million a month is a headache?"

"Do the math, Wolf."

"And me seducing her gets you a discount."

"It's in the prenup."

"This I gotta hear."

He glanced at his bodyguard, who hadn't moved a bloated muscle since being muzzled moments earlier. Then he looked back at me, leaning forward and lowering his voice.

Crunch time.

"We don't have children, thank God. That simplifies things, in more ways than one. So we're down to basics—she remarries, the alimony goes away."

"Slow down there, cowboy. You said seduce."

"I had a hard-on but I wasn't completely stupid. She cohabitates, same outcome. It's in the contract. She keeps the fifty in either case, but the alimony depends on her domestic status."

I whistled again, though no sound came out. I noticed that Steroid Boy was now looking at me, and my eyes shifted between his and Scott's, as if the men were waiting for an answer before the landing gear lowered.

"She's a very beautiful woman," added Scott.

"You've got to be shitting me," I said, feeling my eyebrows converging as my forehead tensed with disapproval.

"I'll pay you a million dollars for the work," he

said, keeping his gaze steady. "Plus expenses, of course, which will be substantial. If you succeed, you earn a four-million-dollar bonus."

That was when the landing gear lowered. The airplane's, and mine. The ambient sound in the cabin escalated accordingly, nearly drowning out the sudden ringing in my ears.

We locked eyes for many disbelieving seconds before I spoke. I felt the flaps extending, and my peripheral vision picked up flashes of real estate outside the windows. Never a good sign, unless you were on final approach.

"Excuse me?"

"The math, Wolf."

"Precisely. Like she's going to walk away from three million a month for . . . hell, I can't even say it. For . . . *me*? Please."

"Why not? You're a hell of a good-looking guy."

The plane flared and touched down on a runway somewhere near what I presumed to be Seattle, based on our time aloft. While we were still braking, the bodyguard got up and went to a closet at the front of the cabin, returning moments later with Scott's suit jacket. The guy was shorter than I'd imagined, but also wider, something along the lines of a Hummer. Meanwhile, Scott had returned to his desktop at the rear, already punching in, presumably to check his email.

"That's it?" I asked as the plane came to a stop. My eyebrows were stuck in the up position.

Scott didn't respond. His eyes were on the PC screen, reading intensely.

"The plane will take you back to Portland," said Bruce, now slipping into his own sportcoat, which could have doubled as a modest pool cover. "We'll expect your answer by this time tomorrow."

"That's it?" I said again, only with a higher pitch.

The hatch dropped open. I could see a massive black SUV parked at the wingtip, the back door open, an equally pumped-up ex-lineman standing sentinel. So this was where all the non-NFL graduating seniors ended up. Judging from the pine trees and little else in the distance, we had stopped at a private field, definitely not Sea-Tac or Boeing Field. Somewhere near Redmond, perhaps. I could almost smell the software.

"Lunch with Bill?" I offered.

Big Bruce actually grinned as Scott brushed past me. No handshake, no eye contact. I honestly didn't perceive it as rudeness—I have a rude meter that could detect attitude from the Dalai Lama himself— just a billionaire's brain having moved on. One of the little sacrifices of life at that altitude is, perhaps, the common courtesy expected from the rest of us.

I guess that was indeed *it*.

Bruce followed Scott from the plane, leaving me quite alone. I vaguely remembered Marni saying something about being back at my miserable life in three hours, including lunch, and found the thought somewhat comforting now.

I watched as they piled into the SUV, which pulled away forthwith. Lunch with Bill. I wouldn't bet against it.

So there I was, sitting in a forty-million-dollar private jet that smelled of Scott's cologne, without a clue as to what might happen next, left to consider a lucrative offer to seduce the wife of one of the world's most successful men.

Just another day in the life of Wolfgang Schmitt.

I couldn't resist. Like an eight-year-old sneaking into his parents' closet, I went to the rear of the cabin

BAIT AND SWITCH   61

and sat on Nelson Scott's immense leather bench seat. My coaches in high school used to say that the other teams, especially the undefeated ones, put their pants on one leg at a time. But this was a whole new level of rarified air. Nelson Scott had personal servants who elevated each of his legs simultaneously as he read a prospectus, while a team of surgically altered female valets wearing wet suits, each recruited from the Miss Hawaiian Tan contest, pulled his trousers up over his ass.

Call me a pig, but that's what I would have done.

It was while indulging in this little visual feast of the mind that I noticed a magazine lying on the seat next to me. It was a back issue of *Redbook*, which didn't strike me as Scott's cup of tea. He was more of a *Kiplinger Tax Newsletter* kind of guy. Then it hit me—I'd seen this particular issue of *Redbook* before. Many times, in fact. There were four copies of it in my desk drawer at home. And not because I was a *Redbook* kind of guy either.

Then it hit me harder. Right in the gut, a sucker punch of Tysonian proportions.

Suddenly, I knew how Scott had found me and why he believed I was just the guy to seduce his wife. This issue of *Redbook* contained an article I had written: "Fatal Detractions—Ten Little Relationship Cancers That Don't Care Who Is Right Or Wrong."

For better or worse, I was a bona fide published authority on how to make a woman happy.

> 11 <

ENTRY #14: LAWYERS—they're like professional athletes: win or lose, they still get obscenely overpaid, they have cool clothes and bad attitudes, they used to be role models but now they're not. All they lack is an all-star game . . . wait a minute, they have Court TV.
—from *Bullshit in America*, by Wolfgang Schmitt

I wrote the article two months before Tracy walked away. We'd been arguing, something about me working out too much, not spending enough time—and money—with and on her, when it dawned on me that the problem wasn't my gym membership at all. It was her *tone*. In fact, our difficulties centered not so much on a particular *issue*, as on the way we dealt with the issue. Seized by a sudden clarity that wouldn't wait until she returned from the Chippendales show to which she'd fled with friends—always a big deal in Portland—I wrote it all down and mailed it off to *Redbook* the next day. It appeared four months later—two months too late where Tracy was concerned—and my career as an author of relationship-salvaging articles for women was born. Who better to counsel women in the ways of wayward men than a card-carrying specimen? They ran my photo in the front pages in the author credit column, and since I didn't have one of those very hip casual poses of me wearing a Sebastian Jungeresque fishing vest, I sent them my modeling headshot, Owen Wilson schnoz and all.

Someone who knew of Nelson Scott's nuptial plight, and of his Machiavellian scheme to get out of it by hooking his wife up with a shill, apparently saw the article and brought it to him. With a little digging they'd found my other two published articles—"Concentric Circles of Relationship" and "Spanking His Inner Child"—and decided to investigate further. Here, they surmised, was a man who understood women. Shortly thereafter, Marni appeared on the agency's doorstep as a perfectly qualified account supervisor, and one month later, there I was, about to become Nelson Scott's best friend.

Who, I had to wonder, would actually have the stones to bring such an idea to fruition?

I didn't have to wonder long. Within minutes, another tricked-out SUV pulled up next to the Gulfstream. From it emerged the longest and most exquisite pair of legs I'd seen since Sharon Stone didn't get arrested for smoking, attached to one of the most beautiful women I'd *ever* seen. She was dressed in a tailored black business suit beneath a dark blue wool overcoat—the kind that costs about the same as a year of tuition at a private school—and kid gloves, and carrying a two-thousand-dollar Mont Blanc briefcase. She approached the airplane with all the confidence of a woman on the cusp of a hostile takeover.

The word "bitch" came to mind, but in a good way.

The jury is still out on women who shake your hand as if trying to stem an arterial hemorrhage, with a Tony Robbins smile pasted on, like she's been dying to meet you and this was the culminating moment of her fiscal quarter. But this lady was pulling it off. Something about the proximity of a million dollars waiting in the wings made her swagger sort of sexy.

"Lee Van Wyke," she announced as she crushed my hand in hers. The plane's hatch began closing before the handshake was consummated, simultaneously with the sound of the turbines starting to spool. Before I could respond, she added, "It's a pleasure to finally meet you . . . may I call you Wolf? That's a fun name. Great conversation starter, I bet."

The coat came off and was tossed fluidly onto a seat as she spoke. She put her briefcase down and sat with great panache. On the off chance that I wasn't sure of the pecking order for this little soiree, I was now set straight.

She was stunning in an evening network news anchor sort of way. A triumph of style and sophistication over genes. Like many beautiful women who no longer frequent bars with their girlfriends, she could have been anywhere from her late thirties to her early fifties. I'd always noticed the difference between women who marry their money and those who make it, and I found the latter far more intoxicating. Women, I still believe, instinctively understand this, the hormonal mystique of power and wealth—it's been the basis of the hunt for centuries—while men approach the game from a different paradigm altogether, one more visceral and, dare I say, visual in nature. Sure, most guys like a little class, a woman who subscribes to both *Sports Illustrated* and *Vogue* and can carry on a solid conversation about the stock market, but let's get real: for the most part they like nice tits and a tight little caboose. More often than not they're intimidated by a woman who is more successful than they are. I've always been weird that way, I guess—give me a woman who can kick my ass at Trivial Pursuit while she's analyzing my portfolio any day. When it's all packaged in a Harvard-bred chassis with a penchant for Halston and a little drama, hey, I'm helpless.

This, in a nutshell, was Lee Van Wyke.

Lee's dark hair nearly matched the leather seats, both in tone and in terms of luster and texture. She wore it shoulder length, just a hint of inward curl at the bottom, very L.A. Her eyes were alert and mischievous, as if she was way ahead of the game, which she was.

"Cat got your tongue there, Wolf?"

"A little speechless, yeah."

I sat in a rear-facing seat and buckled in as the plane began to taxi. It was hard not to look at her, if nothing else because it was as if I were looking at Tracy a few years down the road.

"Let me fill the awkward silence, then," she said. "I'm Nelson Scott's personal attorney, and have been since the day he founded Arielle. I don't run his company but I do manage his personal affairs, which are orders of magnitude more complex, I assure you."

At that moment Monica, who hadn't emerged from the cockpit since she'd welcomed me aboard, hit the throttle, and the plane lurched forward with all the subtlety of an F-18 being catapulted from a carrier.

"You like our little airplane?" Lee asked.

"Oh yeah."

"I bought it for him. Or should I say, I represented him in the transaction. I'm also the person who arranged its lease back to the company, something he still doesn't understand and doesn't need to. Just one of many little arrangements that keep me busy and him solvent while he sucks up to the press. The man hasn't written a check in two decades. He has no idea how much money he has. But *I* know. That's what I do. I run his life."

"Let me guess," I interjected, as much to establish my presence as my insight, "you're also handling the divorce. Which is why we're having this little chit-chat."

She smiled, bringing a perfectly French-manicured hand to her lips. There was no wedding ring, though several other fingers sported what were easily six figures' worth of South Africa's finest. A lipstick-and-fingernail gal, just like my Tracy.

"We've been watching you for a long time," she said.

"That was you?" I said, allowing her to get the joke, which she did. Then I nodded toward the *Redbook* magazine on the seat next to her.

"The article," I said. "Hope you liked it."

"*That* wasn't me."

"Well, your gal Marni deserves a raise. I had no clue."

The little grin that followed had more to it than would be explained to me. Some women have mastered that little trick, and some cynics believe it to be part of the DNA.

She plopped the magazine back down and shifted, re-crossing her legs with perfect feminine symmetry, accompanied by the delicious sound of nylon on nylon.

"So what do you think of our proposition?"

I allowed our eyes to joust for a moment, feeling a bit like Kato Kaelin in the hands of Johnnie Cochran, about to be filleted in front of a national television audience. Despite her smug smile and posture there on the leather bench, which I had a feeling was for my benefit, there was something about this woman that was impatient and cold. Like a certain parent I once lived with.

"I think you're all crazy as hell."

"Well, they say the rich really *are* different. It's true, you know."

"So it seems."

"It's a very serious offer, Wolf. One with more thought and preparation behind it than you could possibly imagine."

We were approaching fifteen thousand feet—the Gulfstream had a digital information board on the bulkhead—and were already well on our way back to Portland. Our time at cruising altitude would be about twelve seconds before we began our descent.

"Try me."

She grinned again, enjoying my defiance. Perhaps they expected me to sit on my haunches like a beagle and wag my tongue at the mention of a million dollars. Then again, if they'd done the homework they claimed they'd done, they were prepared for my well-honed sense of skepticism.

"Nelson's wife," said Lee Van Wyke, "is a very unique woman. Sensitive, emotionally driven, prone to eccentricities. And mean as hell when she's hurt or angry, which she is at the moment. We know exactly what makes her tick."

"And that would be me."

Lee Van Wyke regarded me a moment before responding. "With a little doctoring, yes. Which includes, I might add, a convincing new identity and a net worth of something on the order of five hundred million dollars."

I regarded her back, though in a not nearly as detached way.

"What," I said, "my wit and charm won't be enough?"

This broadened her smile somewhat, as if my comment surprised her. And not in a good way.

"This isn't a game, you know. These people fly above the radar. They get whatever they want, when they want it. Without understanding that context, which you can't possibly understand, you won't know what you're getting into here. Without that kind of financial pedigree, you'll get as much mindshare from the woman as her aquarium keeper."

I didn't like the bitch already.

"And," she added, "Kelly's lawyer is a real snake."

"One bad apple, they say."

With a tired exhale, Lee said, "She's at the center of this whole thing, actually."

"Kelly or the lawyer?"

"Libby Payne, her appropriately named attorney of record, though there's a whole team of man-hating bitches working on this."

I grabbed the armrest as the plane banked nearly ninety degrees, the nose pointing skyward at a forty-five-degree angle. Any more geometry and my breakfast would leave the building.

"I was wondering," I said, "why Mr. Scott doesn't just pay the woman. I mean, three million a month, that's beer money to a guy like him. At least, if you believe the tabloids."

"We don't read tabloids."

"Neither do I. So why don't you just tell me."

She re-crossed her legs. A dozen one-liners flashed before my eyes, but I refrained.

"*Forbes* had us at number nineteen three years ago, at 4.8 billion. Two years ago he was thirty-first with 2.9, and a year ago he was somewhere in the nineties, at about 1.6. It's all guesswork, but it's also all relative and quite accurate. Catching a trend here, Wolf?"

"I did notice there were no peanuts on this flight," I said.

Her eyes narrowed slightly as she said, "We won't even *be* on the list this year."

I nodded slowly, even respectfully. I knew enough about Arielle stock to remember that it had been one of the all-time tankers in market history, falling from a 1999 high of a price in the mid-eighties to a recent price of about seven bucks. I hadn't paused to consider the effect of this on Nelson Scott's credit rating, but now that it was on the table right in front of me, I could see why he was nervous. Poor guy might have to unload that NASCAR team pretty soon just to make his Gulfstream payment.

She was nodding back at me approvingly.

"Libby Payne is nobody's fool. Not now; not when she wrote that prenuptial agreement two decades ago. The contract stipulates that any settlements would be in cash or cash equivalents. Specifically, it countermands any payment tendered in company stock. At the time it was rhetoric, and Nelson had an erection you wouldn't believe. You know how the stock market works, Wolf?"

"Yeah, actually I do, Lee. I put my money in, it goes south. I've got it down."

Her smile was getting thinner with each sarcastic comment I made. I was looking forward to seeing how far I could push before she cracked like a Mormon librarian.

"Arielle stock is at an all-time low," she said, "as you may be aware. When significant shares are put on the market, more selling pressure is applied. Which means the stock cannot go up, at least on technical merits alone. That's freshman stuff. Here's the grad-school take: because of the fifty-million-dollar property division, Nelson will be out of cash the day he writes that check. Which means every month thereafter, he'll have to convert options and then sell the stock to make the three million in alimony, not to mention his personal expenses. That's a double-edged sword right up his ass, Wolf, and I'm not kidding here. This in turn means the stock has that much more selling pressure on a consistent basis, and basically the whole thing spirals to hell in a handbasket."

I duplicated her exasperated exhale as best I could. "All I have to do is get her to marry me. Piece of cake."

She could tell by my tone I was being completely sarcastic.

"That's where Libby Payne fucked up," she said.

I raised my eyebrows.

"Of course Kelly isn't going to marry you or anyone else, not with thirty-six million a year at stake. She's naïve, but stupid she's not. What she doesn't know is that the contract stipulates *cohabitation* as sufficient cause for suspension of maintenance."

She licked her lips like a hyena smelling blood.

"I just have to get her to move in with me."

"Or you with her. There are precedents, some at the Supreme Court level, that establish a benchmark at thirty days of cohabitation. You do that, we go to court, and the whole thing gets hung up in legal toilet paper."

I was getting it now. My eyes fogged momentarily while I organized the data in my mind.

Then I said, "Giving the stock time to pull off a miraculous recovery."

She folded her hands into a church steeple in front of her face. My guess was, it was as close to God as she'd been in years.

"We could drag it out for a year or two," she said. "Meanwhile, Kelly gets a substantially reduced monthly maintenance pending the outcome, and you get paid for a job well done. Hell, we break even on you in three months."

I whistled. They were indeed further down this road than I'd imagined.

"You people are *nasty*."

"I'm an attorney."

"And then what? I just move out?"

"Trust me, when she discovers you're not what you said you were, you'll *be* moved out. If I were you, I'd get a bodyguard."

"That's cold."

"Not as cold as you think. On the surface it'll all add up. Your company will have just filed chapter eleven, and coincidentally—because she'll check—your purported half-billion will have shrunk to a measly five million dollars. She might not ever know you were a fraud."

"Just a failure."

"You'll get your money, Wolf."

"And then I just disappear."

She smiled, nodding with a frightening smugness.

"The recovery of that stock is everything, Wolf. We're making some changes, and we have a good shot at a rebound, but it won't happen quickly. In the meantime we have to put a stop to this alimony bullshit, and we have to get creative to do it. If, of course, you're up for it."

If she'd have been smirking, I'd have thought she was shooting for her own moment of double-entendre. But her otherwise lovely face was as straight as a passport photo.

"Scott's teetering on insolvency, but he's willing to pay cash for my, uh, *services*?" I said.

"People like Nelson understand the concept of risk-reward. And in the scheme of things, you come cheap, frankly speaking."

"Well, that's good to know."

"All relative, Wolf. You in, or not?"

I chewed my lower lip as I looked away. I could feel her gaze staying with me, patient now. The tutorial was over.

"It's a long shot," I offered.

"Not as long as you think. She's lonely, and she has certain, shall we say, hooks. You'll have a team behind you all the way. We don't move until you're ready."

"And of course, I'll have you, too." I smiled slightly.

She paused with a straight face before saying, "Is that a counteroffer, Wolf?"

I hadn't thought of it that way, but I couldn't help but smile at the sudden notion.

Lee cocked her head to the side, sort of like a dog trying to understand its master's words. I knew instantly that my trusty twinkle had just bombed.

"Are you flirting with me?" she asked.

My cheeks filled with regret. I had made a tactical error in assuming she and I were both beneath the lofty station of our employers. It either offended her or I was just plain wrong.

"If you know me like you say you do," I tried, "you tell me."

I waited for her smile to return, but it didn't.

"Let's not play this game. I've been with Nelson for over twenty years, I've met the richest and best-looking men on the planet, out-drunk them, beat them at cards and tennis, slept with a few, and turned down a lot more, and I've made more money than you'll ever see in your lifetime. You think your pretty face can make me all misty, think again. Men like you, you're just another contract. So don't fuck with me, Mr. Schmitt, or I'll squash you like a bug on the windshield of this airplane, and I'll enjoy it."

Now she smiled, and it wasn't pretty. More like the Wicked Witch wringing her hands saying, "Poppies, poppies . . ." I wasn't sure what nerve I'd hit, but it bit back.

Just for kicks, I decided to smile back at her as I nodded my understanding.

"No way you beat me at tennis," I said. "I can promise you that."

She averted her eyes, uncomfortable with being this close to insubordination. I'd been here before, staring down a woman who, for whatever reason, felt the need to assert her superiority right off the bat. Hell, I hadn't really been flirting at all.

The power suddenly backed off and the aircraft's nose dipped. There was nothing coy about Monica's piloting style, and I couldn't help but draw an analogy between it and the world I was being invited to enter: fast, no bullshit, dangerous. And, I had to admit, thrilling.

Lee grabbed her bag from the table and dug around for a moment. Then she handed me a card, which had nothing on it but a telephone number printed in barely legible six-point type.

"You have twenty-four hours. Call this number—it's a service, I'll call you right back, so be sure you're in a secure situation. If you tell anyone about this—including a lawyer, which you don't need—the deal is off. I majored in plausible deniability in law school, so don't test me."

When I looked up from the card, still squinting, she was already punching a number into the telephone pad on the console with one hand, thumbing her Palm Pilot with the other, the receiver pinned between her ear and her shoulder. I had been dismissed, and in a manner not unlike that in which her boss had switched me off earlier.

It was going to be easy to tell these people to go to hell.

The plane landed in Hillsboro a few awkward minutes later. It was raining even harder than when we'd left, and at first I didn't notice that my car, a five-series Beamer which I'd parked in the downtown lot that morning, was now sitting in the middle of the tarmac, hundreds of yards from anything. Which was sort of interesting, since the keys had been in my pocket the entire time.

The airplane came to a stop with its wingtip a few feet away from the driver's side door.

"How the hell . . ." I mumbled as the hatch lowered.

"Presume anything is possible," said Lee Van Wyke, who had joined me next to the door for a bone-crunching farewell handshake. A whiff of her perfume hit me, something all too familiar. "And assume nothing. The old rules no longer apply."

I smiled weakly and stepped out into the rain.

I could have told her my answer then and there. But even my new karmic sensibility, inspired by the pain of Tracy's departure and nourished by the realization that I was alone in the world, was open to a little procrastination. Hell, a million bucks was still a lot of money where I came from. Like she said, anything was suddenly possible.

Except, of course, the likelihood of getting into Lee Van Wyke's pants.

And, I had to admit, I had a thing about breaking rules.

Even if they were my own.

>12<

ENTRY #16: BIG TOBACCO—from the folks who brought you lung cancer, heart disease, litter, smelly clothes, jungle-rot breath, yellow teeth, juvenile delinquents, coffee table burns, and nine-digit litigation. Be sure to send your kids to the Phillip Morris booth on Career Day.
—from *Bullshit In America*, by Wolfgang Schmitt

No can do. Not gonna happen. Not in this lifetime. Not that I wasn't sorely tempted. The million bucks aside, everything about Nelson Scott's proposed gig was compelling—private jets, a new identity as a half-billionaire, the chance to humiliate Lee Van Wyke on the tennis court. The possibility of four million further dollars wasn't even a part of my evaluation, because in my mind there was no way it would ever work.

The whole trip had taken a little more than an hour and a half, door to door. At the airport, on the front seat of my Beamer, there was a white plastic container with a note reading, "Enjoy your lunch." Inside were six escargot swimming in garlic butter and red pepper pasta with a delectable lobster marinara sauce, accompanied by herb bread that was somehow still warm. Their research was spot-on:

these were my all-time favorite dishes, even when served in a plastic container.

Not even that could sway me from my point of view.

The big news back at the office was that Marni had resigned right before lunch. By the time I arrived she was already gone. I tried to feign my great surprise and outrage, but—with apologies to Mike Piazza—I was like a famous jock playing himself in a cheesy commercial: stiff as a board and unconvincing as hell.

Concentration was not an option, and since I had no meetings that afternoon, I left early. This was not altogether unprecedented where I was concerned, so no one noticed. More accurately, I feared, no one cared.

Instead of going home—I live in a small contemporary house across the street from my tennis club—I went to Portland's version of a smoky big-city meat market, which is to say, the only place in town with both hot women and a view.

The City Grill was on the thirty-eighth floor of the tallest structure in town. The view, on the rare clear Portland evening, was of the Willamette River and the expanse of urban sprawl to the east, and the affluent hills to the west. A better view, however, was from the end of the bar, where you could see the front door and the geography of the floor plan with equal discretion. It was here that I hunkered down with a glass of tonic water and a slice of lemon, not so much to take in the scenery as to take stock of my options.

By five thirty, I concluded that not much had changed since my glory days of frequenting such places, a substantial chapter in my life that had come to a sudden halt when Tracy and I had hit our rhythm together over two years earlier. On occasion we'd pop into places like this to meet friends or have a romantic moment—including an evening or two right here at the City Grill—but things are different when you're happily attached at the hip and not scanning for bogeys.

I hadn't come here to cruise. I'd come here to further consider Nelson Scott's offer and the prospect of becoming Lee Van Wyke's personal love slave. And to do so on hallowed ground, a place where my past would speak to me and remind me of my pain. But the fact was, I already knew.

It just wasn't gonna happen. And it was Tracy's fault.

What Nelson Scott wanted me to do was, by my way of thinking, an unthinkable betrayal. Not only of the woman he was asking me to seduce and destroy, but of myself. He was asking me to deceive a woman who, while perhaps not completely innocent in the eyes of her husband or of God or anyone else who knew her, had done nothing to *me*. If it all worked out according to plan, I would break her heart in the end, and though her anger might result in the hiring of some no-neck thug to break my kneecaps, her pain would be the primary outcome of our contrived relationship. That and her loss of three million in monthly alimony, which was none of my business. If you believed in a soul, which I certainly did, the cost would still far exceed the remuneration. Money, by the way, I certainly could have used.

Call me old-fashioned, but this was just plain wrong. In my mind, it was no different from mugging someone for his winning lottery ticket.

In case I was tempted to rethink this noble conclusion—easy to do when there are seven digits at stake—there was something else to consider. Something that, if I were to accept Scott's offer, I would impart to his wife, just as Tracy had presented it to me. I'm talking about *pain*. The dull, relentless ache of a broken heart, the acidic sting of rejection, the humiliation of having *Return to Sender* stamped on your ticker. Four months after the fact and I was still swimming in that pain, I was drowning in it, and I'd be damned if I'd subscribe to the misery-loves-company school of karmic suicide. To deliberately put another human being through what I was experiencing would forever define me as soulless.

So there it was. Either way you cut it—sell your soul, or validate that you never had one—it was a sucker's deal.

Instantly I felt better. Maybe those monks and martyrs were on to something. Maybe God wasn't just in the details—he was waiting just offstage with a hanky and a hug.

It was a warm notion, and I was actually grinning as I sat there lost in thought, staring down into my tonic water, embracing hope for the first time in, well, four months.

But the grin went away in a hurry. When I glanced up, Tracy was stepping out of the elevator with a couple of her girlfriends.

> 13 <

ENTRY #117: WEIGHT LOSS PILLS—eat all you want and still lose weight! Fat blockers, carb blockers—go ahead, have a corndog! Never mind the heart palpitations from the ephedra, and don't pay attention to the small print that says these results are not typical, and the even smaller print that says "Effective only when used with diet and exercise." That pain in your cheek is where the hook is embedded.
—from *Bullshit in America*, by Wolfgang Schmitt

The pedestal upon which we enshrine our lost lovers is high, and over time they become godlike in their beauty and power. Normally, if my friends who had been down this road were to be believed, an unexpected reunion can be wonderful therapy, since the reality simply cannot stand up to these nostalgic standards. But Tracy just blew that little theory all to hell. I'd say she looked like an angel from a long-lost dream, approaching with outstretched arms and an olive branch, but the opposite was true. She looked positively, absolutely, and deliciously poisonous, a one-woman, bite-of-the-apple, soul-devouring sexual sorceress, but with class.

Which is to say, she was every bit as perfect as I remembered.

She was with two girlfriends I recognized but

didn't like—one never likes the co-conspirators of a departing lover—both of whom were close to being showstoppers in their own right. They entered the bar like a shock wave, instantly silencing a dozen or more conclaves of male conversation, pissing off wives and girlfriends, shifting the energy of the entire room. Where would they sit, who would they grace with their cruel smiles? They snaked through the crowd toward a table by the window, trying to appear oblivious to the attention, failing miserably at it. Because they met no one's eyes, Tracy didn't see me—I was the guy at the end of the bar with the unhinged jaw—caught up instead in their protective whispering, as if they had critical business between them.

Yeah, like which of them would con some poor schmo into buying the first round.

Tracy had always been one of those women blessed with both great natural beauty and a killer fashion sense, and she certainly hadn't gone Birkenstock in the four months of my exile. Her hair was a rich auburn—the color of a fine scotch and just as smooth. I'd seen her change it on a whim for a photo shoot or out of sheer boredom, but this was, as far as I knew, the real thing. She'd always worn it long and straight, as she did this night, though when she tied it back or tricked it up for something formal, it was devastating to behold. She had delicate features anchored by a cute little pug nose and explosively kinetic green eyes. Her lips were what men saw when their dreams crossed the line, naturally swollen with a pouty little attitude, framed by dimples that misled you to believe in sweetness.

Then again, I was in love. Someone else might have just said, Yeah, she looked pretty good.

On this night, she chose what I called her neo-goth

Santa Monica look—low-riding tight jeans with the faked bleach fade that showcased her racehorse legs and killer hips, a belt of large metal spheres, well-heeled boots with appropriately witchy toes, a form-fitting black sweater with a deep V-collar trimmed in fur. All of it was worn beneath a long black car-coat sweater that looked as if it had had a prior life as a throw rug in a palace. Her friends were similarly garbed, but frankly they were the Pips to her Gladys Knight. There was no mistaking the true diva in this bunch.

I didn't know what I'd do. There was a better than even chance I'd just sit there and observe, indulge in the torment of proximity without possibility. Watching her, simply absorbing the way she moved, had always been part of the experience anyhow. There was a decent chance that I'd slip away unseen, though I didn't want to think about what that might do to my sleeping pattern for the next few weeks.

Who was I kidding? If nothing else, this was an opportunity to spew a little venom, lay a little Alanis Morissette on her. This was no time for pride; this was all about going for a jagged little guilt trip. And pray that she would respond with something I could construe as comforting.

It was that kind of thinking that got me in trouble with her in the first place.

And so I watched, each minute more agonizing than the last. I observed her laugh, as if her world was without conflict and her dreams were at hand. I saw her flirt, gracefully casting off all comers and then laughing about it with her coven mates. I watched her sip red wine and smoke menthol cigarettes as if she taught that particular class at Hogwarts, generally delighting in the feminine art of being wicked and bewitching, all of which had frustrated and intrigued me back when we shared a digital alarm clock.

About thirty minutes in, just as I was about to make my move, she suddenly looked my way. And judging by her expression—something along the lines of a cerebral hemorrhage—I was the last person on earth she expected to see.

The cerebral hemorrhage, however, would be mine. She put her glass of wine down, excused herself from her friends, and walked right over to me. Upon arrival, she gave me a long, heartfelt hug, freezing the entire bar in disbelief. All laws of time and space were tested, since during those few seconds I experienced enough sensation and conflicting emotion to keep my shrink on Tums for weeks. The familiar—her perfume, the texture of her hair against my cheek, my chemical response—collided head-on with the need to say everything in one thoroughly Faulkneresque sentence. After a few seconds I had to remind myself to breathe, yet I was afraid to do so lest my weakness manifest itself as a shudder. I was doing all I could simply to remain upright.

"You've lost weight," she said as she pulled back, her smile sheepish, her voice still that low sexy purr, like an idling XKE. It was an old joke—people who hadn't seen me in a while were always saying I seemed thinner, despite the fact that my weight hadn't changed in a decade.

"Divorce diet," I said as I patted my tummy, regretting it immediately. "Sans legal fees." I tried for a grin that belied the words.

She nodded, averting her eyes, and I could tell she was looking for a back door. I had to be quick or this would be the shortest reunion since David Lee Roth rejoined Van Halen.

"Business trip?"

"Actually, it is. You still . . . ?"

"A marketing whore? Until tomorrow."

She smirked, thankful to get past that little moment, thinking I was being my typical smartass self. But I was deadly serious.

I pressed on. "So . . . how's life in SoCal?"

"Bay Area."

"I knew that." I actually didn't, but what the hell. "Still with . . . ?"

"No. That didn't work, but the job did, thank God. Things are good."

That one stung. I had made up a story in which her departure was all about the rich new guy from California, inherent in which was the assumption that if he didn't work out, she'd come skipping home, begging my forgiveness. I'd hold out for, say, three or four minutes before caving in.

"You?" she countered with a hopeful tone.

"Me what?"

"Things are good with you?"

I paused, which announced the arrival of the inevitable.

"You want an honest answer?"

"I don't think I do."

She glanced back at her friends nervously.

"Gotta run, right?"

"Listen, Wolf . . . I should have called you long before . . ."

"Stop. You have nothing to apologize for."

"Now you're lying."

"Yeah. Listen, you told it like it was. Greener pastures, chubbier ten-forty . . . hey, you're outta here."

She bit her lip, always a sure sign she was on the cusp of striking back.

"We should talk," she said instead.

"Have a seat." I motioned to the empty barstool next to mine.

"I can't. I'm with . . ."

"Trixie and Boom Boom, I know. I've been watching you smoke for half an hour. Haven't lost your touch, by the way."

I smiled, signaling this wasn't all about carving out a pound of flesh. She smiled back, knowing her inclination to light up in bars had been a bit of an issue with me.

She touched my arm, sending a bolt of electricity straight into my rib cage.

"I mean it. We need to talk. Soon. Will you call me?"

I turned both palms toward the ceiling and shrugged. She hadn't left a number when she bolted, an omission that needed no further elaboration now. I was tempted to remind her that my number hadn't changed, but thought better of it.

"I was a bitch, wasn't I."

"You certainly were."

"You didn't deserve . . ."

"I certainly didn't. But hey, here we are, mending fences, building bridges. Is this a great country, or what?"

She hadn't brought her purse with her, so she pantomimed a writing motion to the bartender, who responded by handing over a pen. She wrote something on the cocktail napkin beneath my glass.

"I go back in the morning. Call me. Please."

I nodded, completely out of witty little bromides.

She leaned in to touch her lips to my cheek. I could feel her swipe the tip of her tongue across my skin before she puckered and burned a kiss that lasted a few moments longer than it should have. To my great surprise, this was all it took to instigate an instantaneous and quite involuntary swelling of certain glands that had forgotten their mission in life.

Damn her.

I watched her return to her table, and the inevitable whispered inquiries from her two friends, who glanced back at me over their shoulders. Then I looked down at the napkin and felt something explode deep in the pit of my stomach.

I didn't expect to recognize the number, and I didn't. But I did recognize the area code: 408. Which wasn't the big city at all. It was the area code for the San Jose–Santa Clara metroplex. The Silicon Valley, the corporate headquarters of Arielle Systems, and precisely the location to which I would have relocated had I decided to take Nelson Scott up on his bizarre proposition.

Just when I thought I had it straight, here was a crooked line, tempting me to cross. Faust, it seemed, was working overtime tonight.

Damn her again.

> 14 <

> ENTRY #51: LOUSY CUSTOMER SERVICE—invented in New York—where eye contact with customers is frowned upon—it has spread to the rest of America, primarily through the telephone companies, who, after deregulation, devaluation, and near disintegration, still don't give a shit.
> —from *Bullshit in America*, by Wolfgang Schmitt

When I met her, Tracy was both a model and a makeup girl working at Nordstrom. It was hardly an original combination, and predictably, the retail gig was explained away as a stopgap until something popped on the modeling front. Portland had never been what you'd call a seething hotbed of undiscovered modeling talent, but Tracy was on a legitimate roll—she was "the face" in a series of billboards and television ads for the city's lame excuse for an upscale suburban mall, Washington Square. Since this was precisely the mall where she plied her trade selling Estée Lauder, she had become a local celebrity of sorts, something of which I was reminded every time we went out in public.

Her notoriety was, I felt, partially responsible for her decision to leave town. And, by definition, me.

We met on a shoot for a local television spot. We were cast as the happy couple shopping for a wedding ring at the neighborhood super shopping center, where the jewelry department is three aisles down from the canned goods—yeah, like *that's* gonna happen—and the director commented on our "chemistry." It was obvious he wanted into her pants in a big way, which gave us something to laugh about in between takes. Between giggles we discovered that we both played serious tennis, shared a wide breadth of musical tastes, hated our day jobs, favored the same restaurants, watched PBS, harbored a jaded sense of politics and a worldview best described as confused, and most critically, neither of us was in an exclusive relationship at the time. I was mid-thirties, she was late-twenties—a perfect spread. She thought I was funny, I thought she was complicated. Most painfully beautiful women I'd known were something less than complicated. Especially in the modeling trade.

We made a date for lunch the next week, and it went from there.

And for nearly two years, it worked.

Our lovemaking was legend. We broke tables in hotel rooms. We beseeched God to the point where He needed earmuffs and a sense of humor. Half the time our postman arrived wearing a shit-eating grin, such was the frequency with which he delivered mail-order goodies in brown paper wrappers. We were morning people, we were night owls, we were afternoon delight-ees, and we were multi-orgasmic. Tracy owned enough leather to upholster half the county, and where candle wax and silk ties and things that go ouch in the night are concerned, let's just say that we have secrets we will take to our graves and leave it at that.

There were also more traditional romantic moments, times when we would lock eyes and move slowly toward the gates of heaven, evoking tears and words with origins neither one of us could explain. She would tell me she loved me forever, and I would tell her she was my angel, my dream come true.

Intimacy wasn't the problem.

Money was.

It never occurred to either one of us that she might, on occasion, whip out her Visa card, too. I was too in love to notice—and she was too ambitious to ignore—one key variable where courtship in America is concerned: I didn't make enough money to keep Tracy happy.

I never saw it coming. In two years, I had yet to see the inside of her wallet, but I wrote it off to her being an old-fashioned girl, and later, to me being an old-fashioned chump. There were a few other minor issues up for debate—I wanted a family one day, she didn't want to talk about it; I didn't drink, she liked to party; I refused to throw games on the tennis court, and she liked to win—but they were routine potholes. Shortly after the Washington Square campaign broke and she was suddenly the toast of the town—a heady experience when your face adorns billboards on all four major freeways in town—there was a slight increase in her evening quiet spells, which I'd always written off to deep thought and PMS. For all I knew, she was struggling with the pressure of sudden fame, anonymous as it was. She started going out with her girlfriends a bit more often than usual—that party thing again—and it was on one such evening that she met Mr. Wonderful.

Cynicism is too often a product of experience, and this was mine: Tracy's departure was a carefully planned sneak attack, an assassination of sorts. In fact, the few weeks prior to her exit—I like to think of it as a desertion—were idyllic, calm, and even passionate, while in her solitary time, she was designing her getaway with all the cold precision of a sniper. The only thing out of the ordinary was a daytrip to California under the guise of a photo shoot, when in fact it was a job interview. I arrived home from work that day, Black Friday, to find her stuff—and some of mine—gone. She was waiting for me at the kitchen table, wearing her coat, and with one look I recognized the tune. I would face the music alone, free to make up the answers for myself.

She left no number, no forwarding address, and no chance whatsoever that her friends would cough up any information. I knew only what she told me, that she had met someone and was moving to California with him, that she had a job and some modeling contacts. Then, with a final thrust designed to pierce my heart, spoken with the calm chill of an admitting nurse, she told me our relationship was going nowhere anyway, and that I would have realized it sooner or later. She simply got there first.

She was wrong, of course. I never got there at all.

> 15 <

ENTRY #25: RACISTS IN THE SENATE—Jesse Helms, Trent Lott . . . waiting until these clowns die in office isn't the solution. There should be a mandatory closet check for Klan robes before the name goes on the ballot.
    —from *Bullshit in America*, by Wolfgang Schmitt

My house was on a cul-de-sac just across the river on the east side of town, on the seventh hole of a public golf course and flanking the driveway of one of the lesser tennis clubs. It was one of six identical contemporary structures lining one side of the street, the other being a creek bordering the fairway. You'd never think this would be a hotbed for the smash-and-grab crowd, but I'd had four break-ins in four years, which was the sole reason for the loaded twenty-two-caliber handgun in my nightstand drawer. Not exactly what Clint would use, but it would slow someone down long enough for me to plant my nine-iron, which was under my bed, squarely between his beady little eyes. A cop told me to be sure to shoot the intruder inside the house, since if I shot him outside I could be sued, spend my entire 401(k) on a lawyer, and lose. He suggested that if I happened to nail him in the driveway or on the roof—they'd entered via skylight twice—I should drag the bastard inside and not worry about the stains on the carpet. In fact, I should plug him again to create an indoor forensic footprint.

Good to know our tax dollars are paying dividends.

So I was a little nervous to see a strange car parked in my driveway when I pulled up. After the day I'd just had—the jet, the job offer, the pasta, Tracy—anything was possible. It was a white Taurus, which could only mean one of two things: someone wanted to sell me insurance at this strange hour, or this was government business.

The car was blocking my side of the garage, so I parked next to it, noticing that there were two people sitting inside. Last I knew, burglars didn't park in the driveway and wait for the homeowner to show up.

They got out of the Taurus immediately. I hesitated long enough to discern that they were a man and a woman of roughly the same size and build. In fact, she looked like she could take him if push came to shove. She had short dark hair and was wearing a black raincoat that definitely wasn't Neiman Marcus. He wore a cheap gray suit—something you'd see at the DMV—adding to the feeling that their business would be civic in nature.

I got out of my car. Never let them smell your fear. Or your opinion of their wardrobe.

"Wolfgang Schmitt?" said the woman, who had been driving. I steadied myself when the man reached for something under his coat. He produced a wallet, flipping it open. I didn't look at it. The woman came around the front of the Taurus, her own wallet open in her hand.

"Special Agents Banger and Short," announced the woman.

Banger and Short. Sounded like a low-rent law firm.

"Which one's Short?" I asked, unable to mask a grin born of the fact they were both about five-five. They didn't answer, allowing their badges to do the talking.

Suddenly I didn't feel so funny.

"I am a special agent with the FBI," she said. "This is Special Agent Short, IRS Investigations Unit. This is a joint investigation matter, and we have questions for you."

I could see this was a moment they relished, when the short jokes bombed and the power shifted. It wasn't the first time a vertically challenged Napoleon and a woman who'd never danced at the prom had looked at me like I was a punch line.

"I must warn you," I offered, "I keep my receipts."

"Can we go inside?" asked the IRS man.

I glanced at Special Agent Banger, the FBI woman, who nodded that I'd heard correctly. I just nodded back and led them toward the door.

"Take your coats?" I said, flipping on the lights. They walked into my living room and sat down without answering.

"We shouldn't be long," said Banger, trying for a smile. You could almost hear the tendons in her face creaking.

I sat on the chair opposite the couch. A recent guest had described the place as "airport waiting lounge meets Woody Allen," the last part because of a print over my stereo of a guy playing a clarinet. The eye was drawn immediately to the 48-inch, flat-screen, high-definition monitor affixed to the wall, my very un-Woody-like bachelor pride and joy.

Short pulled a small tape player from his jacket pocket, setting it on the table with some measure of ceremony.

Banger led off, consulting notes from a small tablet in her hands.

"Today you arrived at the Hillsboro Airport in a hired Town Car at approximately 11:10, give or take."

"Give or take," I confirmed.

"Seven minutes later, a Grumman Gulfstream IV landed and taxied to your location. You boarded immediately." She looked up at me. "How am I doin' so far?"

"It was a G-five, but still very impressive. I have a million questions already."

The two special agents exchanged an expressionless glance before Banger checked her notes and continued.

"The aircraft departed immediately and flew to a private airstrip in Redmond, Washington. Your host, a Mr. Nelson Scott, and his bodyguard, a Mr. Bruce Martinez, deplaned, leaving you on board. You were then joined by a Ms. Lee Van Wyke, and the airplane brought you back to the Hillsboro Airport, where your car and your lunch were waiting for you."

I wanted to challenge them to tell me what I ate, but I was afraid they'd know. I just nodded, looking appropriately blown away.

Banger nodded at Short, who reached out to punch a button on the tape player.

> *Let's not play this game. I've been with Nelson for over twenty years, I've met the richest and best-looking men on the planet, out-drunk them, beat them at cards and tennis, slept with a few, turned down a lot more, and I've made more money than you'll ever see in your lifetime.*

You think your pretty face can make me all misty, think again. Men like you, you're just another contract. I eat your type for breakfast. So don't fuck with me, Mr. Schmitt, or I'll squash you like a bug on the windshield of this airplane.

I watched their faces as Lee Van Wyke's little diatribe filled the room. They were studying me, a trace of bemusement easily detectible, even understandable.

Short said, "How we doing now, Mr. Schmitt?"

I sat back in my chair as my eyes drifted. If I had had any doubt about that power shift, it was long gone.

"How the hell did you get this?" I asked, more to myself than for their benefit, shaking my head for emphasis.

"You underestimate your government's investment in technology," said Banger, her attitude gaining momentum.

"I'm guessing satellite telemetry," I said.

"Actually," interjected Short, who would have made a great Jimmy Olsen in his younger days, the kind of guy who reads a science fiction paperback while standing in line at Kmart, "you need a source transmitter first. The satellite can track anything once it's online."

"Even an airplane," I said, catching on.

"Only way to do it, actually," said Banger.

"Wait till Gene Roddenberry finds out about this."

With a poker face, Banger said, "Do some people find you amusing, Mr. Schmitt?"

"My mother thinks I'm a laugh riot. Then again, she's looney tunes, but you probably already knew that. Am I, like, in trouble or something? Because if

I'm not, I wish you'd tell me why you're here in my living room. Not to be rude or anything."

The lovely Ms. Banger stared at me for the longest time, long enough for the not-so-lovely Mr. Short to look at her quizzically, perhaps wondering if it was his turn.

It wasn't. This was definitely Banger's show.

"We'd like your help, Mr. Schmitt."

"Excuse me?"

"We'd like you to accept Nelson Scott's offer, and to consider going undercover for us in that role."

I felt my brow knitting up tighter than J-Lo's jeans.

"You're shitting me," I said.

"I never *shit* about my work," said Banger.

Upon which I excused myself from the room.

> 16 <

ENTRY #19: THE ALTERNATIVE MINIMUM TAX—you've busted your ass to make a good living, you're in the highest tax bracket the IRS offers, already paying your fair share, and then guess what: you don't get to deduct all your mortgage interest, charitable contributions, and other legitimate write-offs. To get the same deal as your paperboy, you'll have to cheat. Funny, now that they belong exclusively to the wage earners, we don't hear all that bitching about loopholes.
—from *Bullshit in America*, by Wolfgang Schmitt

Cold water, both swallowed and splashed in my eyes, didn't help. I eyed the telephone in my kitchen, but there was no one to call. Besides, I'd just found out they can bug airplanes and listen in from space, so what was the point? I wondered if they knew about my little rendezvous with Tracy that evening—maybe *they* could tell me where she worked—but at that moment I wasn't even sure it had happened at all.

I made a quick stop in the john before going back in. I was itching to know what they had in mind, why the FBI and the IRS were riding in the same rental car, but didn't want to seem too anxious. Negotiating 101: always take a leak in the middle of the action.

Banger and Short were whispering when I returned to the living room. They stopped and sat up when they saw me.

"Interesting," said Short. "We tell you we need your help, you go take a piss. It was me, I'd be all ears."

An odd comment from a special agent of the IRS, I thought.

"What can I say. Ya gotta go, ya gotta go."

"Our first question is academic," said Banger. She hesitated as if expecting a retort, which was lingering on the tip of my tongue. "What are your intentions where Nelson Scott's offer is concerned?"

"Does it matter?"

"Not really. After you hear what we have to say, I don't think it will."

"Then I'm all ears, after all." I winked at Short, and the little bugger looked away.

Banger said, "Mr. Scott is under investigation by the FBI on a variety of fronts. We're working jointly with the SEC, the IRS, and the U.S. Treasury department."

"Name dropper."

"These are serious allegations."

"Such as?"

"We're not at liberty to say," said Short.

Looking at him, I said, "Can you spell 'hypothetical'? Bet you can't."

Sure enough, he looked over at Banger for leadership.

"Tax issues, for one," she responded, as if she were well above petty bureaucratic bullshit. I smelled the beginning of an emerging good cop–bad cop scenario, though the idea of Short as the bad cop was already hilarious.

She continued.

"A notebook full of securities infractions, international tariff violations, and an alleged criminal matter of the most serious nature. Hypothetical enough for you?"

"How about spousal abuse?" I offered, not entirely in jest.

"We're certainly open to suggestions," said Short.

They didn't seem in a hurry to bring this full circle, so I thought I'd give it a go.

"You want me to go through the motions with his wife, and report back to you on anything I hear. How am *I* doin'?"

Short said, "Actually, you'll be wired for most of it."

"Not if Kelly Scott and I hit it off, we won't."

They exchanged another of their private little grins before Scott said, "Why don't you let us worry about that eventuality."

"My government's technology again."

"Something like that."

I squirmed in my chair, impatient with the jockeying.

"Hypothetically speaking," I said, "assuming I was going to accept Mr. Scott's kind offer, which, if I'm not mistaken, is not remotely illegal, I'm supposed to turn my back on a one-million-dollar fee to help you nail this guy? Have I got that right?"

Banger said, "Things aren't always what they seem, Mr. Schmitt."

"That they aren't. Mind if I see those IDs again?"

"Not at all," said Short, already moving for his wallet. I held up an irritated hand to stop him.

"By that, I mean," said Banger, "if you cooperate,

there may be a way for you to keep the money. Provided, of course, we get what we need and you avoid being compromised during the operation."

"As in, *the secretary will disavow, yada yada yada*?"

"I don't think he'll pay you if he discovers you're working on our behalf, do you?"

"Actually, I'm more worried about that criminal allegation you were talking about."

Short said, "We'll have you out of the picture the instant you've been compromised."

"Bet you know all about being compromised," I said.

"Don't push it, sir."

"Right. I just come on back to my little ol' life and Scott'll forget about the whole thing. I don't think so."

"That's well outside the profile. Of course, there are no guarantees."

"Of course. So far, you haven't given me much of a reason to sign up. Except, of course, my civic obligation—which, frankly, doesn't move me to tears."

Banger said, "We can discuss that, if you like."

"Why don't we."

Scott weighed in with, "Ever been audited, Mr. Schmitt?"

I glared at Banger, then at Short, and had to swallow the urge to bodily remove them from my house.

"That's cold," I said.

"That's how it is," said Banger, a hint of impatience now in her voice. "We actually prefer the half-full approach, that being your ability to keep Mr. Scott's money for your time and trouble. Tax-free, by the way, since it can never be on the record, just as your identity will never become an element of the prosecution. We're looking for information, pure and simple. Leads that we will use to further our investigation. These are complex charges, Mr. Schmitt—the most we expect from your efforts will be leverage. We're not interested in the affair with Mrs. Scott, other than what she has to say about her husband. You can see how Mr. Scott's proposition puts you in a unique position to win her confidence. We think she'll dump on the guy, and all you have to do is listen. The potential upside is very generous, and I encourage you to consider it."

"Or you'll audit me to hell and back."

"Something like that," said Short. "Frankly, there are a lot worse things than being audited. You don't want to know."

His pudgy little forehead furrowed with mock concern.

"Is that a threat? Sounds a lot like a threat."

"I'm just saying. We don't make threats, Mr. Schmitt."

"Neither do I. You armed, by any chance?"

He just smiled at me. I really wanted to send him on his merry way via the picture window.

"Listen," said Banger, "I don't expect you to like what you hear, and certainly don't expect you to give us your answer tonight. Talk to your attorney, call your looney tunes mother, do what you need to do, but it is what it is. We need your help, and we're prepared to make it a positive outcome for you. If you don't help us, we cannot officially take any action to coerce you to our way of thinking. But, as you might guess, the auditing of individual tax returns is not a completely arbitrary process, and when necessary, has been and will continue to be leveraged by government interests. That's the official line. You can read between it and any other lines you've heard here tonight."

"Including Jimmy Olsen's here."

She just raised her eyebrows and cocked her head.

"By the way," said Short, "I *am* armed."

"I get it all in writing? That I get to keep the money, tax free?"

"No," said Banger. "There can be no paper trail, certainly not to that effect. You don't exist, the money doesn't exist. We can make that happen. The second this gets put in ink, everything changes—something about the accused's constitutional rights and your obligation to pay your fair share of taxes. Neither of us wants it to go down that way, so we all stay behind the curtain. If you get in trouble, we'll protect you. For the most part, you won't even know we're there."

My vision fogged as I ran it all through my head. My tax situation wasn't all that complicated, but I had cut enough corners and wallowed in enough deductible gray areas in my day to know they would have something to work with if they so chose. As for there being worse things than being audited, I was cynical enough to buy into the unspoken implications of *that*.

But more than anything, I was staring a moral loophole right in the eye. My entire rationale for turning Nelson Scott down was that I couldn't do such a thing to Kelly, his wife. But this changed everything. Helping the Feds nail her husband might actually help the woman make all her gold-digging dreams come true. All I had to do was get her to shack up with me for thirty days or so and let the Feds listen in, and I would be financially independent for life. Hell, chances were the woman wouldn't even like me, much less go the whole nine yards; and in that case I'd have to settle for a cool million just for showing up.

Who was I kidding? The million dollars just got real again.

And of course, there was the newest wrinkle of all, the proximity of Tracy living nearby in my new zip code.

Talk about your dangerous neighborhoods.

When my attention focused back to the room, I was unnerved to see that Banger and Scott had gotten to their feet without my noticing. Banger was grinning, as if my thoughts had been playing like Dick Clark on the Jumbotron in Times Square.

She said, "Starts to pencil out when you look close, doesn't it?"

"I have to think about this," I said.

Banger handed me a business card. It was blank, other than a handwritten telephone number.

"It's a pager," she said. "Leave your number, I'll call you back. When you're ready."

That was interesting. Second time today this had happened. I stared at the card, and once again she read my mind.

"The local office isn't aware of this operation, so they won't know us. You call them, they'll give you the runaround, then they'll call Washington. The local director may or may not get a briefing, but chances are, they won't call you back. So don't bother. A word of advice . . . this is a deep-cover file. Fuck with it, and the cover goes away, along with your money."

"And you can get straight with your accountant," added Short.

I wanted to slap him upside the head with a saucy rejoinder, but the well was dry. I wanted to tell them to go to hell, which was not particularly saucy but was my sentiment of the moment. And, I had to admit, I wanted to tell them I'd do it. Even more than that, I didn't want to give them the satisfaction of an easy close.

I really did need to think about it.

I just looked down at the card and nodded.

"Sleep well, Mr. Schmitt," said Short, his face suddenly alive with pleasure.

"Guarantee me one more thing," I said as they headed for my door. When Banger turned around, eyebrows raised and ready, I added, "Five minutes alone in a room with Richard Simmons here when this is over."

Her smile was almost pretty. I could read between her lines at the moment, too.

"Anything and everything is possible, Mr. Schmitt."

Special Agent Short, however, didn't think it was all that funny.

Only later, lying in my bed, my chest pounding like a subwoofer, did I realize that Banger's parting comment was almost verbatim that of Lee Van Wyke's earlier in the day.

Anything and everything is possible . . .

> 17 <

ENTRY #52: TELEVANGELISTS—tell them to send *you* a check—"whatever you can afford, God bless you"—and you'll pray on their behalf for an early parole.
 —from *Bullshit in America*, by Wolfgang Schmitt

My mother looked back at me with the soft eyes of a woman who loved her son and believed he could do no wrong. That was always her problem when I was young: I could have spray-painted the image of Dan Quayle's ass on the doors of my high school— someone did that, but my name never came up—and my mom would have claimed it was just a phase. Now, her only problem was finding her way back to her room from the dining hall after bingo.

She had no clue who I was.

"I dunno, Mom, it just feels like it's time for a change, know what I'm sayin'?"

She didn't. But she nodded anyway, a peaceful smile on her face. She'd been nodding continuously since I walked into her room, which she shared with a woman named Rose who kept asking me if I was Harvey, her husband, who'd been dead for seventeen years.

"Yesterday I swapped serious attitude with two men I'd never met, neither of whom had any reason to get in my face until I got in theirs first. Which I did, for some reason."

She sat in a wooden rocker which, during the day, provided a nice view of a freeway and a canned goods warehouse. Her room, which if it weren't for the smell of feces and Pine Sol might have passed for a sweet little bed-and-breakfast, was done in pinks and greens, too faded to qualify as pastels. I held her hand, which was shockingly cold to the touch. In the background, Robert Schuler preached salvation from a television perched on a rack high up on the wall.

"I'm just not me anymore. I mean, since Tracy left . . ."

"Who's Tracy?" she asked.

"My girlfriend, mom. The one I almost married? The one who made you bread and brought you tulips? Tall, big boobs?"

She smiled gently, as if that did the trick.

"When I saw her last night I realized nothing is working anymore. Then this thing comes up . . . nothing's ever simple, ya know? I mean, why does everything good have to have fine print at the bottom of the contract?"

"Harvey, get your ass over here now!" beseeched Rose.

I pulled the afghan Tracy had made for her up over my mother's shoulders, wondering if Medicare covered the heating bill in this place.

"I think I'm gonna do it," I said.

Mom nodded back at me.

"I mean, I wasn't at first, and I felt good about that. But then this IRS thing comes up, and here I am between the hard place and the rock. Heads, I win a million bucks; tails, and I end up hiring a tax attorney."

I'd called my CPA that morning, catching him before he got out the door for the driving range. He reminded me that I'd been filing a Schedule C for years, which was the self-employment form for my meager sideline as a model with a broken nose. On it I'd deducted such things as my health club membership, my Nordstrom bill, vitamins, toothpaste, a trip to Palm Springs with Tracy—during which I'd made sure to drop my head shot off at a photography studio—and a host of other questionable expenditures which, when totaled, provided a nifty loss to write off against my day job income. He then reminded me that last year I'd also done a second Schedule C for my writing income—he said this was a red flag the size of Rhode Island—which had amounted to three hundred dollars while affording me the opportunity to depreciate my computer and write off mileage and my Internet costs and a bunch of magazine subscriptions, all to the tune of a convenient sixteen-hundred-dollar loss. He'd refused to put his name on the returns, and quite against his wishes, I'd filed them anyway. Which was why he wasn't all that interested in my inquiries, yet seemed somewhat delighted with his answers.

Tax issues aside, I had another problem. My mother's care was bleeding me dry. If she lived another decade, I'd have no choice but to let her die in a state-funded institution older than the flag. And, it was cold in here . . . the sooner I moved her, the better.

I *needed* the money. I needed it now. Special Agent Banger had been right. The closer you looked at it, the more attractive Scott's proposition became.

"It's complicated," I said.

My mother stared, still smiling slightly, the rhythm of her nodding unaltered.

"I gotta go. I may not be around for a while."

I swore the smile waned a bit. Then I glanced over at Rose, who was beckoning to me with her finger.

I leaned in and kissed my mother on the forehead. "Love you, Mom."

As I stood up, she said, "I love you, too, Dub."

A chill shot up my spine. Dub was my childhood nickname, short for the letter "W," from my first name. She hadn't called me that since I'd reached an age at which I knew the meaning of words like "alcoholism" and "wife battering." It was a piercing flash of light from the midst of the fog.

She was nodding again, the fog back in place.

When I got to the car, my heart pounding—a phenomenon that had taken on a whole new urgency for me lately—I called Lee Van Wyke's answering service. She called me back within two minutes. An hour later, I called Special Agent Banger, who got back to me within five.

I was in. Over my head, on both sides of the fence. Now I just had to think of a way to cover my ass.

PART TWO
>> <<

> 18 <

"Let me get this straight," said Wolfgang Schmitt.

"Straight up," said the man in the suit, who had undoubtedly heard the expression on MTV.

"I can quit anytime I want. No strings."

"No strings. Provided you haven't broken the law."

"I think I have a problem with that last part."

"And what might that be?"

"Call it a paradox. You send me out undercover, with a false identity, pretending to be something I'm not. By definition, I'm lying and stealing every step of the way. At some point, in order to make this work, I may be aiding and abetting criminal activity."

"We're just asking you to listen. Maybe prod a bit."

"See what I mean? If I cross the line, even a little, I'm gone. Deal's off."

"Still having those trust issues. Pity."

"Fine line between blind and naïve."

"You mean, where faith is concerned."

"That's what I mean, yeah."

The suit shifted, tired of the joust.

"We're trying to make this work for both of us, Mr. Schmitt. We'll be with you the entire way. If something goes wrong, you get near that line, you call."

"Or just speak into the microphone."

The suit grinned. "The phone's fully functional. We ran a diagnostic. Be careful what you say."

"I'll try to remember that."

"Until we meet again, then." He offered his hand.

"Counting the days," said Wolf, accepting the handshake.

Then, doing a bad job of pretending he'd just remembered something else, the suit froze, turning back with a pasty little government-issue smile.

"There is one more thing," he said.

"I'm on pins and needles," said Wolf.

"We may ask you to do more than just listen."

"You said, 'prod and listen.'"

"We may need to push that envelope somewhat. But ironically, only if you succeed with the prodding and listening."

"What the hell does that mean?"

"We'll let you know. You want out then, that's fine."

Wolf narrowed his eyes. The suit smiled, smug behind his badge, then left the room.

Before Wolf left the building, another man in another suit approached him. He was nodding as he handed over a cell phone. Then he put his fingers to his lips, signaling for quiet.

Wolf blew into the phone, as if testing a microphone.

The man in the tie shook his head as Wolf walked away.

> 19 <

ENTRY #166: TWO-FACED SEXUAL POLITICS—
in the context of being single and male in this country,
"eligibility" equates to "net worth." Imagine if eligibility for single females was determined by breast size.
Both contexts are sexist, and both still exist in unfortunate abundance. But only one is socially acceptable,
primarily because it was spawned and proliferated by
high society. If anyone with a penis included "impressive net worth" on the hierarchy of his sexual needs,
he'd be locked out of the Elks Club for life.
 —from *Bullshit in America*, by Wolfgang Schmitt

It took three weeks to get to San Jose. Two to resign my position at the agency, one to get my act together. In retrospect, I suppose they could have been done concurrently—they'd be buying me a new wardrobe and setting me up in bachelor nirvana, so I wouldn't be packing much—but Lee Van Wyke said she needed the time, supposedly to get her act together, too. There was, she assured me, much to do prior to my arrival.

At work, I cooked up a story to hand in with my resignation letter, something about taking a few months to bike Europe with an unnamed supermodel, but unfortunately, no one asked for that level of specifics. Unlike Marni, who was out the door within ten minutes of her resignation, I was expected to stick around for the entire two weeks, the objective being a smooth segue to a new account manager. I'd hand over my business to a very capable young woman we'd recently pirated away from the largest account she'd now be servicing, who politely assured me I'd be nothing more than a vague memory before the next billing cycle.

Resigning would be the easiest part of this whole thing.

All the while, I was obsessing about placing a call to Tracy to tell her that the most wonderful coincidence had just happened, that I'd be coming to her neck of the woods, and that perhaps we could rendezvous over a cup of bitter nostalgia. After a few days of working up to it, I actually had the receiver in my hand and was punching in the numbers when sanity hit me: if things went smoothly and our reunion lasted beyond that first meeting, I'd have a little trouble explaining my sudden rich and famous lifestyle. Not to mention all the time I was spending on the arm of the most eligible estranged wife in town. I wasn't sure how Tracy would fit into this little soap opera, but one thing was certain: it wouldn't be out in the open.

Then again, I knew a thing or two about operating below the radar where women were concerned. You can regret the follies of youth—I'd paid more than one tab for such testosterone-fueled transgressions—but only a fool forgets them. Once upon a time, I was actually pretty good at being an insufferable cad.

About a week after my initial call to Lee Van Wyke, I received a FedEx I liked to think of as "Kelly in a Box." Inside were a stack of videotapes, a folder full of Xeroxed photographs, a few newspaper clippings and some neatly typed biographical notes.

There was also a paperback copy of *The Shell Seekers*, by Rosamunde Pilcher, a handful of Anne Rice novels—interesting, Tracy had been a big fan as well—a CD soundtrack to *Somewhere in Time*, and a DVD of *Gone with the Wind*. When considered in total, the package comprised a sort of *Cliffs Notes* on Kelly Scott's life. Mandatory reading for anyone seeking a post-haste insertion into the woman's good graces.

Within the week I felt like I knew Kelly Scott. I wasn't sure I liked her all that much, but then again, that wasn't a prerequisite to my assignment. I wasn't trying to be her biographer, I would be trying to get into her head—and ultimately, her pants.

Like Tina said, what's love got to do with it, anyhow?

There was a reason my initial impression of Kelly Scott was something less than a swooning schoolboy crush. She was attractive enough in a Tide commercial sort of way, and she definitely looked younger than her thirty-nine years. An unlimited spa budget can do that for a gal. She was active and involved, preening gleefully in her many newspaper photos, a fixture on the invitation list for every bash on the Silicon Valley social calendar. A billion dollars in liquid assets does that for a gal, too. Her many fancy friends loved her, her many servants and vendors were loyal to her, the symphony and the art museum and about twenty-two area charities were ever so grateful to her. She was the Princess Di of new money, and she was obviously comfortable in the role.

And now, her husband wanted her cut off at the teller window. I wondered what she'd done to deserve such an exile from the kingdom. Had he been the guilty party in this little domestic dispute, Scott would have done what most men would do, and he was uniquely qualified to do it: he'd throw money at her until she went down. No, regardless of the viability of the stock sell-off story, Kelly had done something of serious adulterous merit to earn her husband's wrath. Which was fine with me, because it would make it easier to look in the mirror as this scenario unfolded.

Amazing, the stories we make up to rationalize ourselves.

Kelly Fisher had been born a true-blue California girl to upper-middle-class parents in Orange County, her father an orthodontist, her mother a music teacher before sacrificing her career on the altar of motherhood. Kelly had been a golden girl from her first piano recital—private grammar schools, leading scorer on the junior high soccer team, cheerleader in prep school—we've all seen the movie in which the spoiled but gorgeous head cheerleader delights in torturing less physically-blessed girls and blue-collar boys with silent crushes—and of course, class valedictorian. All of which was fine and good, except for some between-the-lines characterizations.

For example, Kelly's high school sweetheart had been the son of a studio executive who'd been presented with a spanking new Jaguar on his seventeenth birthday. There was a picture of them peeling away in it, top down, on the evening of the winter formal. Later that year, when the young man went into rehab, she dumped him for the starting middle linebacker at USC—guy had a neck like a sewer pipe—even though she was still in high school and had yet to receive her first breast implants. According to the notes sent with the file, she received a six-figure payoff—Rocky's father was an executive vice president at Lockheed Martin—to have their fetus aborted in the first trimester, a condition of which was that the young couple cease and desist their carnal union. What the hell—it was a long commute, anyhow.

After graduating high school, the young and freshly augmented Kelly headed north to the blue and gold of UCLA, where she promptly beat out several hundred lesser applicants and was named to the football rally squad, and was just as promptly nominated as the main squeeze of a certain fair-haired starting quarterback who would go on to a six-time Pro Bowl career and a spot in the broadcasting booth to this day. The couple was the toast of Westwood, which was why her arrest for possession of an ounce of Colombian was successfully hushed by school officials, who kept a few choice fifty-yard-line tickets on hand for just this purpose.

Alas, that match made in gridiron heaven didn't last, either. Because when Kelly Fisher was a junior, cut from the mold of a young Loni Anderson, she was introduced to the mother lode of all eligible bachelors, the ultimate gold-digger's trophy boy. This, of course, was Nelson Scott, the founder of a software company called Arielle Systems, who at the time was only worth a cool hundred million or so. She dumped her first-round draft choice quarterback boyfriend faster than Anna Nicole Smith dried her handkerchief.

The more I read about Kelly Fisher-Scott, the easier I would sleep.

Most of this was explained in the cryptic notes, with a few photographs—including Kelly's arrest mug shot—tossed in for color. The remainder of the file was an unofficial chronology of the Scotts' marriage, including personal videos of vacations, Christmas gatherings, parties, and otherwise non-specific moments by the swimming pool. If it weren't for the recurring images of private jets, personal valets, and diamonds the size of martini olives, it could have been anyone.

Somewhere along the way, if these videos and photographs were an accurate mirror of her evolution, Kelly had dropped the beach babe thing and gone earthy. Or, perhaps, simply grown up. The breasts were smaller—that could have been a function of underwiring come and gone—the chin tighter, the eyes refreshed. The hair, which had been a Paul Mitchell wet dream in her younger days, was now straight and understated—still the coif of a wealthy woman, but one who didn't need to command the attention of every room she entered. The veneer of youthful ego was gone, replaced by a pleasant face that radiated a tired but courageous energy, the eyes of a woman who was at peace with herself and the certainty she'd never have to work a day in her life. There was nothing remotely icy about her, but you know what they say about icebergs—it was what was below the surface that sank the *Titanic*.

It occurred to me I'd need to armor-plate my underside to get through this in one piece.

As for the paperbacks and the two CDs, I had to assume they held the key to Kelly Scott's unrequited inner Meg Ryan, with a secret penchant for sexy vampires. They were *hooks*, as Lee Van Wyke had called them, little windows into the woman's soul. If the way to a man's heart was through his stomach, the way to a woman's was through flowers, candy, and candlelight—not to mention a few well-chosen dark words of lust.

Kelly Scott was about to meet her fantasy guy, sans fangs, and there would be nothing simplistic about it. The key was in playing against type, in presenting all the trappings of manhood—admit it or not, most women find a strong dose of testosterone a thrilling narcotic—while displaying none of the Neanderthal behavior for which we are famous. I was, after all, a published author on the subject.

All I had to do was learn how to practice what I preached.

There was one more thing. The evening after I cleaned out my desk and departed the agency premises—there was cake and beer in the foyer—I received an email at home notifying me that an account had been opened in my name at the Bank of Bermuda, Grand Cayman branch, in the amount of $100,000.

Suddenly, with a clear and patriotic conscience, I was feeling romantic as hell.

> 20 <

> ENTRY #84: ESTATE TAXES—every dime passed on to an heir has already been taxed. When taxed again as part of an estate, it's actually being double-taxed, which is synonymous with *screwed*. Apparently the government assumes the dead don't care. On a related note, "abuse of a corpse" is still a punishable crime in most states.
> —from *Bullshit in America*, by Wolfgang Schmitt

If cynicism has an upside, it's this: it can be damn near impossible to sneak a curveball past me. Through the entire process of my resignation and the study of Kelly Scott's dossier, there remained a quiet voice whispering doubt in my subconscious mind. It said, *If it smells like bacon and tastes like bacon, it's a pig, ol' buddy*. I knew the odor in question here was my FBI connection, which hadn't surfaced since that night in my living room. With the hundred grand safely in place—not exactly in *hand*, since I could not access the money without a PIN number, which was being held hostage to ensure my participation—I was highly motivated to move forward. But not without the knowledge that it all hinged on the Feds. I needed someone with a bad raincoat and a badge to make an appearance, and soon. If nothing else, to clear the air of the scent of pork chops.

Maybe I'd mumbled this sentiment out loud for all

the hidden microphones to hear, because the next day, my wish was granted.

I was flat on my back on a bench at a gym—Bally's, a case study in what happens when you ask P.E. majors to run a business—going for my sixth rep at 225, when someone moved in behind me as a spotter. From my inverted point of view, the face wasn't familiar. Only when I finished the set and sat upright did I recognize Special Agent Banger of the FBI, dressed in dark blue workout gear with the FBI logo on the shirt. Special Agent Short of the IRS was nowhere in sight.

"Incognito," I said, nodding toward her chest. "The bad guys would have to be able to read to make you."

"You know where the Aurora airstrip is?" she asked.

"I do," I said. "I'm fine, by the way. You?"

"Tell me you can be there tonight at nine."

"Gotta break a hot date."

She grinned. "She'll get over it. Be on time." She patted the bar, then turned and walked off.

I called after her. "How do you know I'm lying?"

She returned with that I've-got-the-law-on-my-side grin, leaning close enough for me to smell her morning coffee.

"Same way I know you've had seven calls in the past three days—four from telemarketers, one from a guy at work who was sick on your last day, one from your accountant, and one from your cousin in Sacramento, which you did not return. I also know that you've been listening to the soundtrack of *Somewhere in Time* between viewings of *Gone with the Wind*, and that you're rather fond of *La Femme Nikita* reruns. Any questions?"

She winked, then walked away again.

"You busy later?" I asked, with far too much volume. But no one seemed to hear, as I knew they wouldn't. The average age of the clientele at Bally's on a Tuesday morning was somewhere near seven decades, so I could have urinated on the squat rack and no one would have noticed.

The Aurora airport is a thirty-three-hundred-foot ribbon of patched asphalt with grass growing from its cracks—I'd seen driveways with more lights—and two metal-frame hangars built in the Eisenhower years. Most of the aircraft that called this place home were crop dusters, with a few tail-gear Piper Cubs and one glass-bubble helicopter with no doors.

It was a typical Oregon fall evening—drizzle, low intermittent fog, cold enough to see your breath. At this hour no one was around. The only light came from a single bulb on the side of one of the hangars. Perfect for a clandestine meeting with my federal employers.

I heard the airplane before I saw it—a small jet, throttling down on final approach. A fog bank hovering over the end of the runway suddenly had an otherworldly glow, which in moments morphed into a set of bright white eyes descending with weightless grace. The small jet, still only a ghostly silhouette, used the entire runway to decelerate, then turned onto the parallel taxiway and headed for the small parking area in front of the hangars, where it stopped. The engines spooled down as the hatch lowered.

Since no one appeared in the doorway, I had the distinct feeling this was my cue.

As I approached, huddled beneath my umbrella and wishing I'd worn different shoes because of the puddles, I saw that the plane had no markings other than its FAA number, and that the cockpit was dark. I could just make out the outline of the pilot's head, the requisite square jaw and headset microphone barely visible in the faint glow of the instruments. Based on the fact that the engines had been cut, I concluded that this meeting would take place here rather than aloft. Other than the splashing of my two-hundred-dollar Ecco loafers through the standing water—I hate it when that happens—the night was once again still.

The plane—a two-decades-old Lear—was significantly smaller than Scott's Gulfstream, more apropos to a gentleman farmer who grows his own wine grapes than a high-technology legend who grows his own subsidiaries.

I stepped onto the ladder and peered in.

A man was waiting inside. Other than the pilot, who remained in the cockpit, he was traveling alone tonight, adding to the surreal quality of this entire setup. He was exactly what you'd expect someone flying solo in a private jet to be: a poster boy for the accounting program at Stanford, his suit nondescript and his bland tie perfectly knotted. The kind of guy whose idea of fun is organizing his closet.

"Thanks for coming out," he said, pumping my hand. "Miserable night. We should pay these guys more."

He shot a look toward the cockpit, and I nodded in agreement. Only an ex–carrier pilot or a maniac—synonymous terms, actually—would land on this airstrip in this weather without so much as a windsock to help him.

"I'm Douglas Crane," he said. "Please have a close look at this."

He handed me a leather business card case. I

flipped it open, seeing what amounted to a badge, sort of an embossed certificate with the IRS seal and his very impressive title: Regional Deputy Director of the Internal Revenue Service. There was also a photograph in which he was wearing the same necktie he was wearing now.

I looked back up and shrugged. "I don't have much in the way of fancy credentials." I handed his back to him.

He smiled and said, "From what I hear, I beg to differ."

I liked him already, despite his tie and his employer. But then, that was the intended response.

We settled in. He was apparently very happy to be here.

"I just wanted to meet you," he said, "let you know how delighted we are with your decision to help us with our little investigation."

I hesitated, unsure how to play this. Like most people who view the world through jaundiced glasses, I tend to hang back a little when someone sucks up this urgently.

"I sure hope this means Special Agent Short won't have to resort to further threats to get my cooperation."

His pleasant expression vanished instantly.

"Short threatened you? I'm very sorry to hear that."

I raised my eyebrows. "I think it was more like a penis deficiency thing with him, actually."

He chewed his lower lip for a moment. I wanted to believe he was barely choking back a chuckle, which, if he knew Short at all, he probably was.

"The statistical possibility of an audit is often brought up as an alternative outcome in situations like this. Pressure, perhaps. But a threat . . . I hope that's not how it's perceived."

"Semantics, you ask me. At any rate, I'm in. Provided the rest of their story floats."

"It'll float. That's why I'm here. To seal the deal, so to speak. Put a face behind the promise."

"I assumed it was to debrief. Swap a few Nelson Scott stories."

The faintest flicker of his good humor returned. "We're up to speed, actually. I'm more concerned about you."

"For a guy operating on blind faith in a wired house, I'm doing pretty well."

His grin was wearing thin.

"I apologize for that," he said. "We do need to take certain precautions."

"Bill of Rights be damned, right?"

"You running for office?"

I shook my head. Back to deuce.

"Didn't think so." He shifted in his seat, as if to savor the point. "You do understand why this can't be a contractual matter. No paper trail, no harm, no foul. As the primary beneficiary of our little corner-cutting, I'm assuming this meets with your approval."

"As long as I get my money and a get-out-of-jail-free card, I'm one happy undercover operative."

He added a smile to his nodding, which I returned in kind.

"That's why we're here tonight," he said. "So you could hear it from the horse's mouth. In case you're experiencing any . . . doubts."

"There was a horse in *The Godfather*, too. It died."

"You're a very clever young man. I think this will all work out."

"Speaking on behalf of the IRS, of course."

"As officially as one can speak in an off-the-record matter."

"I love a good paradox, don't you?"

"This is all you get, Wolf. A personal visit from a senior official of the Service, a review of the terms, a guarantee of compliance. Tit for tat—you deliver, we deliver."

"You bring the tits, I'll bring the tat. Until then, why don't you review the terms for me. Just to be unofficially official."

"Of course. You remain covert, you allow us electronic access to your interactions, you push the envelope before you open it, then tell us what's inside when you can. You do that, you keep all compensation promised by your civilian employer and paid to an offshore account. Tax-free, of course. No different than a district attorney offering immunity for testimony. Happens all the time. We never heard of you, you never heard of us. How'd I do?"

I smiled. "That's what Banger and Short said."

"Pardon me?"

"*How'd I do.* They said that."

Advantage, Wolf.

"Service-speak," said Crane. "You pick it up in meetings, it's hard to lose."

Later I would ponder the likelihood of such jargon cross-pollinating in the halls of two separate and equally monolithic institutions like the FBI and the IRS. I would also ponder why a guy no older than me was referring to me as a *young man*. For now, it just sounded like fraternity president bullshit.

He slapped his hands on both knees—my father did that when it was time to leave—a sure sign the meeting was over.

"Well," I said, "guess that's it then."

He stood and offered that sales-seminar handshake again.

"The horse has spoken. We'll be in touch. Good luck to you, Wolf."

Strangely, I could hear the turbines begin to spool. As if the pilot had been listening in on everything.

An old expression came to mind as I departed the airplane: *don't let the door hit you on the ass on your way out*. The hatch was up and sealed before I got past the wingtip—it was barely light enough to make out the tail number—and by the time I had walked to the hangar, next to which I'd parked, the Lear had reached the end of the runway.

I watched it go, wishing my life had been different, that it was me flying Douglas Crane or Nelson Scott or anyone else around the country in a personal jet, serving bagels and coffee and shining their golf shoes instead of carrying their dirty laundry.

When the Lear's running lights had disappeared into the low clouds, I reached into my jacket pocket and turned off the portable tape recorder I'd brought along.

No contracts, my ass.

Then, because my short-term memory sucks, I made a note of the plane's tail number and stashed it in my pocket.

> 21 <

ENTRY #90: NETWORK MARKETING—what began with soap soon expanded to therapeutic magnets, personal financial services, and overpriced nutritional supplements. Quick, call your friends, neighbors, and cousins—your fortune is just a downline away. Hey, at least the soap actually *worked*.
—from *Bullshit in America*, by Wolfgang Schmitt

I got home just before eleven. I had a half hour before *La Femme Nikita* came on, so I changed into my sweats and checked my email. All three were end-of-day rituals, though the email experience was different now that I was among the gainfully unemployed. Besides the irritating pop-up ads and the occasional spam that somehow made it through the software I'd downloaded to block it—you, too, can start your own Internet marketing business—all that was there were jokes.

Except tonight. I was excited to see that someone had actually written to me, though because of the handle I almost zapped it.

It was from someone calling himself "Deadman."

Cute. A little too Hitchcock, but cute.

I opened the email with some measure of what proved to be appropriate apprehension.

They're playing you. Watch your ass. Take the money and run like hell as soon as you can.
W.R.

My stomach had always reacted to stimuli before my brain could comprehend danger. Something about an aversion to adrenaline, which had until now manifested itself in a longstanding distaste for roller coasters and rock climbing. Reading this email, I was lightheaded and nauseous before I got to the writer's initials.

I stared at the screen for untold minutes, waiting for a reasonable explanation to rise up before my dinner did. The first and most obvious deduction was that the sender knew about Nelson Scott's offer. The next question was this: did they also know about my federal friends? And if they did, to which "they" was the writer referring? I was about to become a sucker for either a billionaire or a government agency, and in my moment of gastric distress, I wasn't sure which was the more frightening prospect.

Being the analytical type that every personality test I'd ever taken had confirmed that I was, I quickly narrowed it down to three possibilities. One: I could do nothing, delete the file, take some Alka Seltzer and go to bed. Two: I could start thinking out loud—literally—and alert those listening in that my cover had been compromised. Which wouldn't be wise if, in fact, my eavesdroppers were the ones I'd just been warned about. And three: I could try to determine who had sent me this little guided missile of an email. I didn't know where to even start on that count.

Without someone wearing a pocket protector to call, all I could think of was to hit the REPLY button. Doing so brought up the appropriate window, already addressed to the sender of the original email. That was the good news. The bad news was that all it said was "To: Deadman," rather than displaying a full email address, which I naïvely assumed could be traced. Not that I'd have known what to do with that information, but it would have at least given me something to work with.

It was at that point I came up with choice number four: answer the email and extend my window of opportunity, hopefully until I had a clue as to how to proceed.

In other words, punt.

Dear W.R.: All my questions fall into the who, what, and why categories. Who are you? Who is playing me? What are they playing me for? What does "Deadman" mean? Why are they doing this? And why are YOU doing this? Don't get me wrong, I appreciate your concern, but put yourself in my shoes here. Why would I place myself and this most unusual business opportunity at risk based on your message? Talk to me, Deadman, I'm all ears.
    Wolf

I stared at my computer for many more untold minutes before putting the cursor on SEND and then, perhaps, clicking a million dollars into oblivion.

That done, I went back to Nikita and a bowl of peppermint ice cream, my favorite stomach remedy. But I was having more than a little trouble concentrating tonight. Besides, I'd seen this episode four times already—Nikita and Michael scheming against Operations between romps in the sack—and my mind was wandering.

Which, in turn, was what led me to the silly notion to check my telephone messages before going to bed.

Good thing.
Lee Van Wyke had called. She didn't leave her name, but I easily recognized the voice and the attitude—both were confident and slightly flirtatious, yet dangerous. She wanted to meet tomorrow morning at eight, at the same place she'd dropped me at our last meeting, which, while unspecified, I knew was the Hillsboro Airport. She added that our trip would last four or five days, and to bring my tennis racket.

Cryptic and untraceable. Also, quite non-negotiable. Let the bullshitting begin.

> **22** <

ENTRY #33: RACIAL PROFILING AT AIRPORT SECURITY CHECKPOINTS—the bullshit is *not* doing it. When was the last time that someone *other* than an angry male of Middle Eastern descent between twenty and fifty years of age tried to commandeer an airplane? Let grandma keep her shoes on and get real.

—from *Bullshit in America*, by Wolfgang Schmitt

The next morning, there was a familiar black Lincoln Town Car waiting in my driveway. My old pal Joe, the NYPD extra turned driver, was reading the newspaper behind the wheel, keeping the engine running to stay warm. I'd intended to drive myself to the Hillsboro Airport, and had I not glanced to the front as I was locking the door to leave, I'd have backed right into him.

The last thing I did was check email, hoping Deadman had again risen from the grave long enough to answer my questions. But there would be no resurrection today.

Joe waved when he saw me, not bothering to get out—the slow death of customer service in this country—and popped the trunk from the inside. I deposited my suitcase and tennis bag, then climbed into the front seat next to him.

"Guess things worked out," he said wearily.

"Guess so."

Nothing more was said between us as we drove to the airport. In the silence, I wondered what, if anything, he really knew.

Next to the Cessna four-seaters and a handful of small jets in attendance this morning, the Gulfstream was as out of place as Shaquille O'Neal joining a bunch of dentists for a game of horse.

Joe popped the trunk, again showing no inclination to handle my luggage. We parted with none of the cross-cultural banter or imparted wisdom of our previous encounter, nothing more profound than a nod between men who had nothing in common.

I walked through the rain toward the jet, a suitcase in one hand, a tennis bag in the other. Walking, as it were, out of one life into the next.

The cabin was empty. Nelson Scott's personal work area at the rear of the library-like cabin was dark and draped off. On a table waited a basket of pastries and a bowl of fresh fruit, with a tray of preserves and several pitchers of beverages. Not bad for no stewardess and an unsociable pilot.

The hatch swung up into place as I settled into one of the seats. Outside, I saw that Joe had stayed to observe the departure. I waved at him through the large oval window, but he remained motionless and expressionless. The engines started up, and within seconds the Gulfstream began to roll. Before we reached the runway, a flat-screen plasma monitor lowered from the ceiling of its own accord, very Kirk and Spock. When the image came to life, I was looking at the smiling face of my new boss, Lee Van Wyke.

"Good morning, Wolf," she said. Had she not

plowed quickly on, I would have responded aloud. It was a recorded message, shot outdoors, though a live transmission wouldn't have surprised me a bit.

"Sorry I couldn't be with you today. I'm actually in transit myself this morning, but I'll see you in California in a couple of hours. Everything is ready, and we've got a busy schedule for you. Intense, but fun, too. So enjoy your flight, have a good breakfast, maybe grab a nap. Trust me, you'll need your energy. Oh yeah . . . before you land, please change into your tennis gear. You're going to start the trip with a sound thrashing from yours truly."

She waved at the camera coyly as the image went dark. Just then, the airplane bolted down the runway with a smooth purring sound. Less than a minute later we broke through a glorious cloudscape, as if someone had flipped the lights on a soundstage. The sky was suddenly an intense blue, the horizon a sea of rolling white billows that made one think of God.

This wasn't another life, it was another universe altogether. And for the time being, at least, I would be the alien.

Nelson Scott would be playing the role of God.

> 23 <

ENTRY #116: PROFESSIONAL ATHLETES' SALARIES—any way you cut it, regardless of the supply-demand economics, when you pay an ill-tempered, drug-using, wife-abusing, gun-toting jock millions to toss a ball through a hoop—regardless of his genetic blessings—and you pay a teacher thirty-five grand, this is truly bullshit in America.
—from *Bullshit in America*, by Wolfgang Schmitt

I have always lied about why I request the window seat on airplanes. I say it's because of my height—six-three is still considered tall in some circles—which makes it impossible to sleep without the window for neck support. Truth is, it's the view. I marvel at the suits who take the aisle seats for a quick getaway, who bury their attention in the financial section from the moment they settle in, never once casting a glance out the window. Somewhere along the line they've lost the love. Their inner child is gone.

The approach into San Jose was familiar yet still exciting. Sitting there in my tennis warm-ups, I picked out hotels I'd slept in, restaurants at which I'd eaten, freeway exits I'd missed, rental car lots I'd frequented. No one over the age of fifteen indulged in this behavior, I was sure, but I didn't care. The day I turn into a Limbaugh-listening, *take-it-apart-so-*

I-can-see-how-it's-made, financial section–reading type who is more interested in watching golf on television than in seeing a killer sunset—in other words, a guy who prefers an aisle seat—just shoot me.

After touchdown, the Gulfstream taxied to a far corner of the field, where I expected to find a waiting car. But there would be no car today. There was, however, a helicopter. A Bell Ranger that seated six, with the Arielle logo on the side.

I decided then and there that I was going to like it here on planet Arielle, or planet Scott, or whatever astrological name by which I would come to know it.

The pilot, who was waiting by the door as we taxied up, welcomed me by name. He made a point of taking my luggage away as quickly as possible, setting it down to help me aboard, then loading it into a compartment somewhere aft. Moving as if we were behind schedule, he hopped aboard and mindlessly hit some switches with one hand while putting on his headset with the other. The rotors began to move, filling the cabin with vibration. Within a minute we were airborne, streaking madly at low altitude over the gridlocked 101 toward the hills to the west.

A commuter no more.

I had no idea where we were headed. Based on the rugged terrain flashing by, it wasn't a corporate headquarters and it wasn't near the neighborhood Walmart. The coast, perhaps. Monterey or Carmel would make sense. We flew a southwesterly heading for about ten minutes before I felt the power cutting—always an alarming sensation when you're nowhere near an airfield. But we weren't descending. In fact, we were actually still in a slight climb.

As the helicopter flared and turned, I saw why. We were landing on top of a significant mountain, with an otherworldly view of the entire valley. A villa, a vast complex of buildings that could be a small resort, maybe something from a Bond movie. The king's castle in all its glory.

This, I knew, was where Nelson Scott lived.

The helipad—every villa should have one—was on top of a building separate from the main house. It was seven thousand square feet of health spa and exercise facility, luxurious locker rooms—including massage suites and several sauna, steam, and inhalant rooms—leading out to the pool deck, and next to it, two lighted tennis courts. The architecture was in keeping with a theme maintained throughout the entire complex: classic Italian, inspired by the oldest Amalfi Coast mansions and rendered in the finest marble. The house itself stood two stories above the landscaped grounds, but descended another three stories down the mountainside, with a waterfall emerging from the roof level that cascaded between arched balconies and terraces on either side.

Lee Van Wyke was waiting for me. She was alone, dressed in her tennis whites, her raven hair pulled back tight and fixed with a white bow. This gave her a somewhat severe aura, Cruella De Vil at the net—and trust me, Anna Kournikova had nothing on this lady. Keeping my eye on the ball would be my most significant on-court challenge.

Once again, her handshake was something of an assault. She came toward me, arm extended, smile in full bloom.

"How were your flights?"

"I could get used to this."

She took my arm and led me toward the stairs. "Don't."

I swallowed that one before I plowed on. "I see you're ready to work."

"It's not all blood, sweat, and tears. Except that this morning on the court, the last two will be yours. Perhaps all three."

"Gotta love a woman with confidence."

By now we had reached ground level. I had been to a few resorts in my day, some of the finest tennis temples in the land, but nothing I had seen, live or in a magazine, rivaled this for pure economic excess. The pathways leading in and out of the recreational facility were made of two-foot-square ceramic tiles embossed with the Arielle logo. Lining each walkway were perfectly trimmed hedges that looked more like green granite than living foliage, as if Edward Scissorhands himself ran the ground crew. The building upon which we'd landed was a busy mass of hand-carved scallops and columns, each window lined with sculpted sills, the walls covered with clinging ivy. Just inside the foyer stood an original life-size bronze likeness of Bjorn Borg, who I would learn had personally christened the court with a private clinic.

And this was just the gym.

"You need to freshen up before your beating? There's food inside if you're hungry."

There was a twinkle in her eye that, if one were looking for an agenda, was quite heavily laden with sexual mischief. This was in marked contrast to the arrogant ice queen I'd met on the airplane three weeks earlier, and I wondered what had changed. Nothing about this foreign planet, I continued to believe, could be taken for granted.

"I'm good. Ready if you are."

"Fresh blood," she said, "invigorates me."

She waved her hand toward the court in an "after you" manner, and together we headed for our first confrontation.

The woman kicked my ass. Straight sets, 6–2, 6–3.

Let me just say in all modesty that I've been known to make club pros nervous in the occasional parks-and-recreation tournament, yet she barely broke a sweat on me. When I hit out, she picked me off in the corners. When I went for finesse, she drove screaming topspin bullets right into my shoelaces. If I tried to run her, she ran me ragged instead. If I stayed back, she'd dink a little drop shot which set me up for a passing shot. And if I came to the net, she let it be known that there was serious potential of an injury that would end my sex life forever.

After the final point—a running forehand lob that landed on the back line—she waited for me at the net with a smile that had no pretense toward modesty.

"Not bad," she said. My chest was heaving, but she looked like she'd just walked out of a Rodeo Drive boutique.

"Sandbagger," I offered as we walked off the court together. A crystal pitcher of water with the obligatory floating lemon slices waited for us behind the players' bench.

"Really? I thought I was rather forthcoming."

"Where'd you play?"

"Stanford."

"Don't tell me. You were the Pac-10 champion."

"Doubles. Runner-up in singles. You were in grade school."

"Like I said—sandbagger."

She poured me a glass of water and handed it to me. Her expression had changed, the smugness gone. I watched her pour herself a glass, which she drained in one pull.

"I'd ask for a rematch, but . . ."

She barked the word "don't" for the second time today.

I just nodded, eyebrows raised, wrists slapped. The

bitch from the airplane was back, all of a sudden. I could see it in her eyes, hear it in her voice.

"Here's the tennis lesson today," she said. "Don't fuck with Lee. Don't challenge what I say, don't try to negotiate with me. Everything has been optimized for the success of this project, which is synonymous with your personal success. Am I being clear, Wolf?"

"Optimally."

A tiny grin emerged on her stern but lovely face. "Sarcastic in defeat. That's good."

"I try."

"Your clothes are in the locker room. Take a shower, dress casual, meet me at the house in thirty minutes for lunch. We have a lot of work to do."

She began to walk away. After a few paces, she turned, walking backwards as she launched a final volley.

"You telegraph your ground strokes. Other than that, you aren't bad for a club player."

I nodded and raised my crystal glass in what was intended to be a mock toast to her tennis wisdom. She, of course, took it as a serious tribute, smiling as she turned and headed for the house.

The final point, it seemed, was mine.

The Scott mansion defied both belief and description. It would be tempting to conclude that one needed to have more money than God to design and build such a temple—God just might live down the street from here—but that was precisely what people said about Nelson Scott, so I guess it made sense. Later I would absorb the numbers—nineteen thousand square feet if you didn't count the rec center and the ten-car garage, eleven bedrooms, twenty bathrooms, forty-four televisions and, rumor had it, a working dungeon doubling as a wine cellar—but my first impression was pure, numb awe. Every doorway was arched, every floor had a different marble design, the vaulted ceilings were straight out of an Italian cathedral, and every wall seemed to be laced with carved mosaic pieces. There was enough original art to furnish a new wing at the Met. Scott had a particular fascination with sculpture; every hallway had a recessed alcove containing something very Michelangelo. Many had exposed penises, which, if my art history served me, meant they had been imported from Italy.

I was met at the door by a fellow who could have been a cousin of Nelson Scott's no-neck bodyguard from the airplane. He didn't introduce himself, didn't smile either, but he did politely ask me to follow him in.

Lee was waiting on a deck overlooking the entire expanse of the South Bay. Lunch was already on a glass table with a centerpiece of freshly cut orchids: cold Gulf shrimp the size of small dachshunds which had been flown in that morning—as they were *every* day—on a bed of organic greens, with warm bread containing toasted seeds and pieces of dried fruit. A glass of ice tea was in front of my setting—Limoge china, of course—while Lee sipped a fine chardonnay from one of Scott's own vineyards. I didn't know it then, but three of the better California wine labels were his.

She greeted me with a soft smile as she leaned over and pulled out my chair.

"Will our employer be joining us?" I asked as I sat down.

"No," she said, without looking up.

"Well, he's missing a fine lunch indeed."

"That, I doubt. Nelson travels with a personal chef."

"I see. So, you whipped this up?"

She smiled, though somewhat patiently.

"No. House chef. He has a traveling chef because the house chef won't fly. There's a physician on staff who attends exclusively to Nelson and the employees here at the villa. Mr. Scott's personal valet is a former Miss California, whom, by the way, he's never touched. He owns twenty-two major shopping malls—a little sideline of his—and he's never set foot in any one of them because, as he says, she does all his shopping for him, so why waste the time. He employs two full-time masseuses—one a craniosacral specialist with a chiropractic degree, the other who does acupressure and Jin Shin Jyutsu, which I highly recommend. He has a feng shui master come in weekly, a Pilates instructor with tits like satellite dishes—never touched her, either—a hypnotherapist to stem his craving for sweets and oral sex, which his wife refuses him, a sparring partner for tae kwon do workouts, and six personal secretaries. That's not counting his office and other personal assistants. I believe there are twelve of those. Shall I continue?"

I whistled appreciatively, then said, "What, no live-in exorcist?"

"Nelson's an atheist. His personal staff fluctuates between forty and sixty, his six-billion-dollar business is in the toilet, and the ex-wife who won't blow him is trying to ruin his life. The man doesn't have time for God."

There were many things I wanted to say to that, none of them sarcastic—okay, the blow job reference begged for a one-liner—all of them sincerely preachy and judgmental. How anyone who had been blessed with all this good fortune could turn his back on the source from whom all blessings flow was beyond my understanding. But that's just me.

As if reading my mind, Lee added, "And he gives

about ten million dollars a year to some very good causes, not all of which involve oboes or tutus or art galleries. We're talking children and battered women. In case you were wondering."

"I wasn't," I said, "but thanks anyway. Good to know."

I smiled, she smiled, and we began to eat.

After lunch and an overview of my agenda for the week, we got down to business. The purpose of this trip, I learned, was twofold: to familiarize myself with the carefully crafted identity of the wildly successful and flamboyant high-tech tycoon I was slated to become, and, later in the week, to dig deeper into the complex psyche of Kelly Scott. For our introductory session, we hunkered down in the library, a two-story circular cavern lined floor to ceiling with books—not a dust cover in sight—which were accessed by a remote-control ladder on runners. The wood accents and the leather on the chairs, I noticed, were identical to those in the Gulfstream.

Lee placed her hand on a stack of materials that had been piled on the floor near a desk. She retrieved them, one by one, with a carefully scripted explanation for each. Whoever put this scenario together should have been running the CIA.

The first was a bound folder, about three inches thick.

"This is a five-year summary of your company, which we are calling *Diatech Systems*."

"Snappy. What business am I in?"

"Root-level systems diagnostics. Something she wouldn't understand even if she was interested, which she won't be. It's far above the retail arena, which explains why she's never heard of it or you. She and Nelson never talk business."

"What happens if *I* don't understand it?" I asked. "I hate all that shit."

"Read and memorize. Besides, you were the CEO—you're expected to be clueless."

"Is Mr. Scott clueless?"

She shot me a withering look before leaning down to retrieve another item, this one resembling a photo album.

"Dummy press kit. Five years' worth of bogus magazine articles and trade press clippings on the astounding success of your enterprise."

She handed it over. Inside were several dozen very believable forgeries from publications such as *Fortune* and the *Wall Street Journal*, which don't appreciate being forged. Now I *knew* the perpetrator of this little ruse had once run the CIA.

"Anything Kelly might want to know is here, so get deep inside this stuff. Go between the lines, as if you'd written it all yourself. She'll be far more interested in your generosity than in your technology."

"I was sort of hoping she'd be interested in my sports package, actually."

Lee just smiled.

Still looking through the fake articles, I said, "This'll get us five to ten at Chino if we get caught."

"We won't *get caught*, as you put it. This is primarily for your eyes, and on the off chance she needs a little documentation to ease her doubts, here it is."

"Who wrote this shit?" I asked, looking up.

"Just understand what it says."

"Maybe we should go public, make some real money."

Lee's face remained straight as she said, "Stranger things have happened."

She bent down again, bringing up a box this time.

"Your life in a box. Everything prior to age eighteen, you stick to the truth. Same name, parents, hometown, schools, social security number. She won't check that stuff, and you won't get caught in a lie."

"Too bad. I was looking forward to creating a happier childhood."

"You get plenty happy later." She patted the box for emphasis. "It's all here. Résumé, education, early jobs, a logical career path leading you to the founding of your company. She checks any of it, she'll find a paper trail corroborating every element of your life."

"Some day you'll have to tell me how you pulled this off."

"Some day I might. *If* we pull it off."

I thumbed through the box, seeing a pile of files, each labeled according to subject. It would be a long night of reading at the Villa Scott.

"The most critical part is in here."

She lifted one last leather-bound notebook to the tabletop. It was about four inches thick, reminiscent of a medical dictionary.

"The buyout," she continued. "Arielle purchased your company for six hundred million dollars in cash and stock. As the holder of seventy-seven percent of your firm's equity, that makes you worth something on the order of four hundred sixty million dollars, not counting five or ten million in outside assets you've accumulated on the side. The entire contract is here, and it is imperative that you memorize and understand every detail of how the transaction went down. We've even created a gap between the rumor, which is alluded to in some of the magazine articles, and the supposed truth. You can clear it all up for Kelly to cement the viability of your identity."

I nodded, staring at the notebook. Even as a fraud,

there was a compelling narcotic effect to the very notion that this *could* happen to someone. Until the dream ended, that someone would be me. I wondered which NBA franchise I would buy.

She said, "A little overwhelming, isn't it."

It was perhaps the first empathetic expression I'd heard emanate from Lee Van Wyke.

"This is why I'm getting the big bucks," I countered.

"The good news is, we have time. Kelly is involved with someone now, but that's about to end. She isn't one to jump into something heavy all that quickly."

"Why do I have the feeling you're involved in *that*, too?"

She turned away without expression.

"What's the bad news?" I asked, feeling the need to fill the sudden silence.

"The bad news is it's all still a roll of the dice. Based on what we know about her and what we've created, I'd say there's about an eighty percent probability that you'll be able to get to her. That's a bet we're willing to make."

"You a statistician, too? I'm impressed."

She must have been tired, since all of a sudden nothing I tried was working. Maybe my tennis game had taken something out of her after all. Then again, it hadn't seemed like it, based on *those* statistics.

"Your room is upstairs. You have a nice balcony view, access to the Internet, your own hot tub on the deck. You can get started, take a nap . . . your call. Dinner is at seven, casual chic."

I winced. "*Casual chic?* Tell me you're shitting me."

"Slacks and a shirt, Wolf. Tonight, we'll talk about what you've read. Tomorrow, we'll go see your condo, which I think you'll like, and we'll see about dressing you like the rich and sophisticated man that you are. Perhaps a few surprises, too."

I surveyed the stack of reading material.

"You'll be around?"

"No. Have a good time, Wolf. You can do this thing."

Then Lee Van Wyke did the strangest thing. She came to me for what I thought was a hug, a gesture that seemed out of place, yet sort of sweet. After all, we were partners in crime, and there was much at stake for both of us. I stood, accepting her into my arms.

Then she kissed me softly on the cheek, a bit too sensually to qualify as a good-luck moment. As she left, she seemed pleased with the look of utter confusion on my face.

In that respect, she was like every other woman I'd known.

> 24 <

ENTRY #26: INVESTMENT BANKING—we allow underwriters who risk millions in bringing a stock to market to recommend that same stock to its retail brokerage customers. This is like allowing your insurance agent to list himself as your beneficiary.
—from *Bullshit in America*, by Wolfgang Schmitt

It fooled even me, and I was the protagonist in this little independent production. Whoever had written the lifelike contract for Arielle's acquisition of Diatech Systems, the company my sophisticated alter ego had founded nine years earlier, sure knew how to sling the legalese. No one would ever be able to see through this façade because no one with a life would be able to read the damn thing, much less understand it. There were twenty-eight beefy chapters, each with an abundance of schedules and exhibits and sub-schedules and attachments and consents and non-competes, wherein the party of the first part, heretofore known as the "seller," subjugates and warrants all representations to be free of expressed or implied liabilities or liens or other forms of claim which might cause the party of the second part, heretofore known as the "buyer," to, in the event of independent audit, and in alignment with general accounting principles, be adjudged a value less than that attested to and warranted by the seller herewith, with such meanings to be equally applicable to both the singular and plural forms of the terms defined.

To wit, my ass. My guess is, someone took a contract from a prior acquisition and, thanks to the miracle of Microsoft Word, swapped out a few names and numbers. Probably Lee herself. Fewer witnesses for her to kill later.

No less impressive was what she had called *the dummy press kit*, which was anything but. The articles were mostly technical mumbo jumbo about the product my fictional company sold, the root-level diagnostic software of which I had been the brilliant architect. Good idea for me to know my own stuff. Actually—and this was smart—I would be positioned as the entrepreneur behind the propellerheads who did all the real work, which was standard practice in the high-tech game.

There were, however, a couple of "profile" articles, and they made my skin crawl—perhaps the same sensation felt by celebrities upon viewing their waxen image at Madame Tussaud's. There were even photos, most of which I recognized from my very thin modeling portfolio, no doubt scrounged up by the same flunkie who'd boosted my car back on day one. One shot—it had appeared in the local Sunday supplement five years earlier—had been Photoshopped to convincingly show me glad-handing prospects at a Comdex booth.

Most intriguing of all, of course, was the box containing my life before the money. It was a stroke of genius to leave my biography untouched prior to the age of eighteen, but from there it went from weird to positively H. G. Wells. Apparently I had shipped off to Arizona State University, majoring in marketing and, according to a little narrative biography for my eyes only, the seduction of tanned coeds. From there, I began to climb the Intel ladder at their Chandler facility, before I was fired for insubordination. It seemed I'd referred to Andy Grove in a staff meeting as "that little gnome from Vienna," and that was it. In a career comeback move John Travolta would envy, I'd cashed in my 401(k)—this was long before the stock tanked, turning more paper millionaires into thousandaires than Michael Milken—and scraped up enough outside capital to found Diatech, partnering with a genius type-B programmer who just wanted to build things and leave the PR stuff to me. A timeline of company milestones, such as patents, product releases, and capital investments, would make me convincingly fluent in the midst of the lie.

There was even a "cheat sheet" showing several addresses in Tempe and Scottsdale where I had supposedly lived as my career flourished, including what cars I'd owned, with—this truly gave me the creeps—Xeroxed copies of the titles.

I planned to tell my hostess that it took most of the afternoon to get through it all. The truth was, however, that between chapters, I did indeed avail myself of the spa—I was officially working, Anne Rice novel in hand—and the Internet, where I researched other diagnostic software companies, a base left uncovered in my tutorial materials. I'd make equally sure Lee knew of my initiative, and that my butt was covered in case Kelly had the presence of mind to ever ask about my competitors. Then again, if it came to that desperate level of conversation, chances would be I wasn't getting too far past first base with the woman anyhow.

As I was getting dressed for dinner—my best casual chic by Saks—I yielded to an urge that had been gnawing at me since boarding the jet that morning. Being in Tracy's neighborhood was having a narcotic effect on my memory and my attention span, both of which I needed intact. My only rationale for waiting until now to call was that I was "in the area"—I actually rehearsed saying this out loud—which I thought sounded less desperate than "just wanted to say hi," which I'd also rehearsed.

A folded cocktail napkin emerged from my wallet, even though I'd already memorized the number. Without giving myself time to change my mind, I punched it into my mobile.

Amazing, how audible one's own heartbeat can be.

Moments later, I was rocked by the recorded news that Tracy's line had been disconnected.

Frankly, and much to my surprise, I was relieved.

I dined alone, in casual chic splendor. Dinner was served by an attractive woman named Regina, who apologized on Lee's behalf without further explanation. She was so beautiful I almost invited her to join me, but thought better of it. Still insecure after all these years. No apology was necessary, however, for the filet mignon and accompanying garlic-sautéed scampi.

As Regina brought me my crème brûlée for dessert, she notified me that Lee was waiting in the study when I was done—a room I had not yet encountered in my brief stay. Guess she decided to stick around after all.

"This come with a map, too?" I asked as she placed the silver dish before me.

"Up the stairs, hang a left, double doors on the right. How was your dinner?"

"Would have been better if you'd have joined me."

She grinned as she departed without a response, as if she'd been warned about me.

* * *

The study reminded me of Wayne Manor, with a huge walk-in fireplace—there's a piece of architectural logic beyond comprehension—and a gargantuan black leather couch, where Bruce and Alfred might wax nostalgic on the decline of Gotham City over cognac in noir lighting. Lee Van Wyke was sitting in the accompanying overstuffed chair, her pants precisely matching the shimmering leather of the furniture as they both reflected the fire, giving her a somewhat menacing aura that was not altogether unattractive, if you like that sort of thing in a woman. She was reading, ironically, a copy of *Architectural Digest* when I entered the room, and I wondered if her raven feathers were ruffled by having to wait for me. I certainly hoped so.

"Good evening," I said, noticing that she was already nursing a glass of white wine.

She looked up and smiled warmly. "How was your dinner?"

"Lonely."

She motioned toward the couch, which was ready to swallow me into a black hole of lumbar support.

"You look richer already," she said.

I would get the Good Lee tonight, at least for a while. Based on her outfit, the Evil Lee would show later, I was sure.

"Interesting reading," I said coyly.

"And you have questions."

"I do. Such as, you really think this can work?"

"Don't you?"

"I did. But after reading your little missive, I realize just how many things can go wrong."

"You're absolutely right about that."

"I am?"

This made her laugh, though that wasn't my intention.

"You think you were chosen for that nice tight little butt of yours and those oh-so-pretty eyes. You think this was just another audition and you got the part, that your witty repartee and your refreshingly jaundiced take on the world is so very irresistible as to lock you in. Close?" She raised her eyebrows to punctuate the question mark.

"Something like that," I said.

"Your humility is misplaced but refreshing. Actually, that *is* part of it. You underestimate your powers of, how shall I put it . . . going with the flow."

She was using her hands to emphasize the latter point, which I was beginning to get.

"You think I can make this up as I go along. That if this is going to work, I have to be light on my feet."

"Precisely. Which, I might add, is why we're willing to pay you this outrageous sum of money to do this for us."

"It *is* above scale."

"If you make this work, you'll have earned every penny. You're the juice, Wolf. Without you, or someone like you, none of this flies."

"Thanks, now I can sleep nights."

Lee just grinned, waiting for my next question.

"So what you're saying," I said, "is basically that I was chosen for my ability to bullshit."

This made her smile widen somewhat.

"That's ironic," I added.

"Go on."

"I'm writing a book called *Bullshit in America*."

"About time someone did."

"I'm serious. Sort of a collection of injustices and outrages, like . . ."

She held up a hand for me to stop. "You said you have questions."

"Why was I fired from Intel for insubordination, of all things? Why not have me quit to pursue a dream, reach a higher goal, some bullshit like that?"

Lee took a sip of her wine, shifting in her chair with a wonderful leather-on-leather sound effect. You could almost see the transition, the Good Lee lowering her eyes and shuffling out of the room as the Evil Lee swept in on her German-model broomstick.

"You appreciate irony, Wolf, so here you go: Kelly has a bit of an attitude about corporate America. A real Democrat at heart. She's a crusader, a regular pit bull, and she believes in getting even. It's a religion for her. She'll relate to your story, and she'll admire your moxy almost as much as she'll admire your pedigree. Make sure she hears about this part of your life, the oppressed foot soldier who comes back to stick it up the boss's ass."

"Not sure I like the sound of the 'getting even' part when our little *Joe Millionaire* thing hits the fan."

"At the risk of insulting you, when she finds out you're worth less than her annual flower budget, she'll forget you exist. She'll go after Nelson, but by then the damage will be done. Besides, at the core of this entire thing is her secret fascination with, for lack of a better term, the *bad boys*. She might actually like you more for your seamier talents. A theme, I might add, that pops up a lot in the text of your new résumé."

"Like my college exploits."

She shook her head, lowering her voice to say, "You were a bad, bad boy, Wolf."

"Why Arizona? I hate the place. It's like one big ashtray, but with a killer baseball team."

"Because she's not familiar with Arizona. We put your past in a location with names and places she can't recognize. She'll take whatever you say about them for granted. My advice is to memorize those addresses, in case it comes up. In the dossier, you still live in Scottsdale, in fact. You have a place here because of the sale to Arielle and your contractual obligation to consult with them going forward. This should make you breathe easier, because you can disappear for extended periods, and it'll explain why you don't really know that much about this area. She gets to show you around and show you off, and she'll like that."

"What if she wants to see where I live? It could happen."

"It could, and we have that base covered. How does eleven thousand square feet at the base of Pinnacle Peak sound?"

"I'll have to get a tan."

"You're going there next week for a long weekend to familiarize yourself with the landscape. You can work on the tan then."

Woman had an answer for everything.

"What if she has me checked out?"

"She will. Question is, to what extent? There's documentation in place at ASU, the DMV, the Social Security Administration, even at Intel. On paper, you *exist*. If she goes too deep, chances are she's become suspicious anyway, so we're dead in the water."

"You hacked into the Social Security system?"

"Anything and everything is possible."

Something wicked stretched its limbs in my chest.

"I think we just crossed the line into prosecutable territory."

Her smile was appropriate to a woman wearing black leather. "Sue me," she said.

"Good to have friends in low places," I countered.

"Excuse me?"

"It's from a song. Garth Brooks. You probably never heard of him."

"Beat him in straight sets, actually."

"You're lying."

"You'll never know, will you."

Our stares squared off, hers tinged with vague amusement, mine with caution. Like someone who handles snakes for a living, my respect for this woman was growing at a rate equal to my fear of her. And—I didn't want to admit—my attraction.

She ran her fingertip around the rim of her wine glass for a moment, thinking deeply, as if listening for a tone.

"There's something else you need to know about Kelly Scott. The coup de grace, so to speak."

"Meaning what?"

"Meaning, once you get your mind around this one, and if you can pull it off, the game is ours."

"A secret weakness, perhaps?"

"Her secret *desire* is more accurate."

"I thought only men had secret desires."

Her eyes twinkled with delight as she drained the last of her wine from its glass. I half-expected her to snap her fingers to summon a servant, but it didn't happen.

"Men," she began thoughtfully, "have fantasies. Fetishes, fascinations which have nothing at all to do with romance or the women in their lives. Women have them, too, but they are almost always much more complex, and they usually have something to do with her primary relationship. With *romance*. For most women, however, these needs are subordinated to more basic life requirements."

"Such as money."

Lee nodded in approval. "In essence. Kelly is fortunate in that she is free to pursue fulfillment on an entirely different level than most women. Which has allowed her desires to, shall we say, become obsessions, even goals. When a man walks into her life with the qualities she desires, and the pedigree to match, she will have died and gone to heaven."

"I hope to God you're being metaphoric."

She hesitated, a bit of that twinkle returning.

"It's very subtle. Simple to describe, challenging to understand, incredibly complex to implement. And frankly, something most men simply aren't capable of grasping."

She paused, studying me.

"How do *you* know what Kelly Scott wants? I mean, on that level."

"Please. Nelson's been sleeping with this woman for nineteen years. He *knows*."

"Most men sleep with their wives their whole life and don't know what the hell she wants."

"I couldn't agree more," she said.

I whistled softly. "Nothing like going to the well for the good dirt."

"We think you can do this," said Lee.

"Is that a compliment? I'm not so sure."

She glared at me. "More than you know."

I waited. She held my gaze for a moment, then got up and went to a desk in the corner of the room. She returned, handing me several books wrapped in plain brown paper.

"Your reading for the evening."

"Kelly wrote a book on her fantasies? Cool."

"No. Anne Rice did."

"I'm not biting Kelly Scott's neck. Sorry, I draw the line."

She actually chuckled out loud. It is a wise woman

who laughs at a man's jokes, and her timing was perfect.

"Context, Wolf. One of your favorite words. If you have to ask, you don't get it."

Now I smiled, signaling the truth at the end of the joke.

"I get it. It's a style thing, a certain gothic panache. Dark romance, the Phantom of the Opera, sexual hunger in an over-the-top metaphor, sweet submission and loving dominance, take-me-I'm-yours, all in mediocre prose with a slightly purple hue. I *get* it."

She had no idea how I got it. Tracy, whose dark side would have made Anne Rice run for her rosary beads, had taught me how to speak this particular dialect in the language of love.

Lee got back to her feet, picking up the empty wineglass to take with her.

"What remains to be seen, then, is if you can do *this*."

She tapped the books, which were resting on my knee. "Have a nice evening. We'll talk tomorrow."

I watched her exit, which she was in no hurry to complete. Some women know how to work a room, and a proper exit—especially in black leather pants— was part of this exclusively feminine discipline.

It was early, and I assumed I was expected to retire to my room and read the Great Key to Kelly Scott's mind and heart.

I tore the wrapper off the books before my butt hit the mattress. There were three paperbacks, each by a writer named A. N. Roquelaure, which sounded like a salad dressing, and thankfully wasn't the author's real name. Above it, in smaller print, were the words: "Anne Rice writing as . . ."

Metaphor, indeed. The first thing I needed to know

was this: who would be tying up whom, and where did the fine line between fantasy and reality reside in Kelly Scott's mind? One thing I knew about sexual fantasies—and after my time with Tracy I knew a thing or two—it was best when it remained right there, in the mind. An artfully composed word picture was worth a thousand clothespins in bed.

What was true for me at the beginning of this journey was, in many ways, just as true now, FBI or no FBI. The bottom line was this: I had limits, and I had a mirror into which I intended to gaze for the rest of my long, long life.

As I lay in Nelson Scott's guest bed on his 380-thread-count linen sheets, struggling to clear my mind of the vivid images lifted from Anne Rice's lucrative imagination—these are not books one reads to relax—I was stricken with a sudden and unrelated thought: how in the *hell* did Lee Van Wyke know that *context* was one of my favorite words?

After two hours of rolling around, counting heartbeats, I decided to check the Internet and see if my hundred grand was still handy in that offshore account. It was, allowing me to finally drift off to sleep with a smile.

> 25 <

ENTRY #144: THE ELECTORAL COLLEGE—something is wrong when the guy with the second-most votes can win—a phenomenon no one can explain or defend.
—from *Bullshit in America*, by Wolfgang Schmitt

I was awakened at eight the next morning by a soft knocking on the door. It was my old pal Regina—who cared not in the least that I had answered wearing only my briefs—carrying a silver tray with an offering of fruits and warm breads, the same as those that had awaited me on the airplane the previous morning. Watching her place the tray on the desk, wondering if she was ever allowed to leave the premises, *The Stepford Wives* came to mind, reminding me that I was indeed not in Kansas anymore.

Half an hour later, someone knocked on the door again. I assumed it would be Regina, come to fetch the tray after a quick recharge from a 120-volt outlet, but I was wrong.

This new visitor made Regina look tepid. I was speechless, and it showed. Thankfully, I had progressed from my tighty-whities to a pair of Dockers and a Young-Republican Polo.

"Good morning. I'm Lynn, Mr. Scott's personal valet."

Lynn, the former Miss California who did Scott's shopping when she wasn't helping him put his pants on one leg at a time. Lynn, who for some mysterious reason Nelson Scott had never touched. Lynn, who looked so much like Elizabeth Hurley that for a moment I thought I was watching a rerun of *Bedazzled*.

"I'm Wolf. Bet you knew that."

She was carrying a notebook and a tape measure, the color of which went well with her flowing pantsuit and heels. Which is precisely how I'd dress my personal valet if I had one.

"Ready to be fitted?"

"For what, a respirator? Please."

This made her smile, and I knew I'd be okay. We had just acknowledged the sexual tension, which I was sure was a one-way street this morning.

"May I come in?"

I moved back, pulling the door with me.

"I assumed Mr. Scott traveled with his personal valet. What do I know?"

"I do sometimes. Vacations, mostly."

"Nice perk."

"Works for me. Can you put on some shoes?"

"We going out?" I knew better, but I was relaxing quickly.

"Lee said you were a wiseass," she said, while pulling a length of the measuring tape between outstretched arms.

"What else did she say about me?"

"That you'll be easy to fit."

"Forty-six long. Will there be anything else?"

"Stand here." She pointed to a spot in front of the full-length mirror which doubled as my side of the bathroom door. I complied, and she went to work.

Inseam, waist, hips, arms, chest, neck, bada bing. It was over in less than what proved to be a very quiet minute. Having such a creature kneeling at my feet, intent upon serving me, deserved a moment of silence.

"What are we wearing in this movie?" I asked when she was finished.

"Couple of custom-made suits, tops and sweaters from Milan, linen slacks from Neiman's, a pair of killer jeans from Melrose Avenue. And a tux. What's your shoe size?"

"Twelve D. I don't do wingtips."

She made a note of it. Then, with a businesslike smile, she looked up and promptly extended her hand.

"Nice to meet you," she said. "Hope you enjoy your stay."

Why is it that beautiful women, when they're smiling at you, make you want to believe they are reading your mind? I shook her hand, which was firm and warm. Nelson Scott was either a saint or a big fan of the Village People.

As days go, this one was scripted by Robin Leach, with a little doctoring by M. Night Shyamalan for that surreal touch.

The helicopter ferried me and Lee back to the San Jose airport, where a car and driver awaited us. The agenda called for a tour of the area, including stops at my new luxury condo, which was still being redecorated to something suitable for a man of my means—I was looking forward to understanding what *that* meant—and a drive-by of Kelly Scott's penthouse digs.

"We gonna talk about the books?" I tried several minutes into the ride, seizing a moment between her phone calls.

She smiled and patted my knee. "Down, boy."

"I have questions about the part where they use human beings as furniture."

Without looking at me, she said, "It's not like that."

"Not my idea of a good time."

"Not to worry. We'll talk."

On cue, her mobile phone rang, and that was that for now.

Over the course of two hours, Lee showed me where people with my checkbook stayed while they were in town, and where they ate when they wanted to be seen and where they ate when they wanted to dine in finer style—which was rarely the same place. She gave me the obligatory high-tech e-ticket tour: First Avenue, north to Mountain View and the Fairchild building where the integrated circuit was invented; the Cupertino house where Steve Wozniak invented the personal computer that would be the Apple; the Oracle campus with its Larry Ellison–designed twin towers—on a cocktail napkin, urban legend holds—which, in a nobody-tell-the-king-he-has-no-clothes classic, were supposed to emulate disk drives but looked more like pre-Nixon apartment buildings; the bars where the venture capital deals were signed and some of the most notorious gold diggers in the history of nail polish plied their trade; the hillside road where one high-tech tycoon killed himself in his Maserati nine hours after taking his company public and pocketing ninety million dollars; and assorted other silicon trivia that I hoped I'd never have to discuss with Kelly Scott. I'd rather talk about my future as an ottoman, to be honest.

Speaking of Kelly, her flat was atop a seventy-year-old six-story office building that was remarkably underwhelming. There was a doorman—also underwhelming—and a parking lot attendant who, upon penalty of death, would require a note from the Pope before allowing someone inside, but that would be no problem once I'd broken through into Kelly's inner circle. How *that* was going to happen remained undefined, and frankly, I was in no hurry to know. Especially since Lee and I hadn't had that furniture discussion yet.

We lunched at a California bistro specializing in pretension and stuffy waiters, the kind of place restaurants in Oregon tried to emulate but ended up simply being overpriced. California cuisine just doesn't fly in Klamath Falls. The conversation remained, as Lee put it, "offline," centering on the resurrection of the stock market and the power elite who run it, with whom she was quite familiar and had no doubt beaten in straight sets.

I was bored and she knew it.

"I went out with someone like you once." She pointed her fork at me for emphasis, her eyes playful.

"Lucky you."

"He was smart, gorgeous . . ."

"I like it so far."

"And completely incapable of getting past an irritating propensity to mouth off."

"Ouch."

"Precisely."

I used my fork to toy with the ravaged skeleton of the unfortunate Cornish game hen on my plate.

"You pay a steep price for your saccharine wit."

I started to say that I hadn't had too many complaints to date, but stopped myself. It was a lie, one that would make her case. Instead I mimicked her body language, shoulders hunched, hands folded contently in my lap.

She grinned, seeing through me. "See? It's a wall you put up, a defense."

"Against what?"

"Intimacy. Getting real. You can't go there."

In the ensuing moment of quiet I felt my entire biology shift into a lower gear.

"It'll be your undoing with Kelly," she said.

"I'll try to watch it."

"What you should *try* to do is understand why."

"I'm all ears."

The waiter made a timely appearance, offering coffee, which she accepted and I, of course, declined.

"Most people misunderstand the game," she said, and I could tell she was going deep for whatever followed. "Which is why most people inevitably fail at it."

"Which game is that? I need a program here."

"The game of love. Try to keep up, Wolf."

I nodded with a straight face.

"It's all so easy at first," she continued. "You flash your credentials, show your pecs, haul out your best mask, the one your father taught you to wear, and you do it proudly because you are a *man*, and then, being the player you are, you risk the revelation of your weaknesses with a filter on what will fly and what won't. That is, if you're looking to score."

"You sound like Dr. Phil. You beat him in straight sets, too?"

She shot me a look that could boil the bottled water.

"Initially it's all about compatible assets. Chemistry. Before long the game changes, it becomes about compatible *liabilities*. A killer one-eighty. To make it really work, to make the turn, you have to have compatible flaws, compatible vulnerabilities, compatible tolerances."

"I should take notes, write an article about this."

"Feel free."

"Please, go on. I'll use the napkin." A little joke, since it was made of linen.

"All of which brings me back to *you*."

The waiter was conveniently passing our table at that moment, so I asked him for a pen, which he produced from his pocket. It was another joke, one which prompted my companion to shake her head in soft disapproval.

"Can't help yourself, can you, Wolf."

I put the pen down and placed my hands in my lap.

"Kelly will laugh at your jokes and she'll admire your ability to poke fun at the bullshit around you. But very soon—because she'll definitely find you attractive, and if you push her buttons like we plan on helping you push them—she'll want to see the serious Wolf, the vulnerable inner Wolf, the guy who has needs and dark secrets. Only then will she assess whether those secrets are compatible with hers. At that level, your comedic gifts will kill you rather than serve your purpose."

"Lee, I'm trying to seduce the woman, not marry her."

"Typical bullshit male perception. You really think there's a difference where she's concerned? She's not looking for a piece of ass, Wolf. She's looking for *you*. Or better put, the *you* we'll put in front of her."

I nodded, understanding her point.

"Kelly doesn't want a suave comedian with nice cheekbones. She wants a lover who will rock her world in a way she may not even be able to describe to him. When she does, she'll toss the prenup in the toilet and move in. But he has to bring it to the table himself, and she has to feel like she's discovered a dark prince beneath all that attitude and posturing. Like most women, she wants it both ways: all man on the outside, all passionate and sincere on the inside."

I whistled at the sheer complexity of it all. I felt like I'd been kicked in the gut by an ex-girlfriend who'd figured me out. I also realized that, brick wall and all, Tracy and I had been perfect for each other, since she was no more inclined to pull back the kimono and be real than I was. Perfectly compatible weak points. We had been codependent on each other's inability to get real, to go deep, surviving on the heat of a doomed fire. Tracy wanted it both ways, too: hunky on the outside, financially overwhelming on the inside.

Lee was right on the money. If I couldn't change, become someone far more evolved than the man Tracy had left at the ATM, I wouldn't get out of Kelly Scott's batter's box.

"You can do this," said Lee, once again reading my thoughts. "You *need* to do this."

Another kick to the midsection. My face betrayed my confusion, perhaps my pain.

"You're not a happy man. You're not done yet, and you know it. Your friends still get excited about beer and football, but you want more, you hunger for meaning. This is a crossroads for you, isn't it, Wolf. A milestone. Which is why you said *yes* to something your programming tells you to walk away from. That's a good sign—it means you've got a shot. The money you'll make will enable you to become anyone and anything you desire for the rest of your life. What that is, where that road takes you, is completely up to you."

"You should go on Oprah."

"Am I right? Or is this just more bullshit in America?"

I wanted to tell her that *I* was the expert on bullshit

at this table, to challenge her credentials in life and romance and the doublespeak of personal growth. I wanted to get the upper hand back, flash a sizzling smile and try to take her down, validate my existence with my ability to smother her arrogance with sexual prowess. This was my wall, a reliable defense in the game I had played so well, the game that had left me alone on the court while the world moved on. And I recognized it, was pounding my head against it—the very fact of which confirmed everything she had just told me.

I was a guy. And despite my magazine articles, I was still as dumb as a box of gym socks.

"Let me ask you something," she said, a definite shift in her energy easily detectible. Dr. Phil was gone, replaced by someone far more playful and hard to read.

"Careful, you're cracking my wall here."

She leaned forward and grabbed hold of my hand with both of hers. The temperature of her skin was shockingly warm.

"Do you find me sexually attractive?" she asked.

I felt my lungs seize up as my stomach did a double camel.

"Is this a trick question? Because if it is, you're not playing fair."

She brought my hand to her face, using the backs of my fingers to caress her face, which was just as warm.

"I'd like an answer," she said.

I managed a breath or two. I wanted my voice to sound cool, under control. In other words, I wanted to perpetrate a complete fraud possible only by the likes of Daniel Day Lewis.

"Why do you ask?" I said.

"That's a good question. I'll answer it when I hear your response."

"I think you already know the answer."

"Say it."

I swallowed. Hard.

"Yes. I find you sexually attractive. Who wouldn't?"

She parted her lips, using them to massage my knuckles. I could sense other patrons watching, making the moment all the more uncomfortable.

"We're playing a game here, aren't we, Wolf."

"If you say so."

"It sucks, doesn't it. The game."

"I certainly hope so. Sorry. I mean, yeah, it sucks."

She was using her teeth now, pinching the skin between my fingers.

"It's better if we just get real, say what we want."

"I get it. You're making a point in a spectacular way."

"Am I? Maybe I'm just spinning you up."

"That's a game, too."

She released my hand, her expression infuriatingly superior. I could feel heat assaulting my cheeks, feel my stomach constrict into an even tighter ball. She seemed to be finished with whatever it was she'd just started.

"What was *that* all about?" I asked.

"Just a little taste."

"Taste? Of what, bullshit? I know how *that* tastes."

"What you want me to say now is, a taste of what's to come."

"Don't tell me what I want. Trust me, you don't know."

Her smile expanded to the precipice of laughter. "A taste of how it feels. Like it or not, you enjoyed how that felt. For a moment, I dropped the façade, got real, or what you perceived to be real, and you could feel the power of it. Am I right?"

I just stared. Damn her.

"You wanted to go with it, just hop on, let me do all the work, take you someplace. I know you find me attractive. That's not the point. The point is how my sudden shift into intimacy made you feel, and how much you enjoyed the sensation. It's like a drug: you get high on it, you want more. Tell me I'm wrong, Wolf. Tell me this is just more bullshit."

God, I wanted to. But I could not. I nodded.

"Here's the takeaway. Are you listening to me? Right now is when you take notes, you brand this moment into your brain and use it going forward."

"I'm listening."

She leaned in, as if to reveal the secret of all Creation.

"Kelly Scott is addicted to that drug. She yearns for it, she's powerless in its presence, she swoons at the prospect of it."

She allowed a few seconds to pass, studying everything about my eyes and my face to be sure I'd heard her clearly.

"Think about it, Wolf. It's the key to Kelly Scott. The key to everything you desire."

With that, Lee Van Wyke rose to her feet, fetched her purse from where it hung over the back of her chair, and headed away, winding through the tables like a movie star walking through the lobby of the Polo Lounge.

Like a puppy, I knew I was expected to follow, and I did.

> 26 <

ENTRY #149: FOUR-WAY STOPS—this is without doubt the definitive IQ test for people over sixteen years of age. Too bad, too, since people under sixteen would do better at it. When the meek inherit the earth, traffic's gonna be hell.
—from *Bullshit in America*, by Wolfgang Schmitt

After lunch we drove to a cheeky neighborhood called Los Gatos Hills. These hills were alive with the sound of money. You had to have a German car or a driver to get in—preferably both. My condo was behind large iron gates, which were guarded by an ex–pulling guard with a frown and a big gun. We stopped across the street, allowing him to stare at us, and we at him. There was a view of the Valley, not remotely in the same league as Casa Scott's—but then again, my alter ego wasn't quite a billionaire yet. I would have to be content with perfectly groomed boulevards and magnificent palm trees aligned by anal-retentive landscapers.

"We going in?" I asked.

"Not today. I just wanted you to see the neighborhood, get a feel for the commute. Trust me, you'll like it."

"Color me a cynic, but I have questions."

She smiled patiently and nodded. Expectantly, even.

"You said I don't live here, I just come into town to fulfill my obligation to Arielle."

"That's correct."

"So why do I own a condo? Why not stay at a pretentious resort with room service and a masseuse named Ursula?"

"Because you're rich and you like your privacy. Ursula comes to you. Think of it as investment. A modest one, for a man of your means."

I nodded. "That'll fly. I think."

She stared, considering something, then said, "You want the real reason?"

"No. I always prefer the rhetorical bullshit over the real bullshit."

"Because you'll need a place to take Kelly before she lets you into her world. And the less people see you, the better."

I issued a little wave at the guard. Lee slapped my hand away like a mother disciplining a child reaching for forbidden cookies.

"So why aren't we going in?"

"Because it's not ready, and you're not here. And if you don't stop with the twenty questions, you won't get your surprise."

The expression on her face was playful, so I assumed my surprise had nothing to do with Anne Rice's sexual fantasies and my impending role as a footstool. I still wondered when that would become relevant, but for now I was content with my tutorial on the art of being obscenely wealthy.

"Consider me silenced," I said, and the limo began to move.

Robin Leach's scriptwriters had outdone themselves.

We drove straight back to the San Jose airport, where the Bell Ranger sporting the Arielle logo awaited us with open doors. A building sense of realization began to overwhelm me as we drove through the cyclone fence gates onto the tarmac, so much so that Lee patted my knee—her way of acknowledging and perhaps sharing my excitement.

Parked next to the helicopter was a gleaming black jewel of a car, shimmering in the afternoon sun. It was a spanking new Mercedes SL 55 AMG, the tricked-out two-seat coupe with an engine designed by NASA, outfitted with twelve thousand dollars' worth of oversized chrome wheels. Positioned in front of the helicopter, it looked like a layout for the cover of *Automotive News*.

Had she not touched my knee, I would have clung to doubt. But by the time we stopped, I knew. This was my new ride.

"Pinch me," I said.

"Later. For now, go get into your car."

I whistled again—something I'd be doing a lot of while I was in town.

"I'm gonna hate giving this up come quittin' time."

"Tell you what," said Lee. "You pull this off, you keep the car. Fair enough?"

I tore my eyes away from the Benz long enough to see if she was sincere. She was, and for a moment I was once again in love.

"One question," I said as we got out of the Lincoln. "How are we gonna get this thing into the helicopter?"

This didn't quite rate a laugh, but it made her smile.

"There's a map on the seat. Be back at the Villa in time for dinner. Give yourself thirty minutes for the drive, and watch the curves. Don't want you messing up that pretty face before the party begins."

"Where am I going?"

"That's entirely up to you. Anywhere you like. Except Kelly's building, of course. Drive around, check out the geography. Get comfortable. You'll be here a while."

She was already walking off toward the helicopter, leaving me and my hanging jaw next to the car. Make that *my* car. The top was down, and the interior was a creamy shade of gray leather that went nicely with my personality.

"That's it?" I called after her.

"Not really," she said, barely turning her head. "You have a date tonight. Be on time."

"I have a *what*?"

All she did was wave as she climbed aboard, the gas-turbine jet engine already spooling up, the giant blades slowly commencing their first rotation.

Needless to say, I took the long way home.

> 27 <

ENTRY #195: THOSE LITTLE KETCHUP PACKETS YOU GET AT FAST-FOOD PLACES—honestly, have you or anyone you know ever used only *one* of these things? With all our science, why can't they make them twice as big, and while we're at it, easier to open?
—from *Bullshit in America*, by Wolfgang Schmitt

There were two things waiting for me on my bed when I returned from my afternoon test drive, which I'd managed to stretch into a fifty-seven-mile experiment in high-speed cornering. Regrettably, neither of them was Lee in a black teddy and heels. One was a spanking new tuxedo, with a very Hollywood black shirt and appropriately uncomfortable shoes. The other was a typed note instructing me to be in them and waiting on the helipad precisely at six thirty.

Since it wasn't Oscar night, I concluded I was meeting my heretofore undisclosed "date" for dinner.

Another note awaited me on the seat inside the helicopter. I was the sole occupant for tonight's flight, and I waited until well after liftoff to open it, allowing myself to appreciate the panoramic view of Nelson Scott's hillside kingdom.

This note read: *Wolf— Your companion tonight knows*

all that you seek to achieve. Listen and learn. Most of all, obey.

Wonderful. I would be swapping hors d'oeuvres with Dr. Ruth. I had assumed, and frankly hoped, that it would be Lee, wearing that teddy beneath something gloriously devastating. The recent sensation of my fingers between her lips had left an indelible impression.

Like all of the notes in my life lately, it was typed and unsigned.

It was nearly dark by the time we descended toward a patch of black somewhere near the San Francisco International Airport, where the requisite limo was waiting.

This was only my second day on Planet Scott, and already I was losing the ability to be surprised. So when I saw that a woman was waiting in the back of the car, and that her legs were straight out of a Victoria's Secret catalog, I was more pleased than struck dumb with shock.

Dr. Ruth this wasn't.

Her legs were crossed in that *dig me* way some women have mastered, and her grin was of the same egocentric bent. She extended an arm sheathed in a black satin glove and a bracelet Harry Winston would have been proud to have had in inventory, presenting a hand expecting to be kissed rather than shaken. She wore a black gown with one buffed shoulder exposed, and a fur coat that had been pulled back for just this purpose. A spectacular necklace encircled an Audrey Hepburn neck. She was of partly Asian descent, her hair jet-black and cut in a perfect bob, tucking inward at the chin line—perhaps she and Lee used the same guy—framing scalding dark eyes that contradicted her smile. This was a woman who, at a glance, would be as comfortable hosting an embassy bash as she would interrogating a prisoner with a butane torch.

All of it was straight out of a Bond movie. My job now was to determine which team this dark angel in a black dress was playing for. And, whether we were headed for the embassy or the dungeon.

"I'm pleased," were her first words. "You live up to your photographs and your endorsements. Not many do."

I acknowledged a dash of embarrassment with my eyes. There's not much to say when a woman comes at you that directly.

"And you," I said, when the moment had passed, "are she who must be obeyed."

I handed over the note from my room, which was in my left hand. I watched her eyes morph from curiosity to amusement as she read.

"I'm Amanda," she said, looking up.

"I'm Wolf," I countered. It was then that I realized I was still holding onto the hand I had kissed in greeting. I gently released my grip, and she folded her hand with the other in her lap.

The limo was already under way. The driver was a young woman, her blond hair tucked beneath a silly hat similar to the one Joe had worn. The glass partition was in the up position.

"How much did Lee tell you about me?" she asked, her eyes twinkling, as if the answer was dicey.

"Just this," I said, flashing the note again.

Amanda nodded and looked ahead. A woman who knew far more than she intended to reveal, at least for now.

Taking my next cue from her playful energy, I said, "She should have added great beauty to the list of your attributes."

If it was a game they wanted, let it rip. It occurred to me this was a test of sorts, a dry run to see how I'd do with a woman in Kelly Scott's league.

"I'm thinking she's said too much already."

She studied me as the limo was pulled onto the 101, heading north. Straight toward the mouth of the beast that was downtown San Francisco.

"So, what *do* you do?" I asked.

Her smile was that of a hunter who hears rustling in the grass.

"Think of me as a therapist of sorts. Behavior modification, for lack of a better term. Tonight, I'm a teacher."

"Not much money in *that*, I hear."

"*Au contraire*, sir." Her smile softened, then quickly hardened again. "We're going to a ten-thousand-dollar-a-plate fund-raiser at the St. Francis. In my day job, I'd have to work less than a week to get us in, but this is my lucky night. You're my date, which means you're also my host."

"Not to mention your student. Expensive class."

"Class is always expensive."

"I'll try to remember that."

Stacks of what looked like Monopoly houses were lined up in neat columns heading up the hills to our left, and to the right was the mysterious black expanse of the Bay. Ahead I could see the silhouette of 3Com Park, the house that Barry Bonds built with seventy-three swings and an attitude.

"You want my first impression?" she asked. "I'm never wrong."

"Bring it," I said.

"You will succeed. You're glib but humble, confident yet not particularly needy. Kelly Scott is going to think she's met her dark prince."

"Thank you. You know her?"

"No. I know *about* her, which is better."

"I get it. You know what she likes."

"I know what she *loves*. She's going to be there tonight, at the neighboring table, in fact. She'll notice you. All the women will. They'll ask who you are. Some might even make a few discreet inquiries."

I nodded slowly. "And so it begins."

"Don't be nervous. You look every bit the new rich guy in town, which is precisely what they'll discover if they care to check. The one thing you shouldn't appear to be is nervous."

"They'll wonder who you are, too."

"That won't be an issue."

"Because they won't know you."

"The women won't, no."

"Ah. The men, then."

"A few."

"The ones who avoid eye contact at all costs."

She put a gloved finger to her grinning lips, as if to call for quiet. Then, aiming to raise my pulse, she put that same finger to my mouth and playfully parted my lips.

I froze, afraid to breathe.

She grabbed my arm and snuggled closer. "Are you uncomfortable?"

"Should I be? I have a feeling you'd enjoy that."

She leaned close, the smile melting into something softer, our first kiss inevitable. Her lips radiated warmth, and my body chemistry responded, right on cue. Good to know the old plumbing was in order.

My hand found the back of her neck with a pressure that seemed to vie for some of that power. I was comfortable with this particular mode of sexual shorthand, when the narrative of seduction changed from implication to invitation. Tracy had taught me well. The verbal joust had been one of our more evolved forms of foreplay.

Amanda tightened her grip on my arm as she slid one of those killer legs over mine, kissing me deeper while forcing me back in the seat. I sensed there was suddenly a smile behind those busy, highly experienced lips.

God, I thought, how I loved this job. At least so far.

Political fund-raisers draw the coolest people. The governor of California was there, still far more muscular than his bodyguards. The vice president of the United States was there. An aging action hero with his own mayoral mystique was sitting next to him, and it appeared they were bored with the entire flagrant affair. I did the math—the gross was somewhere near five million dollars.

All that, and the steak cut like a catcher's mitt.

Amanda and I hung at the fringes of the crowd, watching with fascination as the jockeying grew more heated as the cocktail hour wound down. There was a photographer from the *Examiner* in attendance, and it was hilarious to observe the maneuvering for his attention. There were no nametags in this club, which in our case resulted in plenty of *wonder-who-they-are* stares and a few outright incredulous squints from across the room. I answered the first of several *and-who-might-you-be?* queries, posed by a woman with hair a pale shade of blue, by telling her with a straight face I was with the Secret Service, prompting Amanda to plant the heel of her shoe squarely on the top of my foot. When similar inquiries came—which they did throughout the course of the evening—I simply said I was in the high-tech business, and that I had recently sold my firm and was looking forward to scoring some 'Niners tickets at my earliest convenience. No one asked the name of my company, which I found interesting in a *what's-that-have-to-do-with-me?* sort of way. Several people did, however, want to know my name, and I looked upon my answer as part of a process of planting seeds in what Amanda assured me was an insidious and highly fertile garden of good and evil.

Toward the end of the cocktail hour, a city councilman approached, introduced himself, and, bringing Amanda's hand to his lips, told her it was nice to see her again. Something about his manner gave me the creeps, perhaps because he was old enough to be her father, perhaps because of the somewhat medieval visual that popped into my head. As he walked off I shot her a look, spiced with raised eyebrows, in response to which she simply said, "Don't ask."

Kelly Scott was fashionably late, arriving between the crab cakes and the Caesar salad, on the arm of a guy who looked like he should have been a studio executive. Slick, a bit full of himself. His hair, however, confirmed the suspicion that you can't make chicken salad out of chickenshit.

As for Kelly Scott, it was like spotting a celebrity. What surprised me was how attractive she was—one of those women the camera couldn't quite capture and men couldn't quite get out of their heads. Her allure was largely in the way she carried herself, floating through the room, oblivious to the scandal on her arm—enough money and rumors evaporate like a presidential indiscretion—chatting up the minions and spewing charm. As for her gown, Halle Berry would kill to wear this little number to the next Golden Globes. It was black and shimmering, liquid night, with a sash encircling her neck that followed behind her like smoke. Her blond hair was worn up, crafted by a room full of well-schooled *artistes* with fake French accents, framed with jewelry everyone in the room knew she hadn't borrowed. Someone should write a novel entitled *The Billionaire's Wife* and put Kelly Scott on the cover.

While my eyes feasted on her entrance, Amanda's were fixed on me. I could feel the weight of her stare.

"Behold, her majesty arrives," she whispered to me.

"My money's on you when the catfight starts."

"Take away the net worth and she just disappears. There's nothing remotely remarkable there, Wolf, other than her tax bracket. Which is precisely why this will work."

I watched as Mrs. Scott passed our table en route to her own. For the briefest instant our eyes met, but it was a fleeting moment, and quite by design. I could tell immediately that she was a woman with an eye for the opposite sex.

"One leg at a time," I said.

"Pardon me?"

"What the coaches used to tell us about players on teams that were bigger than life, undefeated teams, the Goliaths to our David. They put their pants on one leg at a time."

We watched her date hold her chair for her, saw her greeting others at her table as she settled in.

"What we're talking about here is taking them *off* one leg at a time," said Amanda, still leaning close so our conversation remained discreet. "Except in her case, I think *tearing* them off would be the better approach. Same metaphor, Wolf. The instant you start believing she's better than you are, you're toast. She'll smell your insecurity like bad caviar."

"Maybe you should leave the metaphors to me."

"Agreed. But hear this clearly. The stronger the

woman—in fact, the stronger the person—the more they crave to be dominated. Believe me, I know."

She put her face on my shoulder, holding my arm tightly. Anyone watching would discreetly elbow her escort and comment on how very much in love we appeared to be. I was conscious of that thought, and for the first time since I'd set foot on a private jet, I felt in need of a hot shower.

We ate in silence, waiting for the designated Republican comedian—now there's an oxymoron—to entertain us with the keynote stand-up. My unspoken assignment was to study my mark, which I did with as much discretion as possible. It was quite by design that I allowed her to catch me in the act, smiling shyly as our eyes met. I wasn't sure who looked away first, but I was now positive she knew I was there.

So did her date. I had made the mistake of forgetting he had eyes, too, and he had pegged me as something other than a gawker from the moment they sat down.

In the middle of the meal, Kelly excused herself from her table and made for the lobby. Before she got there, Amanda squeezed my arm, shot me a coy look, and got to her feet.

"No," I said.

"Obey," she whispered, and she was off.

A discreet glance toward the neighboring table confirmed, judging from an expression more appropriate to a root canal, that her date didn't like me at all.

Ten agonizing minutes later, Amanda returned, and I could tell from her expression that she had achieved whatever mission she'd set out to accomplish. Children receive applause when they return from the bathroom with such news, but this was

Planet Scott, and the report would be far more terrifying.

"Buckle up," she whispered as she sat down, me having risen to hold her chair and replace her napkin.

"You didn't," I said.

"I did."

"I thought you didn't know her."

"I do now. And so will you before this is over."

"So much for training day," I said, sensing that my pulse had pumped up the volume a bit.

She leaned in.

"You want training . . . when we get home, I'm going to show you how to make love to a woman in a way that parts the ocean and infects the mind. For now, just sit there and be beautiful and shut the fuck up."

Her smile was sweet, that of a child expecting applause. Mine was nervous, that of a child anticipating his spanking.

> 28 <

ENTRY # 133: STARS PLAYING AGAINST TYPE—
Robert DeNiro doing comedies with Eddie Murphy and Billy Crystal . . . that's like asking Pavarotti to sing *La Boheme* with Kid Rock.
    —from *Bullshit in America*, by Wolfgang Schmitt

It was between the entrée and the dessert—whoever dreamed up the notion of boiled pears ought to be glazed—that I felt a soft hand touch my shoulder. I tried not to gasp, but when I saw that Kelly Scott was kneeling next to Amanda and me, my suspect heart skipped a beat.

She was looking at me when she spoke, but she was clearly directing her words at Amanda.

"You didn't tell me he was a hottie, too."

I looked at Amanda, whose eyes sparkled. It was a conspiracy of estrogen, hatched in the ladies' room as the war paint was being touched up.

"Too?" I inquired.

Kelly extended her other hand, clearly that of a wealthy woman.

"Kelly Scott. I'm eating next door."

"Wolf Schmitt," I said, accepting the handshake. "Welcome to the neighborhood."

"Wolf . . . sounds kinda dangerous."

I mustered my best complex expression as I said, "Depends on the game, I guess."

Amanda decided it was time to weigh in. So she said, "I believe the game is tennis," which made her sound like my slightly threatened date instead of my pimp. The fact that neither Kelly nor I looked at Amanda as she spoke validated this little dynamic for all. The game wasn't tennis at all.

"Amanda says you play," said Kelly.

Amanda snuck in a wink as I glanced at her.

"Been known to bat a few around."

"And you've just moved to the area."

"In a manner of speaking. I commute. You?"

"I don't commute."

"I mean, you play tennis."

"Dangerously."

Amanda feigned indignation perfectly by clearing her throat before saying, "I think your date is hyperventilating, dear."

We all glanced over at Mr. Hair Club for Men, who was humiliated enough to turn away without a smile. Deduct five points for lack of cool.

"He doesn't play," said Kelly, without a trace of humor.

"Pity," I said.

"Listen, I'm hosting a charity doubles event weekend after next, one of those 'Tux 'n' Tennies' deals . . . and I need a partner." She turned toward Amanda and added, "That is, if it's okay."

"Don't mind me, we're just fuck-buddies."

I rolled my eyes toward Kelly's table and said, "Is it safe?"

"Same deal, just fuck-buddies. What I need is someone who's good at the net."

I looked at Amanda and raised my eyebrows, which any gentlemanly date would do in such a moment. She touched my arm and said, "Knock yourselves out."

Back to Kelly now. I said, "Looks like we're on."

Kelly was ready with card in hand. She pressed it into my palm, allowing her fingers to linger longer than necessary.

"Call to confirm."

Kelly put her hand on Amanda's shoulder and expressed her thanks, then extended it toward me for a manly handshake. When I took it, she put a second hand over mine and squeezed. As nonverbal communications go, she'd just recited a soliloquy.

We both watched her retreat, and then how her date welcomed her back to their table with all the warmth of Sean Penn signing an autograph. Cracking this lineup would be a piece of cake.

"Wasn't ready for that," I said, barely moving my lips.

"You did fine," she said, placing her chin on my shoulder, which allowed her to speak with very little volume. "What you're not ready for is what I'm going to do to you later."

I barely heard a word the comedian spoke. Partially because of my suddenly very engaged imagination, and partially because Amanda had her hand on my thigh under the table the entire time, her pinky in full writhing contact with the forbidden.

Oh yeah, the plumbing was just fine, thank you.

On the way out of the hotel, I detoured to the restroom. I sensed someone was behind me, but then there usually is during a mass exodus such as this—though ages-old rules of men's room etiquette forbid eye contact of any kind.

Those same rules say that one stands at the urinal at full attention, eyes fixed on the porcelain squares in front of you, or at the ceiling. Then, simultaneous with flushing, one must spit into the urinal as one zips up.

I accomplished all this with practiced grace, all the while aware that someone—the same someone who had followed me in here—had been staring at me.

At the sink, using the mirrors in a strategic manner, I saw who it was.

"Special Agent Short," I said, punching the soap dispenser for emphasis. "Come here often?"

"Special Agent Schmitt," he responded with a quiet voice. "The enemy has been engaged, I see."

"You here with Banger?"

"Back table. Who's the fortune cookie?"

He was referring to Amanda, and I didn't like his tone.

"You don't know?"

"Actually we do. Question is, do you?"

We were at the paper-towel dispenser now. Though there were men all around us, those rules of crapper etiquette were coming in very handy, allowing us to converse with confidence.

"What do you want, Short?"

"Come with me." He started to leave the bathroom.

"You're not exactly my type," I said, drying my hands on a paper towel.

He mouthed a silent *fuck you*, then motioned with his head that I should follow. He didn't wait for a response as he opened the door and walked out to the foyer.

Only now did I notice that he was carrying a briefcase.

Short led me through the deserted lobby, around a corner and down a hallway, and finally into a deserted room filled with boxes of supplies destined for

BAIT AND SWITCH 189

the concession stand. He reverently put the briefcase on a box and opened it, revealing a laptop among other electronic paraphernalia.

He held out his hand and snapped his fingers. My father used to do that when he was scolding our dog.

"Cell phone," he said, his eyes on my pocket.

I was tempted to ask which one, since I had two. Lee had given me a phone as a lifeline to her, and though no one knew it, I had brought my own with me for emergencies. Tonight I was carrying Lee's in the breast pocket of my suit jacket. I dug it out for him and handed it over.

Working with the dexterity of a committed techno-nerd, he quickly plugged the phone into the PC and hit a few keys. Data appeared on the screen, which I presumed was the digital fingerprint of the phone, including the number.

He unplugged the phone, then opened a compartment in the lid of the briefcase. There were about ten other mobile phones there, each a different make and model. One of them was exactly like the one Lee had provided me, your basic cheap Nokia, which he attached to the wire leading to the PC. He hit a few keys and waited a moment for a screen report.

I didn't have to ask what had just happened. He had just programmed the new phone with the number of the first phone.

"We're already in your fancy new car," he said, "we're in the helicopter, and we're in the Villa. We know what you eat, what you say, when you shit, when you snap your wire."

"Now *that's* entertainment."

"We need to extend our reach into your new domain. This will do that for us. Same functionality, same number, same digital signature on their end. Except now, we hear everything you say within a ten-foot radius, and we hear everything they say to you."

He unplugged the phone and tossed it to me. I snagged it from the air without looking, holding his eye contact instead.

"Were we in the john when my date told Kelly Scott I played tennis? I'd like to hear how she pulled that off."

He leaned closer, despite our solitude. "I advise you to remember that we are listening to everything you say and do. For your protection, of course."

I whispered back, leering over him. "Somebody had the French onion soup. Whoa."

He drew a breath, nodding toward the phone in my hand. "It'll clear any scanning technology they have. Unless you're military intelligence, the signal is basically undetectable. Keep it in your pocket, on your nightstand, wherever. If someone doesn't like it, stick it up your ass where they won't see it. Are we clear?"

"Thanks for caring," I replied.

He turned off the PC and clicked the briefcase shut, then said, "Earn the money, asshole," and walked out.

I held the phone close to my mouth as I headed back toward the lobby. I whispered, "Banger, if you're out there, just know that whatever happens in the next couple of hours, I'm just serving my country. And that I'm thinking of you, sweetheart."

I stashed the phone in my pocket and went to find Amanda, very much looking forward to earning my money.

> 29 <

ENTRY #6: CATHOLIC GUILT—imagine empowering Congress to dictate the price of admission to heaven, creating hierarchy, ritual, and rules as they please despite a complete absence of Biblical foundation. The Catholic Church has been doing that for thousands of years, except we don't get to vote on who wears the robes.
    —from *Bullshit in America*, by Wolfgang Schmitt

The ride back to Amanda's purported den of iniquity was quiet. At least at first. Maybe it was the bug in my pocket. Maybe it was the lingering taste of asparagus on my tongue, or an emerging sensation of motion sickness as our limo meandered through the streets of this city without a blueprint. We were acting more like a husband and wife on the heels of a social disaster than student and teacher on the cusp of a sexual epiphany.

I sensed she was watching me as we drove.

"Nervous?" she asked as we climbed into the hills.

"That a trick question?"

"No. Wanna talk about it?"

"That's right, you're a behavioral therapist. Remind me to ask to see your sheepskin."

She lowered her voice to a purr as she said, "I must warn you, it's printed on black leather."

"Had a hunch."

"We can go that route, if you want."

"I'll pass, thanks."

She paused. Her eyes were on me like a vinyl catsuit. Finally, she said, "You haven't had sex since your girlfriend, have you."

I hadn't been looking at the lovely Amanda throughout this bouncy dialogue, but I turned to her now.

"Is there *anything* you don't know?"

Her smile widened. "No."

Our eyes remained engaged for a few moments of telling silence, during which we both felt the tables turning.

"I'm not sure what this is about," I said.

"Coaching. Showing you how to reach into Kelly Scott's soul and carve your name. Making her fall in love with you."

I nodded. I'd been avoiding the latter realization, which remained my One Great Regret of this entire sordid affair, rationalized only by the presence of Special Agents Banger and Short on the playbill.

"You assume I don't know how to get it done," I said. "Because I'm a man, you think I can't possibly understand the complex romantic shadings of the mysterious female psyche."

The sarcastic energy in my voice made her grin again.

"Not when that psyche is twisted into clever little knots like Kelly Scott's. No. You can't possibly understand."

"She's submissive. So what. Half the world is submissive. You make a living off that half, remember?"

"You've read the *Beauty* books?"

"Anne Rice's masturbatory phase."

"Many women regard them as erotic poetry."

"Good sex is always poetry, with or without the nipple clips."

"And you think, after reading these books, you know how to make Kelly Scott sing."

Amanda was shaking her head, her smug grin causing my blood pressure to head towards the redline. Women like this made me crazy, women who brought a sense of genderized fascism to their God-given hormonal superiority. So be it. She was used to reading the simple minds of men like a label on a beer bottle. What really pissed me off was that she was probably right about the frustratingly male tendency to simplify the eternal sexual tango, to regard all things romantic as either a strategy or an obligation, something to be tolerated in order to get laid, something to which men rarely brought passion or creativity beyond flowers and candlelight.

But it was simply a statistical tendency, not an X-chromosome absolute. Amanda the professional dominatrix didn't know *me*. Nor did she know that Tracy the amateur dominatrix had already schooled me in the seductive power to be found in embracing the inexplicable with utter abandon. All lovers have their secrets, and if they don't, chances are it won't last—they'll bore each other to death. Tracy had shown me that the human mind was, in fact, the most sensitive and responsive sexual organ in the body, with or without testicles. But, irrespective of the psychology, you had to *read* that mind first. You had to crawl inside those dark nooks and crannies and listen to the whispered pleadings, which never lie.

"Those books," I went on, "poetic as they might be, are just fantasies. Nothing more. When you write the script of the stage play, one should understand the difference. Otherwise, you're destined to be embarrassed."

"Sounds like you've been there."

"More than you know."

I shifted my position so that I faced her squarely in the back seat, leaning forward as I lowered my voice. She seemed amused by this at first, but moments after I mounted my soapbox her expression went blank.

"Let me tell *you* what this is about. This is about dancing to what Andrew Lloyd Webber so aptly calls the 'music of the night.' It's about embracing the fine line that separates fantasy from reality, proactively blurring the edges of that line, seeing where it bends, pausing to give it a lick now and then, blowing a little warm air on it to see what happens."

Her eyes held mine, rapt with fascination. I inched closer and took her still-gloved hand.

"For men, that means you wear a pair of killer heels in bed, maybe a leather teddy or a mask. The way you hold a riding crop while he watches. The line moves forward, the dance changes tempo, and the props and the dialogue evolve with it. Suddenly, the music is deliciously dark."

I heard a little moan emanate from her throat, sounding a lot like concurrence. We exchanged wicked little smiles that signaled our journey should resume posthaste. I caressed her hand through the fabric of her glove as I spoke, stroking each finger individually.

"But with women, you see, it's different. It's about knowing how the entire dance connects to her past— a father who was cold and distant, a mother who smothered and disapproved, a boy in the neighborhood who went too far too fast. It's about needs, about caressing them, swallowing them whole. It's about fear, which, like some poisons, is medicinal and even sweet in moderation. You can't acknowledge the psychology because it's like pouring weed-killer on caviar, so you pretend it's all just an inexplicable craving, some dark forbidden pleasure, when you know it's much more, that it's the salving of old wounds, the feeding of demons, and that it's never going away."

I sensed her breathing becoming deeper. I was singing to the choir, and she liked the melody.

"I should ask to see *your* sheepskin," she said.

I put my hand behind her neck and moved so that my face was within inches of hers. My voice was barely a whisper now.

"It's all about giving while making it *seem* like taking. It's about becoming what she wants while convincing her it's what *you* want. It's about understanding that your selfishness is intoxicating for someone who desires to be selfless . . . about knowing that the keeper cares for his pets, just as the hunter honors his prey . . . it's a balancing act between worship and consumption, between possession and obsession . . . it's about absorption, devouring that which inflames your lust."

Her eyelids were at half-mast, her lips parted. I began tracing them lightly with my fingertips as I pressed onward, my breath hot on her cheeks.

Hell, I was turning *myself* on.

"In the end it's simply about intimacy, about wallowing in naked honesty behind the curtain of your worldly competence, about not being alone with your fear and your need. You know about fear, don't you, Amanda. You dole it out like heroin, you take them to the edge of terror just to see it in their eyes, and then you take their money along with their gratitude."

She raised her free hand to my shoulder, her breathing deep and rhythmic, her eyes half-lidded. If I'd have touched her just so she could have climaxed within seconds, but then this was all about teetering there on that edge, delaying the inevitable.

As I went on, I put my cheek next to hers, so that my lips touched the folds of her ear.

"You and I know that Kelly Scott wants to lose herself in that desire, in the embrace of the vampire, at the cost of her blood, in the bonds of the cruel master, with the gift of her suffering . . . the darker the better, because there in his darkness, she has no accountability for her own, she is a little girl again, a victim to her own beauty."

I used my teeth to pull gently at the lobe of her ear.

"I see you understand the poetry part," she purred.

"It's so twisted up in explanations, in right and wrong, in shame and guilt, when in fact she just needs one thing . . . to be desired . . . to be consumed . . ."

She let out a little whimper, then whispered, "I'm so fucking wet . . ."

"She just wants to be kissed . . . like this . . ."

I moved my fingers to Amanda's chin, raising it slightly. I pulled back momentarily so I could engage her eyes before moving back in, brushing my lips lightly over hers, lingering there, using them to grasp her lower lip and knead it, then the upper, brushing them with the tip of my tongue, tasting her, then backing away when I sensed her urgency.

Without breaking contact, I continued whispering through the kiss. "Here's what I think, Amanda."

My tongue went deeper now, but just for a moment.

"To swing the whip as you do, to take your lovers to that dark place and make them quiver for more of you . . ."

Still holding her jaw with one hand, I used the other to suddenly grip a nice fistful of her hair, pulling it down firmly in order to raise her surprised face to mine. Not enough to hurt her, but enough to show that I could.

There it was again. It was all about context. A little postgraduate contextual seminar for the teacher herself.

This was getting to be fun. I continued.

"You have to know that place yourself. You have to know the ecstasy in willingly handing over your will and even your pain to a dark lover, one who licks and savors your tears while he wraps you in a protective embrace."

"Oh, my . . ." was all she said.

"How am I doin' here, *Mistress* Amanda?"

I kissed her deeply, not allowing an answer. Then I pulled back to more casual contact, again whispering through playfully jousting lips. I had her on the ropes, if not *in* them, and it was time for the TKO.

"I'll know what Kelly Scott needs in the very moment she needs it, and I'll give it to her in ways she's never imagined, ways that transcend books, transcend imagination. She wants a dark prince of passion, then that's what she'll get. Because of what I know about her, which is a distinct advantage I do admit, I'll plant those nasty little seeds from the first kiss and go from there."

Then I kissed her deeply once again, releasing my hold on her hair in favor of a more traditional embrace, which she returned with squirming enthusiasm.

"Take me home, my teacher," she said.

I pulled away. "I don't think so."

Immediately her expression flipped from drug-like lust to bitch-like indignation.

"You fucker."

"I'm not going to sleep with you, Amanda. Tell me what else I need to know, any specifics required to set the stage, but that's it. Mission accomplished, lesson over. No nookie, no spanking, no enema, no whatever it is you do."

I could tell she was fending off an emotion she hadn't confronted in a long, long time. Her smile was as contrived and bold as it was unconvincing.

"Something I said?"

"No. Something *I* said. To myself."

"Well, I'm sure it's every bit as profound as what I just heard. And just as full of shit."

I shot her my most sincere expression of regret.

"Listen, I'm not in this to get laid. And I'm not here because of you. You're beautiful, you're sophisticated, and you take money from men who want to lick your footwear. I'm sorry, I'm just not gonna go there."

She was nodding now, already having composed her response, reassuring herself that this was all my problem, that her seductive powers were in full glorious tact after all.

"Wolf fucking Schmitt, Boy Scout. How special."

"Really, it's nothing personal."

"Never is in our business. Oh, does that surprise you? *Our* business? Because the way I see it, you're taking a big old shit-pile of money to prey upon the weakness of your particular client. But unlike me, you're going to leave her in a heap of suicidal tears as you slither back to wherever it is you came from."

"Well stated. You're pretty good at this humiliation thing."

"You make me want to puke."

"Have at it. They're not my shoes."

She tapped on the glass, which lowered in response. She instructed the driver, who still wore that inexplicable hat, to drop her off, then take me back to the helicopter before it turned back into a pumpkin.

She left the car without another word, or even a glance back. Then again, I wasn't looking, just in case.

The woman her wealthy clients referred to as Mistress Amanda stood at a window looking out over the great city, watching the limo pull away. When the taillights disappeared, she punched a number into a phone, then put it to her ear and waited.

It was a recording, which was according to plan.

"He's ready," she said. "And by the way, when this is over, send him back to me, preferably in one piece. Consider it a tip."

> 30 <

> ENTRY # 109: EMAIL/ISPs—don't you just love it when they merge and your email address changes without notice or your permission, turning all your business cards and letterhead into scrap paper? And then, just to really piss you off, they refuse to forward email sent to your old address. Oh, that's right, they used to be part of the phone company . . . that explains everything.
> —from *Bullshit in America*, by Wolfgang Schmitt

When I arrived back in my room at the Villa after my near miss with a cat-o'-nine-tails, there was a little surprise waiting for me, and it wasn't under my pillow. It was on my computer, another cryptic email from Deadman, about whom I had almost forgotten, and it completely ruined my otherwise eventful day:

Hi again—Can't take a hint, or what? Don't say I didn't warn you. You ask a lot of questions. All will be revealed in time. I just hope it's not too late when it happens. For now, ask yourself one: whose place are you taking?
    W.R.

Nothing like a little digital intrigue to bodycheck a guy's shot at a good night's sleep. I tossed for at least two hours, coming up with little besides the obvious. One, W.R. wanted me to find him. Why else use initials? There would be enlightenment in the discovery. I pondered the ways I might go about discovering my pen pal's real identity, coming up with only one viable idea, which would have to wait until the next day. Two, he was close by. He knew about Kelly Scott's boyfriend, whom I was soon to render obsolete. I was being pointed in his direction for a reason, and I was curious enough to take the bait. That, too, would have to wait until morning. Three, I was either being protected from some as-yet-to-be-identified threat, or I was being set up. Which meant, I needed to watch my ass on either count.

Unable to solve the riddle of Deadman, I resorted to the mental picture of my new car, which I'd visited upon departing the helicopter. I drifted off to sleep with visions of twenty-two-inch chrome wheels dancing in my head, along with the realization that I had no idea what Lee Van Wyke might have in mind for me tomorrow.

The next day was huge.

After a continental breakfast on my private veranda—a guy could get used to this—I placed a call on my private mobile phone—the one that wasn't wired—to my best shot at uncovering Deadman's identity. Blaine Borgia was the IT Director at the agency from which I'd recently bolted—*IT* meaning Information Technology, which translated to Propellerhead Extraordinaire in Blaine's case—who had proven on more than one occasion that he could sidestep obstacles as irritating as federal law to achieve minor digital miracles. In addition to his role as silicon savior for a cast of creative types who knew only enough about computers to be laughable, he was the company's resident goth afficionado of the tragically hip, a guy who wore black dusters during summer and drove a restored '64 Impala, who collected backstage passes from the Dead and the Stones going back to the seventies, and who, in defiance of all that was predictable, was married to a second-grade teacher. He claimed he had papers tracing his ancestry back to the notorious Borgias of Catholic Inquisition fame, that Lucretia herself was his great aunt times nineteen. I believed him, too.

And, best of all, the dude liked me. He really liked me. Just for laughs, and in return for lunch, he used to print out a list of all the pornographic websites and chat rooms frequented by our fellow employees on a weekly basis. We could have blackmailed the firm's partners for millions.

There are no secrets from an IT director. None.

He wasn't in this morning. So I left a detailed message, then forwarded him both of my Deadman email messages, pleading for his assistance without the slightest explanation. I was confident he'd dive in, because there was nothing my pal Blaine Borgia liked more than sticking his digital nose where it didn't belong.

I had two requests of the guy, actually.

That done, I was heading for the rec center for a workout when the house bouncer, whom I'd met upon my arrival, intercepted me at the front door. He instructed me to be on the helipad in thirty minutes, dressed casually. And he didn't say *please*.

Just another lofty commute—ten minutes by helicopter to the San Jose airport, a ninety-foot walk to the open hatch of one of Arielle's jets, and it's off to another day of buying and selling companies. Nelson Scott, whom I'd yet to see on this trip, had the

Gulfstream today, or so I assumed. Either that, or I'd been demoted to an older Learjet.

Lee Van Wyke was already aboard. She was on the phone, though she greeted me with a warm smile as she motioned for me to buckle in. We were airborne and nearly at cruising altitude before she concluded her call, which, from what I could tell, concerned a tax claim from an unnamed third-world country with no case and a lot of balls.

"I hear you were quite the hit last night," she said from the seat across the aisle from mine.

"What I think you mean is, I somehow *avoided* getting hit by your friend Amanda."

"She liked you."

"She said that?"

"Actually, she implied that. What she did say is that you have a tennis date with Kelly Scott. Congratulations."

"Thank you. You have interesting people working for you."

"That's what Amanda said, too."

Lee's smile was mischievous. Looking at her, it occurred to me that Lee just might have taught Amanda everything she knows.

"Where are we off to today?"

"Wichita."

"Of course, I should have known. Mind if I ask why?"

"Not at all. We're going to pick up a certain capital asset. Thought you might enjoy coming along for the ride."

"Thanks, I was getting a little tired of the Mercedes and the view from my balcony."

"It's *your* ride, actually."

Her expression was smug enough to take the sarcasm right out of my mouth, which simply remained open. I had enough awareness of the civil aviation industry to immediately see where this was going.

"Wichita, Kansas, as in the home of the Cessna plant, Wichita, Kansas?"

She nodded, genuinely pleased by my dumbfounded expression, which included a sudden inability to pick my lower jaw up off the floorboard.

You haven't lived until you've stood on the pavement before a set of eighty-foot double doors and watched them slowly open, allowing the sun to bathe your spanking new Cessna Citation X long-range executive jet in biblical light as it rolls out into the world for its first day on the job.

"Thank you, Jesus," I said softly, and I wasn't kidding.

Lee stood at my side, and even she seemed impressed by the sight.

"This, I never get tired of," she said with equal reverence. We both stared at the gleaming white airplane, which had no markings yet other than the serial number. The lines were muscular and voluptuous, a centerfold in the world of private aircraft.

"Ready to take her home?" she asked. She'd left me alone on the older jet in which we'd arrived for nearly half an hour while she went inside to finalize the delivery arrangements, the details of which, she assured me, remained far below the radar of an important capitalist gentleman such as myself.

"Don't I have to, like, sign the pink slip or something?"

"Taken care of. Officially, she's all yours, in case anyone with a nosey lawyer decides to check it out. Of course, we'd like the keys back when your work with us has concluded, but perhaps we can work out some visitation privileges if all goes well."

BAIT AND SWITCH

If you think a new car smells fine right off the showroom floor, try a fourteen-million-dollar private jet sometime. We even had to remove the plastic from the leather seats ourselves, seats which Lee claimed cost some twenty-five thousand dollars each, given their electronic and ergonomic capabilities. The manufacturer threw in a bottle of Dom Perignon for the trip home, and although this was officially not on the roster of permissible Wolf indulgences these days, I figured this wasn't your average deadheading journey, so what the hell.

She opened the champagne with the practiced hands of a seasoned maître d'.

"To Kelly Scott," she said, hoisting her crystal glass for a toast.

"To Kelly," I said, clinking mine to hers.

As we drank, our eyes met, exchanging messages which eluded me. If I didn't know better, I'd say Mrs. Robinson wanted to play.

"Tell me everything," she said, reclining in the new leather chair, crossing her legs with feminine precision.

"Everything?" I asked.

"Everything about how you're going to seduce Nelson's wife. Everything you told Amanda last night. And leave nothing out. I want to hear it all. I'm your boss, and you must do as I ask."

"You mean *obey*. You sound just like your friend Amanda."

"All of it."

I sipped, waiting for her to play out her hand.

"Especially," she said, pausing and leaning forward to make sure I didn't miss a beat, "how you're going to kiss her like the vampire Lestat himself."

To say I was one happy megamillionaire would be the understatement of the Bush era. Either of them.

I was given the evening off, encouraged to don some of my new Italian threads and drive into town in my new German car and flex my new bohemian identity in some of the hotter spots in town, a list of which was in my pocket. I'd just taken delivery on a new fourteen-million-dollar airplane, I'd exchanged stimulating mind games and bodily fluids—of a sort—with a woman who was both bewitching and tormenting me on a daily basis, and I was liking myself for not being led into temptation by the devil's mistress the night before. The only thing that could top this would be running into Tracy dressed to kill.

Guess what.

Like I said, the day was huge.

The bar where I had gone to celebrate my day—alone—was crowded, the place having experienced renewed social cache after a decade of being "so last year." I took a table in the restaurant section bordering the lounge, with a great view of both the door and the bar, with its seven-level display of colorful spirits, which was precisely the description of the occupants of the lounge in front of it.

Someone tapped me on the shoulder.

"Hey, mister, got a light?"

Tracy stood before me, a hand bearing a white-filtered cigarette in front of her face. Her other hand held a lighter, which she expected me to take to execute her odd request. As a means of flirtation this was as obvious as it was de rigueur—she used to do this just to piss me off—but the charcoal leather pants and a bare-waisted top made me a forgiving soul on a night when I, the new owner of a fourteen-million-dollar airplane, was just happy to be here.

Her grin was smug as I struck the flame. My hand trembled so badly she had to steady it with her free hand as she lit up, something she found amusing. It was a sick, sensual, unhealthy moment, one we'd shared many times before in places just like this. She playing the bad girl, me hating it and loving it simultaneously.

She blew the smoke to the side, smiling as she took the lighter back. She mounted the seat across from me, pulling the ashtray close.

"What the *hell* are you doing down here?" she asked, perky as a cheerleader.

I wasn't ready for any of this, so the answer had no chance. I avoided it, hoping she would think me playing coy.

"I called you, like you asked."

She cocked her head, taking a graceful puff on her Virginia Slim, as if I'd just spoken to her in a foreign tongue. I was sure she practiced doing this in a mirror.

I embellished. "Up in Portland last month? You gave me your number, practically begged me to call you."

"That was *you*?" she said, already laughing.

"Such a cute girl."

"I moved. If it makes any difference, I did wonder why you didn't call."

"I *did* call."

All humor had left the building. Amazing how quickly the tone can change, especially with a little history to kick its ass on the way out. She glanced at her watch, which I noticed was a gold Rolex I'd never seen before.

"What'd that take, forty-five seconds? Shit."

Her cancerous drag this time wasn't nearly as glamorous. She stared out at the crowd, either cooling her heels or planning her exit strategy.

"So what *are* you doing here?"

There was no question her sudden good cheer was contrived, but rather than being overtly sarcastic, I took it as a sign she was willing to give this conversation another go.

"Just some business."

"You left the agency. What business?"

"How'd you know that?"

Her grin was suddenly genuine.

"Spies. I was up in Portland, I called. They said you were gone."

"You should have called my house."

"I'm not *that* eager, Wolf. I just wanted to say hi."

Having taken that little dagger to the heart, I struggled to maintain an expression of indifferent cool.

"So, what business?" she asked again.

Heat assailed my face, which I tried to cover by draining what remained of the ice tea I was drinking.

"I'm interviewing."

It was the best I could do. She nodded, not completely pleased with my answer.

"Coincidence," she asked. "Or convenience?"

"What do you mean?"

"Cut the shit, Wolf. Suddenly you show up in my backyard interviewing for a job? All the cities on the West Coast, and you pick Santa Clara?"

"I have, or should say *had*, clients here. Friends, even. Don't flatter yourself, Trace."

She tapped the table with her long nails, stared out at the bar, then took another drag on her cigarette before stamping it out. I had created another moment, this one arising from a desperate little fabrication that meant nothing. The irony was almost amusing, and completely definitive of the final days of our relationship.

"Would it be that bad? I had no idea you were so

comfortable having me a thousand miles away. Or that my very presence makes your skin crawl."

When she looked back at me her eyes were red and moist, ready to burst. Seeing it made my heart leap to attention, four months of pain suddenly validated by this evidence that there had at least been something worth grieving.

She reached for my hands, taking them both.

After a few seconds of silence, I said, "A genuine Hallmark moment, folks."

She was all too familiar with my sick wit, and she knew I meant it as an acknowledgement of the tension, rather than some indictment of the circumstance.

"God, I've missed you," I said, surprising even me.

She lowered her eyes in what I preferred to believe was shame.

"Say something," I said.

"How long are you here?"

"Not long. But I'm coming back."

Suddenly, as if a bird had shit on my sleeve, reality hit me with a splat. There was a wired mobile phone in my pocket, and somewhere out there Banger and Short were slamming their fists into the side of an unmarked van. Everything I was here for was suddenly, in this very moment, in dire jeopardy of imploding. And I was risking it without cause, without the slightest indication from Tracy that there might be a shot that would make it worthwhile.

I could actually see the linen shirt I was wearing pulse with each adrenaline-fueled constriction of my heart. If the calcium didn't kill me, a moment like this just might.

"I have to go," she said.

"Of course you do."

"No. I mean, I'm with someone. See that guy in the blue blazer?"

As I looked, Blue Blazer shot me a little wave, but he wasn't smiling. He looked like a fat window mannequin, all wax and glue, a walking cliché with a wallet.

"Great. You're dating Rush Limbaugh."

"I want you to call me," she said. "When you come back. We'll have dinner, talk it out. We need to get this straight between us, move forward as friends."

There it was, the dreaded "F" word. Agenda had just collided with hope, hers head-on with mine. A thousand thoughts coalesced at once, the pain of finality at that next dinner, the dreadful mystery of Tracy as my friend, the proximity of my new money juxtaposed against her criteria for romance, the ghosts of the past refusing their graves.

"For that I'd need a phone number."

She got to her feet, bending to kiss me on the cheek. I made no effort to turn my head, to divert her intention toward a more intimate kiss. My way of displaying a little prideful chill in this moment of truth.

I watched her walk to the bar, where she borrowed a pen and wrote her number onto the ever-present cocktail napkin. I had a friend once, one of my eternally single hopeless seeker friends, who'd actually wallpapered his bathroom with phone numbers written on various bar media around the world. A great place to sit and ponder your life.

She returned to the table and slid the number under my wrist, which I didn't move. Then she said the strangest thing, proving she still had that touch of feline cruelty that gnaws at the back of a man's mind like heroin.

"You can trust me, Wolf. I don't hurt my friends."
My eyebrows arched like the McDonald's logo.
"Just your lovers," I countered.

She squeezed my hand in understanding, offering one of those *be strong* smiles before turning back toward the crowd, through which she slinked toward the embrace of Mr. Been There, Done That, who hadn't taken his beady eyes off of us the entire time.

Walking to my car in the parking lot behind the building, I said aloud, "Hope you enjoyed the show, kiddies," wondering if Banger and Short would ever forgive me. "Always remember, friendship is forever."

I drove straight back to the Villa, up into the mountains where it waited in all its over-the-top glory, taking the corners at speeds not recommended by the State of California, truly not caring if the new Michelins failed their manufacturer-guaranteed cornering capabilities.

I went to bed with a dull ache in my heart, both metaphoric and real. Each, I decided, was equally capable of killing me before dawn.

Trust Tracy? Been there, done that.

> 31 <

San Francisco, California

Despite what was about to arrive on his doorstep, this definitely wasn't Boyd Gavin's week. Last night, while he was watching his girlfriend flirt with some square-jawed pretty boy at the next table, someone broke into his bayfront condominium. They got his stereo and his collection of adult DVDs, which he thought was secure in a locked cedar box stashed behind the entertainment center, and because not much else was worth lifting, the assholes decided to trash the place. The police, of course, said there was nothing they could do, which was true enough since they offered no explanation as to how the intruders breached the secure parking lot, the elevator code, and then his double-bolted front door, which was without evidence of tampering. A neighbor did say he had seen a suspicious-looking woman with short hair on the floor, but she hadn't been the approachable type. The icy demeanor of the cops suggested they were suspicious he'd done it himself for the insurance, but then, paranoia had always been one of his more endearing traits. Yeah, like a guy making two-sixty a year would own up to a stack of kinky DVDs just to up the claim. They did inquire about any ex-lovers who might be in possession of a key

BAIT AND SWITCH

and a grudge. There were none, and while Kelly did indeed have a key, she had been with him last night and would be best served by keeping her name out of it.

Gavin was asleep on the couch, wearing sweatpants and a 49ers shirt, when the security buzzer went off. He got up and punched the visitor in without asking who it was. It was four o'clock, and he knew precisely who had come to call.

Lee Van Wyke entered the condo and walked directly to where Gavin reclined on the couch. The lack of a formal welcome didn't surprise her—this had happened the first two times she'd come—and she knew it was a statement, and that it rhymed with *kung fu*. She put the Neiman Marcus bag she'd brought with her on the floor at her feet.

"I've buried people who look better than you."

Ignoring her comment, he reached for the bag, placing it on his chest as he peered in. It was filled with bundles of crisp new one-hundred-dollar bills. Fifty of them, in fact, an even hundred each. Which, his accountant's mind already knew, equaled a half-million untraceable dollars. He reached inside, running his fingers over the money. The first two times he'd taken a few stacks out, even tossed some around the room just to piss her off. But not today. That was a million and a half dollars ago, and a few million shy of where he'd end up. Today, he knew his nonchalance would piss her off even more.

"We need a completion date," said Lee, avoiding his eyes as she looked around the room with an expression of distaste.

"Tell your boss I'll let him know."

"He's never been known as a particularly patient man."

"That a threat? Sounds just like a threat. You his

mouthpiece on this, or is the threat from you personally?"

Now her eyes drilled him as she said, "You blackmail him, you're blackmailing me. Same game, same risk to your health."

"Then you can both kiss my ass. I'll let you know when the buzzer rings."

They locked eyes, and for a moment, Gavin thought he might have pushed too far. He knew that the woman was capable of anything, and that, indeed, it was his health at risk here.

She broke the staredown with a tiny smile.

"Your little insurance strategy isn't that good. Maybe we should lean on it, see where it breaks."

"Your funeral, sweetheart."

"On the heels of yours, lover."

"Let's just stick to the agreement. You pay me, I stay discreet. I stay healthy, your boss stays clean."

"I know the terms."

"You and my lawyer," he said with a smile of his own, one designed to test her limits. From the way her eyes narrowed, he knew he'd hit the intended nerve.

Lee understood that Boyd Gavin knew where the bodies were buried. Singularly speaking, in this case, since the body in question was burned and dismembered, on a road between San Jose and Santa Cruz, resulting in a final audit report for Arielle Systems that was clean enough to use as sheets in a delivery room. She also knew there was an as-yet unidentified lawyer out there with the audit file and instructions to blow the whistle if anything suspicious happened to his client.

As soon as Lee's people found out who he was, it would be a whole new ball game.

"I'm thinking five years," said Gavin, his voice stronger.

"Expensive."

"Worth every fucking dime, too."

Lee shook her head and turned for the door. Until the lawyer was found, half a million a month was a reasonable amount to keep the kitty in the bag.

"I almost forgot," she called without turning back, "how are things with Kelly?"

"Ask her."

"One wonders what she'd say if *she* knew," offered Lee.

Gavin laughed out loud. "Now here's a kick in the ass . . . maybe she already knows. Maybe she thinks it's hilarious."

"Wouldn't surprise me. She's playing the same game, only for a lot more money."

"Birds of a feather, sweetheart."

Lee opened the door, leaning on it as she spoke. "She's going to shit-can you, you know."

"We'll see."

"Way I hear it, the next batter is already in the dugout."

This one drew blood, judging from his expression.

"You've never been anything but a placeholder for Kelly. Until a prettier face and a fatter checkbook came down the pike. Something to play with, fill the empty hours. You're just a way for Kelly to push her husband's buttons. How's that feel, knowing you can't play in this league?"

"Play? Hell, I'm the quarterback, you ask me."

He patted the sack of money for emphasis.

"That's just it, Boyd. Nobody's asking you."

She blew him a kiss, then stepped out into the hallway. Then she laughed when she heard him yell the word "bitch" from behind the closed door.

> 32 <

The Saturday morning after the ball—happily, the Mercedes hadn't turned back into a butter squash and the Citation X still smelled like money—Wolf met with Lee over scones to go over the next step in his transformation.

Wolf would fly to Scottsdale later that morning to get the lay of the land in what would become his facsimile home. An escort would meet him and take him to a rented eleven-thousand-square-foot, five-acre spread at the base of the McDowell Mountains. It was, Lee said, a tad on the modest side for a man of his means—Wolf wasn't at all sure she was being sarcastic—but he had purchased the place before selling out to Arielle, and he was in no hurry to spend his winnings.

Or so the script read.

His escort would be an Arizona Cardinal cheerleader named Evelyn who doubled as an aerobics instructor when she wasn't doing personal favors for Nelson Scott. Over the course of two days, she would school him in the ways of Scottsdale life: the abundant restaurants and style-conscious clubs, the sheer insanity of their drivers, as well as the site of his old firm, a now-vacant building near the Scottsdale Air Park. Digitally altered photographs showing the place with the now-removed Diatech logo would be available, in case Kelly was less than convinced.

Once the charade got underway, he would commute between San Jose and Scottsdale every few days, in case Kelly was more cautious than they expected and had him followed. Stranger things had happened—she'd once had Nelson tailed through Europe when she suspected he was nailing his tai chi instructor. She had her own advisors and lawyers who had their own private investigators and undercover specialists, and most of all she had a full plate of insecurities and personal agendas. Anticipating contingencies would be the key to their success.

Admittedly, it was a house of cards, a lie built upon a foundation of illusion, perpetrated by the sheer force of deceitful will, funded by a billionaire's greed. Nobody would be going to heaven for this one. Nonetheless, it would be Wolf's job to keep the winds of suspicion away from this fragile structure, at least long enough to have cohabitated with Kelly Scott for a minimum of thirty days, the documentation of which, according to Lee, would be none of his concern.

After that, it would be every man for himself. Heaven, as they say, could wait until the checks cleared.

Wolf, who this morning was wearing loose-fitting slacks which effectively hid the cell phone in his pocket, asked astute questions that demonstrated a sense of confidence and seemed to please Lee Van Wyke. He had a tendency to verify facts and logistics, particularly times and places, in a way that came off as efficient rather than suspicious.

Lee bid him farewell and headed for the helicopter and a meeting with Nelson Scott on another matter.

The Bell Ranger would return to fetch Wolf within the hour and take him to the airport. Lee suggested he pack his things—he would not be returning to the Villa, at least as an overnight guest—and if he had a few minutes left over, perhaps work on his serve.

But rather than take that advice, Wolf spent his free remaining minutes checking his offshore account balance online. An additional four hundred thousand dollars had been deposited there. He had now been paid half his guaranteed fee for the work.

Sixteen minutes later, the helicopter deposited Lee Van Wyke on a pad near the Arielle corporate headquarters in Menlo Park. She entered the building and brushed past the security console without so much as a glance—she was one of two people in the place who could get away with that, the other being Nelson Scott himself—and within two more minutes was sitting in front of the boss, a cup of very hot coffee in her hands.

Scott was on the phone—a headset, actually—pacing behind his desk. The office was huge and decorated very much like his airplane, an old-world mahogany motif that was out of place in the block-and-tackle architecture of high technology. Books lined the walls, and the leather guest chairs, one of which Lee occupied now, were oversized and gleaming from a daily spit-shine. Scott hadn't acknowledged her presence since her arrival, but she knew he was aware of her presence by the tough talk he spewed at the unfortunate underling on the other side of the call. He always did that in front of Lee, as if to show her who was boss, when in fact both of them knew the truth of the matter.

He ended the call as he did all his human exchanges, without a parting word or a good-bye or,

God forbid, a thank-you. He simply hit a button, having already moved on to the next thing on his plate. Which, at the moment, was Lee and the progress report she'd come to deliver, which was too sensitive to handle over the phone.

He hit another button, an intercom this time.

"Hold my calls," he said, with all the charm of Ike Turner asking Tina for his damn dinner. "But let me know when she's here."

That done, he came around the desk and sat in the matching guest chair next to Lee. He crossed his legs and leaned forward, a childlike expression on his face.

"So . . . he's good?"

Lee sipped her coffee with a look of contemplation, making him wait. It was a small thing, but she took her pleasure from Nelson Scott where she could.

"Better than good. He turned Amanda into a sponge just by talking hot to her. She doesn't go down easy."

"A good sign."

"He's smooth. Smart, too."

"The airplane?"

"The paperwork is in place. Anybody looks, they'll see only what we want them to see."

"I'm glad you're on my side."

"I'm not on your side. I'm on your payroll."

This made him smile. Her attempts to scratch at him had, over the years, taken on an amusing context.

"That makes you somewhat morally ambiguous, doesn't it."

With a saccharine smile, she said, "Did I mention he's a great kisser?"

The intercom buzzed, followed by a disembodied voice. "She's here, sir."

"Thirty seconds," he barked.

Scott leaned even closer and lowered his voice to a whisper.

"The money?"

"Delivered this morning."

The two of them locked eyes, sharing the unspoken.

Just then the double doors swung open, held there by Scott's secretary. A woman entered, wearing a natty blazer and carrying a briefcase. She approached, the door closing softly behind her. Scott and Lee watched as she pulled up a chair from the conference table a few feet away and joined them.

"Traffic. Sorry."

Many an MBA had been fired for being mere minutes late to meetings with Nelson Scott, traffic or no traffic, even on weekends. Then again, this woman, who did not have or particularly need an MBA, had graduated to a whole new level of intimacy with her employer.

"Your boy didn't disappoint," said Scott.

"Except on the tennis court," added Lee with a smile. "Other than that, he's everything you said he'd be."

"You slept with him."

Lee just smirked, allowing the woman to believe whatever she wanted.

"Congratulations," said Lee. "You're a rich woman."

The woman basked in the glow of their approval, which didn't happen often in this office. While you played the game for money, you happily took your strokes when they came.

Scott's energy shifted to something more comfortable, that being the waving of a big stick.

"I'm holding both of you responsible for the success of this project. I don't need to remind you what's at stake."

Whereas this comment had been directed at both women, the next was focused solely on the newcomer.

"You're sure he's in? You'd bet your career on it?"

Tracy Ericson, the woman who had so recently broken Wolfgang Schmitt's heart, smiled at them.

"I've got him just where we want him," she said. "I promise you, on my life, and on his, the last thing he wants to do now is leave."

Nelson Scott and Lee Van Wyke locked eyes, again exchanging meaning without a word.

"Well then," said Scott, holding his arms aloft in a very Charlton Hestonesque manner, "let there be love."

PART THREE
>> <<

> 33 <

"Where the hell have you guys been?"

"We're professionals, Mr. Schmitt. We're supposed to be covert."

"Yeah, and I'm supposed to have my ass thoroughly covered. Just wondering how you're following me when I'm flying around in helicopters and private jets."

"I don't believe we said we'd follow you. We said we'd protect you if you get in trouble, and we will."

"Semantics. You write Clinton's speeches, too?"

"We know where you are at all times."

"That's right. The bugs. The cell phone. Your so-called satellite technology."

"That's correct. And since you bring it up, I might remind you we're not in this exclusively for the purposes of, as you put it, covering your ass."

"Had a feeling you'd say that."

"You haven't exactly been pushing the envelope."

"Soon as I get back, I'll be sure to ask Kelly about her husband's fraudulent activities."

"I'm just saying."

"I know why I'm here."

"That's good. You're being handsomely compensated for your services."

"And you expect a return on your investment."

"That's accurate."

"But it's not exactly your investment at all, is it. I

mean, technically, it is Scott's money. You're just letting me keep it. If I do the job."

"If you do the job. Technically, that's correct."

"I don't think Kelly knows a lot about her husband's business."

"That could be. Just keep the objective in mind."

"That it?"

"Yes. For the record, you're doing a good job."

"Thanks. Really makes my day."

"When this is over, we should talk."

"When this is over, I promise you'll hear from me."

"Not if you hear from us first, Mr. Schmitt."

> 34 <

ENTRY #122: WEALTH-BUILDING SEMINARS—promoted on late-night infomercials, held in second-rate hotels, they inevitably conclude with a high-pressure pitch to shell out thousands for the *real* four-day seminar to learn "a proven technique" for getting rich in real estate, options, starting an internet business, or brokering worthless notes. The only guy getting rich here is the one putting out the stale cookies.
—from *Bullshit in America*, by Wolfgang Schmitt

Where I come from, they call it *hit and giggle*. Four suburban hackers playing mixed doubles in a charity tournament, seriously decked out in Fila, new Nikes, a Rolex, and a sweatband. There would be about twelve hundred bucks' worth of rackets between them, the men politely letting up on serves to the women—set point being the exception—while blasting away mano a mano. Partners confer in hushed whispers between points, as if strategy actually means something when the odds against anyone placing the ball within ten feet of an outright winner are right up there with a Bjorn Borg comeback.

The philanthropic tennis affair being held at the Villa cost five grand a person, which, if one did the math, averaged out to about fifty bucks a serve. None of the posturing, however, would change to accommodate the tax bracket of the participants. That aspect of the experience was priceless.

I had called Kelly Scott four days earlier, getting through to an assistant who had no idea who I was. I left a message that I would be delighted to be Kelly's doubles partner at her Tux 'n' Tennies bash, leaving the number of the new mobile phone Lee had provided me. Which was, of course, registered in my name at my Scottsdale address, in case anyone cared to check. Lee suggested—which in Lee-land means, do it or your ass is grass—that I consult caller ID on each incoming call, and unless absolutely necessary, allow Kelly to leave a message rather than actually answering.

Made sense to me. Wouldn't want to take a call with my mouth full of fries at In-N-Out Burger.

Which was precisely the case when it came. It was comforting to know that my federal friends could hear the message, which was from Kelly's assistant, confirming my attendance before dictating an address and directions to the Villa. At the end, she gleefully tagged on a reminder to bring a check for five thousand dollars, payable to the Scott Foundation.

I'd deal with that later. Right after I called Lee Van Wyke with the news. The game—and I'm not referring to mixed doubles here—was on.

From my very first junior-high sock hop on, I had been a fraud at every party I'd ever attended. I could work a room like a Merrill Lynch rep just out of training, I could break the ice like Darrell Dawkins shattering a backboard, and from the giddy smile on my mug, you'd swear I was wallowing in my God-given element. That he had put me on the planet to eat canapés while chatting up strangers. But the fact was, I hated every bacon-wrapped minute of it. I much preferred the company of a good book and a lap dog.

This irony—it wasn't even *me* faking it on the deck at Villa Scott—was not lost on me as I waxed charming and pretended to not see more than a few wary stares while waiting for Kelly to appear. Being fashionably late to one's own bash was, it seemed, all the rage this season. Meanwhile, the word was out: there was a new kid on the block, and he simply reeked of new money.

I had spent enough time boning up on my fictional self to somehow pull it off. Humility was the key to survival, deflecting tricky questions with a self-effacing crack that made it obvious that my ego, if not my wit, was safely in check. I recognized a few Villa employees from my brief stay here, serving tonight as purveyors of fine cocktails, but my coy little nods were returned with empty eyes. It was a beautiful spring afternoon high above the smog, perfect for double faults and forehands into the net.

I caught my first glimpse of Kelly Scott, who'd slipped in without much notice, holding court with the press—today represented by a woman named Heloise who'd nipped and tucked one too many smile lines. Her photographer, a walking Benetton ad, stood dutifully silent at her side. Watching her, it occurred to me that this must be a frustrating event for women who traditionally tried to out-coif each other at every turn, since there isn't much you can do with tennis whites other than accessorize them with the creative use of trinkets and a hair ribbon. Still, Kelly looked every bit the billionaire's wife, resplendent in a shimmering off-white warm-up and the latest rave in designer sunglasses.

I kept my distance, hoping to catch her eye while I trolled the buffet. Which didn't happen. In fact—

having a keen sensibility about such things after too many years of practice in lounges from coast to coast—this was precisely how I knew she was aware of my presence. Oh, the games people play. I was playing one, too—if I kept moving, plate in hand, I would be harder to intercept and pin down.

Somewhere between the Grecian spa bathroom and the ice sculpture I lost sight of her. It was then that I felt a hand grasp my elbow and turned to see Kelly Scott beaming at me from arm's length, a water bottle in her other hand.

"Thanks for making it."

"My pleasure. It's a good cause."

I could already sense her perfume. A nice start.

"Oh? You're familiar with the foundation?"

"Not really. Just the name."

Our respective smiles acknowledged that this was, beneath all the charitable bluster, all about hormones. At least where she and I were concerned.

"I had you checked out," she said, running her eyes up and down my body as if I were on a hanger.

"You go straight at it, don't you."

"Anyone as good-looking as you has to be up to something."

After an obligatory eye roll, accompanied by a full gainer somewhere in my stomach, I said, "And?"

"You're quite the mystery man. My husband buys your company and suddenly you're the shit around town. Specifics, however, are much harder to come by."

"Just ask. I like to fly under the radar."

"In your new Citation."

I'd seen this expression before. Women were good at it. It meant *I'm way ahead of you, sucker, and you know you like it.*

"You *did* check me out."

"Bring your 'A' game? We're going to need it."

"A, B, and C. Always."

She took my arm, turning as if to face the crowd she knew was watching us. "Then let's kick some ass."

She kept her hand in the crook of my arm for everyone to see as she led us straight to the tennis court. I had noticed that Boyd Gavin, her current squeeze, was not in attendance today, which made this little waltz toward center court all the more intriguing. Scandal on the social page.

We would be the first match of the afternoon, the sequence of which was displayed on a massive grease board showing the tournament bracket. There were thirty-two teams—three hundred twenty grand for the Scott Foundation, an amount the Scotts surely spent on dog grooming annually—sixteen first-round matches, all of which would utilize an eight-game "super set" instead of the regular two out of three sets to save time. Good thing—with this field we'd be chasing balls until midnight.

Our match took nineteen minutes. Kelly and I played the CEO of a venture capital firm and his date, whose background remained undefined but clearly included breast augmentation. We took them 8–2, both losses coming on Kelly's serve. At one point, after I hit an overhead that ricocheted off Mr. ROI's foot, I sheepishly asked Kelly if I should ease up. Her face became taut in a way more suited to an announcement of impending gas.

"Tell you what—I'll buy you a new Jag if you nail him in the balls next time."

"You're serious?"

"Do I look like I'm kidding?" She was sweating—

sort of sexy, actually—and her expression was pure Sun Tsu. "You're my ringer, so keep ringing. No matter who gets hurt."

The kamikaze smile changed to Mata Hari–devious, and I knew we had an understanding. From that point onward we were a team on a mission, exchanging high-fives and inappropriate little pats to the derrière. Amazing how effective flirtation can be on a tennis court, a year's worth of chemistry in nineteen short minutes.

After shaking hands with our pissed-off opponents at the net, she rewarded me with a quick kiss, all to the applause of the guests, many of whom were already on cell phones.

We didn't exactly hang out between matches. The distance was part of our private little game, actually, a game which was far more intense than the tennis. This was cat and mouse, classic hard-to-get, all spiced with occasional eye contact to show we were very much aware of the other's proximity. The rules of this game never change from high school, where we all discovered it.

Before our next match, as I bounced from one shallow conversation after another—nobody wanted to talk diagnostic software, it seemed—I learned that Boyd Gavin was home in bed, sick with a stomach bug. I wondered how the dynamics of the day might have been different had he been around, but the point was moot. As moot as he would soon be if everything went according to plan.

We sailed through the next two matches, 8–3 and 8–1. Our on-court chemistry was heating up, a certain frivolity free to express itself given the certainty of the outcome. She made a crack about the view of my backside from the service line being a bit of a distraction, and I commented—somewhat strategically—that if she continued to miss those easy put-aways I'd have to punish her. Judging from her response—similar to the guttural moan one makes when biting into an éclair—the strategy was dead on.

Never too early to plant a few seeds.

The third-round match was a different story altogether. Our opponents had both played college tennis—they were the only married pairing on the court today—and they took us to six-all before Kelly and I huddled at the baseline prior to what would be my final service game.

"You've been letting up on her," she said.

"He's letting up on you, too."

"Don't." There was no negotiation in her eyes.

"Okay."

"They won it last year, on their court. It's my court, and I want this."

"Okay," I said again. A classic type-A/type-B conversation.

"We win, there's a reward."

"You have my attention."

"We win, you spend the night."

I nodded, adding a grin as I leaned close and whispered, "You smell nice."

She grinned back, almost embarrassed. "Down, Wolf. I mean, we get to know each other, share a fire on the deck under a blanket, nice bottle of merlot, talk till dawn. Rated PG."

"We can always re-edit. If we lose?"

"You go home and work on your game."

"Ouch. You sure know how to hurt a guy."

She winked. "Count on it."

I served out, a love game, two screaming aces on the lady, two forced return errors on the guy. Then we broke his serve at love, me poaching twice. Not exactly the Queen's tennis—more like McEnroe's tennis—but effective. The crowd loved it. So did Kelly. So did I.

As we walked off the court, she asked, "You always that easy, Schmitt?"

"Count on it," I replied, and I could tell she approved. Once again, she kept her arm around my waist as we walked off the court.

We won the next and final championship match, 8–4. By now, those who had been eliminated were two or even three sheets to the wind, and the seafood buffet had kicked in with serious Wolfgang Puck panache, as had a live band. These billionaires sure knew how to party. A hundred-dollar bribe to the photographer got him off my ass—he being among the snockered—though thankfully the columnist seemed more interested in Kelly than in me. You had to earn your stripes on this sociological battlefield, and my rumored money was far too new and undefined to warrant editorial attention.

By ten the crowd had dispersed, and other than a handful of Villa employees already well into the cleanup, Kelly and I were finally alone. It was time for my reward.

The real game would now begin in earnest.

"To quote Glen Frey," she said, "I'm already gone. Nelson's traveling, no doubt screwing some starlet on the Gulfstream, and for now my key fits the lock, so screw him."

I had stumbled across a litigious nerve, so I had to tread lightly. We were completely alone, the staff having retired to wherever help goes at night, the other side of the tracks. I wondered what they thought of my presence, if in fact they noticed at all.

"Not exactly amicable," I offered gently, stroking her hair.

"I caught him in bed with a staff writer from the *Wall Street Journal*. 'Amicable' is not gonna happen."

"Ouch."

"That's what he said. And I'm not done."

She took a hefty swallow of her wine, fighting off a change in mood which would have been entirely my fault.

"So . . . are you living at the Days Inn, or what?" I tried to inject some levity into my voice.

"We have a building downtown. One of many I'll own before this is over. You?"

"Little condo in Los Gatos Hills."

"Nice."

"Beats the Marriott. I come and go a lot."

"In your Citation. From Scottsdale. I've never been to Scottsdale." Whatever shadow had loomed was gone.

"We should go sometime. Catch the Diamondbacks."

"That an invitation?"

She looked up at me with a grin I hadn't seen since high school, her lips parted slightly. The only plainer invitation came on embossed stock in a white envelope.

I put a hand on her cheek, stroking slightly with

> 35 <

ENTRY #70: TELEMARKETERS—we should thank them for the most hilarious presumption in the history of insulted intelligence: when you say you're not interested, they provide an 800 number to call in case you change your mind.
—from *Bullshit in America*, by Wolfgang Schmitt

The fun began with the second bottle of wine. One of the concessions of my deception—I didn't like to think of it as a *compromise*, though that was probably the more accurate term—would be to bluff my way through bottle after bottle of fine wine over the coming weeks, this being one of Kelly's passions. We cracked the second bottle of merlot just after midnight, in a setting exactly as she'd described: a nice fire on the deck, a patio lounger, a cashmere blanket, and a view of the valley available elsewhere only on final descent into a local airport. We quickly dispensed with the obligatory twenty questions about our respective lives and turned the corner toward chemical exploration.

"So," I said during a lull, "are you planning on staying here when this is over?"

"This?"

"Your divorce. None of my business—I withdraw the question."

BAIT AND SWITCH

my thumb. My other hand gently cupped her cheek, holding her jaw up as I moved in, alternating my gaze between her mouth and her eyes. The first touch of our lips was feather-light, allowing our breath to meld between us. After a moment I felt her hand behind my head, pulling me closer. Instantly our sweet, cinematic first kiss had swelled to full blown drive-in movie passion. A barely audible tone emanated from deep within her throat—it was that éclair sound again—like a cat's purring, a vibration really, something I'd never heard before.

Somewhere in the middle of the kiss, she found room to whisper, "That's nice."

"Yes, it is," I returned.

This went on for a minute or two, luxuriating in our closeness, which was enough for now.

Finally, I said, "I should go."

"Why?" she responded, without pulling away.

"I'd say it's complicated . . . but it's not."

"I don't like rejection. I throw little-rich-girl fits."

"That's not what I'm afraid of."

She pulled back, a playful expression on her face.

"You're afraid of me already? How sweet."

"No. I'm afraid of me."

She forced another kiss. Twisting my arm was not required. Without pulling back, she said, "Maybe I should be afraid of you, too."

"Maybe."

"Try me," she breathed.

We were turning another corner now, from Ice Breaker Avenue onto Foreplay Street. I had no intention of parking here for the night, but I was happy to pull over and plug the meter.

"I think you know," I said.

"Tell me anyway," she said.

I smiled—always interesting with your tongue in

someone else's mouth. I cupped her face with both hands and pulled back, just enough to allow eye contact.

"I should go because every cell in my body is screaming to stay. To lose myself in you, right now."

She smiled. "What if I promise you won't get lost?"

"My cells can be very insistent."

I gave her a little extra squeeze for emphasis, prompting the return of the lovely little moan. With a little help from my friends, I had broken the code.

"I should shut up," I said.

It was at that moment I remembered the spy phone in my pocket.

She whispered, "I don't think so."

Hoping to demonstrate that the body and the mind were in sufficient conflict, I began pulling gently at her upper lip with my teeth. She elevated her chin in response, accompanied by The Moan. A moment later I stopped and began running the tip of my finger over her lips.

"Wolf knows what Kelly likes," I whispered.

"Wolf is cocky, too."

"Tell me I'm wrong."

"Tell me what Kelly likes first."

I leaned in and touched my lips to her ear, taking a few heated breaths before whispering the answer.

"Words," was what I said.

She shuddered, melting into me with a sigh—I could just see the IRS boys in a van exchanging high-fives—and I knew I had discovered the keys to the kingdom. I would talk my way into Kelly Scott's bed and, shortly thereafter, her heart. From there, it was a short dotted line to her townhouse and a multimillion-dollar payday for *moi*.

But the key would not slide into the lock tonight.

No sale. Within ten minutes she was sound asleep, her head on my shoulder. She would awaken in a few hours, quite alone with a headache, to a glorious California sunrise and a note of gentlemanly apology on the table under her empty wineglass.

> 36 <

ENTRY #74: REALITY TELEVISION—suffering and humiliation for the entertainment pleasure of the masses. Zoom to a closeup of those tears; more survival and social ostracization right after the break. Didn't the Romans try to decimate an entire religion with this concept, with live lions as props? Stay tuned.
—from *Bullshit in America*, by Wolfgang Schmitt

A guy like me, with more sudden money than he knows what to do with, needs a condo from an episode of *MTV Cribs*. A money-is-no-object, meet-my-interior-designer, this-is-a-reflection-of-my-inner-art-student respite from the pressures of tax optimization. Six thousand square feet of minimalist, electronically enhanced splendor done in a tropical motif, as if Tommy Bahama himself had been brought in to choose fabrics and wall coverings. Everything, down to the toothbrush and a drawer full of boxer shorts, even a fridge stocked with protein drinks and half-consumed condiments, had been made ready for my arrival, as if I'd been living here for weeks. All I had to do was park my butt in front of a forty-eight-inch plasma wide screen and flip channels like the man of leisure that I was. The Benz was in the garage, next to a Harley that Lee thought might come in handy, and all was right with the world.

The first thing I did upon arrival from my night at the Villa was phone in my report. Lee had provided a number, answered with only a beep, to which I would dictate the nature and progress of my time with Kelly Scott, and make any special requests which might grease the skids of our fiction. My first report was void of much detail—"We won hands down, you'd have been proud of me"—other than my belief that I had breached the first level of her womanly resistance and my conclusion that she was a kick-ass kisser of the first order.

The last part, by the way, was true.

That done, I went into the bathroom—four tons of embossed marble and opaque glass bricks—and started a shower. With the water on full, I put the juiced cell phone on the counter next to a Bose stereo tuned to the local rock station. I left the room, taking my shaving kit with me.

I took it back into the kitchen—more embossed marble, this time with enough granite to outfit a small cemetery—where I placed it on the counter and dug out the mobile phone I'd hidden there. The ringer had been muted—I was certain these walls were crawling with bugs—but I saw that one call had come through.

The caller ID showed a familiar number. Blaine Borgia, my technical sounding board and great white hope back in Portland, had finally called me back.

"Dude, it's fucking dawn," I heard him say, though I knew he'd been up for at least an hour. Blaine tried to get in a half hour of meditation and another half of tai chi before donning his pocket protector—he actually wore one, just for grins—and heading for work at the agency.

"Yeah, and you called at two a.m."

I was outside, taking a secure morning stroll.

"Sleep is for sissies."

"So I hear."

"Got your guy."

"Never a doubt."

"Very low-tech. Fucking Yahoo, it's like Fort Knox."

I knew he was referring to the fact that W.R.'s cryptic emails had been sent to me using a Yahoo email account, rather than a normal Internet service provider with a traceable IP address. It was like getting a postcard with no return address from the Twilight Zone.

"Talk to me," I said, already excited. Blaine never met a firewall he didn't like.

"You owe me a steak."

"And lobster. Go."

"Morton's, man. No Ruth's Chris bullshit. For two."

"Blaine . . ."

"This dude I hang with, he knows a guy works at Yahoo."

"Thank God for chat rooms. Go."

"You want the bits and bytes? It's pretty cool."

"Blaine . . ."

"Okay, here's the deal. Your email came from a remote node on a discreet encrypted network."

"English would be good."

"An intranet. A fucking server. You got a pen?"

I told him I did. He dictated an address. He didn't have a company name, just the address of a downtown building.

"That's it?"

"No. Here's why you owe me *two* steak dinners. Got you a name. Tapped the dude's cache and cross-referenced his surfing history. We got you a name, and, thanks to some smokin' decrypt algorithms, a credit card and some other shit. Like, what books he orders, what kind of porn he prefers. Interesting thing, though. Yahoo's not his primary email. In fact, he just opened the account. Only email sent on it was to you."

"What's that mean?"

"Hard telling. Maybe nothing. If he's on a company server, then he probably uses that for his day job. Guess is, he knows what's up, uses Yahoo to mask his identify. From you."

"I'll take that name."

"W.R.—Wayne Rogers."

"AKA Deadman. Never heard of him."

"Seems he's heard of you."

"Blaine, you rock. Thanks, man. May tap you again."

"Wolf?"

"Yeah, Blaine."

"Careful, dude."

> 37 <

ENTRY #23: THE PLEDGE OF ALLEGIANCE—
what, it's okay to pledge allegiance to the flag, but not
to God? Does the Constitution really tell us *what* to
worship? What is allegiance, anyway, if not a statement of what you believe in?
—from *Bullshit in America*, by Wolfgang Schmitt

Two hours later I was standing on a street in downtown San Francisco during the morning rush hour, a piece of paper in my hand, a confused expression on my face, and a buzzsaw in my stomach. I was looking up at a building I'd seen many times, trying to convince myself that the address was correct, that Wayne Rogers had really sent me two ominous emails from the bowels of the Transamerica tower, the world's largest monument to the penis.

The pit in my stomach was justifiable. On the drive up the 101, I held the cell phone to my mouth and said, "In case anyone cares, I'm going into the city to play tourist. Have a nice day." Then I turned up the radio to establish the background ambiance that would sustain this charade while I was out of the car. I parked in a pay lot, leaving the phone on the seat and portable radio on—I knew the car itself was bugged, too—hopefully loud enough to mask the sound of the door opening and closing. With any luck, they'd think I was driving around town, at least for the half hour I planned on being away. I then made a hasty and quite illogical retreat on foot, in and out of buildings and obscure stores in an effort to lose any tail I might have recently grown. Call me paranoid, but I was now officially operating outside of the box.

The building directory in the lobby offered too much information. There were dozens of companies on dozens of floors, any of which might employ the elusive Wayne Rogers. Assuming small firms don't have a *discreet encrypted network* server, that narrowed the choices to the bigger players. Further deduction inspired by the word "encrypted" led me to assume the company would be involved with client-confidential issues. Like a bank. Or an accounting firm.

I hit pay dirt on the second try. After being told by the security guard in the lobby that nobody named Wayne Rogers worked at the Transamerica offices, I asked him to try the accounting firm that was the building's second largest tenant. I tried to keep my poker face in place as he consulted a computer and directed me to the forty-ninth floor. This, in turn, brought me face-to-face with another receptionist, this one unarmed and with breasts, who didn't need to consult a computer upon mention of Wayne Rogers's name. In fact, her face went slack at the moment I said it.

"Are you a, what, a client?"

"Well, sort of. A friend. Both."

She pondered my response before nodding, and I had the distinct feeling this was a wrong answer. But rather than confront me with her doubts, she decided to call someone.

That pit in my stomach was suddenly knocking to get out.

"Hi, I'm Steve Gilroy, Human Resources."

A young man in a cheap suit appeared from the woodwork, offering his hand and a plastic smile.

"Wolf Schmitt." I said it quickly, slurring the words. It sounded more like *bullshit*, I'm sure.

"And you're here to see Wayne Rogers?"

I nodded, eager eyebrows appropriately raised, as if to ask what all this drama was about.

Gilroy glanced around the lobby, presumably looking for a secure place to have a little chat. There wasn't one—the chairs were already occupied by more suits, who in their boredom were watching us intently—so he settled on moving back toward the elevators, motioning with a flick of his head that I should follow.

He was looking me right in the eye now.

"You're a friend of Wayne's?"

"In a way. More of an acquaintance. He'd written about some tax stuff a while ago and I haven't been able to reach him. I was in the neighborhood, thought I'd see if he was in."

Vague, yet reassuringly noncommittal.

"How long ago was that?" he asked.

I had to guess here. "Quite a while. Last year."

Gilroy nodded, then glanced back at the receptionist. I could see relief seeping into the lines around his eyes.

"Listen," I said, "I can come back . . ."

"Wayne isn't here."

I nodded. Steve held my gaze hopefully, as if this might be enough. It wasn't. I stared back, eyebrows still raised.

He lowered his voice. "Mr. Rogers has . . . passed away."

"You're shitting me."

A solemn headshake. "I'm afraid I'm not. Car accident last year, up on 17 halfway to Santa Cruz. I'm sorry."

A silent moment passed. Then he said, "Is there anything I can help you with?"

My eyes drifted as I shook my head in a dazed fashion.

Deadman. Of course.

I snapped back into the moment, offering my hand in thanks. Then I turned toward the elevator doors with the body language of someone who'd just been hit by a train. I had the feeling this wasn't the first time Gilroy had been in this position, and I didn't envy him. First-year HR guys get all the shit jobs.

A bolt of inspiration crashed into my mind just as the elevator doors slid open, and it had a question mark behind it.

Whose place are you taking?

Gilroy was disappearing around a corner when I called out his name. He stopped and smiled back, all too happy to help.

"Is Boyd Gavin in today, by any chance?"

Boyd Gavin, I suddenly recalled being told, was an auditor with a big-time firm. Two neuro-synapses, passing in the night. Worth a shot.

Gilroy's smile wavered. Our eyes locked, the outcome teetering on the precipice of disaster. I wondered what can of worms I'd just tapped into.

"Boyd's out sick," said Gilroy, clearly conflicted. "What did you say your name was?"

"Smith," I said. "Ralph Smith. Tell him I said hi."

That sounded a lot like bullshit, too.

Gilroy just stared as I stepped into the elevator with a little wave of gratitude, hoping I didn't throw up before the doors closed.

What to do, what to do.

My first notion, constructed and then discarded before I got back to the car, was that Boyd Gavin had been sending me the Wayne Rogers emails in order to scare me away from his girlfriend. But why adopt the identity of a dead guy, and why pose the self-incriminating question, *Whose place are you taking?* Not only that, the emails had occurred before I ever showed up on Kelly's radar, so this made no sense at all. Certainly, given the fact of their shared employment, Wayne Rogers was connected to Gavin in some way. Perhaps someone on the inside, who knew about my impending crash through the gates of Kelly Scott's life, was warning me *about* Gavin. Question then would be, why?

Without any visible means of discovering that answer, I was left with two alternatives. One, share today's news with my federal friends, see if they had any light to shed. Or two, simply ride it out, see what happened next. Maybe Deadman would once again rise from the grave and lead me to the next revelation. He just might, after all, be on my side.

I liked number two best. I'd wait and see.

What happened next was waiting for me when I got back to my condo. There was a message from Kelly, asking me to call as soon as possible. She wanted to apologize for last night, for being, as she said, a bit on the aggressive side. And, to seal the deal, she wanted to take me out to dinner.

More games. The rhetoric of chemical attraction.

Wayne Rogers and Boyd Gavin and the IRS could wait. For now, at least, Kelly Scott and I were in business.

> 38 <

- ENTRY #91: DEAD NOVELISTS—the stiff that keeps on giving, new books from embalmed authors. Proving once again that you don't need talent; you don't even need a heartbeat. You just need an editor with balls and the name of a hungry copy guy.
  —from *Bullshit in America*, by Wolfgang Schmitt

And so it began.
A limo ride to the city that evening. A rendezvous for drinks at the Fairmont. Dinner in Chinatown, heavy on the from-the-heart banter. A hand-in-hand walk along the Bay. A movie kiss by the rail at Pier 39. Cruising used bookstores in Old Town. A veiled invitation to spend the night, a chivalrous decline.
Soon, I said. Soon.
A good-morning call the next day, just to say thank you. From her, to me. Not only for the evening, but for being such a gentleman.
So far, so good.
Flowers sent to the Villa—from me to her, unsigned—with a cryptic note alluding to the limits of my gentlemanly nature.
A day off, just to keep it cool. I drove up to the Arielle complex to debrief with Lee—she was most pleased with the progress of our project—in the hope that someone in Kelly's employ was observing my

every move. As a consultant, I'd be expected to make an appearance now and then.

Next day: a shared ball machine at a terribly elite tennis resort—the kind that actually furnishes ball boys and towel girls—followed by lunch. After that, we sat on the deck for two hours and killed a pitcher of ice tea, trading stories—lies on both sides—from the days before we had money.

Another day off. I spent the majority of it at the gym, trying to flush the toxins of deceit from my body.

My turn now. A call to Kelly's assistant—three minutes on hold before I was connected—an invitation to catch a ballgame at PacBell. The fact that we'd have the Arielle suite to ourselves seemed to please her immensely. The game, to which we paid little attention, stretched into dinner at Dwight Clark's restaurant—the former Forty Niner, he of the immortal 1982 NFC championship game-winning reception—and her hand in my lap all the way back down the 101. Serious mashing in the loading zone in front of her building, another invitation spurned. I didn't want to screw it up early, I said, with something as mundane as casual sex, and it was too early to have anything but. She wasn't sure what to make of this—she asked if I was gay—allowing me to imbed the harpoon even deeper.

"Nothing about how I make love is casual," I said, quietly speaking the words through her hair into her ear. The doorman was watching us, but when I winked at him he turned away. "I'm *very* intense. I wouldn't want to scare you away."

"Scared? How exciting."

My teeth pulled at her ear. "A little fear adds an element of interest, I think."

She moaned, that little sound I had come to love.

"So," she said, her tone apropos to a late-night FM disk jockey after a shot of amaretto, "just how dark are you, anyhow?"

I knew we were on the same wavelength.

"I could lie, tell you I'm a missionary man."

She turned in her seat without disengaging her mouth from mine, pushing me back to assume the dominant position. "Maybe it's you who should be afraid."

I offered my own version of a guttural moan, the best answer I could conceive.

"Until then," I said, ending the evening by pressing my lips against her forehead for a prolonged time, during which I nodded toward the doorman. He approached and opened her door.

As she got out, she looked back and said, "Who the hell are you, and where have you been all my life?"

"Working," I said. "I'll call you."

"Soon. Or I'll have you killed."

I gave her my best deadly smile. "We'll see who kills whom."

With that I drove off, noticing that the doorman, who perfectly defined the term "curmudgeon," was shaking his head.

On the seventh day, he rested.

I took the Citation up to Portland—a private airstrip south of town where we could slip in and out without questions—to visit my Senegalese fighting fish and then spend the afternoon with my mother. The trip, like all my travel these days, was facilitated by a call to Lee's private number, resulting in a call back from someone I'd never met specifying a time to be at the Mountain View airfield, where my fourteen-million-dollar toy was housed in the shadow of a massive World War II zeppelin hangar. There was a different pilot every time, but mine was not to reason why, mine was simply to call and fly.

My mother was her usual vacant, confused self. She kept mumbling about having to return some hose to Meier & Frank, the working man's Nordstrom. Maybe it was because I hadn't seen her in a couple of weeks, but I was stricken by the dark poetry of slow death, the abandonment of hope. An existence among a cadre of the condemned, served by the well-intentioned who nonetheless regard you as their day job.

As I was leaving—when I kissed the top of her head, she looked like she wanted to belt me with her bedpan—the head nurse stopped me to say that my mother's emotional well-being was declining, and that some out-of-plan prescription drugs would go a long way toward maintaining her level of comfort. Bottom line: another hundred and a half a month.

Wolf needed to get back to work.

> 39 <

Boyd Gavin was on the telephone with an angry client—they were all pissed off these days—when Kelly Scott walked into his office, closing the door behind her. She plopped into one of the pretentious chairs positioned before his pretentious desk, which was roughly the size of a pool table. Partner-sized, he liked to tell visitors. He hadn't been expecting her—she'd only been here once before, in fact, on his birthday to take him to lunch—and based on two unreturned phone calls since the unfortunate circumstance of his stomach flu, he was pleasantly surprised. That is, until he saw the tension in her manner as she waited for him to finish, the way she avoided eye contact, the way she bit at her lip as her hands fidgeted in her lap.

He knew what this was about. Everyone in their social circle knew she'd been spending time with the pretty-boy new guy from Scottsdale, but he'd clung to the hope that it was a crush, that the fact that his claws were still in her husband's throat would bring her back into his arms.

He ended the call prematurely and hung up, trying to muster a smile in the face of imminent dismissal.

"You look unhappy."

"I'm happy."

"Then why do you look unhappy? Like you just ran over your dog."

She drew a deep breath, her eyes finally fixing on him. Kelly prided herself on being direct; in fact she seemed to delight in the imposition of her power.

"I'm seeing someone else, Boyd."

"Rumor has it."

"I didn't want you to hear it from someone else."

"Too late for that."

"I'm sorry."

"You don't look sorry. You look . . . impatient."

"I'm hoping we can stay friends."

"We never were friends."

"No. I guess we weren't."

Gavin wasn't ready for the wave of emotion that descended on him in the obligatory pause that followed her words, which had no logical response. Their eyes remained locked for a moment, but he had to look away.

"We had a good time," she said, her idea of comfort.

He allowed a nasty grin to emerge. "This doesn't change anything."

She knew what he meant. "I know."

"Just makes it a little less . . . sweet."

"That's between you and Nelson."

"None of your business."

"That's right."

"Unless I tell him . . ."

Kelly narrowed her eyes and said, "Don't fuck with me, you pencil-dicked little parasite."

"Ouch." His smile broadened.

She had to fight to contain a smile of her own. This was precisely the direction she'd hoped this conversation would go. Among other things, it made it easier to walk away.

With that, she rose to her feet. On his desk was a ceramic cup with the Arielle logo, full of pens and pencils, tools of his trade. She picked it up, then looked up at him. He was still smiling.

"He'll kill you," she said.

"One wonders how that will make *you* feel."

Now she smiled. Then she turned and hurled the cup toward the closed door behind them, the pens and pencils taking to the air in a symmetrical pattern. The cup shattered upon impact.

"Very nice," he said, shaking his head.

He watched her departure, saw her swing the door open with enough force to make it bounce off the doorstop, a sound almost as loud as the impact of the cup had been.

Just outside the door, Gavin's secretary froze at the sound of something smashing into the closed door, then nearly jumped out of her seat when it flung wildly open. Though Sarah had never met Kelly Scott other than a few minutes earlier when she'd arrived, she certainly knew who Kelly was and, because Sarah was so close to the subject of the most spirited rumor in town, why she was here today.

Judging from the expression on Kelly Scott's face as she stormed through the room, things hadn't gone well.

Her buzzer rang within seconds.

"Does Pat Healey still work over at Dun and Bradstreet?"

"I have no way of knowing that."

"Find out."

"Yezzuh." Being African-American, Sarah often adopted an appropriately Ebonic tone when her marching orders were delivered with something less than diplomacy and tact. Which they often were, particularly of late. She wasn't sure if this was good or bad, but Boyd Gavin had no idea he was being dissed when she did.

"Tell him there's someone I want checked out."

"Yezzuh."

"Name is Schmitt. Wolfgang Schmitt, from Arizona."

> 40 <

ENTRY #8: TWO-PARTY POLITICS—the issues be damned, let's play team ball. Minority leader, majority whip . . . sounds more like a party at R. Kelly's than efficient government.
—from *Bullshit in America*, by Wolfgang Schmitt

And so it continued.

A gallery opening in Palo Alto. A fund raiser at the St. Francis. Cruising for cocktails on El Camino Real. Mixed doubles with a fabled movie star couple, whose asses we thoroughly kicked.

I was public now. Which meant, highly at risk.

The story never went deep. My little privately held Arizona company had been swallowed by Arielle for cash, end of tale. No one asked much beyond that, "cash" being the secret word that opened the door to this clubhouse. The only real exposure resided with Kelly herself, and I had no idea if she was sniffing around my resume or not.

Kissing, yes. Hand-holding, often. Snuggling, when appropriate, whenever possible. More to the point, it was easy. Kelly was an affectionate woman. She liked me, I liked her. She smelled nice. There was enough sexual chemistry between us to interest Abbott Laboratories.

Almost enough, in fact, to make me forget about my job.

My mid-week call—I was still phoning in progress reports after every Kelly episode—was the first in which someone actually answered. Lee was in her car somewhere, to which she'd forwarded the message phone.

"I want to know how *you* are," she said, after listening to a narrative of my latest amorous adventure.

"So glad you asked. Life is, in a word, tough. Price of fuel for the jet, all those lobster tails, and what am I, a boy toy? Please. You're asking a lot of me, you know."

"You like her, then."

Her tone was no-nonsense, so I paused before answering, long enough to extract the armor from my voice. There would be a certain satisfaction in telling Lee the truth.

"Yeah. She's sweet to people. Generous, too. And she likes my ass. Can't keep her hands off it. Yeah, I like her."

"Kelly has a lot to offer a man," she said quickly.

"You're making a point, Lee. I'm a guy, you have to lay it out for us."

"That ass she likes so much, I want you to keep an eye on it."

"Meaning?"

"Wolf, listen to me. You're doing a great job. From what I hear, Kelly is falling for you. Hard. Rumor has it she dumped the man she was seeing. With the bad hair."

"I didn't know that."

"Of course you didn't. She's playing you just as hard as you're playing her."

"You have spies."

"Everywhere."

"Question is," I offered, "who's zooming who, right?"

"Precisely. I'm worried about you. You're bright, you're ambitious, and more than that, you have a heart. A *big* one. She's going down, Wolf, and when she does, I need to be sure you aren't in the way."

"Just say it, Lee."

"You fall for her, you let her in, we're dead."

There was silence on the line for several seconds.

"Oh shit," said Lee, reading into the moment.

"I'm okay. No uniforms will change on my watch."

"Like hell. Frankly, it's not a bad option for you. She wins, she can outbid us. Greener pastures. And we can't touch you."

"Hey, there's an angle."

"Like you hadn't thought of it."

"Actually, I hadn't. Tell me something—just what did she do, anyhow? Who fucked over whom in this little domestic dispute?"

"You don't want to know."

"Hell I don't."

"She's a bloodsucker. *That's* what you need to know. Nothing else matters."

"Does to me."

I could hear her exhale, exasperated.

"I tell you it was Nelson, you'll feel sorry for her, and that makes you weak. I tell you it's her, what she did, and I promise you'll have trouble getting past it. You're not that good an actor. Either way, we lose."

"That's supposed to make me feel better?"

"No. The money is supposed to make you feel better. You want out, Wolf, tell me now. Before you fuck it up."

Quiet again, other than ambient traffic noise from her end.

"It's a five-million-dollar decision on your part."

"I'm good, Lee," I said. "Really."

"You haven't had sex with her yet."

"No."

"But you're close."

"I'd say so, yeah."

"That'll test you. Your heart will forget your wallet, argue with your head."

"I can handle it."

A pause, then, "Five million dollars, Wolf. That buys back a lot of guilt."

"Thank you, Ms. Dante."

I heard her chuckle, and it gave me chills.

"Go to bed, Wolf. Decide who you are, who you want to be, and call me in the morning."

I hung up, though I didn't move for several minutes. The truth was, I didn't know what to think. The truth was that I'd been looking forward to my time with Kelly Scott with increasing anxiety, not because of a crack in my charade, but because I found myself enjoying the woman's company.

Hormones are a powerful drug.

I held the cell phone in front of my mouth and said, "And so, boys and girls, the plot thickens. Stay tuned."

I went to bed, though I was unable to sleep for hours.

> 41 <

ENTRY #100: THREE WORDS—Anna Nicole Smith.
    —from *Bullshit in America*, by Wolfgang Schmitt

The soundtrack from *Somewhere in Time* was playing in the background. She'd asked me to put some music on, something soft, and this was what I'd selected. The movie we'd just watched together, *Interview with the Vampire*, was scrolling credits from the DVD. That selection had been hers, and we'd talked through most of it, dissecting the metaphor of the undead at some length. She seemed fascinated by my thoughtful analysis—submission as freedom, thirst as desire, darkness as eternal penance. The need to consume, the willingness to be consumed—they were two sides of the same medieval coin. In the end it was just lust, simple and entirely human, disguised as forbidden lore, dressed in black.

Then again, she didn't know I had had the benefit of having three weeks to rehearse what I'd say.

As I returned to the couch from my duties at the CD player, Kelly was lighting candles around the room.

I knew our time had come.

Kelly had invited me up to the Villa for the evening, asking me to pick up microwave popcorn and a nice bottle of merlot on the way. The staff had been sent home, Nelson was reportedly in Australia buying a software company, Tom Cruise and Brad Pitt had done right by Anne Rice, and all was cool with the underworld.

"You don't talk about him," I said once we'd settled in, her head resting on my shoulder. I stroked her hair, both of us staring into the fire that blazed in a fireplace larger than my childhood bedroom.

"I don't think about him," was her reply.

"The sad little lies of the domestically doomed."

"You don't know women, do you."

"All too well, I'm afraid."

"Then you know we look the other way, we tolerate, we even forgive, time after time, year after year . . . but we never forget. Sooner or later, if the abuse continues, we snap."

"I've heard that sound a time or two."

"When that happens, it's over."

"And you snapped."

She reached for her glass of wine from the coffee table in front of us, draining what remained.

"Nelson is special. Brilliant beyond comprehension. Very generous, in his way. For eighteen years I had everything a woman could possibly want, but only on one level. My husband has delusions of godhood. I could take the isolation while he built his empire, I had all the friends money could buy, access to the entire planet any time I wanted to go."

"Doesn't take Miss Cleo to guess what's next," I said softly.

"I even forgave that, for a while. We fought about it, he crawled back with an olive branch in his teeth, he bought me ridiculously expensive gifts . . . then he went out and did it again. More times than I can admit to myself. I never actually caught him, I never *knew* . . . but in my heart I was sure. I blamed myself. There must have been something about me that wasn't enough. It's a tough life to walk away from, Wolf, you have to realize that. I cut myself a lot of slack for just that reason. But after a while I realized, it wasn't the marriage that was deteriorating, it was my pride, my self-respect. I was losing me."

She paused, swallowing hard. I pressed her tighter to my chest, tight enough for her to feel my pulsing heart.

"I caught him with one of his assistants, some bimbo with an ass like a racehorse, right here, in our bedroom. They were . . . I can't say it. I'm sorry. It was obscene."

I put my mouth against the top of her head.

"Kelly, don't. Please."

She was sobbing now, softly. It was the worst kind of sorrow, the uninvited kind that resides beyond hope. Holding her, I felt my own sense of upheaval, my entire basis for being here suddenly cut adrift, left to find its own way back to something to which it could anchor. A moment in which you turn on yourself.

I was on the wrong team. One of the bad guys.

She calmed down, the fire exerting its soothing magic, and for a while I thought she was asleep. After a few minutes, though, she stirred, turning her face toward mine as she put her hand behind my head, pulling me down. We kissed gently, and in the yellow light I could see where her tears had fallen on her cheeks.

I wiped them away with my thumb.

"Make love to me," she whispered.

It certainly seemed like the right thing to do.

"Welcome back," I whispered. We had been silent for several minutes, our chests still heaving somewhat. Hers looked substantially better than mine doing so. My opinion.

"How do you feel?" she asked.

I was about to ask the same question. We were lying on the rug in front of the fire, entwined in each other's arms. I was happily running the tip of my finger up and down the depression along her spine, which was moist and smooth.

"Close. Satisfied. Maybe a little embarrassed."

"Never apologize," she said. "I loved it."

"I noticed."

"You said you were intense, but . . . damn."

I made sure she was smiling, then relaxed.

We took a moment to play it back. Submission as freedom, thirst as desire. I had played her like an instrument, gently caressing the notes at first, building toward a frenzied crescendo. She had been consumed, and I had worshipped my prey. Her word, muttered in the heat of the moment.

Damn, I wondered, where did *that* shit come from?

"You?" I asked.

"Weak. Wonderful. Safe. Maybe a little afraid."

I touched her face, brushing back the hair. In the firelight she looked like a Scavullo photograph. Perfect.

She put her finger to my lips, cutting short my response.

Then she kissed me.

"Afraid," she said, "in a good way."

I nodded. "Talk to me."

She gathered her thoughts, and I marveled at what I was feeling as I watched it happen. This, I knew, was trouble.

"That was, and I'm being honest here, the most incredible experience I've ever had."

Didn't know what to say to that, for a lot of reasons. I just smiled self-consciously.

"The fear I'm talking about has nothing to do with what just happened. *That* fear was . . . delicious."

"What then?"

Her eyes drifted. "I'm just a little nervous about what I'm feeling right now."

When I started to respond, she again put her finger on my lips. It was warm to the touch as I took it into my mouth.

"Just hold me," she said, her eyes moist.

Once again, it seemed like the right thing to do.

> 42 <

ENTRY #55: ADVERTISEMENTS IN MOVIE THEATERS—this is why concession stands don't sell tomatoes . . . they stain the screen. Show up twenty minutes late and you won't miss a thing you paid to see.
   —from *Bullshit in America*, by Wolfgang Schmitt

I flat-out lied to Lee. I came clean about the crossing of the much-anticipated sexual threshold—she seemed pleased and quite hungry for details, about which I also lied—and to hear me tell it, you'd think I had already carved a notch in my fine Italian leather belt. But nothing could be further from the truth. The only carving that had taken place had been a pound of flesh separating from my heart. I was in over my head, and my only alternative was to bide my time, hoping that the forces of good would eventually emerge victorious, and that Kelly would forgive me my trespasses.

I just hoped the FBI wasn't getting impatient, and that they too were in a forgiving frame of mind. I hadn't exactly gotten around to plumbing the depths of Kelly's knowledge of Nelson's dubious business activities—which was, after all, their objective. I hadn't heard from either Banger or Short in a good while, to the extent that I had to remind myself that every word I spoke, not to mention every tinkle I took, was overheard by someone in a cheap suit.

Strangely, Lee didn't seem to be in any greater hurry than were my federal eavesdroppers. Her anxiety about my loyalty apparently quelled—though not, I had concluded, her jealousy towards Kelly Scott—the coast was now clear to press forward in quest of an invitation from Kelly to cohabitate.

The only person with any urgency to get this thing done, it seemed, was me.

Week Four, and things were heating up.

We flew to Scottsdale for a thirty-six-hour whirlwind of contrived nostalgia. It was her idea—"Show me your life," she'd asked—and what was I supposed to say? *Sorry, the jet's in the shop.* I was reassured by my behind-the-scenes team that all would be made ready, but I was nonetheless nervous when the Citation touched down at the Scottsdale Airport. My fears, however, were unfounded. My domicile was housekeeper-clean, my Land Rover and my Jag appropriately bacheloresque. We drove past the now-vacant address where my company had once done business, where I casually extracted the photograph of the old Diatech marquee from the glovebox. Hard to impress the wife of a high-tech legend who had beaten Bill Gates at Nintendo, but she was polite. We ran into old friends at the Ocean Club, one of my supposed hangouts—among them was Evelyn, the ex-Cardinal cheerleader who'd hosted my training visit, full of hugs—and Kelly seemed playfully concerned that Evelyn and I had been more than friends. Good to leave her thinking my tastes ran toward the genetically gifted. Next morning we climbed Camelback Mountain, made love in the Jacuzzi, and, later that afternoon, shopped The Biltmore. That night we dined at Banderas, then caught a Diamondbacks game, followed by another soak in the tub, this one with the original cast recording from *Les Misérables* playing in the background.

We were back in the Silicon Valley by lunch the next day. I highly recommend this private jet thing, by the way.

I finally made it past the doorman at her townhouse digs, which frankly looked as unlived-in as my Arizona estate and didn't seem to match her flair for things Mediterranean. Something about career housekeepers keeping the ravages of domestic minutiae at bay, I guess. We made love in her bed, testing the limits of her imagination and the design specs of the bedframe in ways that surprised even me. In the afterglow, I told her about a mother in a nursing home in Portland—if she looked for family, she'd now find one. It also justified any trips I might make there, in case she had me followed. We talked about God and George W.—*that* certainly got her collar up—and the state of grace in the Middle East, of which there was little. None of it led to either conclusions or collusion, but we had crossed them off of some unwritten list new lovers were obliged to address, and we had emerged unscathed.

At the end of the week I told her I had to fly out for a few days of business—thank God she didn't ask—and that I'd see her on Monday, if she'd have me. Kissing me good-bye in the parking lot where we'd rendezvoused for dinner, she unwittingly threw open the door Lee Van Wyke had sent me to knock down.

"I'm falling for you, Wolfgang Schmitt."

"You're a married woman, Kelly Scott."

"Details. Not for much longer."

"You don't know lawyers," I said. "Especially in your tax bracket. I'm a patient man, but I'm not that young."

"You don't know *my* lawyer," she said, and from her flirty smile I knew this was a Ping-Pong match she had already played in her mind.

I mustered the most sincere expression in my bag.

"I don't know if I can wait."

"*Wait?*" Confusion washed over her face. "For what?"

"I'll tell you. I like making coffee in the morning, for two. I like having to explain where I'm going and when I'll be home, and getting in trouble if I'm late. I like going to bed with someone warmer than me, and if we're too tired to make love it doesn't matter, because there's the next night and the next night and the next. I'm waiting to be with a woman I love, twenty-four/seven."

Her confused look melted away.

"Sometimes," she said, "you seem too good to be true."

A small nuclear event detonated in my stomach.

"Ah, but then I have this dark side," I said.

"I know. I think I like *that*, too."

We kissed, in no hurry to part.

"Hurry back to me," she said, the playfulness in her voice yielding to the sincere. "When you get back, we'll talk."

"About?"

"Making coffee. Twenty-four/seven."

"Just talk?" I said playfully, fearful that I'd gone to fast.

"If you're good, maybe I'll show you *my* dark side."

"And if I'm bad?"

"Even better," she said. "Hurry home."

I watched her drive off. When I was sure she was gone, I called Lee to share the happy news.

> 43 <

ENTRY #137: SINS OF THE FATHERS—racism, sexism, alcoholism, social elitism, intimacy issues, sexual inadequacy, career paralysis, misplaced machismo, rage . . . gee, thanks, Dad.
  —from *Bullshit in America*, by Wolfgang Schmitt

My "few days of business" began with a quick trip to Portland to sign some consent forms at my mother's care facility. She was napping when I arrived—the naps were getting a little bit longer every day, I was told—and I justified an early departure with the certainty that she'd think I was the new janitor and I'd be depressed about it for days. When I phoned the pilot with the news that I was ready to leave—this was protocol, a quick call and the turbines would be running when I arrived—he asked where we were going next.

"I don't know," I said, sounding as if I'd just awakened from a coma.

"Pardon me?" said the pilot, a real stiff named Rex who'd been raised in military schools before his stint in the Air Force Reserve.

"I'll let you know," I said, hanging up on him. I wanted to say that his distressed leather flight jacket from Kmart looked more than a little ridiculous with pleated Haggar slacks and wing tips from Florsheim, but I hadn't been rich long enough to insult the help. Soon, though.

As I drove the rental back to the plane, I realized I *did*, in fact, know where I wanted to go. You can run, but you can't hide from the truth of the heart. And at that moment, where my employer and my deception were concerned, my heart had other plans. I wanted to fly straight back to San Jose.

I wanted to be with Kelly. Not Tracy or my mother or my Senegalese fighting fish. Kelly.

The toughest part, you see, was not playing hard. I'd come from the school of thought that holds goals as sacred, to be pursued with passion, omitting such wimpery as subtlety and tact. Over the years this approach hadn't served me all that well as I traversed the minefield of romantic relationships, and it was certainly challenging me now. When I saw something I wanted, I tended to cast all caution aside and enter the frame with a flying tackle. But this thing with Kelly was more like chess than a team sport requiring pads. And I'd always sucked at chess.

Which explains why I was pretty proud of myself when I refrained from calling her immediately upon my return on Sunday evening. I'd spent the past thirty-six hours in Las Vegas, much to the delight of Rex the Pilot Boy, who was as anxious to be rid of me as I was him. When we'd met at the hangar earlier that evening, I'd had twenty-two hundred dollars in my pocket that hadn't been there when we landed, and he'd had a hangover that was very much against FAA regulations.

The rich, it seems, really do get richer.

After watching a little bad television—the reality shows were taking over the world in an alien plot—I went to bed. I was almost asleep in my faux condo when the telephone rang. It was the faux gate guard. I had a visitor.

Kelly.

Amazing, how quickly one can wake up. Kelly hadn't been to my condo before, and I didn't recall telling her when I'd be back from my weekend of business. She either missed me in a way that was going to blow this whole charade to kingdom come, or the Schmitt had already hit the fan, so to speak.

As it turned out, it was neither.

For the first few seconds after I opened the door, the only thing that seemed odd was the way she just stood there, staring with no expression whatsoever. She had no coat, though one was appropriate to the evening air, and the tennis shoes were a good clue she hadn't come to surprise me with something from Victoria's Secret.

I noticed two things right off. Her chin was quivering. As I stepped forward to offer comfort, I saw evidence of blunt-force trauma on her face. Her nose was swollen and bright red, her upper lip cut, and the area surrounding her eyes puffy and pink, as if she'd been slapped repeatedly. Or worse.

I only caught a glimpse, because she quickly buried her face into my shoulder and began to sob. I asked all the right questions as I held her in the doorway for over a minute, but if she heard at all, she wasn't ready to answer. Then I guided her inside, toward the ridiculously expensive leather sofa Lee told me she'd hand-picked for my bachelor digs.

I parted her hair gently, positioning her face toward the light. I drew a deep breath, as much to calm my racing heart as to keep a sudden light-headedness at bay.

"Who did this?"

"You don't know him."

"Did Nelson . . ."

She shook her head, exasperated.

"You should see a doctor."

"Right. For what, a Band-Aid and an Advil?"

I didn't know what to say to that, and I didn't like her tone. But she was here, and I liked the tone of *that*.

Sensing my stung reaction, she pulled me close, and we held each other for another few minutes. This time, I softly asked the questions that still demanded attention, and she answered without impatience.

"Are you injured?"

"No. Just a fat lip."

"Are you going to tell me who did this?"

"A man I was seeing. Before you."

A moment of panic made me shut up. Thanks to Lee, I certainly knew about Kelly's relationship with Boyd Gavin, but I couldn't remember if Kelly had spoken about him. The default position, itself risky in case I was wrong, was to play the ignorance card, and if she had, in fact, told me about Gavin, I could always say I forgot.

Whose place are you taking?

Based on what I'd recently discovered about him—the fact that Gavin worked at the same accounting firm that the dead-yet-still-emailing Wayne Rogers had worked—I was understandably anxious to see where this might lead.

I made a little production out of exhaling loudly, more emphasis than acting. I was legitimately mad as hell.

"Don't even think about it," she said.

She pulled back, facilitating eye contact.

"Okay," I said, using a little *tone* of my own. "You're pressing charges, then."

She shook her head and looked away. "I broke it off, and he flipped out. End of soap opera."

"Meaning what? He slaps you around and walks away?"

"That's what it means. He's just upset."

I shook my head. "Sorry. Doesn't work that way."

"Wolf, listen to me . . ."

"What, you gonna say this is none of my business? You're *here*. That *makes* it my business."

When I said "here," I was pointing at my chest. Seeing this, her eyes welled up and we embraced again.

"Run me a bath?" she mumbled into my Mariners T-shirt.

I kissed her forehead lightly, the scent of her hair filling me, and she smiled back in a way that told me it was time to back off. I had flared my tail feathers, notice taken.

As I got up to start her bath, she said, "Nice place, by the way."

"You like?"

"Yeah. Looks like you've been here for years."

I left the room, certain I'd throw up before reaching the john. I hoped the sound of running water would mask the sound of my shame.

I held Kelly in my arms through the night, sleeping very little, content to listen to the deep rhythm of her breathing. In the morning light her face looked much better, the swelling gone, the redness more a reminder of her tears than the open palm of Boyd Gavin.

Everything between us was different now. Context had been redefined. She had broken it off with her lover, and I had to assume it was for me. She had come here not so much for safety as for comfort.

She'd missed me, and I her. We had shared a bed without the slightest sexual intention.

She'd come home. And I didn't want her to leave.

Over coffee and toast—the best breakfast this flighty bachelor could manage—she made me promise to let it go. She had lawyers and muscular friends and other means to deal with Boyd Gavin should he reappear, and she didn't want any shadows obscuring the horizon of our relationship. He was litigious as hell, she said, and with my new money, I was a lawsuit waiting to happen.

But I knew better. I knew enough about women to sense she was lying through her teeth. In matters of romance, the princess and the gladiator have a pact as old as the parchment paper upon which it was first written. Wrongs must be righted. Honor defended.

The entire kingdom would be waiting to see who survived the joust.

> 44 <

ENTRY #188: RESTROOM ATTENDANTS—an unnecessary tip for an unnecessary and entirely American service. Next step—they handle the paperwork, too. Wonder what that'll be worth.
—from *Bullshit in America*, by Wolfgang Schmitt

Somewhere deep in hell, Johann Wolfgang von Goethe—the creator of Faust, and for whom I was named—was laughing his ass off. I had become that which I most despised—one of those guys who talks on a mobile phone while riding a stationary bike at the gym. While I drew the line at walking through airports talking aloud to a hands-free phone—just shoot me—this was close. But Lee had stressed that I should have the phone nearby at all times when I wasn't with Kelly. Including the gym, which she mentioned specifically. Luckily, other fit but lost souls were doing the same, so I was right at home.

"Listen to me," she said, after I had debriefed her on Kelly's visit the night before. "This is critical."

"I'm salivating."

"You sound like you're humping something."

"Thanks for the visual. Shoot."

"You've got to confront him, Wolf."

"You mean, like, *step outside* confront him?"

"Whatever. And she has to see it."

"What am I supposed to do, hunt the guy down?"

"Leave that to me. Just be ready for it."

"I promised Kelly I'd let it go."

"This is a promise you need to break. Trust me, there isn't a woman on the planet who would hold you to that. No matter what she says."

"The beast within, that which cannot be restrained, yada yada yada."

"You know what I'm talking about," she said.

I did. I just hoped Kelly did, too.

The battlefield, it turned out, would be a small seafood restaurant in Sausalito, with a killer view of the city, the bridge, and Alcatraz—the trifecta of Kodachrome. Last place in California one would expect to run into an old boyfriend—we flew in with another couple on the Scott helicopter—but I knew that Lee Van Wyke was never to be underestimated. The woman was manipulative on a global scale.

Which was why, during the sautéed langostino appetizer, I was not at all surprised when Kelly muttered "oh shit" half under her breath, her hand clamping her forehead as if a migraine had permeated her skull. We had been engaged in a lively conversation with the Kragers—he a venture capitalist, she a fledgling philanthropist who loved seeing her name in the paper—about the Rolling Stones, no less, when the course of the evening took a decidedly southern direction.

"What?" I said, touching her arm.

"Don't look," she mumbled.

I knew.

I also looked. Standing next to the maître d' was Boyd Gavin. He was scanning the room with his eyes, a deer-in-the-headlights look on his face.

Looking, I had to assume, for Kelly.

"No way this is a coincidence," said Kelly.

"Who'd you tell about tonight?"

The Kragers were looking at each other as if we had just switched to Mandarin and they couldn't read the subtitles.

"No one. I was at the Villa picking up some clothes. I think I might have mentioned something to Rita. I don't know."

Rita, the maid. Lee, the bitch with the big tip.

"What's he doing?" she asked, still shielding her face.

I tried to be discreet, but there was no place to hide. If he'd had a good squirt gun, we'd have been easy money.

Nonetheless, Gavin didn't seem to see us. And instantly, I knew why. We weren't the ones he was looking for. He was looking for Lee. Or someone she'd sent him to meet.

"Let me do this," I said, putting my napkin on the table.

Kelly touched my arm, but seemed to choke on whatever words were at hand. In that instant of hesitance, in which wisdom collided with the aphrodisiac of chivalry, I knew I would never doubt Lee Van Wyke's well-honed, vicious feminine instincts again.

Our eyes locked. I knew this was an investment that would pay off. Perhaps to the tune of five million langostinos.

It wasn't all acting, either. Gavin had roughed up my girl, and we needed to have a little man-to-man chat, he and I.

The bar where he had gone to wait was elevated by a few steps, providing a nice view of the dining area. And, conveniently, vice versa.

Gavin saw me approach. From his face, I could tell he knew who I was. Our eye contact at the fund raiser had been brief, but apparently enough, especially in context to what came of it. I stole a look back at the table—Kelly and the Kragers were wide-eyed and motionless. Kelly had her hand over her mouth as if she were watching a De Palma film.

I extended my hand like the gentleman I intended not to be. "Wolf Schmitt," I said with a perky voice.

He looked down at my hand, then back at me without accepting the gesture.

"That a name or a joke?" he said, smiling falsely.

"Okay, we can do it that way. Your call, pal."

"I get it," he said. "What I don't get is *why*."

"Why what?"

"Why she put you up to this. This is bullshit."

I wasn't completely sure which *she* he was referring to, or even which *this*. My only choice here was to change the direction of the conversation. I'd mull it over later while icing down my bruised knuckles.

But Gavin preempted this strategy.

"She told me what you said."

"She did? That's interesting, since I didn't say anything. I don't even know you."

If it was a mind game, it was a good one. I still wasn't sure to which woman he was referring.

"What are you doing here?" I asked.

"You tell me. You seem to be the man with the answers."

His tone was what you'd expect, full of contempt. The questions in my mind were coming too fast, the answers even faster, and he could easily misinterpret my hesitance as fear.

"Maybe you should go," I said. "In fact, I insist."

"Who the fuck are you, anyhow?" His voice confirmed what my sense of smell had suspected: this wouldn't be his first cocktail of the evening.

"The guy replacing you," I said. I added a little smile just for effect.

"What does *that* mean? You're just the dick of the week, *pal*. With a big fucking mouth, from what I hear."

Somehow Lee had planted a seed in Gavin's brain, one supposedly sprouting from my own words. Because of that, there were two matters of honor on the table tonight, one fact, one fiction—me confronting his violence toward Kelly, him confronting some disrespect I'd never actually uttered.

Gavin suddenly stood up. He moved closer, invading my space. If I edged back, with Kelly watching, the moment would be sacrificed. If I didn't, my heretofore clean slate with the law would be in imminent jeopardy. And if *they* looked close enough, the house of cards would come crashing down.

In the background I could hear Uncle Wolfgang, still cackling from the cheap seats in hell.

I was four inches taller than this man who suddenly wanted to kick my ass. I used that as inspiration and pressed forward. Entering the frame with a flying tackle, as it were.

"You gonna hit *me* now, or what? Give it up, man."

"What the *hell* kind of shit are you talking?"

"Look, I came over here to ask you to leave. You're making my date uncomfortable. And you're pissing me off."

"Your *date*? Oh, that's good. That's *rare*."

"You want to talk about Kelly, we can go there. I suggest you just get out of here."

"That a threat? Must be forty, fifty people in here watching you threaten my ass right now."

He inched closer, our chests nearly touching. Because of the difference in our respective heights—I use the term loosely in his case—he had to crank his head nearly all the way back to maintain eye contact.

There was nothing left to say. Go time.

My father the abusive drunk always told me to never take the first swing, unless you saw the other guy twitch. We both stood motionless, apparently having received identical parental advice, probably from similar abusive drunks.

In that awkward moment the cavalry arrived in the form of the maître d'. He was about five-six, with a bald head that reminded me of that fake butler from *Joe Millionaire*. But he was the man with the hammer in this situation, because he was the man with the telephone if things got out of hand. Which they very nearly had.

"That's it, guys," he said, wedging himself between us.

He turned to Gavin first. "You," he said, "out of here."

Then he turned to me. "You, pay your bill, get your friends, leave. You wanna beat each other to death in the parking lot, be my guest."

Gavin and I maintained eye contact like two contenders in the ring at the prefight referee spiel. And like two street fighters wanting to impress their respective crews, we were both smiling, too cool for the moment.

Then Gavin shook his head, as if giving up on something that was no longer worth his time. There was no way to depart the scene of a street fight gracefully, and he had the burden of walking away under the gaze of the entire room.

He stopped near the door and turned back. He spoke loud enough for the entire hushed throng to hear, including Kelly.

"I don't know who you are, Mr. Wolf-man, but I know this—you aren't who or what you say you are. You're a poseur. And I'm gonna find out why."

His eyes found Kelly in the booth. His expression changed, dissolving into something sad.

He said, "I owe her that much, at least."

Just when you thought the shit couldn't get any deeper, I was up to my ass in a new subplot.

> 45 <

The inner sanctum of Nelson Scott was as impenetrable as the Pentagon War Room on Veterans Day. The last and most imposing measure of security was the presence of Bruce "Rashod" Martinez, who occupied a sturdy chair in the lobby outside the explosion-resistant and thoroughly soundproofed walls of Scott's private office. Strapped to the bottom of the chair was a significant automatic weapon, but no one in the building knew this except him and his employer.

All Boyd Gavin had to do to gain entry today was give the receptionist his name. And although Martinez would stare a hole through Gavin as he passed, the bodyguard wouldn't say a word.

Just prior to Gavin's arrival this morning, Scott and Lee Van Wyke had been sipping coffee while discussing sensitive matters of personal cash flow. Things were getting tight, and with a monthly nut that could finance a small university, urgency was the watchword of the day.

Lee was in mid-sentence when she noticed a dull gaze arrive in her boss's eyes, a sure sign he had checked out. She'd seen this a thousand times over the years, and she knew she'd have to wait until he was ready to open whatever can of worms had hijacked his immediate mindshare, that he wouldn't hear a word she said until he was.

"Talk to me about Kelly," he said, setting the cup down gently before folding his hands in his lap.

"She just might be in love," said Lee, trying to restrain an inappropriate smile.

"You mean lust," Scott fired back. His ego, combined with his disdain for his wife, refused her the capability of love.

"Whatever. I'd say we're very close."

"And our man Schmitt?"

"Problematic. He's too good. Very quick on his feet. I think he's falling for her, too."

"Why is that a problem? They move in, we swoop down, he gets paid. If they're in love, they live happily ever after."

"Don't let anyone tell you you're not a romantic fool, Nelson."

"I don't let anybody tell me anything," he said. Then he smiled, very slightly. "Except you, of course."

That was when the intercom announced that Boyd Gavin was in the lobby.

Lee and Scott shot each other a stern glance. Lee shrugged to affirm her surprise, and perhaps her innocence.

"Show him in," barked Scott.

A moment later the door opened. Martinez entered the room, holding the door for Gavin. He closed it, remaining inside.

Gavin looked as hung-over as he felt. He wore a suit, though it was much too early in the day for his tie to be askew and his shirt half untucked.

His eyes fixed on Lee.

"That was some stunt last night."

"You play with fire, Gavin . . . there you go."

"It'll cost you." His eyes moved to Scott now. "Actually, it'll cost *you*."

Scott shrugged in a *so what?* kind of way. Lee, however, looked somewhat less composed.

Gavin cracked a grin. "I know about your guy. This Schmitt character. Haven't figured out why yet, but I know he's not who Kelly thinks he is, and that somehow he's connected to you."

"And how might you know *that*?" asked Lee.

Gavin snorted contemptuously. "Trouble with you people is that you're always underestimating people like me. I *made* the guy, okay? People talk, they've *seen* you with him. What you have to ask yourself is, what's Kelly going to say about it? That's the very expensive question here."

"And why," said Scott, "would I give a good shit, much less five hundred grand, what Kelly thinks or says about anything?"

"Call it a hunch. How am I doin'?"

Scott closed his eyes for a moment, a billionaire's eccentricity, summoning some zen-like calming energy before he sprang from his chair. The presence of his highly schooled, 240-pound bodyguard tended to make Nelson Scott a courageous and often combative man.

Gavin sensed the sudden tension, his smile widening.

"Hey, I'm a reasonable guy. I think a bonus is appropriate, more than fair. Say, double the next installment? A one-time-only special, then we're back on plan."

Scott leaned forward in his chair. "You want a half-million dollars to keep this Schmitt thing to yourself."

Gavin flashed a grin at Lee. "He's quick, this guy."

"We'll let you know," answered Lee, her face blank. She nodded at Martinez, who took a step forward. That was all Gavin needed, as he immediately began to back up toward the door. As he turned, he pointed a finger at Scott and said, "Nice doing business with you."

He smiled as he hurried out of the room, nodding at Martinez as if they were old friends. The smile was not returned.

The bodyguard closed the door, leaving Lee and Scott alone once again. Both of them stared at the door for several seconds.

"I want this finished," said Scott. "Pay him. Shut him up."

"I think shutting him *down* is more like it."

"Whatever. Get it done."

With that, Scott got up and went around to his desk, his eyes quickly engaging with some papers waiting there. Lee knew the meeting was over, her marching orders clear.

She left the room without another word.

> 46 <

ENTRY #46: THE POWER OF THE PRESS—this just in, Ted Koppel's hairpiece declared a hazardous substance. Film at eleven.
—from *Bullshit in America*, by Wolfgang Schmitt

Wolf, here's your second question: who's on page seven of last Thursday's Oregonian Metro section, and why should you care? Pay attention.
W.R.

The email was on my computer the night after my little man-to-man with Boyd Gavin, which, as it turned out, had ruined the evening. Kelly had seemed preoccupied through the remainder of the dinner in Sausalito, and later, after the helicopter had landed and the Kragers had departed in a flourish of air kisses and overwrought handshakes, we'd argued about it on the drive back to her flat. I should have known better—in my experience, ex-boyfriends were touchier subjects than religion and group sex. I wasn't surprised when there was no curbside invitation to come up and massage away her headache—I offered—and in that instant, I knew what it was like to be in conflict with a woman whose wish was everyone's command except mine.

I wondered if she'd heard Gavin say the word "poseur," and if she had, whether she was processing the possibilities.

The next morning Kelly's assistant called to cancel our tennis-then-lunch date, citing the continuation of the headache with a tone I suspected to be infused with a certain *I-know-something-you-don't-know* smugness. I'd never set eyes on the woman—couldn't quite get the image of the fat lady with the eyeshadow from the *Drew Carey Show* out of my head—and, call me small-town, no matter how long I survived here on Planet Scott, the notion of an unemployed woman having a personal assistant would still rub me the wrong way.

You're a poseur . . . and I'm gonna find out why . . .

I slept in, worked out all afternoon, then went to cheap dinner and a late movie. Two movies, actually. After finding that I had no voicemails—my mobile phone hadn't rung all day, either—I checked email and found W.R.'s cryptic message. It was just after midnight.

"Wolf, you gotta get a life, man," said Blaine, whom I awakened once again with a request for assistance. I used my personal mobile phone, which I knew was clean, pacing the driveway in front of my condo. Lee's cell phone, the one Short had bugged, was on my nightstand with the TV going.

"Tell me you keep your newspapers," I said.

"Okay, I keep my newspapers. What the *fuck* are you talking about?"

I read him the email from Deadman and signed by "W.R.," whom we now knew to be someone named Wayne Rogers, who was indeed dead.

"Hang on," he said. I heard him put the phone down, followed by some ambient background noises. Blaine lived in an apartment in Portland on Twenty-third Avenue, which fancied itself a sort of Santa-

Monica-Boulevard-meets-Georgetown haven for the tragically hip. I'd never been to his place. Waiting for him to return to the phone, it occurred to me that over the entire course of our relationship, I had always needed Blaine far more than he needed me.

I heard the rustling of papers before he picked up the phone.

"You're lucky," he said, slightly out of breath. "I used Thursday to line Blanch's cage."

"You keep your girl in a cage?"

"My bird, asshole. Metro, you said?"

"Yeah. Page seven."

More rustling. I pictured him in his underwear with the receiver tucked between his shoulder and his ear.

"Got it," he said again.

"Go."

"It's the fucking obituaries. Whole page. And a few ads from funeral parlors. Used caskets, half-off."

A pain that was indistinguishable as either my heart or my stomach suddenly stabbed at the base of my rib cage. There was a distinct possibility that my prophesied cardiac event was at hand, which, in context to the moment, would be more than a little ironic.

"You want the names?"

My voice was barely audible as I said, "Yeah."

He read off eighteen names of the recently departed, none of which rang a bell.

"Start over. All of it, the whole entry."

"Dude, I charge by the hour."

When I didn't respond, he began. Somewhere in the middle of the oration something clicked. I asked him to start over . . . again.

"Shit, man . . ."

"Just that entry."

"Joseph Kasanski. Family and friends mourn the passing of a devoted husband, loving father and loyal friend. Mr. Kasanski was killed in a traffic accident. He was fifty-seven." A pause. "More?"

"Please."

"After a career in the military, Mr. Kasanski had worked as a chauffeur for the last fourteen years, the last with Classic Limousines."

At least I knew my heart was fine. Nothing beating that fast could be in ill repair.

Blaine kept reading to the conclusion of Joseph Kasanski's obituary, but I didn't hear another word. I pictured the man who had driven me to meet Nelson Scott's jet on the day this all began. I remembered thinking he looked out of place for Portland, more like a New Yorker, a sweaty neck and an attitude. I recalled how he had eyeballed the Gulfstream with the wide eyes of a boy, how I decided I liked him for that, despite his refusal to tell me who had sent him that day.

"Wolf, you there, man?"

"Yeah."

"That your guy?"

His voice sounded distant, coming from a tunnel.

"Yeah. That's my guy."

He asked me to forward him the email, then said he'd try to dig up something on Joe Kasanski's traffic accident and get back to me.

Blaine. I still needed him more than he needed me.

My mobile phone—the clean one—rang from the nightstand at six thirty, sending a jolt of adrenaline through my system that nearly lifted me off the mattress. I had been asleep for an hour at the most—

time has no meaning during a night in hell—the long dark hours having been a nightmare of second guessing and regrets.

For some reason I thought it might be Kelly, but quickly realized she wouldn't be calling on my private line. I'd left the hot phone in the refrigerator for the night. She, too, had helped fill the eternity of minutes since I'd hung up with Blaine. There was too much I didn't know, and she was at the top of the list.

Number two was why I was even there.

"Dude, wake the fuck up," said Blaine. "Payback's a bitch."

The other phone—the bugged one—was on the nightstand next to the phone. Nothing I could do about the ringing now. I stuffed it under the mattress and took the clean phone into the bathroom, closing the door. I ran the water in the sink just in case.

"Tell me you're not calling just to piss me off."

"You taking a fucking shower?"

"No. What's up?"

"Joe Kasinski. Limo went off the road up in Forest Heights a week ago Saturday."

"You found that out in the middle of the night?"

"Internet, man. Wake up and smell the silicon."

"He alone?"

"Quite. Coming home from a job, a bachelorette party. Apparently shared a few pops with the girls, blood-alcohol to the moon. Wrapped his Lincoln around a tree."

The stabbing pain returned to my rib cage.

"There's more," he said after a moment.

I drew a deep, painful breath. "Go."

"The email, it wasn't sent from the same computer as the others."

"But it was the same Yahoo account."

"Pay attention, Wolf. You can access Yahoo from anywhere, any computer. This came from a company server in Menlo Park."

I held my breath.

"Arielle Systems," he said. "Ever heard of 'em?"

He was being sarcastic, though he had no way of knowing how acid his wit had become.

I thanked him profusely and promised to keep him posted.

After I hung up I remembered something Joe the dead limo driver had said to me that day on the way to the Hillsboro airport. He told me he didn't drink, that he hadn't touched a drop since he'd sobered up over twenty years earlier.

I was on the road fifteen minutes later. Just in time to catch the rush-hour northbound traffic on the 101. Which gave me plenty of time to think about what to do next.

I left the bugged mobile telephone in the fridge.

> 47 <

ENTRY #62: CELEBRITY POLITICS—it's a free country for them, too, but here's the deal: they're like telemarketers calling at the dinner hour. No one cares what they're selling, no one wants to hear it. Just shut up and read the lines somebody else writes.
—from *Bullshit in America*, by Wolfgang Schmitt

Standing in front of Steve Gilroy, the human resources cowboy for the once-prestigious accounting firm occupying four floors of the Transamerica Building—none of the companies was terribly prestigious anymore—I had to stifle a smile. He was studying the item I had handed him moments before, and as I waited for his response, I suddenly and inexplicably flashed on Clint Eastwood as Dirty Harry Callahan saying, "Personnel? Personnel's for assholes." Steve Gilroy certainly hadn't been demoted because he'd roughed up his clients, which was Clint's excuse. No, Steve Gilroy was *born* to process timesheets.

Strange, how humor finds its way into even the darkest moments. Like this one.

Gilroy looked up at me with a blank expression, one more appropriate to the accountants for whom he worked.

"Sure. That's Wayne Rogers's girlfriend."

He handed back the picture I'd extracted from my

wallet. Call me sentimental, but I just couldn't bring myself to remove Tracy from my life that completely. I'd like to say I'd forgotten the photo was even there—a snapshot of her on the beach in a killer suit—but that wouldn't be true. The only respectably macho thing I can say about it was that I sort of liked having her near my ass all the time.

"Anything else I can help you with?" said Gilroy.

I wondered what he was thinking, staring at me like a postal clerk. He had made me as a jealous lover who had come to confront the past—the picture was a dead giveaway—and that I was just now piecing it all together, a year too late. That much, at least, was all too true.

"No. Thanks." My expression was appropriate to the moment—the devastation of the betrayed.

Gilroy nodded, then turned and walked away. As I had done last time, I pulled another Columbo and called him back.

"Any chance she kept Wayne's laptop?"

For a moment I wasn't sure he'd answer. HR guys, none of whom had heard of Dirty Harry, guarded company secrets with their lives. Then his expression cracked.

"Possible," he said, cracking a weak smile, as sympathetic as it got here.

Probable, I thought. Despite having ample time to think about it on the drive up, considering just this outcome, the news rocked me. Wayne Rogers had probably kept a computer at home, through which he could log onto the company server to work on weekends, as every accountant worth his pencil lead does. It would have been easy enough for Tracy to lift it from his worldly goods, especially if it was a laptop, before she disappeared from the landscape of his life. Which meant that in all likelihood, it had been Tracy sending me the Deadman emails using the firm's server, which in and of itself created more questions than answers. Could have been Gavin, too, for that matter, trying to scare me away from Kelly, though I had discounted that option since the emails arrived before I'd invaded Gavin's sexual space. If Tracy's purpose had been to protect me from something, why hadn't she just come to me? And what was there to protect me *from*? If anything, Tracy would want a piece of the action, which still might be the point after all. Then again, she hadn't exactly been shadowing my every move of late. On the other hand, she *had* come to me, twice, in fact, if that was the spin I wanted to attach to our two supposedly haphazard reunions.

Coincidence? I think not. Cluster fuck? I think so.

One answer today did provide was this: Tracy worked at Arielle. I hadn't known that. And what a tasty little morsel of context it was.

All of this jelled in one long, awkward pause, Steve Gilroy staring at me patiently the entire time.

"Anything else?" he asked.

I had further questions, a dozen or more, but none that were ready for prime time. I shook my head.

He said, "Have a good day then," the smile waning.

I nodded my thanks and disappeared into the safe harbor of the elevator, where a Muzak rendering of an old Police song was waiting.

This was something the Feds needed to hear. Especially since my role in this thing had ended.

It was over. As of that very moment, I quit.

PART FOUR
>> <<

> 48 <

"You can't quit, Mr. Schmitt. Not now."

"Used to be a free country."

"Used to be gas under two bucks, too. Write your congressman."

Wolfgang Schmitt had been here before, squared off with some pencil-neck whose tax-subsidized balls had been fortified by a certificate of completion. Even the functional dynamics of the meeting were obvious—him seated, his interrogator perched on the side of the table, looking down at him. If Wolf stood up, the guy would be staring straight into his sternum.

The agent, wearing an infuriating little smile quite inappropriate to a civil servant, said, "Someone doesn't like being told what to do."

"Bet that's why they call you Sherlock. They teach that at Quantico?"

The smaller man's smile vanished. He collected himself, then said, "Why back out now? Just curious."

"Let's just say I'm emotionally involved."

"No stomach for it, Wolf?"

Wolf's eyes narrowed. The truth hurt.

The Fed Schmitt had come to know as Sherlock pressed. "Not about the money anymore, Mr. Schmitt?"

"It's about a dead guy in Portland."

"Could be a coincidence."

"That what you think?"

"What I think is that we're interested."

"Which is why you won't let me quit."

"We had an arrangement. We still do."

"The arrangement didn't include dead people."

The Fed shifted from one butt cheek to the other, feigning boredom. He looked at the wall as he spoke.

"We can call it off if you want. You have a lawyer, Mr. Schmitt? A good one?"

"More threats? I didn't like it when Special Agent Short went there, and I don't like it now."

"Not a threat. But there are options on both sides. Yours is to quit, if you want."

The ensuing eye contact finished his train of thought. After a moment the agent smiled, signaling a transition.

"Just for grins, let's say you experience a sudden fit of civic duty and don't walk. What's next up?"

"You tell me."

"Happy to. You go back in, move it along, play stupid. Maybe pull the trigger on this thing, see what fish jump into the boat."

"I can't do that to her."

"I see. Because she's emotionally involved, too."

Their eyes locked again. But this time, the agent's expression was almost empathetic.

"What the hell do you want from me?" asked Wolf.

"What we've wanted from the beginning, Mr. Schmitt. The bad guys. Just the bad guys."

"You figure out who the bad guys are, let me know."

"Funny," said the interrogator, *"that's just what I was going to say to you."*

Wolfgang Schmitt waited until he was several miles away—he felt foolish checking the rearview mirror, but he did it anyway—before reaching into the pocket of his jacket to turn off the tape recorder. Once again, the dumbasses hadn't bothered to check.

Our tax dollars at work.

> 49 <

Portland, Oregon

Raining again. Mid-May, and there hadn't been a ballgame around here in weeks. No wonder no more than a handful of major leaguers had come from this area code. Mickey Lolich, Rick Wise, Dale Murphy, that was about it. John Jaha, but nobody ever heard of *that* guy. The rest were just a bunch of minor-league washouts, and damn few of those worth a shit, guys destined for day jobs and a lifetime of wishing things had been different. That they had grown up in the sun.

Just like the poor schmuck who owned the house he was about to break into. A minor-fucking-leaguer.

God, he loved baseball. He'd grown up in Florida, been a spring training junkie until the military thing happened. He loved it almost as much as he loved what he did now, which included researching the hell out of his marks. Like a pitcher who keeps a book on hitters. The more you study, the better your chances of working out of a jam.

The weather would make things harder for a normal B&E guy. There would be tracks out of the woods behind the house. Footprints on the roof. More footprints inside. A hundred little ways to screw it up.

But not him. He was no ordinary two-bit smash-

and-grab man. This intruder had skills. In and out in less than four minutes. He would erase any evidence of his presence when he reversed his steps, leaving without anyone ever knowing he was there. His record was perfect. Tonight would be the same.

He waited for half an hour after the closest neighbor's lights had gone out, crouched behind a tree on the wooded hillside behind the houses. Then, just after midnight, he slipped unseen from his cover and approached the back of the target house.

First thing: bypass the phone line. Install a device that maintains the connection but blocks any outgoing signals, like the one made by the security system if he was too slow tonight. Dumb fucks at the phone company would never know. He'd done it a hundred times, practiced it a thousand. Took him six seconds tonight, once he had the box open. The government had trained him well.

Then, with the agility of the Special Forces washout he was—yeah, he could relate to all those busted minor-league dreams—he used the air-conditioning unit as a platform and was up on the roof in seconds. He was well aware of the alarm system and its roof sensors. He'd have thirty seconds to get inside and disable the alarm at the code box. While the call would be blocked if he fucked up, the noise would be a problem. Better to get there first. He much preferred to go about his work in peace.

Easy game. Easier money.

It took fifteen seconds to loosen the skylight with the special power tools he'd brought along for this specific task. Zip here, zip there—some genius actually designed it for roof access—splice the wire connection, pull it open. Four seconds to put protective clean-room booties over his shoes—definitely the low-tech part of the evening—three seconds to drop down into the hallway without breaking his ass. Four more to get downstairs to the back door, where—if his source data was correct, and it always was—the code box would be located.

He punched in the four-digit code he'd memorized with one second to spare. Source data again. Expensive, but accurate.

The house was quiet, a crematorium before dawn. He savored the moment, breathing it in, listening to his pounding heart. God, how he loved his job. Better than baseball, at which he'd sucked once upon a time.

The first package—he dug all that movie special-ops talk, even though it was bullshit—would be in one of four places: the nightstand, the dresser, the closet, or under the mattress. Statistics supported that particular order of probability, in context to a ninety-five percent likelihood it was in the bedroom in the first place. If it wasn't, it would be in the bathroom, which made no sense at all. Less than one percent chance it was somewhere else. In that case, he was screwed; he'd just leave without completing the mission.

After the second package, of course. That one was easy.

He'd be in and out in less than a minute and a half. Hell, he wouldn't even have to open anything to find it—he'd brought a handheld metal-detecting wand along for that job, sensitive enough to detect a skull-plate in a crowded movie theater, which he'd done once just for kicks.

The smart money was on the nightstand. Where the minor-league dude with the shattered dreams could get it quick.

Bingo. Statistics, man. They never lie.

Next up: package two. It would be in the bathroom, if it was there at all. Not a sure thing, but he'd do what he could.

Bingo again.

Getting out clean was the fun part. Skylights were tough—you had to use both walls to shimmy up like a circus performer. Too easy to scuff the paint, maybe knock a picture down. Jobs like this—*ghost jobs,* they called them—were more challenging. In and out with no trace whatsoever. Only the real pros did ghost jobs. Better to use a door, double back to the roof to secure the hardware. After resetting the alarm, he simply walked out the back door, went around the air conditioner, and scampered back to the roof, where he reinstalled the skylight and its alarm sensors in less time than it had taken to take it apart. Then, he pulled the bypass unit off and went back into the woods.

In and out in three minutes plus. Both packages were safely in his pocket.

He was worth what they paid him, every significant dollar. Paid him like a major-fucking-leaguer, man. If they gave out bubble gum cards for ghost breakers, he'd be one famous guy. He'd be in the fucking Hall of Fame.

> 50 <

ENTRY #4: DISCRIMINATION—racial, sexual, gender, age, reverse, social, geographic, economic, whatever. It's indefensible in a country founded by poor white immigrants who stole the land from proud natives and then plowed it with kidnapped African labor. News flash: reversing it doesn't make up for past sins.
—from *Bullshit in America*, by Wolfgang Schmitt

The resurrection of Wolfgang Schmitt, quasibillionaire from Scottsdale, would begin the next morning. Easier said than done, too, since apparently Kelly was taking her PMS-induced mood to extremes. Something about my little altercation with Boyd Gavin had pissed her off, and I wasn't being allowed a fair trial. Two days now and no messages, no returned calls. Same story with Lee, whom I'd phoned to report my frustration, and perhaps call her on her bad judgment with the Gavin thing. If Kelly decided I was suddenly something less than enticing, then the curtain would fall and I'd be a pumpkin again faster than you could say *sociopathic liar*. I had to get that glass slipper back on her foot, and fast.

I called the townhouse first thing, after another night of fitful sleep. Cruella the assistant from hell answered, and I was in no mood.

"Morning. Kelly in?"

"May I ask who's calling?"

This was bullshit.

"Come on, let's cut the crap, okay? She's in or she isn't."

I heard an extension pick up, followed by a familiar voice. Kelly's.

"It's okay, Lynn."

Then came the sound of Lynn hanging up, followed by pure silence.

"Good morning," I said.

"I've been pouting," she replied. The words and the tone combined to untie a knot that had been in my stomach for the past thirty-six hours. Amazing, the power women have over us.

"I've missed you," I said, surprised at how serious I was. Nothing about the *next* thirty-six hours would be easy, either.

"I'm a poop," she shot back.

"My thoughts exactly."

"You should have hit him."

"Also my thoughts exactly. Ever figure out how he knew you were there?"

"No. I've got a mole, I think."

"A rat, more like it. Mind if I ask you a question?"

"I apologize," she shot back.

"Excuse me?"

"You were going to ask me why I went high-maintenance on you, what you'd done that was so wrong."

"I was thinking PMS."

"Not so wrong, Mr. Monk. It's kinda scary, actually."

"So scare me."

Her voice changed here, a dash of sudden schoolgirl.

"I'm serious. Watching you with Gavin, I felt . . . something. I've been in denial, Wolf, but it hit me then. Hard." She paused, then added, "Right in the heart."

Damn that Lee. Just when I thought I had her by the tennis skirt, she pulls out another ace.

Before I could respond, she said, "Can you come by? I want to see you." When I didn't answer immediately, she added, "Please?"

"I've got a meeting," I lied. Only thing I had to do was find Lee and tell her that payday was right around the corner.

"This afternoon?" she tried.

"I have a lunch. How's three?"

"I'll make it up to you," she said, the schoolgirl now gone compellingly bad.

"See you at three," I said, summoning a hint of ice to my tone. I'd never been good at the hard-to-get thing, and I was stinking it up now, to be sure.

We hung up simultaneously.

Back in the saddle. Why, then, did I feel like horseshit?

I knew. And it was complicated.

> 51 <

ENTRY #13: SMOKERS—rights or no rights, say what you will, for the most part they have one thing in common: the world is their ashtray.
—from *Bullshit in America*, by Wolfgang Schmitt

"You need to know, I'm pissed at you guys."

I was driving to Kelly's downtown penthouse that afternoon as I spoke the words. Thing was, there was nobody in the Benz with me. I was talking to the mobile phone on the center console, and anyone else who happened to be listening in. Despite a perfectly sunny California day, the top was up, to make sure my ramblings were easily heard. Besides, I had to admit, I really liked playing with the retractable hardtop.

It was time for Wolf to bare his soul.

I'd just returned from a drive north to Menlo Park to check in at the Arielle building, and my dander was up. Lee wasn't in—she still hadn't responded to my last eight phone messages—and on something slightly more premeditated than a lark, I asked the robotic receptionist if Tracy Ericson happened to be in. She'd never heard the name. I suggested a quick check of the employee phone book—for a good time, try second-guessing a career receptionist—which bore the same discouraging result. She suggested I have a nice day; I told her there wasn't a chance in hell of that happening, which seemed to make her happy.

So much for my conspiracy theories. Then again, I'd always thought Oswald acted alone, so what did I know.

I had made it to the parking lot when I got another idea. I went back in, this time holding the picture of Tracy in my hand. She studied it a few moments before her eyes widened in recognition.

"Yeah, I've seen her a few times. Tracy, right?"

"Tracy Ericson."

"Sure. She works for Mr. Scott. Personal staff."

I nodded, trying not to show a reaction. "So, what does that mean?"

Just as quickly as it had arrived, the pleasure in her eyes melted away.

"What is this in regard to?"

Maybe I was tired, maybe I was caught up in the infamous tangled web we weave, but the question froze me. I just backed away from the counter, mouth open.

I left quickly, before security arrived.

And now here I was, heading north on the 101, talking to Banger and Scott, wherever they might be.

"I'm pissed because you've put me in a no-win situation here. You send me in to play Nelson Scott's game, fine. You ask me to listen for incriminating evidence, I do that. I listen, you listen, and guess what, we get zilch. Nada. You tell me to stay in there when things get tough, and because there's a pot of gold at the end of the rainbow, I hang. Then a body turns up, and you guys disappear on me. What you didn't tell me was that Kelly Scott would make me rethink my motives. Pot of gold, hell, it isn't worth it. This isn't working. There is no dotted line to her husband's illegal activities. Hell, there probably *aren't* any illegal activities. It's no longer my problem. I'm done."

On that note, I let a few miles go by, composing my close.

"I'm going to see her now, and I'm pulling the plug. For her. She deserves better."

I paused, clipped by the emotion in what had begun as a sort of therapeutic unloading.

She *did* deserve better. High maintenance and all. She had been nothing short of sweet and generous with me. She had taken me into her bed and into her heart. And in doing so, she had shown me how to feel again.

Oh, what a tangled web, indeed.

I picked up Lee's phone and brought it to my mouth, blowing into it, as if testing a microphone.

"Goodbye, Banger. You've got a nice smile for someone so smart. So do you, Short, for someone so low on hormones. I'm outta here. See you kids in tax court."

I rolled down the window and threw the phone out, wondering how that was sounding on their end.

And wondering how long it would take before they came for me.

I wasn't sure about the logistics of parking in the lot under Kelly's building—there was a guard, and in my two visits I'd not noticed a guest parking stall—so I grabbed a one-hour meter across the street. I had a pocketful of quarters, so what the hell.

"Hey, what's up?" I said, flashing my best Dale Carnegie catalog smile to the doorman. I recognized him from the parking garage, where he apparently did double duty. He should have recognized me, too, since he'd done a once-over on my bogus Arizona driver's license.

"Help you, sir?"

What *was* it with these people? I took a deep breath and tried again.

"I get it. It's pretend-you-don't-know-who-I-am day, right?"

"I know who you are, sir."

I nodded. Judging from the expression on his face, you'd think I was here to check his green card. Judging from his teeth, he had his picture in the lobby at RJ Reynolds.

"So you know why I'm here. Sir."

His blank expression morphed into impatience, like he had something better to do. He picked up the telephone and buzzed the penthouse. I heard him announce me by name, the prick. Guess his memory was fine after all.

Then he listened for a few seconds, his eyes brightening somewhat before he hung up. Good news, from his point of view.

"Mrs. Scott isn't here."

Our eyes engaged, two men on the verge.

"She's expecting me," I said.

"Apparently not."

"So who was that?"

"Mrs. Scott's personal assistant. Who is *not* expecting you."

"Let me talk to her." When he didn't move, I added the word "now," with no lack of attitude.

Same look as he picked up the telephone. This time he turned his back to me, covering his mouth with a hand while speaking in hushed tones. He nodded as he turned back to face me, replacing the receiver as he did.

"She'll be right down."

He held my gaze. We were the same age, same build, but I knew I could take him. It was something men knew with a glance, barring something unpredictable like martial arts training or a severe mean streak. I could kick this guy's ass, and right then I desperately wanted to do so.

I stepped off the landing to the sidewalk to wait for Cruella. Last thing I needed right now was to put Kelly's doorman in the hospital.

Five long minutes later, the door opened. Lynn wasn't at all what I expected—I had her pegged as matronly, a Miss Moneypenny type without the flirty personality. But she was a peer, the girl from the yearbook you can't remember.

She charged me as if I'd threatened one of her children. Her hands were on her hips and she was standing in my space, close enough so that I could smell the gum she was chewing.

You can't coach class, even in this league.

"What is it with you?" she asked.

"Nice to meet you, too. Kelly invited me, here I am." I held my hands out to the side, palms up in humble supplication.

"She's not here."

"So it seems."

"What part of *hit the road, Jack* don't you understand?"

The doorman had joined us on the sidewalk, just in case. I wasn't sure which one I wanted to clock first.

"I think there's a misunderstanding," I said.

"I'd say that's correct."

"Sir," said the doorman, stepping between us with a sudden Bruce Willis swagger, "it's time to go. Right now."

He was willing to lock asses if I was. Instead, we

locked eyes, contemplating choices with career implications and beyond.

Then I made my move. Only a knee to the groin would have been more effective in the moment. Oldest trick in the book.

I smiled. A *this-isn't-over* smirk, with *I'll-see-you-around-pal* overtones. His face remained void of expression; if he'd been any cooler he'd have drooled on his cheesy Universal Studios–issue uniform.

It was a long ride back to Los Gatos Hills. I desperately wanted to hit something, but hey, it wasn't my car.

I could hear my phone ringing as soon as I turned off the engine in the garage. I vaulted over the door without opening it and sprinted inside.

Missed it.

I slammed my hand on the granite counter. The pain reminded me I was losing it, that if I didn't find a way out of this mess quickly, I would snap.

I would test the rumor that the truth shall set you free. We'd see about that.

Then the phone rang again. It was Kelly. "Wolf, thank God I got you."

"Thank God you did."

"Lynn told me what happened. I'm *so* sorry."

"Lynn needs a pay cut. A haircut, too."

"She's overprotective. I'm having trouble with her."

"No shit."

"I'm sorry I wasn't there. Something came up."

"No shit," I said again.

"You're mad." Little-girl tone. Probably been working like a charm for decades.

"I must be," I said, spinning a decent return I hoped she'd interpret correctly.

"Let me make it up to you."

I let her hear me exhale loudly.

"Please?"

"Will you *be* there this time?"

"You have no idea how I'll be there. What would you like me to wear?"

"You think I'm easy," I said, softer now.

"I *know* you're easy. Nelson is gone, doesn't fly in until morning, and he'll go straight to the office from the airport. Let's meet up at the Villa. I have a meeting early evening. I'll send the staff home. We'll play vampire games. I suck you, you suck me."

"Kelly, listen to me. We have to talk."

A moment of quiet. Then her voice sounded genuinely frightened.

"You ditching me, Wolf?"

"No. We just need to talk. Scary stuff, waking-up-together stuff. You remember scary, right?"

"I love scary. We'll talk. Say, nine thirty?"

"Nine thirty. You'll be there."

"Oh yeah. See you tonight."

She hung up before I could say good-bye.

I pulled the tape recorder away from the receiver and clicked it off.

> 52 <

San Francisco, California

Boyd Gavin thought he was dreaming. In the half-light of dawn there were ghosts in his bedroom, moving without sound.

Then one of them sat on the bed next to him.

Gavin opened his eyes and tried to sit up, but something stopped him. Something hard. Within moments his brain comprehended that it was the barrel of a gun—the click of the hammer was a telling clue—pressing against his skull right behind the ear. Pressing hard, forcing his head back onto the pillow.

"Not quite yet," said a calm voice, a man, positioned as a gray silhouette in the periphery of Gavin's vision. The hand not holding the gun rested gently on Gavin's shoulder.

"What the hell . . ."

The free hand moved to his face, a finger pressing against his lips. He heard the intruder whisper, "Shhhh," like you would to a child waking from a nightmare.

"Not quite yet," the man said again. His voice was low and textured, like a cheesy FM radio promo.

Noises were coming from his closet. He pivoted his head against the pillow for a better angle, seeing that the door was open. Someone was inside, rooting around.

Shit. The money.

The gun pressed harder against his skull. Hard enough to cause pain, more than just a reminder to remain still.

Gavin watched the closet, trying to weigh his options, finding none. Whoever was in the closet now stood up, turning to face the room.

"Got it," said the closet guy. No, not a guy at all. A woman. Holding the suitcase that contained the Nelson Scott cash. A million and a half. He had meant to move it soon, but hadn't solidified a plan he liked. Money like that left a trail, and it was harder than you'd think to move it quietly.

Bloody hell, he was being robbed.

He felt the man lean closer now, the pressure on his skull even greater than before. He could smell foul breath, coffee and cigarettes, something rank from deep within the tissues.

"Now," said the man, almost sadly.

Gavin tried to pivot, make a move of some kind. But instantly he felt a pillow clamp down over his head.

And then it hit. Like a driver kissing a Titleist on the screws. Like Barry hitting another one into the Bay. With a scalding flash, the world went white, and then he spun, tumbling through an abyss of time, wind roaring through his being. The sound of screaming.

His flesh was gone, already a fading memory.

Other than a moment of intense heat, there had been no pain. Only the sensation of falling.

He didn't hear the second shot at all.

The woman from the closet put the bag full of Nelson Scott's cash down at her feet. She nodded at her partner, who immediately turned his attention to

BAIT AND SWITCH

the man on the bed. She then withdrew a plastic sandwich bag from her jacket pocket. She didn't look up as she heard the sound of the gun, two quick pops, loud but not alarmingly so. Especially when you knew it was coming. A neighbor might have heard, but maybe not. That didn't matter either way.

There were tweezers in the bag. Along with several strands of hair taken from a house in Portland by a man she'd never met, and never would.

Kneeling by the foot of the bed, she withdrew the tweezers and used them to extract one of the strands of hair. Like her partner, she wore blue latex surgical gloves purchased at a Rite Aid in Oakland the previous day.

Then she waited. She knew better than to rush him.

Her partner moved away from the dead man, pulling the pillow back with him. A mass of tissue that had once been Boyd Gavin's head was soaking into the mattress. The eye that remained intact stared into eternity.

The man carefully put the pistol he had used into a plastic bag.

The woman stepped forward, holding the tweezers at eye level. Then she released their hold, allowing a strand of hair to float downward, landing on the dead man's neck.

Several other strands were left behind in a similar manner, all very forensically sound, based on proven data.

The data never lied. The data, if you honored it, could save your ass.

> 53 <

ENTRY #2: THE SINGLE-GUNMAN THEORY—
the real bullshit here is that we'll never know for sure.
Despite the significant evidence, we still need someone
to tell us it's okay to believe what we see, rather than
what we were told.
—from *Bullshit in America*, by Wolfgang Schmitt

I'd learned a few things from women. Like how to skin the cat using various and sundry means, the most effective of which involved centering the crosshairs of your strategy right on your opponent's jugular. Thinking of all the creative ways that I had been manipulated like a sycophantic Muppet by the women in my life, I placed the following call to Lee van Wyke, making sure my tone sounded as if I'd just stumbled back to base camp after a failed assault on Everest's summit.

"Hey Lee, Wolf here . . . listen, I don't know what's going on—you've obviously got more important things on your plate—but, ah, this just isn't working anymore. At least, not for me. And by the way, Kelly's not buying what I'm selling. I'll leave the phone and the Benz keys on the counter. Tank's full, by the way. Thanks for all you've done. You've been very generous, and your tennis game rocks, but life's too short for unreturned phone calls and a diminishing sense of self-respect. That's my story, and I'm stickin' to it."

I hung up.

She called me back within three minutes.

She opened with, "Whoa, slow down, cowboy."

"You remember when you were a kid," I said, maintaining the same oxygen-starved tenor, "there was always this one poor schmuck who'd get invited to meet the crowd somewhere, all the cool kids, but nobody was there when he arrived?"

"That happen to you, Wolf? I'm so sorry."

"Matter of fact, it did. That's how I feel now."

"No wonder you have issues."

I really wanted to ask *what* issues she was referring to, but that was another conversation. She took the pause for drawn blood and continued.

"I've been out of the country," she said. "I assumed from your messages that everything was copasetic. Sorry, but I never was much of a cheerleader. Or a babysitter, for that matter."

"That your version of an apology?"

"I haven't apologized to anyone since 1984. So what's this horseshit about quitting?"

"Kelly isn't going for it," I lied.

"That's not what I hear. And since when did you turn into the all-seeing interpreter of the mysterious female mind?"

She made a good point.

"Listen to me," Lee went on. "There's something you don't know, exciting news. Are you listening?"

"You sound like a babysitter to me."

"Libby Payne called, Kelly's lawyer. They may be willing to renegotiate the prenup, and I think it's because you have her client's full and hormonally charged attention. I'd say Kelly's rethinking the consequences of her greed. She'll take a reduced settlement in exchange for her domestic freedom."

Consequences of her greed. That was precious.

"Right. Hey, what's a few hundred million dollars between friends, I always say."

"Wolf, think about what this means. You've done your job, better than we dared hope. Talk about consequences. Don't walk now—you'd be deserting yourself more than anyone. You're not that stupid."

I allowed a moment to pass, giving the impression the news had stunned me into silence, that I was suddenly overwhelmed by the self-serving logic of it. Or perhaps I *was* that stupid.

Actually, she did have my attention.

"I get paid?"

"Every dime. Trust me, you're still cheap."

"That's exactly how I feel."

"Have you checked your account lately, Wolf?"

"No. I've been too busy trying to reach you."

"You might want to check. I'm meeting with her attorney tonight over dinner. If I can get her to initial an agreement, then I need to meet with you to sign a release. Tonight. I'm leaving the country again tomorrow morning."

A yellow flag went up in my mind. I was no law student, but my signing a release at this stage of the game would be like Oswald trying to cop a plea. And we all know how *that* turned out.

I said, "I'm supposed to be with her tonight."

"I thought you said it was going south?"

You could almost hear my coronary artery dilating.

"I don't know what she wants."

"Midnight, your place. By then it won't matter, especially if she's dumping you. If she's not, get a headache. Either way, you be there."

BAIT AND SWITCH

This certainly complicated things. It wasn't what I'd expected to hear, and as I had learned from my involvement thus far, the best course of action was to step back and let the chips fall where they will. In this case, right into the dumper.

But I had other chips. Ones Lee Van Wyke had no idea existed.

"Midnight," I said quietly.

She hung up without saying another word.

Within minutes, I had the laptop booted up and online. Seconds later, I was on the website of my Cayman bank, punching in the series of codes I had so lovingly memorized earlier.

A half-million dollars was there. Four hundred grand had been deposited earlier in the day. All in my name.

Like they say in Sin City, money talks, bullshit walks. And I was suddenly in the mood for a romantic stroll down Main Street.

Besides, it was far too late for yellow flags.

Lee Van Wyke hung up the phone, unable to keep a dark grin off her face.

"He bought it?" said the woman in the room with her.

"They always buy it. Someday I'll meet a man who isn't significantly less complex than my African Grey parrot."

The other woman smiled back at her. "No turning back now, is there."

"Unless someone rolls away the stone and a new religion is born, you could say we're committed."

Lee intended it as dark humor, but Kelly Scott's face showed signs of the stress and doubt she'd been harboring since this whole thing began. Lee saw it and went to her, embracing her like the mother the years had taught her to be where Kelly was concerned.

"Wolf thinks you're not interested. That you're dumping him tonight."

"The man is no dummy."

Lee rocked her gently back and forth.

"Nelson has no idea how lucky he is."

Kelly spoke into Lee's shoulder, the jacket of a very expensive linen suit.

"To have the both of us," she said.

Lee pulled back to make eye contact, her hands gripping each of Kelly's shoulders, a posture of emphasis.

"It's critical that Byron sees the two of you arguing. You need to throw Wolf out on his ear. Maybe have Byron do it. That'd be a nice touch, I think."

"I understand," said Kelly, though Lee had her doubts. Kelly had been second-guessing every part of this since day one. Other than Byron, Kelly's bodyguard, she would be on her own tonight, and that put the entire project at risk.

"It's almost over, sweetheart," said Lee, pulling her back into the embrace while stroking the younger woman's hair.

"I'm glad," said Kelly. "He's sort of sweet, you know."

Lee said nothing in response. Her face was a statue, beaten bland by decades in the wind.

Ten minutes later, Lee Van Wyke was airborne in the Arielle helicopter, streaking high above the developing gridlock of the Valley—the ants, she called them—toward a dinner meeting in the city. But not with Kelly's lawyer. Libby Payne was in Maui working on her tan, and had no intention of renegotiating Kelly's prenup. Tonight's dinner meeting was with representatives of the San Francisco Symphony, making their annual pitch for more of Nelson Scott's money.

Conveniently, it would provide her with a bulletproof alibi when the shit hit the fan, which it was about to do.

In a matter of hours, in fact.

> 54 <

ENTRY #177: TIMESHARE SALES PITCHES—a free dinner for coming to a presentation, or a free weekend in Vegas for sitting through two hours listening to a knee-breaker giving you his cash-flow analysis. Just try saying no. Go ahead, we dare you.
—from *Bullshit in America*, by Wolfgang Schmitt

I figured black was the fashionable thing to wear. I had some Pierre Cardin slacks and a tight-fitting Nino Cerruti sweater—just what the modern vampire might wear to a romantic tryst in a medieval castle. It was eight thirty and the day had gone slowly. All the players were accounted for now, so there was nothing for me to do but await my fate.

In fact, I had taken a nap in front of the television. I awoke hungry, ordered pizza—Domino's, just what every young capitalist eats on his nights alone—and watched a movie to kill time. Nine thirty couldn't come soon enough.

As I fell in and out of my unscheduled catnap, and then throughout the course of the movie, I kept having to remind myself that this thing had to end ugly. My salvation—my only choice now—was in coming clean with Kelly. Someone had died, an innocent, and I had to assume it was to cover a loose end that connected to Scott. To complicate things, I had developed feelings for her, and to take the charade any further would be an unthinkable betrayal, not only of Kelly, but of myself. This much gave me a sort of giddy high—the valiant knight doing the right thing, music up, credits roll, break out the hankies. But just when that movie review started to feel all warm and fuzzy, I realized she'd be outraged at having been subjected to such a Machiavellian scheme, with me as the point guard. I was the guy trying to bilk her out of three million a month, no way around it. She'd have me bounced down the mountain on my ass, or worse.

I changed back into Dockers and a Polo. No more bullshit from Wolf. At least I'd have a nice down payment on a killer sailboat in Aruba, where my broken kneecaps could mend in peace. As soon as I got out of the hospital where Kelly's bodyguard would put me.

The doorbell rang while I was turning off the stereo to leave, perhaps for the last time. The grinder in my stomach was already going full-bore, but the chime put it on red-zone adrenaline overload. A dozen possibilities raced through my head as I went to answer, none more unlikely than the face that greeted me when I swung open the door. A million and a half for a remodel, and they forgot the little peephole.

"We have to talk," said Tracy, brushing past me into the condo, leaving me next to the door with a jaw fallen wide enough to park a minivan.

I'd never seen her like this. She had aged ten years since our last chance encounter, the coven thing long gone, replaced by the eyes of a woman whose ambitions were desperate. Her hair was pulled back and tied with a nondescript band. She wore jeans and a light jacket, all very Target instead of her usual Neiman Marcus edge. Even her nails were short and plain, something I'd never seen on Tracy before.

"Where to start," she said, sitting on the couch, her eyes scanning the condo as if she knew what she was looking for. "Do you have an ashtray?"

"No."

Her eyes snapped to me, locking on.

"It's over, Wolf. The whole thing . . . it's done."

My expression teetered between confusion and the keenest interest.

"I know where you're going tonight," she said, "and I know what you think you're going there for. But you don't know *shit*, Wolf. Trust me."

"You're Deadman. Wayne Rogers's girlfriend."

Her expression was instantly complex, the name obviously surprising her. Or perhaps stinging her. But I could also sense she was pleased that I had followed the scent, the trail leading us to this bizarre reunion.

She nodded, averting her eyes. "Before I say any more, there's something I want you to know. Everything I've done, everything I'm about to tell you, I've done for us."

"Well now, there's a can of worms."

"I mean it," she said. "This is all for us, Wolf."

No matter how smooth the scar, how neatly the past has been tucked into its crypt, such words tend to tear the heart right out of someone who'd been lying to themselves for months.

"You have my attention," I said, fighting back emotions I didn't want her to see. Not yet, at least.

She started with what I had already surmised. That she had been seeing Wayne Rogers when he'd died in an accident on a highway leading to Santa Cruz. That she'd had his laptop, and that she had used it

BAIT AND SWITCH

to send me the Deadman emails, warning me that all was not as it seemed. To keep my head out of my ass when going forward.

"Let's start there," I interrupted. "Why warn me? How did you even know I was involved at this point?"

"Because I *got* you involved."

Neither of us flinched, maintaining solid eye contact. I was glad I was sitting, because the room began to move.

"You think Nelson Scott sent someone to check you out based on your glowing reputation, because of some ad you were in or a magazine article you wrote? Please. I knew exactly what he needed and why, and you were the perfect choice."

"How, may I ask, did you know that?"

She averted her eyes again. "Because it was all my idea."

I drew a deep breath, hoping to still a wave of vertigo. The air was suddenly scalding hot, sweat breaking under my collar. It occurred to me that the condo was in all likelihood bugged, and that the cavalry might just swoop down on us at any moment. Then again, whoever was listening would want to hear all this, too. Question was, would they be wearing white hats or black hats when they arrived? I wasn't at all sure any more.

"Because you worked for him," I said. "On Scott's personal staff."

She nodded, not particularly proud of the answer.

"Okay. There's a million more questions, but back to number one. Why the cryptic warnings? Why not just come to me, tell me what's going on, if you wanted me to cover my ass? Why hang me out there?"

"Because you're a fucking Boy Scout, Wolf, and

you'd have never signed on. You had to discover the truth for yourself, and when you did, when you realized it was me in your corner all along, maybe then you'd trust me."

She bit her lip, carefully considering her next words.

"It was the only way we'd both get paid."

I wanted to rip into that one, but more important things were at hand. If I got an explanation, fine. If I didn't, well, that was fine, too.

Perhaps ol' Schmitt was making progress in his quest for peace of mind. Now if he could just stitch up that bleeding gash in his heart, which had been torn open yet one more time.

"I have to go," I said.

"You're not going anywhere tonight," she said. "If nothing else, because your car is gone."

"Say that again?"

"Go look. They took the car."

I squinted at her, noticed that she seemed embarrassed, perhaps ashamed. I got up and hurried to the garage.

Which was empty. I'd slept right through the heist.

I came back and plopped onto the couch in the same place. I leaned forward, covering my face with my hands. Tracy didn't know it, but I was scrambling to think of a way I'd get up to the Villa without being late. She came over and sat beside me, putting her arms around me in comfort. A familiar smell came with her, and for a moment my sanity was in question.

"It was never yours," she said.

It was then that I felt the slight sting in my back, a pinpoint of pain. For a moment, I thought it was nothing, a little muscle twitch, but then I knew. She had plunged a hypodermic needle into my shoulder, holding me firmly as she depressed the plunger.

I spun away, springing to my feet. She sat back on the couch to miss my swinging arm, a syringe in her hand, her eyes wide and frightened.

"What the hell . . ."

"Listen to me, Wolf. You only have a few seconds."

A few seconds, hell. I was already going down. I leaned over to steady myself on the coffee table before involuntarily sinking to one knee.

"I had to choose," said Tracy.

"Choose? Choose what?"

"You or her," she said, her voice further away than before. "She's dead, Wolf. I'm sorry, but I had to choose."

I opened my mouth, but no sound escaped. I fell slowly back to the carpet, the room now in full rotation. I prayed I would pass out before throwing up—literally, amen—an event which was right around the corner.

Tracy followed me down, leaning over me, her hands touching my face with a tender caress.

"She's dead, Wolf. You killed her. I'm so sorry . . . I had to choose . . ."

Then a black cloud materialized in the air, swallowing her whole.

> 55 <

Kelly Scott's doorman was actually a bodyguard by trade. He had a small office just off the entry foyer in the Villa, with a clear view of the circular courtyard and, several hundred yards beyond, the gate to the estate. A panel, which guests liked to marvel reminded them of something in a nuclear reactor control room, displayed several LCD screens, with live feeds covering the eight-car garage area, the gate, the pool, and the courts, and a scanning view to the other side of the house. There were also communications links to the police and fire departments, a direct line to the Arielle offices, and a radio hookup for the helicopter. Next to the security panel was a small portable television, presently showing an NBA playoff game, Lakers versus Kings, Kings by six.

The big man's heart skipped a beat when a tone signaled that the front gates were opening. No one had called from there, which meant that whoever was approaching knew the code. Mrs. Scott had not told him to expect anyone, and because of the hour, he was immediately tense.

He turned his attention to the appropriate monitor. Floodlights, triggered by the opening gate, illuminated the entire drive, and he quickly recognized the car. It was a new Benz SL, black on black, the one driven by that pretty boy Mrs. Scott had been banging lately. The one Ms. Bitch Van Wyke had been doing before Kelly took him. Who knows, maybe they just traded the dude back and forth, like some toy from an adult store. White people were crazy sometimes.

He watched the car pull into the brick-paved circular landing in front of the door. Strangely, the boy toy wasn't driving. Two people, a man and woman he didn't recognize, got out and approached the front door. Maybe it had something to do with the car—maybe the guy just split and they were bringing it back.

He turned his attention to a different monitor now.

The screen showed them standing on the porch. If he didn't know better, he'd think the Seventh-day Adventists had come to pitch salvation, but there hadn't been a door-to-door solicitor since he'd worked here, going on five years now, and it was damn late. Besides, no Seventh-day Adventist on the planet had a ride like that one, and no one who had a ride like that would be caught dead in those Kmart threads.

Whoever these people were had some serious explaining to do. And fast, since it was the fourth quarter and he didn't want to miss a shot.

His name was Byron, but, like his mobile bodyguard counterpart, Rashod, he'd adopted an Islamic name, "Jamal"—something he'd come to regret because it was no longer cool, and certainly not politically correct. Jamal checked his weapon, making sure the safety was off, and went to the front door.

He opened it boldly. He was six-seven, and he knew the effect he had on people at first blush. Even Mrs. Scott's new boyfriend, who wasn't so small himself, had a look of respect on his face when his eyes first set on Jamal. Respect, man, that was the name of the game in this business.

"Hi," said the woman, smiling broadly. She was wearing what appeared to be a raincoat, three-quarter length, and her hair was a couple of decades out of style, sort of Billie Holliday in need of a cut and curl.

"Help you?" he said, trying for an expression that straddled impatient and cordial.

The bullet hit him in the throat. He'd been looking at the woman and hadn't seen the man, who was shorter than her, going for a gun at all. The guy'd had it in his hand the entire time, hiding it behind his back.

He should have seen it. That thought—his last—and the anger that came with it, was clear as could be as he realized he'd been hit.

Jamal stumbled backwards, both hands clutching at his throat. It was the force of the impact that caused him to go down, rather than the trauma of the wound itself, which would actually take nearly a minute to affect his motor skills if he could just keep breathing.

None of that would matter. Jamal was already fumbling to get his own gun out of its holster when the next bullet struck him in the temple. The gun never made it out, and Jamal never felt the impact of his head cracking against the imported marble floor in the foyer.

The man and the woman stepped over the body as if they were hiking and had happened upon a downed tree. At the end of the hall, they exchanged hand signals with stealthy military precision, the man proceeding into the house on this floor, the woman drawing her own handgun as she went up the stairs.

BAIT AND SWITCH

Kelly was on the deck outside the master suite, nursing a glass of wine. A fire was burning in the huge brick outdoor hearth, and a movie soundtrack was playing in the background. She wasn't, however, nearly as placid as she appeared. Wolf was well over an hour late, and no one was answering his phone. Any number of things could have happened, none of them good.

She didn't hear a sound as she considered the possibilities, which was why the touch of someone's hand on her shoulder made her scream out loud.

Wolf. Finally. Thank God.

She turned to see a woman she did not recognize. Her eyes immediately scanned the rest of the room, perhaps looking for Jamal, who would have announced any visitors. Her attention went back to the woman, who was holding a latex-gloved finger to her lips, asking for quiet.

It was then Kelly saw the gun in the woman's other hand.

"Who . . . what the hell . . ." But her voice tailed off. Robbery was her first notion, but nothing about this woman supported that idea, and the logistics of her getting this far didn't compute. Instinctively she realized this had something to do with Wolf and Gavin and the deception at hand, and for a fleeting moment, she thought the woman might actually be here in support of that objective. Violence was, after all, on the agenda for the evening. Wolf's absence was somehow at the root of this intrusion.

Kelly started to get up, but the woman shook her head, raising the gun for emphasis. When Kelly started to speak, she again put her finger up to her mouth.

In that moment, Kelly realized that she had been betrayed. And she knew who had done it.

A man entered the bedroom a few seconds later. As he walked toward Kelly he raised his gun—this one was smaller than the one held by the woman—to eye level, stopping within arm's reach.

Then he lashed the pistol out, striking Kelly on the side of the head. She went down immediately, an arc of blood from her mouth spraying across the tile on the deck.

The man quickly knelt beside her.

"A crime of passion," he said. Then he backhanded the gun against the other side of her head, knocking her momentarily senseless.

She regained enough of her senses to realize that she was looking straight into the barrel of the gun in the man's hands.

"Now," she heard him say softly, almost gently, as if he wished it could end some other way.

But it couldn't. The ending had been written and paid for weeks ago.

The assassins made one more stop before leaving for the evening. In Jamal's security office by the front door, in a cabinet beneath the counters, were several digital recording devices, one for each monitor. The man sat at the computer console and began typing in commands, while the woman stood by the window, looking out at the still-illuminated drive and the car parked at the base of the steps leading to the front door. She now held the gun that had been used to kill Jamal and Kelly.

Working with the confidence of someone who knew his way around a security panel, the man brought an image to the screen. He hit a key, and an image filled the monitor. It showed the Benz they'd arrived in coming through the gates and heading down the drive. The car moved out of frame and was gone.

The man hit a few more keys, bringing a new angle to the screen, images recorded from another camera. This one showed the Benz entering the frame and coming to a stop in front of the doorway. Just as it was clear there were two people inside, he hit another series of keys. The image reversed to the point at which the car was just about to enter the frame.

He worked for six more minutes, erasing disks, the house with its two dead bodies as quiet as a morgue after hours. When he was satisfied, he held out his hand, and, like a nurse giving the surgeon a scalpel, the woman wordlessly handed over the gun she'd been holding.

The man fired into several of the recording devices, destroying the hard drives. All the police would find intact would be an image of the Benz arriving, with the time of day seen in the lower right-hand corner. The killer, who'd obviously intended to destroy this evidence, had been sloppy, or maybe just unlucky.

The only fingerprints in the car—which was registered in Kelly Scott's name—would belong to the new boyfriend, the mystery man from Arizona. Everyone on the Villa staff, and everyone in Kelly Scott's life, knew he'd been driving the new Mercedes that Kelly had, on a romantic whim, bought for his use several weeks before.

> 56 <

ENTRY #6: CHARLTON HESTON AND THE GUN LOBBY—"Guns don't kill people, people kill people." That's like saying crack doesn't kill kids, dealers do. So let's just legalize the drug and arrest all the bad guys. Same bullshit, different lobbyists.
—from *Bullshit in America*, by Wolfgang Schmitt

Having never been under the knife, I didn't know much about anesthesiology other than the fact that its perpetrators all drive new German cars. A couple of colonoscopies—not my idea of a good time—were thankfully the closest I'd ever been to that particular narcotic experience. Which was why I was so thoroughly confused when whatever Tracy had stabbed into my back began to wear off. I had no idea what time it was, or even where I was. My first comprehension was that it was dark outside, that the lights were off inside, and that my head and stomach felt as if I'd spent the last month test-riding roller coasters. At first, my only certainty was that I was lying on a strange sofa in a strange room. Only after sitting up and seeing the illuminated screen of my laptop computer on the granite kitchen counter did I piece together the particulars of my whereabouts. I was still in the condo where I'd been living the lie of

Wolfgang Schmitt, wealthy high-tech playboy from Scottsdale.

That, and the sudden awareness that someone was in the room with me.

"Please don't move," said the silhouette sitting in the facing chair. It was a man's voice, but because of my state of medically-induced fog, it sounded a lot like Barry White after too much Jack Daniel's.

"No problem," I said, slumping back into the cushions. If I'd tried to stand up, I'd have tumbled nose-first into the plate-glass coffee table separating me from my visitor.

I squinted at the man, but everything in the room was in motion. When I looked toward the kitchen, I now noticed that someone was sitting at my computer, and that it was in all probability—nothing was yet a sure thing—a woman. It was then that I remembered it was Tracy who had been here when I went under. That, and the memory of what she had said— *She's dead, Wolf . . . you killed her*—led me to the conclusion that I was as good as dead, too.

But the woman at the table wasn't Tracy. It was Banger. Banging away at the keyboard. And the man in front of me was Special Agent Short, her partner in crime.

"Lemme guess," I said, the words spoken without spaces between them. "Suicide note. How am I doin' so far?"

Short didn't answer. Instead, I saw him look over at Banger, as if she were the one to answer my question. I saw her nod at him. Then, inexplicably, she got up and walked through the door leading to the garage.

Time to go. No way was this a good thing.

Short stood up and came toward me. He was holding a gun in his hand, pointing it at my face.

"Guess you're still pissed off about the microphone thing," I said.

I tried to move, some valiant effort to save myself, but quickly realized that the modern miracle of anesthesiology was a formidable adversary in such a situation.

He pressed the barrel of the gun against my temple. Then his smile went away.

"Now," he said calmly.

I closed my eyes, too stoned to give a shit what happened next.

The man fell on top of me. In the darkness behind my closed eyes I heard an incomprehensible sound, a cross between a sack of flour dropping on kitchen tile and the quick exhalation of breath usually accompanying a sucker punch to the gut. Despite the noises—I was expecting a gunshot and a choir of angels—and the sudden heaviness on my chest, it was still difficult to open my eyes.

When I did, I saw that Tracy was standing above me, already pulling the dead weight of Special Agent Short off of me. The tennis racket she had used—mine, which had been in the garage—to club him behind the head was still in her hand. She wore gloves and a different jacket than before.

"You all right?" she asked, not looking at me as she picked up the gun from where it had landed on the floor.

"If the headache doesn't kill me," I said, struggling to sit up again. "Nice forehand, by the way."

Tracy ignored Short for a moment and helped prop me into an upright position. Then she cupped my face in her hands, brushing back my hair in an expression of what would otherwise have been affection. Her eyes were wildly intense.

"Listen to me. You have to do precisely what I tell you. Are you awake? Do you understand what I'm saying?"

I nodded, though not sure that I was doing so truthfully.

She held the gun up in front of my face. Not pointing it, just showing it to me.

"Recognize this?"

I squinted. The gun looked vaguely familiar, as she knew it would. Then the vagueness went away in one sickening wave of clarity.

It looked familiar because it belonged to me. It was the gun I'd planned on using on the asshole who kept kicking in my skylight. Last I saw of it was in a drawer back in Portland.

"Wolf, listen very carefully. Kelly is *dead*. They took your car to the Villa tonight and they killed her . . . with *your* gun. Do you hear that clearly? *Your* gun."

The pudgy little body on the floor at her feet suddenly let out a moan, twisting like a snake beneath a boot. Tracy made a face, quickly setting the gun on the coffee table. She reached into her pocket and withdrew a syringe, which she uncapped and plunged into Short's neck without hesitation. She capped the syringe and put it back into her pocket.

Short was no longer moaning.

Call me easily impressed, but I was markedly more alert than I had been moments before. Her attention returned to me as if none of that had happened.

"You don't see it, do you, you big naïve schmuck. The whole thing's been a sound stage from day one. Just step outside yourself and take a look. See what they put on the screen for the world to watch. Lee Van Wyke brings a new loverboy to town, a hot stud nobody knows. Handpicked for the role."

"That would be me," I said, my eyebrows raised.

She nodded with a comfortable old twinkle in her eye.

"That's not news in the Valley—the woman's a slut. She introduces him to Kelly Scott, who moves in when Lee is done with him. Not the first time that's happened, either, both before and after Kelly and Nelson separated. She buys you a car, lets you use her fancy new airplane, squires you around town like a side of beefcake. You, the new trophy boy with the big serve. Everybody assumes she's just making her husband jealous, that it'll never last. Nobody asks questions, nobody cares. Only person who thinks the paper trail is real is you."

I was already shaking my head.

"You fingered me for this," I said. "You were sleeping with Scott, scored some points by bringing me in."

She looked away, busted. That look, too, was familiar.

"But I'm here now, aren't I? I chose you. You want, I'll apologize later, make it up to you on a beach somewhere. For now, we have to get moving . . ."

"Time out. What about Scottsdale, the house, the plane, the pilot . . . ?"

Tracy's head was shaking more emphatically than mine had been. As if she was barely tolerating my need for clarity.

"Employees, loyal and very well paid. Some of the players on the periphery are in on it, others aren't, but nobody will talk. They never do. Money and fear are a very persuasive combination."

Like that hopeful young boy arriving at an empty house, party invitation in hand, I suddenly realized nobody was home. That I had been the centerpiece of an elaborately staged fiction worthy of a seven-figure advance. The Ashland Shakespearean Festival was already negotiating for the rights.

Staring off into space, I whispered, "Why?"

"Because Boyd Gavin was bleeding them dry."

I added, "Because Boyd Gavin audits Arielle. He and Wayne Rogers. Lemme guess: Gavin's dead, too."

Tracy had started nodding halfway through my oratory.

"Your gun, Wolf. Wake up and smell the embalming fluid."

"Wait . . . you said Kelly was dead . . ."

Her soft expression had *you poor, dumb child* written all over it.

"Wolfgang snapped. Kelly was dumping you, going back to Gavin, whom she seduced months ago to set this whole thing up. In the script you went over the edge at the news. You killed Gavin, you killed her, and then in a fit of psychopathic guilt you killed yourself. They find your gun, they talk to people and unearth your motive, they find your sad little note, end of program. What they *don't* find is a shred of the life you think you're living now. None of it can be traced."

She watched me process this for a moment.

"The fight at the restaurant," she went on. "You think that was coincidence? Lee got Gavin there with some line about Kelly wanting to see him, and you read your lines perfectly. Sixty people saw you almost cold-cock the poor bastard."

"The jealous new boyfriend."

Tracy was nodding again.

I began a fast-forward of the movie, all the scenes with Lee and me, with Kelly and me, and saw what the audience already knew. With my head up my ass, smelling all the money, I had no real vantage point to perceive the truth.

"But I don't understand . . . I mean, Kelly . . ." I began, the words trailing off.

"Deus ex machina," said Tracy, always one to bludgeon a perfectly good quote. "Nelson wanted her gone. It was part of the plan from the beginning. The play within the play. She had no way of seeing it coming."

"But you did," I said, suddenly sick to my stomach.

Tracy paused, her eyes drifting to the side. "I had to choose. I could stop them from killing her, or I could stop them from killing you."

Shaking my head, I said, "Wait, start over . . ."

She put up a hand, signaling a course change. "I'd love to stay and chat, but I have work to do. Can you stand up?"

Despite my shaking head, she helped me to my feet. I was steady, though not quite up for a set of doubles.

"Help me get him out of here." When I didn't move, she added, "Please?" with a sincerity that surprised me.

There would be time for answers later.

She went behind Short's head and hoisted him up under the shoulders. I took his feet, and we half-carried him through the kitchen and then into the garage, his ass and his limp hands dragging along the ground the entire way.

My SL 55 AMG—or what until tonight *had been* my SL 55 AMG—was back in its spot, trunk open. Banger and Short had taken it out from under me earlier in the day while I was napping, driven it to the Villa to kill Kelly, then returned to finish me off. Who would I call to report it stolen, anyhow?

Tracy shuffled toward the car, hoisting the still-unconscious man up onto the bumper when we arrived.

"We need to talk about this," I said, as out of breath as Tracy was.

"Go read your computer," she said between gulps of air. "You want to give back the money after that, you go ahead. My bet is, you're not that stupid. Get his feet."

I shoved Short's feet into the trunk, simultaneous with Tracy doing the same with his torso. When she slammed the trunk, I saw that someone was in the front seat of the Benz, passenger side. I went around to look. Special Agent Banger of the FBI was there, as unconscious as her partner, a huge lump visible on the side of her head.

"Same drug," said Tracy, patting her pocket. For the first time, her expression was as evil as her agenda was turning out to be. A chill shot up my spine, recalling how many times I'd seen that look, and how delicious it had once been when the dark lady bit was all leather and make-believe.

Steadying myself against the car, I closed my eyes and drew in a deep breath. Whatever the drug was, apparently it hung in there. When I began to slump to the floor, Tracy was quickly at my side, supporting my weight.

She kept her arms around me when I was stabilized, her mouth near my ear. She spoke softly, patiently.

"Here's what you do. You stay here, you hear me? Nobody would find you until morning anyway. You rest, get your head back. Read what's on your laptop,

Wolf. Read it carefully, and don't erase it. Then check your email. You decide. But do it knowing that I love you. That I did all this for us."

I pushed her back so our eyes could engage.

"For a moment there, I thought you said *us*."

Her eyes were actually moist. As if she'd just closed the cover on the latest Nora Roberts. I'd seen *that* look before, too, and I had always been helpless against it.

"I love you," she whispered. "I never stopped."

Like I said, shit happens.

So far, so good. For a while after she drove off in the Benz, one unconscious bad guy in the trunk and the other unconscious bad guy next to her, I felt pretty good about my chances. In fact, other than the headache and the departure of the car of my dreams, and the quite unexpected twist of Kelly's murder, this was playing out just like I'd hoped it would.

Then I remembered that the microcassette recorder I'd been using to cover my ass, along with the last few tapes that would do that job, were in the center console of the Benz.

I had to call someone, and quickly.

> 57 <

ENTRY # 241: HUNTING FOR SPORT—this is no different than some redneck ex-linebacker hitting the local tavern looking for a good fight, just for the sport of it. Where's your big gun then, Hunter Boy? You want meat, go to Safeway.
    —from *Bullshit in America*, by Wolfgang Schmitt

There was a suicide note on the computer screen. Banger had been putting the finishing touches on it just as I was waking up on the couch. According to the note, I had killed them all, just as Tracy had described, and the guilt was drowning me. I was sorry, so very sorry.

I saved it for later—wasn't sure why at the time—and opened up Outlook Express. As usual, I was simply doing precisely as Tracy had wished.

There was a new email from Deadman, but this time the text went straight at it.

Wolf—Here's what you don't know. On the day Wayne died, I went to his place and took his laptop, which had the Arielle audit file on it. My apartment was broken into twice soon thereafter, but they never found what they were looking for. I knew they suspected I had it, and if I didn't do something quick I would end up dead, like Wayne ended up dead. I was already work-

ing for a subsidiary of Arielle (this was how I met Wayne), and I took what I knew straight to Nelson Scott. Easy to get an appointment when you have that kind of leverage. I told him I'd erased the disk because I knew what it would do to the company, and also that my ass was covered if anything ever happened to me. I told him I wanted in, that what I'd done proved I was a company woman, and that I was dangerous, just his type. He hired me as a personal assistant, basically two hundred grand a year to lie by his pool with a laptop and a phone, moving money around for him. We got close, and soon we were sleeping together, which was implicit to our agreement. Not proud of that, but it is what it is. Gradually, over time, I got on the inside of a lot of scary shit, including the fact that Boyd Gavin was blackmailing the hell out of Nelson with the audit data. Gavin was part of the Wayne cover-up, too—he knew about it before it even happened—and part of the blackmail was to keep him quiet going forward. For an MBA from Stanford, the guy was stupid beyond belief. Now he's dead.

If your Catholic guilt is kicking in, get over it—the idea to get rid of Gavin was Kelly's. She'd seduce him, then they'd kill him and frame someone for his unfortunate demise. There is no pending divorce, never was—only a pending financial nightmare that would ruin them both. All they needed was a jealous lover to frame, someone who fit the Kelly Scott profile, and I knew just the guy. I'm so sorry, Wolf, but you have to believe me that I was working an angle all along. I wanted them all to burn for killing Wayne. And the more I was away from you, the more I realized I had to find a way to bring us together again. I wanted it all—my revenge, Wayne's justice, and a big pot of money for my trouble. And you. My plan and all that has occurred since evolved from that feeling, from my love for you. When

I saw you up in Portland, I knew I had made a terrible mistake in leaving you. But by then it was too late; I was in this thing with Nelson too deeply. But I saw the potential upside. An upside which is now well within our grasp.

Wolf, you must be strong. The police will come for you. But you will be cleared of suspicion, because I will give them something else to chase. You must tell the truth about everything that has happened—EXCEPT FOR THE MONEY. One of my jobs was to handle that aspect of the deal, and believe me when I tell you the money is there, that it's yours, and that it cannot be found unless you tell them. Admit you were hired by Nelson and Lee to seduce Kelly for the purpose of blowing up the prenuptial agreement. Kelly's lawyer will verify that such an agreement indeed exists. Tell them how Lee trained and prepared you to seduce Kelly. Be the patsy you were set up to be. You had nothing to do with Kelly's murder, other than your role as the ignorant patsy. Leave the rest to me. It's best if you don't know the details.

You must believe in me now, Wolf. You MUST trust me. I will get you out of this, and THE MONEY WILL BE OURS when I do. We will be together again.

If you do not believe me, check the balance in your account at noon tomorrow. If you still don't believe, take a look at the new world I will have created by the time they come for you. And ask yourself why I would do what I did, risk what I risked, when I could have simply let them burn you. Ask yourself about your account balance. Ask yourself until you know the answer.

If you love me at all, just hit REPLY. If you don't, then you have what you need. I am trusting you with my life. I believe in you. Believe in me. Believe in us.

    All my love, always—
    Tracy

As my dear dead grandmother used to say: *well, knock me over with a feather duster*.

I stared at the screen for thirty minutes. The condo was deathly quiet, except for the blood rushing through the capillaries in my ears, propelled by a cardiac locomotive on a mission.

What to do, what to do. I positioned the cursor over the button, caressing the button with my fingertip.

Defining moment, Wolf.

I hit the button. Then the unexpected happened—the screen flickered, then froze. I couldn't close the email, couldn't turn off the machine without unplugging it from the wall. Even then, because of the mobile battery, I couldn't shut it off for a reboot without actually pulling out the battery completely.

When I finally restarted the thing—or should I say, *tried* to restart it—I discovered just how brilliantly devious my Tracy truly was.

The computer had crashed and burned. My entire hard drive was fried. Windows was gone. All my data was gone. My Golf with Tiger Woods game was gone.

And, the email from Deadman was history. As were all the earlier emails Tracy had sent me using Wayne Rogers's account.

Viruses can do amazingly nasty things. This one had been the digital equivalent of the reel-to-reel tape that had given Mr. Phelps his marching orders at the beginning of every episode of *Mission: Impossible*. That particular piece of archaic media self-destructed in three seconds, right after saying, "*Good luck, Jim."* In my case, the hard drive had gone up in smoke at the first touch of a button—any button—after the infected email had been opened.

Ah, but Wolf, we hardly knew ye.

It hadn't been the Reply button I was touching. I had my finger on the Forward button, intending to send the email to Blaine Borgia for safekeeping until I decided how to handle this.

Apparently it had been decided for me.

But I had other ways to skin a goddamn cat. My sweet dead grandmother used to say *that*, too.

> 58 <

The Mercedes-Benz SL 55 AMG drove west on Highway 17 out of San Jose, winding into the hills that separated the valley from the ocean, carefully negotiating the turns that on so many other nights had claimed the lives of the distracted and the chemically handicapped. A little over halfway to Santa Cruz, at shortly before one in the morning, the car slowed and turned onto a dirt road. There was no traffic at all tonight at this hour, so no one saw it. Had there been a car, the Benz would have driven past and then returned minutes later. Just in case, though, the driver cut the lights, navigating the single-lane dirt road—once a notorious lovers' lane until two teenagers had been knifed here a few years earlier—using only its parking lights and the driver's memory.

Tracy Ericson had been here before, earlier that very day, in fact, preparing for this very moment. A moment that, for her, signified the turning point of her life. And of her passengers.

She parked the car, stopped the engine, and got out. There was significant cloud cover tonight, but the ambient light would serve her purpose. Her position was not visible from the highway, nor was it visible from any structure in the distance. She would have preferred to do this on the exact location where

Wayne Rogers had been forced off Highway 17 months earlier, but there was no way to shield herself from passing cars, and the guardrail on that curve had been secured with enough resistance to ward off the impact of a small tank. But she could see it in the distance, a wall of black against the paler shade of dark of the sky, where Wayne had tumbled into eternity.

This would have to do. This would do nicely, in fact.

She went to the trunk and opened it. The man Wolf knew as Special Agent Short was still unconscious, though he had moved slightly from the position in which he had been inserted into the car earlier. She took his feet and pulled them over the edge of the trunk. Then, using all her considerable strength, she hoisted him up by the arms until his body teetered on the edge. A final tug and he fell to the ground just under the car's exhaust, motionless.

Next, she went to the passenger side and opened the door. This body—the woman's—was easier to disengage from the car. A good pull on one arm and she tumbled out, landing face-first on the ground.

Tracy pulled the syringe from her jacket and carefully extracted a dose from another bottle, different from the one she had used to render them unconscious. She had to be careful here: too much and they would regain momentary strength, enough to make this harder than it needed to be. What she wanted was their consciousness, enough to experience their moment of justice—the same fear and pain Wayne had felt—but not enough to regain motor skills. The friend of a friend from whom she'd acquired the narcotic had showed her the precise dosage to use, and the obscene amount of money she had paid him would effectively erase any memory of the transaction. Hell, the guy never really knew who she was, anyway.

In two minutes, the man and the woman were able to balance upright on their haunches without falling over. They were unable to speak, but she could tell from their eyes that they recognized her, and that they comprehended their fate. After cleaning their pockets of money and weapons and false ID—Wolf's gun, the one used to kill Kelly Scott, was safely in her pocket—she moved them to the edge of a three-hundred-foot cliff, a sheer rock facade guarding a canyon that was not adjacent to any roads or trails. Because no one would be looking for them, the odds of their bodies being found in the near future were acceptably miniscule. Even then, there would be no identification, and on the odd chance that some forensic wonder boy did manage to unlock the secret of their identity, it would be written off as a mob-related hit with no explanation. Such were the conveniences of the truth in this case—the couple most recently known as Special Agents Banger and Short had effectively erased their own histories as part of their own marketability.

Now she would erase them altogether.

She went back to the car, returning in moments with a can of gasoline. She took off the lid and poured the contents over the heads of the condemned, holding it until the can was empty.

She took out her cigarette lighter. She thought of Wayne and she thought of Wolf, how the promise of one countered the grief of the other, and how this moment signified a new beginning for all of them. Wayne would finally rest, hopefully in the heaven of which he so often spoke, having been avenged by the woman who loved him. And she and Wolf could live a life of dreams, the life she'd interrupted with her foolish greed.

She struck the lighter, wishing she had a cigarette. Wolf wouldn't approve—a thought which made her smile. What Wolf did and didn't know no longer mattered. In fact, it was what Wolf didn't know that would save his ass.

She leaned down and touched the burning lighter to the woman's hair.

Tracy jumped back as the body exploded in flames, enough to immediately ignite the man next to her. She listened to the roar of the flames, not unlike the bonfires from her childhood camps. Both bodies writhed slightly—the dosage had been perfect—like paper folding into itself on hot coals, though no screams were heard.

A pity, that. She had selected this place for the privacy it would afford, including the soundtrack.

After thirty seconds, she moved forward. The heat was more intense than she'd anticipated, but thankfully, she'd positioned them just inches from the edge. All she had to do was land one solid kick to each flaming torso to send it tumbling over the edge.

First one, then the other. Two falling stars, unseen in the night.

Next to her in the car was the duffle bag containing the money that had been recovered from Boyd Gavin. Her job had been to rendezvous with the two operatives after they'd killed Wolf, relieve them of the cash—their compensation took the form of an offshore deposit—and send them on their merry way.

Tracy smiled, realizing that she'd done exactly what she'd been instructed to do.

> 59 <

Lee Van Wyke arrived at Tracy's apartment in Cupertino just before three. The last thing she'd wanted was to get up in the middle of the night and answer an undefined panic call, especially from Nelson's little twit of an assistant, but she had no choice in the matter. Tracy had said it was critical to the project they were working on, that the whole thing was in jeopardy—"in the shitter" were her exact words—and couldn't wait until morning. Because of the possibility of a wiretap, their conversation couldn't be any more specific than that. But Tracy's voice had been full of fear, and that meant trouble.

Lee had to respond. Besides, there would be no sleep tonight. All the switches had been thrown, the wheels set in motion. By now Kelly Scott was dead, Wolfgang Schmitt was dead by what would appear to be his own hand, and the two covert operatives had given the cash taken from Gavin's condo to Tracy and were long gone, their fee safely in an offshore account as planned. She had expected a phone call, but not this early, and not from Tracy.

Something had gone wrong. Tracy had said this was something only Lee could fix, which in all likelihood meant it connected directly back to Nelson.

And from the beginning, this was above all else what they had sought to avoid.

Tracy lived where all Silicon Valley staff seemed to live—generic earth-tone stucco townhouses behind ridiculous coded gates, the parking lot full of midsized cars with credit union liens that consumed a full third of their take-home pay. It depressed her to even get near these kinds of places, which reeked of crass mediocrity. These were trailer parks with fountains. What Nelson, who could have any woman on the planet, saw in this little tart was beyond her comprehension.

Then again, Nelson was certainly a pig of the first order. One with a weakness for fast food and cheap pleasures. Perhaps the slumlike nature of his sexual tastes made him feel a part of the human race—Caesar's nocturnal roaming among the tents.

Lee knew the code from a prior visit—her memory was photographic and unforgiving—and punched herself through the gate. She parked in the quiet lot and hurried to the second-floor apartment, banging hard on the door.

Tracy answered, wearing panties and a T-shirt. What Lee would have worn to bed, had this not been the night it was. Tracy held the door and stood aside, allowing Lee to enter.

Lee immediately smelled smoke and stale cooking odors, and made her facial expression appropriate to her disapproval. The room was dimly lit from the kitchen and the hall, leaving the living room in shadow.

"You don't look as upset as you sounded," said Lee, sitting on the edge of a couch she guessed was from Wickes.

"Oh, I'm not," said Tracy, sitting in the facing chair.

"Then what the hell is this?"

Tracy reached behind herself and pulled out Wolf's gun. She held it up, a tiny smile on her face.

Lee squinted, her mind in full scan mode.

"It's Wolf's," Tracy clarified.

Lee's gaze snapped from the gun to Tracy's eyes, posing the inevitable question.

"And guess what?" Tracy added. "He's not dead."

Lee closed her eyes as her head hung for a moment. "What happened? What went wrong?"

"I was thinking about it," said Tracy, her voice sarcastically analytical now, "and it didn't make sense. I mean, they'll figure out he knew *me*, right?"

Lee looked up again, her expression stern.

"What are you driving at, Tracy?"

"Think about it. Wolf kills Gavin, fine. Jealous lover. He kills Kelly in a fit of passion and rage because she's dumping him. I might buy that. He kills himself in his guilt, okay, that flies, too. But wouldn't he cover all the bases? I mean, wouldn't he kill the woman who broke his heart in the first place? The woman he couldn't have, who was right under his nose the whole time?"

Lee said nothing, her eyes narrowing.

Tracy nodded, eyes wide, as if urging Lee to keep up.

"He'd kill *me*, too, don't you think? Before he went home and wrote his suicide note and shot himself? Think about it, Lee. Of course he would."

"Why do you have Wolf's gun, Tracy?"

Tracy got up, looked at the gun in her hand.

"I'm actually sort of surprised you didn't go that route. Have your two goons come here, do me with the gun, then go visit Wolf and finish it."

Lee was chewing at the inside of her lip, a nervous tic Tracy recognized from many tense meetings. She had to move fast now, before the tic turned into a plan, which it always did.

"You're part of the team, Tracy. You know that. We couldn't have done this without you."

"That's true, isn't it. But if you'd *wanted* to, you could have done it that way, saved yourself a cut of the pie, tied off a loose end in the process. Aren't I right, Lee? That you could have done it that way?"

Lee shifted her weight, as if preparing to make a move.

"What are you saying? You've been drinking."

"No, no, you're wrong. I'm just thinking, you see. Thinking that it could have gone down that way. It makes sense. It supports the entire façade we've already built. I mean, hell, Kelly was on the team, too, right? She's dead, never saw it coming, not for a moment."

The two women stared at each other, one with a gun, the other with only her mind, a weapon that had served her well.

"Say it," said Tracy. "Tell me I'm right."

"It could have gone down like that, yeah."

"But it didn't."

"No. It didn't. Tell me why you have the gun."

"Because you brought it here."

Lee's eyes flicked toward the door, measuring the room.

"Where's Wolf?"

"You brought it here to shoot me," said Tracy.

"What, you want a better deal? We can talk. There's plenty of money, Tracy, if that's it. Talk to me."

"What if there weren't any goons posing as Feds? Work with me here. What if they just disappeared, as if they never happened?"

"It's the money, isn't it. You've got Gavin's cash."

She did indeed, though Tracy seemed not to hear. She was staring into space, keeping her distance from the other woman, who, despite her age, was more athletic.

"*You* killed Gavin," said Tracy. "Then *you* killed Kelly. You stole Wolf's car, killed the guard, shot up the video system to cover it. Then you came here to kill me, to make it look like Wolf had snapped even bigger than the original plan called for. You were going to kill him, too, all of it with this gun. *His* gun."

Tracy's eyes snapped onto Lee now. "But you never got there, did you, Lee."

"Name your price, Tracy. Give me a number."

"Maybe Nelson knows," said Tracy. "Maybe he's buying this ticket. He turned on Kelly—maybe he's turning on you, too."

Lee was shaking her head. "Don't insult me."

Tracy turned, feet squared, raising the gun toward Lee, holding it with two hands like she'd seen on television.

She suddenly lunged forward, slamming the gun against Lee's shoulder as it fired. The force of the bullet knocked Lee back to the couch, as Tracy stepped back to arm's length.

Lee looked at the wound in horror, then back at Tracy in disbelief.

"We fought for the gun," said Tracy, backing away toward the end table, where she swung her hand, sending the lamp crashing to the floor. "It was terrifying—you came at me, but I surprised you, fought back, and as we struggled for the gun it went off. Close range . . . the CSI boys will verify that part, won't they. You like that show, Lee? I do."

Tracy fired again, from several feet away this time. The bullet struck Lee squarely in the stomach, just above her navel and at the base of her sternum, blasting cleanly through her body, leaving an exit wound the size of a peach. Lee doubled over, her hands reflexively covering the wound.

Tracy approached and knelt at her feet. She put the gun on the coffee table, then took one of Lee's bloody hands in her own. Holding the fingers rigid, Tracy brought the hand to her throat and slashed the nails across her own flesh, drawing her own blood.

The cushion under Lee's hips was already soaked with a sticky crimson sheen.

"Damn, looks like we hit an artery," said Tracy, getting to her feet. She then grabbed Lee by the hair and pulled her head back, exposing her face. She took her other hand and raked her nails down from Lee's forehead over her eyes, embedding them in the flesh of her cheek. Then she violently threw Lee's head to the side, the momentum causing Lee to slump over. Her face was that of a woman who had fought for her life.

She didn't move, other than a fruitless effort to right herself. After a moment, she just relaxed, her chest heaving.

"The first shot only hit your shoulder, but it allowed me to take the gun away from you. But you kept coming at me—I mean, you're one tough bitch—and then I fell back . . ."

Tracy looked over her shoulder, then fell across the coffee table behind her, sending a candle holder, a vase full of flowers, and some books flying. While on the floor she kicked the coffee table to the side, as if a fight had unfolded in that spot.

"That's when I shot you again. Got you good this time, and tough as you are, you stopped. That's where you ended up, there on the couch, bleeding. God, there was so much blood . . ."

Tracy was on her knees now, the gun back in her hand. She pressed Lee's weakened palm and fingers to the barrel, smearing it with blood, mixing it with her own fingerprints, as if they'd struggled for it after the first shot had gone off.

"Of course, I called 911 right away, but I was scared, so I ran outside and waited. A neighbor heard the shots, and she waited with me. Carrie lives across the landing. She's a light sleeper. My guess is she's already up."

Tracy got back to her feet.

"I think you were already dead, Lee. I really do."

Tracy stood in front of Lee for several minutes. The body didn't move once. The breathing was very shallow and infrequent. She'd be dead by the time an ambulance arrived.

Tracy drew a deep breath, then went to the kitchen and picked up the phone. She dialed 911 and waited, wondering where Wolf had been when she'd returned the Mercedes to his garage. Her own car had been parked outside the property, a half-mile down the street at a busy club; she'd scaled the fence twice that evening to come and go from Wolf's place. The security guard never saw a thing, other than Wolf's car departing and returning. Twice.

Amazing, how long it takes 911 to pick up sometimes.

Damn that Wolf. She'd told him to wait until morning, to play it straight when they came for him, but the chickenshit bastard was already gone. With millions of dollars riding on this, why couldn't he do what he was told, just this once?

Then again, in the long run, when the shit hit the fan, he'd do just as she wished. He always had, and some things just don't change.

> 60 <

ENTRY #96: JERRY SPRINGERESQUE PROGRAMMING—it's a free country, and even the lowest common denominator of humanity gets a time slot. Too bad they can't just pipe it straight into the trailer park and spare the rest of us the embarrassment. Scariest thought of all: this guy used to be the mayor of a major American city. Second-scariest thought: he has imitators.
   —from *Bullshit in America*, by Wolfgang Schmitt

I figured I had twelve hours, fifteen tops. Even if Kelly's body was discovered before morning, which was highly unlikely given the staff's schedule, it would take them a good while to tie the murder to me, using the synthetic thread of the contrivance at hand. I visualized a tearful Lee Van Wyke standing on the porch, as in the background the body bag was being loaded into the coroner's van—straight out of prime time—telling them who I was and where I lived, that I seemed like such a nice guy, though, on second thought, a bit odd at times.

I wouldn't be on hand when they came for me.

It took less than five minutes to pack. One suitcase, a duffle bag, and a tennis racket, and I was ready for the road. Of course, with my car gone, there was the problem of transportation, but Lee had inadvertently facilitated that solution—there was a perfectly good Harley Davidson in my borrowed garage. I'd fired it up about a week earlier, and I knew the tank was full. If I didn't plow into the guard station at the property gate, I had a good shot at surviving the night.

One thing was certain: the neighbors all knew of my departure shortly after two o'clock; it sounded like the Blue Angels were doing a touch-and-go in the cul-de-sac.

At this time of the morning, every third vehicle is a police car. A Harley with a suitcase strapped to the bitch-seat tends to get their attention. So my strategy was simple—stash the bike until morning, stay out of sight, then blend into the commute in quest of my next destination.

El Camino Real is the quintessential American street: six lanes and a succession of strip malls, strip clubs, used car lots, and fast-food emporiums, in that order, all the way north to the outer vestiges of South San Francisco. I parked the bike at the first all-night establishment I encountered—a Denny's—and took a seat at the back of the lot, next to a Dumpster that smelled like ammonia. From here I could keep an eye on the bike and the street, and easily disappear from sight if necessary. Which it was. Two squad cars pulled through the lot, an hour apart, but they didn't seem to care about the bike, and they didn't notice a shadowy figure lurking near the garbage, breathing through his mouth.

Shortly after dawn I went inside, had some breakfast, and cleaned up, a quick shave and a good flossing.

I wanted to look sharp for my meeting. I remembered Kelly had said that Nelson was flying in this morning, that he'd head straight for the office from there. Knowing what I knew now, it was a good bet he was nowhere near the Villa during the night, so I was hoping she had no reason to fabricate this particular detail. Liars have a tendency to mix as much truth as possible into the stew of their deception—a fact I was counting on now.

I always loved that shot in *Top Gun* in which Tom Cruise is on his bike at dusk, paralleling a departing fighter jet seen in the background while raising his fist in cinematic exultation. And suddenly there I was—I had the bike, the airport, and a dawn that was similar enough in hue to Cruise's dusk. No fighter, but a Gulfstream wasn't a bad stand-in. All I lacked was his twenty-mil-a-movie smile and a way onto the airport grounds.

The latter appeared in the form of an open gate with no guard, just off the executive aviation building and across the strip from the commercial passenger terminal. In this age of terrorism, one could simply drive one's car onto the tarmac and drag-race an MD-80. I waited until I saw the Gulfstream touch down to give it a shot. Several cars had entered and parked in a very exclusive lot, and I pulled in behind an Escalade and just kept on going.

Amazing, the freedom that comes with having nothing left to lose. One grows balls the size of casaba melons.

I caught up with the Gulfstream as it turned onto the taxiway for the parking tarmac. I paralleled the airplane—a sight I'm sure the pilots immediately radioed to the tower. I could see faces in the cabin peering out at me, one of them dark-skinned and pissed off.

I knew I'd only have a minute or so to say my piece. The airplane suddenly stopped, still on the taxi strip, a quarter-mile from the hangar it called home. I didn't know if this was a good thing or a bad thing, but I realized it had everything to do with my presence. I hoped it was because Nelson Scott didn't want a crowd any more than I did.

I pulled in front of the wing and shut down the Harley's engine. I pulled off the helmet and put it on my knee and waited, posing like an ad in *GQ*. If nothing else, they now knew who they were dealing with.

The hatch opened. Rashod Martinez was the first one off, hopping to the pavement without using the steps, his expression apropos to someone having called Christina Aguilera a ho-bag.

Nelson Scott was right behind him. They approached quickly, like an offense breaking huddle for the line of scrimmage. Rashod stopped with his nose approximately three inches from mine. I had him by six inches, he had me by forty pounds. Do the math.

"I promised him I'd let him break your back in thirty seconds," said Scott, pulling his suit jacket sleeve up to reveal his watch in a gesture of supposed drama. "That's about thirty seconds before the police arrive, whom we've already called."

"You've got quite a day ahead of you," I said.

"If you're referring to Kelly, I've been advised."

"You've been advised. What a sweet, sensitive man you are."

"Twenty seconds," said Rashod, already hyperventilating.

"Three words," I said. "Wayne Rogers's audit."

I saw his eyes betray him, but only for an instant. If Tracy had been straight with me, I wasn't supposed to know about this. Not unless something had gone south, which it had.

"Fifteen," said Rashod, now loosening up his neck muscles.

"Three more words," I said, imitating the precise movement Rashod was making. "I've got it."

"Bullshit," said Scott.

"Oh, I've got it, all right. Tell your second-string linebacker here to hit the showers and we'll talk."

Scott hesitated, but only for an instant. He put his hand on Rashod's shoulder, nodding when the bodyguard looked at him for guidance. I could see that Rashod's stepping back took every bit of willpower in him.

"Thirty more seconds," said Scott, who had taken Rashod's place in front of me. I had this guy by several inches *and* forty pounds.

"Good, then the police will be here. Maybe I should wait, let them hear, too. Got a killer story to tell."

Without averting his eyes, Scott told Rashod to radio the gate and hold the troops.

"Anything else?" Scott said sarcastically.

"Pretty simple, really. You hired me to do a job. I did that job. The base was one million dollars. The job is over, I want my money."

"You're shitting me."

"Do I look like someone in a position to shit you?" I asked, gesturing toward the meathead waiting a few feet away. "I didn't earn the bonus, so that's not what I'm asking for. I've seen what happens to people who blackmail you. You've paid me five hundred grand so far, I want the other five."

"In exchange for the audit."

"Sure, if that's what you want. You can duplicate a file in about six seconds, or maybe you didn't know that. What you get for your million is the peace of mind that comes from knowing you won't hear from me again."

I was careful how I worded that one. I didn't want

to be put into a position of telling an untruth. This was Wolf's Great Reinvention still in progress, complete with a spanking-new moral code.

"What if I said I don't have a clue what you're talking about?"

"Then I'd say you're in about as deep a pool of shit as me. Interesting, too, because you built my pool, and I'm about to build yours."

"Not if no one believes you. Not if you're missing."

"The dead tell tales, Nelson."

"Go on."

"I've got it all documented. Taped, witnessed, backed up, and ready to hit the beach. You, Lee, Tracy, how you set me up for Boyd Gavin's murder, and then how you turned it on your wife and had her killed, too. I've got the audit because Gavin saw it coming, and he gave it to me."

Okay, one little lie. I was a work in progress.

He hesitated, then said, "You're bluffing."

"God, how I'd love to get you across a poker table, you arrogant piece of shit. Try me."

Watching his face was like watching Clinton suggest multiple interpretations of the word "is."

Finally, he said, "Tell me what you want."

"I want the money in that account within an hour. I want to drive this thing out of here and not be followed or otherwise interfered with. At that point, we're after the same thing, you and me—my complete and utter disappearance. Which brings me to another point. I don't call my attorney in thirty minutes, you go up in flames. Or should I say, your company does. You burn later when they tie you to the murders of Boyd Gavin and your wife. We clicking here, Nels? Or is that dumb expression on your face standard operating procedure?"

The man hadn't gotten where he was in life without a keen sense of self-preservation, usually disguised beneath a textbook win-win veneer. At the very least, I hoped he was still on top of his game enough to see it that way.

Otherwise, me and Rashod were about to dance.

"Agreed," he said.

"You have the account data?"

He nodded. "I hope you're very good at disappearing, Mr. Schmitt."

I nodded back. "Count on it."

I fired the Harley, then put on the helmet. I gave Rashod a little wave as I drove off, but he didn't as much as twitch in return. It would have been a good time for a wheely, but frankly, I had no idea how to do one and would have ended up on my head if I'd tried. I was just glad to get out of there with my strategy and my vertebrae intact.

I waited until I was cleanly out of sight to turn off the new microcassette recorder in my pocket.

The bit about the attorney was something I came up with on the spot. As I drove off, it occurred to me that I ought to get one on my team, and fast. Despite what the government boys had said—if they even *were* government boys—all bets were off now. Considering my next stop, this seemed like the prudent course of action for a desperate man such as me.

I drove to the downtown San Jose police department, parking the Harley in a "Police Only" zone. I went inside and showed the receptionist both of my identifications—Arizona and Oregon. I told him I was here about the Kelly Scott murder investigation, and he looked at me as if I were seeking donations for the Free Willy fund.

Of course, this was after stopping at a gas station

phone booth near the freeway exit to make several calls. The person on the receiving end of the first call—who was not an attorney by trade—advised me to turn myself in. The second call was to Blaine Borgia, who didn't answer, but who would receive notice of the impending shit-storm when he checked his messages. The third was to my mother's nursing home, advising them to charge whatever they needed to my account in the event they didn't hear from me in the near future, and to tell my mother that I loved her. This, too, was a message left on a machine, and I had no confidence whatsoever in the fulfillment of my parting wish.

I hoped to God Tracy had been telling the truth about pulling a rabbit out of her Prada bag.

The San Jose police had no idea what I was talking about. They asked me to wait in their Naugahyde-themed lobby, and at any time in the ensuing two hours, I could have moseyed out the door and simply driven away.

That's how long it took to get their attention. There's something wrong with this country when you can't even turn yourself in for a capital crime without a bureaucratic fuck-up of the first order.

From the moment that a woman with a very shiny badge came to fetch me on, however, they certainly did want to talk to me. I was suddenly, as they put it, "a person of interest."

They would soon find out just how interesting I could be.

Not even I, however, had any idea of the magnitude of the so-called shit-storm that lay ahead. Tracy, it seemed, had been a very busy—and a very bad—little girl.

> 61 <

> ENTRY #1: THE VIETNAM WAR—fifty thousand dead, a war lost, and the regime we were sent to "disarm" is still in power to this day. Over thirty years later, and that regime hasn't harmed a hair on a single American's head. Look up "bullshit" in the dictionary, and this is what you *should* see.
> —from *Bullshit in America*, by Wolfgang Schmitt

I didn't get out of the police headquarters until nine that evening. Astoundingly, the Harley was still there, parked illegally right where I'd left it, the helmet perched on the seat in anticipation of my return. If they'd bothered to check the license and title, I'd have been in the deep end of the pool much sooner than I'd planned.

As it turned out, I had to tread water for only a short while.

By noon, the bodies of Kelly Scott and Lee Van Wyke—which had been discovered many hours before Don Knotts at the front desk seemed to know about it—had been moved to the county coroner's icebox. By three, the Portland lawyer I'd requested—a local legend I'd seen many times in the news but had never met—had designated a local representative from a partner firm, who was scoring three hundred dollars an hour to tell me to keep my trap shut until the attorney of record arrived the next morning.

Only later did I find out that Tracy was a mere forty feet away in another room, singing like a bird.

I kept the faith. In spite of my lawyer's urgings to keep quiet, I had a lot to say and couldn't get it out quickly enough. The lawyer's context was that I was indeed hiding something of an incriminating nature, and mine was that of someone reading a carefully written script who couldn't get enough camera time. I outlined the entire scheme to squelch the Scott prenuptial agreement, told how I'd been recruited and hired for the job by my ex-girlfriend, and professed great sadness and horror at the revelation that Kelly Scott was dead because of it.

Yeah, I was one scared puppy, and I couldn't bark loud enough. Were it not for the hourly boost, my lawyer would have gone home by the dinner hour.

Or so I thought.

Three different detectives questioned me. Yeah, I'd certainly heard of Boyd Gavin, had even seen the guy, and yes, there'd been a run-in at a Sausalito restaurant. But I feigned complete surprise at the news of his death, almost as much as the utter stunned stupor that temporarily overwhelmed me at the revelation of Lee Van Wyke's unfortunate demise.

Tracy, Tracy, Tracy. I'd had no idea what she meant when she said she'd fix things. She'd always been a bit of a drama queen, but this was the Metropolitan Opera of manipulation. All the while I was speaking the truth, my confession was in perfect symmetrical contour to the smooth curves of her lie.

There had been some attempt on the part of the police to withhold these various and sundry revelations in the hope that I'd show my hand, but this was where I took the lawyer's advice and played stupid. I simply stuck to my thin but plausible story of being Nelson Scott's well-paid gigolo, nothing more, nothing less. I was the perfect patsy, blinded by the money, blindsided by the frame-up.

This was precisely what I'd been instructed to do.

When they let me go that evening, they asked me where I was staying, the prologue to the inevitable *don't leave town* speech. I had no answer other than the condo, which was sitting empty with leftover pizza in the fridge, the rent pre-paid. Since everything about my presence in town was now out in the open, I saw no reason to pony up for a room at the Days Inn.

When I got back to the condo, I was totally dumbfounded to find the Mercedes back in the garage. In the center console, right where I'd left them, were my microcassette recorder and a stash of very interesting tapes.

God is indeed alive and well in His heaven, working overtime.

The story was all over the news. My name, however, was never mentioned, other than a reference to an unidentified "person of interest" who was being questioned.

Tracy, however, was in the first televised moments of her fifteen minutes of fame. Her dream, it occurred to me, was at last coming true.

I remained a "person of interest" for many weeks, as the investigation proceeded and the story began to unravel. The lead detective, it was said, had already scored a book deal, and a producer from *48 Hours* was seen sniffing out rights and releases from anyone remotely involved.

Three people were dead: Boyd Gavin, Kelly Scott,

and Lee Van Wyke. Tracy, who could prove she'd received training in the martial arts, had killed Lee in self-defense when the woman came to her apartment with a gun—my gun. The purpose of Lee's visit had been murder, and the ensuing framing of yours truly. Because Tracy had been identified—by me, and by Nelson Scott—as the person who'd brought me into the scheme, however innocently, she was then a credible source of skin-saving information about how Lee had been forwarding her own agenda all along. Why? Because Lee was in love with Nelson Scott, and felt that if Kelly were dead she'd have a shot.

The media freaked.

From my point of view, things just got better and better.

Because of the botched attempt at destroying the security videos at the Villa, several seconds of digital footage were recovered, clearly showing two occupants of the Mercedes—the one Kelly had loaned to me, it turned out, exactly as I'd claimed—approaching the entrance of the main house. Clearly neither of the occupants was me, though it was never discovered just who the hell they—a man and a woman—were. However, Tracy did testify in a deposition that she'd seen Lee Van Wyke meeting with two people who fit this description, and Nelson Scott provided evidence that funds had been disbursed from a private account accessible by Lee, all without his knowledge. The search for their whereabouts continued.

Tracy, Tracy, Tracy.

Then there was the matter of my alibi. The Domino's pizza guy remembered the precise time of his delivery to my condo—my generous tip turned out to be a karmic life-saver—which happened to coincide with the coroner's time-of-death estimate for Kelly Scott. Couldn't have been me.

A crackerjack forensic team swarmed my house back in Portland, much to the amazement of my neighbors. They found evidence of a rooftop break-in, corroborating my contention that I'd not had the gun in my possession since I'd left Portland, that someone must have stolen it in anticipation of the frame-up. Once again, Nelson Scott was only too happy to provide records that showed unauthorized distributions, payable to a complex network of offshore accounts, roughly coinciding with the time the break-in was believed to have occurred. A little digging would link those accounts with Lee Van Wyke, making the district attorney a very happy little lady.

Nelson Scott was quietly questioned many times, but somehow remained out of camera range. He was only too happy to corroborate my story about the plan to hire someone to seduce his wife and break the prenuptial agreement, and he reluctantly had to blight the memory of Lee Van Wyke with stories of her alcohol-fueled jealous fits of rage and increasingly unstable behavior. It was a broadside hit to the Scott PR ship, to be sure, but it beat the hell out of the truthful alternative.

I remained in the condo for the entire course of the investigation, driving the SL for several more weeks, until it simply disappeared from the garage without explanation. The whole thing was like a paid vacation in a resort, complete with a car and a Harley hog. I had plenty of time to write it all down, and to finish my manuscript for *Bullshit in America*, which had taken on new meaning for me over the course of the past few months.

It wasn't all that long before I became a bit player,

the butt of inside jokes at the police department, an embarrassment to Nelson Scott that he'd just as soon forget.

The feeling, I assured the press, was mutual.

Almost forgot. Back on the day when the entire house of cards had tumbled and I'd been detained at the police station until nine that night, I hadn't had a chance to get my hands on a computer. So on the way home, I stopped at a Kinko's—my laptop being fried and useless—and for thirty cents a minute, was granted much-anticipated access to the Internet.

I was a few keystrokes away from discovering just how sincere Tracy had been in her promise to set me free.

The day before, there had been five hundred thousand dollars there. Now there was $2,500,000 in my account. This is something one has to experience to understand, the way all those zeros wink at you when you stare at them. The way the adrenaline cuts loose and makes you believe in orgasms again.

Five hundred thousand dollars had been deposited that afternoon. Nelson Scott had kept his word—I had been paid in full. And I would keep my word to him—he would not hear from me again.

Semantics, my dear Watson, semantics.

But that wasn't all. One million five hundred thousand had been deposited that morning. I had no idea where it had come from, but I had a pretty good idea. The Boyd Gavin estate had been settled.

Tracy, it seemed, really did love me after all.

> 62 <

> ENTRY #40: CAR ADVERTISING—never in the history of the newspaper has an advertised car price been one penny lower than a customer with balls could, with patience and skin thicker than Paul Allen's tax return, negotiate for themselves.
> —from *Bullshit in America,* by Wolfgang Schmitt

Seven Weeks Later
Key West, Florida

Mom was fine. On the honor of my esteemed and exquisitely expensive attorney, I was allowed to make a trip to Portland in the middle of the investigation to see her. I flew commercial, by the way, with no idea whatsoever what had happened to my beloved Cessna Citation-X. Probably absorbed into the Scott fleet, destined to fly propellerheads and marketing pukes back and forth to Comdex every year.

As usual, my mother had no idea who I was. But at least this time, I did. I kissed her good-bye on the forehead, promising I'd be back before too long. Before I left, she asked if I would please change the channel to *Gunsmoke,* which of course hadn't been on the air since Lyndon B. Johnson was lying to the country through yellow teeth.

Whatever. Some things you just can't influence. Life, I had learned, really does go on.

Which was precisely what I was thinking about as I sat on a beach a few miles down the road from the quaint little burg of Key West, Florida, where my particular sexual orientation was in a vast minority. The sun had just gone down—one of the nice things about the Keys is that the distance between a sunrise and a sunset is only a few miles—and I was sitting on a log before a fire I'd built within a perfect circle of rocks.

A pile of eight-and-a-half-by-eleven papers sat next to me in the sand. About two hundred of them, each bearing a number followed by words I knew to be all too true.

She was late. We had agreed on sundown, planned on sharing the grand solar drama of another day's demise, complete with marshmallows.

I picked up a random piece of paper. *Number 44: HMOs. Easy to hate 'em, for sure. But what are ya gonna do, take up Christian Science? Write the check and eat more chicken, I always say.*

I wadded up the paper and tossed it into the fire. The edges glowed orange, then began a final dance of death as the paper twisted into itself, a sort of fetal return, ashes to ashes, never to be recycled again.

Bullshit to bullshit, as it were.

Tonight, I was drinking wine. A nice cabernet from an Oregon vintner, something I thought she'd enjoy. People in the east are crazy for Northwest wines, as if all the rain imparted some magic to the grape. Hell, the explanation wasn't magic at all; most of the time it was just too damn gray in Oregon to do anything but drink, so a few folks cashed in their Tektronix stock options and started growing their own.

I took a swallow from the paper cup I'd brought

for the occasion, feeling the sweet burn of its descent. I didn't know from bouquet or which pallet was which, but it was nice.

Life's too short, I told myself not so long ago, *to not savor the wine*. My reasons for not doing so before now were just more bullshit.

I sensed a presence behind me, felt it as much as heard it, and I knew she'd arrived. I didn't look up from the fire when she sat next to me, placing her hand on my shoulder. Despite the breeze, I immediately caught a whiff of her perfume, an old favorite from the days before the fall.

All these months, and she was still reliably late.

"You want some gum?" I asked, offering her a pack. She was amused—I used to force gum on her when I knew she'd been smoking—and took a piece, popping it into her mouth.

"This is terrible!" she said.

"Chlorophyll. You get used to it."

I hadn't seen Tracy since San Jose. We had run into each other a couple of times, but always with people around, her lawyer, a journalist, some of her new friends. One day there had been a note in my mailbox—I'd moved out of the condo after a few weeks—asking me to meet her here, in this place, on this date. To plan the first day of the rest of our lives, she'd promised. She had done her part, and I had trusted. It was time to move forward.

The police and the district attorney finally bought her story. She had acted in self-defense. Lee Van Wyke's twisted plan, the one that had resulted in the tragic deaths of Boyd Gavin and Kelly Scott, had failed before its ultimate objective had been met. Lee had tried to fuck with the wrong girl.

The lights of a cruise ship were visible in the distance, having just departed Key West, bound for the

Cayman Islands. I wished to God I was there instead of here.

Soon, perhaps.

I took another piece of paper from the pile. *Number 122: Wealth-building Seminars.* I'd shelled out ninety bucks for a day-trading workshop, and within two months I was nine grand in the hole. I got the idea for my *Bullshit in America* book shortly thereafter.

"What are you burning?" she asked.

"The past," I replied.

"Sounds heavy."

"Getting lighter by the page."

She took my arm with both of her hands, putting her head on my shoulder. We watched the cruise ship shrink into the night, listening to the soft crackling of the wood I'd used to stoke the fire.

"It's good to be here," she said.

I kissed the top of her head, inhaling the scent of her. Dozens of solitary nights flashed in my mind, when I'd done this in my imagination, inhaling the same ghostly aroma, praying for a chance to smell it again.

They say be careful what you pray for. Amen to that.

"You know we have to talk," I said, staring at the sea.

"I know that."

"You saved me. Like you said you would."

"I love you, Wolf. I told you I never stopped loving you, and I meant it. I would think that it would be easy to believe me, after all that's happened."

"You never hurt your friends," I offered.

She nodded, remembering our conversation in the bar that night in San Jose. Nobody ever said love made sense.

"People died, Trace. Hard to get that out of my head."

"Evil people. Worse than you even know. People

who would have killed you in a heartbeat to serve their own agenda. I got *involved*, Wolf, or you'd be in a box right now."

"You got paid, too."

"Don't hear you complaining, chief."

I hadn't touched the money. Sure, I'd checked it frequently—okay, I checked it daily; it was accumulating nicely, despite the prevailing interest rates, which frankly sucked—and to be honest, I wasn't sure what I'd been waiting for. Maybe tonight. Maybe I never really believed.

"I won't lie to you," she said. "It started out about the money. It's why I left Portland, left you. But I was miserable right away, and frankly it pissed me off, Miss Gotta Have It All, that I couldn't have you and the lifestyle I'd always dreamed of."

"And then there was Wayne."

She nodded. I knew I'd hit a nerve.

"He was a lot like you. That's what drew me to him, I think. Straight-up guy, nice abs, worshipped the ground I walked on."

"Don't we all?"

She softly put her head on my shoulder.

"When he died, it rocked my world. Made me stop, rethink the girl-on-the-make thing. My sugar daddy wasn't out there; he was spoken for—either married to someone he'd be cheating on or a job he'd always love more than me. The fantasy wasn't real. The loneliness, that was real."

She lifted her head, pivoted on the log we were sitting on. I turned to meet her stare.

"That's when I knew. I'd made a mistake. But I didn't have a clue how to undo it."

"Rocket science, Trace. You pick up the phone, you punch the number, you say *Hi, I'm a confused self-centered bitch, take me back*."

She laughed, though sadly. Too true.

"That was the problem, I think. The great Wolfgang paradox. You'd have said *Yes, come home,* and ultimately I wouldn't have respected you for that."

I whistled out loud.

"Complicated, aren't I."

"Fubar, more like it."

We both knew what that meant: fubar—*fucked up beyond all repair.*

"So I went for the money. I saw an angle, I worked it—boy, how I worked it—and here we sit. Fabulously rich."

"Cake's on the way. We get to eat *it,* too."

"I can't change what happened, Wolf."

"I know that."

"But you're struggling. I can feel it. Something's not right."

She was stroking the back of my neck. I'd always been plagued with muscular tension there—downside of too much time in the weight room, something I intended to get back into.

"I need to understand, Trace. I'm sorry. I just need to know. What was in your head, what you *did.* Maybe then I can make it okay, because now I'll know why."

She turned her attention to the sea, and we were quiet for several minutes.

"You still don't trust me. After all this."

I just stared.

"Ask me anything," she said.

She talked for over half an hour, her voice low and even the entire time. How she met a guy who worked high up in channel marketing at Arielle, who flashed a few million in stock options, how she thought she was in love and moved down there to be with him. How it lasted a month or so, and suddenly she was alone and single in a place where the game was played at a whole new level, where the sharks had teeth and she was just another pretty fish in the aquarium. And so she changed her game, grew some teeth of her own, found a few weak spots and burrowed in, making the right friends, doing the right parties the right way, ending up with a finance job at an Arielle subsidiary, close to the action, to the players.

That was when she met Wayne. He was a refreshing change from the Valley boys, a guy with soft eyes and brass balls, a guy who liked the same things she liked. Wayne made it easy, if not to forget the past, then to put it on hold while her career moved ahead and she figured out what she really wanted out of her life besides the money.

And then he was killed before the question had been answered, and suddenly she had her hands on the holy grail. She described the Arielle audit in detail, how Wayne had unearthed covert fraud going back four fiscal years, to the tune of four billion dollars in overstated profits. Enough to ruin the company if it ever leaked.

The audit file was on a CD in a safe-deposit box in downtown San Francisco. Only her lawyer knew where it was, and what it involved. If anything ever happened to her, the lawyer had instructions to take the whole thing to the *Wall Street Journal*, who would be all ears.

And now I knew, too.

She was sleeping with Nelson Scott within days of approaching him. There was a cash payment up front, plus a sweet job on his personal staff reporting to Lee Van Wyke, helping Scott move personal funds between accounts in the states and offshore. She had crossed the line, her soul had a SOLD sign on it, and soon she was brought into the dark loop of Scott's inner circle. She saw it all—the payoffs and the bribes, graft and political leverage, the occasional anonymous persuasion, ten-thousand-dollar-a-night hookers for VIPs with kinks, the infrequent payback disguised as justice. She had proved worthy. It wasn't long before she'd earned his trust.

When the issue of Boyd Gavin had come up, she was there with a plan.

Yes, getting rid of Gavin had been her idea. One that Nelson and Lee both understood and endorsed. Kelly was brought on board as the idea grew legs; she thought it would be fun to sleep with a man she was deceiving, to ultimately send him to his doom. It was right out of the gothic novels she adored. What they needed then was a patsy.

A few other insiders knew, too. By now they were buried in other conspiracies—Marni had probably already slept her way into the executive suite at Oracle, Arielle's chief competitor; and Douglas Crane, the supposed Regional Deputy Director of the IRS with the rented Learjet, was probably running a purchasing department in Encino. Both were richer than most U.S. senators.

All along, Tracy swore she had other plans.

Other than an initial bounce or two, Lee had had no idea that Nelson and Tracy were having a full-blown affair. It was Nelson's idea that the plan expand in Kelly's direction, that the same mechanism used to frame me for Gavin's death could now embrace Kelly's murder as well. Then, he promised Tracy, the two of them could be together.

Yeah, right. Never shit a shitter. The guy was clueless.

He gave her two million dollars to make it happen.

And, she could keep the money that would be given to Gavin, if she could get it back. Independent contractors were brought in to help—freelance military intelligence agents from Europe, whose English was as perfect as their record—including the recovery of the cash they would pay to Gavin. She explained how these were the same thugs who'd killed Wayne, how they'd engineered the accident on Highway 17, and how she'd arranged the delivery of her poetic justice, trial, and execution by fire. She'd left their bodies at the base of a cliff less than a mile from the site, where they remained, so far undiscovered.

She ended with Lee: how she'd lured her to her apartment with a panic call on that fateful final night, then how she'd shot her—twice—in the midst of explaining herself.

She seemed pleased with the precision of her execution. A quiet shudder skidded down my spine as I listened.

She was suddenly quiet, having said it all.

"That's it," she finally said. "I'm not proud of what I did, but I'd do it again."

"For love," I offered.

"For us," she said quietly. "I've forgiven myself. I hope you'll do the same."

I stared out at the ocean, which was glowing under a nearly full moon. I had no idea what to say to her now.

"Scott won't come near us," I offered quickly, hoping to change the subject, "because you have the audit."

"He thinks *we* have the audit. He's paid me for my silence, and he thinks he's paid for yours. Deal's a deal with that man. In the scheme of things, it wasn't all that major a transaction. He knows I have too much to lose to sell him out."

"Smart businessman," I said.

"That was some piece of work, by the way, bluffing the shit out of him at the airport that day. The man doesn't bluff easily, you know."

I smiled again, easier this time. "Maybe you're not the only person on this beach with huge, impressive balls."

She liked that, as if it signaled my willingness to play on her team. She snuggled close, one hand snaking down between my legs. We had turned a corner, perhaps burying the past.

"Maybe we should compare notes on that," she whispered.

Then she put her hand on my jaw, turning me toward her. We kissed—a moment I had been visualizing since the moment she'd cracked open my heart like a morning egg.

I cut it off. Before my nerves failed me.

"Let's go," I said, the only avenue open to me now. "Consummate our deal with the devil."

"There can't be the devil when there's this much love," she said.

Once again, a chill swept through my body.

As she got to her feet, I tossed the remaining pages of *Bullshit in America* into the fire. It was time to bury the past, to burn the negativity and cynicism that had been consuming me, a cancer of the soul. What better way to symbolize the first day of the rest of my life than by incinerating the past.

"What *was* that?" she asked as we walked arm in arm toward the street, where the only two cars—both rentals—were ours.

"Just bullshit," I said, smiling to myself in the dark.

> 63 <

ENTRY #5: CAMELOT—that slight tremor you feel is Jackie and Marilyn rolling over in their graves every time someone refers to the assassinations as the end of an innocent age.
    —from *Bullshit in America*, by Wolfgang Schmitt

We took my car. I told her we'd come back for hers in the morning, and if it wasn't there, we'd just write a check and forget about it. Such was the mindset of the newly-minted rich.

She wanted to go to her place. She had a suite at the Marriott, with an ocean view and an in-room Jacuzzi. I had a little cottage just a short walk from the bar district, with a mosquito net over the deck and a resident lizard named Jake that liked to occupy the sidewalk right in front of the door.

She didn't press it when I insisted we go to my place. I told her I had champagne on ice, which did the trick. Based on the things she did to me in the car, she was too hot to care where it happened. Only that it was soon.

I lit the candles while she opened the bottle of Dom, which I did indeed have in a bucket of ice. She was pleased that I was now sharing her love of fine wine, which had always been something I'd belittled and she'd complained about.

Everything, it seemed, was different now.

My heart was beating so fast I had to sit down, choosing the bed as my destination. In my mind, I saw my calcium deposits disintegrating into saltlike sprinkles of cardiac death.

"What's wrong?" she asked, reading my expression.

"Just a little nervous."

She came to me on the bed, smiling coyly. She'd always preferred me a little on the nervous side, I think.

"Medicine," she said, handing me a glass, holding her own in front of me. "To money. To forgiveness. To the great sex in which we are about to imbibe. To us."

God, she was beautiful. My eyes actually welled up as we clinked the plastic glasses together, witnessing the joy she was sharing with me at that moment.

We began to kiss. Tracy had always been the aggressor, the one who pushed me down, working her lips south from my neck as she undid the buttons on my shirt, usually stopping for a good nibble on my oh-so-sensitive nipples.

She got to the third button of my Tommy Bahama shirt—bought at the Miami airport two days ago—when I felt her freeze. Hanging from a thin gold chain, directly between my greatly diminished pectoral muscles, was a metal disk about the size of a quarter. Which, on any other Caribbean stud, would have been fashionably routine. But my Tracy had an infallible memory, and at this moment, it was telling her I wouldn't wear a gold chain around my neck unless I was doing a Wayne Newton impression. Not ever. A latent self-image bugaboo of mine.

BAIT AND SWITCH

She held it up, turned it over. It was obvious this was no St. Christopher medal. Too high-tech. Too James Bond. And thanks to the word "Motorola" imprinted on the back, too obvious. She tapped it with a fingernail. Then she looked up at me, the smug smile gone, comprehension washing over her like unwanted rain.

"Why?" she asked, her voice betraying her.

It was the tapping that did it. Within moments, the door burst open, admitting four federal agents to the room, all with drawn guns. The first guy in was flashing a badge.

One of them pulled her off me, gently at first, then with impatient force when it was apparent she would not go without a struggle that involved the clawing out of my eyes. He quickly pulled her upright, cuffing her wrists behind her back.

"Why?" she repeated, her eyes blazing.

I wanted desperately to look away. But that would betray us both, lend the moment a sense of cowardice it didn't deserve. I had nothing to say to her; I owed her nothing at all. Except, in homage to our past, the courage to engage her eyes.

That, I owed to myself.

"Tracy Ericson," said one of the agents, the one I'd been working with all these months, "you are under arrest, to be charged with the murders of Boyd Gavin, Kelly Scott, and Lee Van Wyke, and other federal crimes to be specified at your arraignment."

Without pausing for breath, he went on to read the obligatory Miranda rights.

With her eyes locked on mine, she again mouthed the word "Why," hearing nothing the man said. Her face was all raw and passionate rage, tempered with the pain of betrayal. I knew the feeling. Mine had done the same on the day she'd walked out, telling me she just didn't love me enough, that I wasn't "the one."

I continued to hold her gaze. That wasn't the reason we were here. I'd gotten over *that* weeks ago.

No, this was about the first day of the rest of *my* life.

They guided her toward the door. The agent I'd come to refer to as Sherlock because it made him laugh looked at me and said, "You're good, despite the rumors."

I nodded, our eyes cementing a deal struck weeks ago in an office with bad furniture and dull lighting.

Tracy fought, not to escape so much as to linger another moment, struggling to keep her line of sight on my eyes.

"Why, dammit? Answer me!"

I did. Not because I felt I owed it to her, or that I gave a damn what she thought. I answered because I owed it to me.

"One of us needs to get a life," I said.

Finally, efficiently, she was gone. I knew I wouldn't see her again until I testified at her trial. I wondered if she'd still look me in the eye then.

By that time, everything would be different. Hell, it was different already.

I had cut the deal with the FBI myself, sans lawyer, shortly after my meeting at the Aurora airport with the man passing himself off as the regional FBI honcho. Something about it hadn't clicked for me, so I wrote down the serial number on the tail and called the ever-vigilant Blaine, who happened to have a buddy who happened to be a civil servant in Idaho, and he traced it to a charter service working out of the San Jose airport. Not exactly an IRS hub, and not likely the regional honcho would charter a twenty-year-old Lear and pass it off as his personal transportation. I also suspected that the only thing special about Agents Banger and Short was the sheer audacity of their schtick, so in spite of their caution, I contacted the local office of the FBI—and you thought I just waltzed into this mess with a thumb up my ass—who, to my great surprise, already had pictures of the imposters in their possession.

They were, of course, way ahead of me. People going around impersonating IRS officials just wasn't right. They asked me if I would consider playing along for a while, see where it all went, be of service to my country. When I explained that I was already committed, and at a very nice price indeed, they dropped the bomb that would eventually change my life.

Just as Banger and Short had promised—but with no connection to them whatsoever—I would get to keep whatever money Nelson Scott paid me. As long as I didn't break the law, as long as I cooperated with the Agency, and as long as I paid my fair share of taxes on the proceeds. Whatever was left in the offshore account at the end of it all would be mine to keep. Call it a consulting fee, for purposes of my Form 1040. They would grease it with the IRS to look the other way—hey, they owed me one—in case some ambitious young auditor in Salt Lake City got a little loose with his inventory of red flags.

It was a one-time-only offer, and I jumped at it. For me, it was a one-time-only opportunity to reinvent myself.

I never told anyone about my feelings for Kelly Scott. Those warm emotions had certainly been cooled by the news that she was delighted to have a role in my demise. And while it certainly validated my place as the chump in this *Masterpiece Theatre*, it also told me my heart, pre-disclosure, was not as dead as I'd feared. That maybe I could love again, put Tracy behind me, and move on.

Amazing, though, how quickly a little homicidal intent helps you to get over it.

I was as surprised as the next guy when the bodies started dropping. What the San Jose police thought was a quick call to my lawyer was in fact a call to Sherlock, my federal handler, who arranged the Portland attorney for me as a way to buy some time and make everything look like standard operating procedure. The stand-in lawyer for my first day of questioning had, in fact, been a rookie FBI agent acting the part, who coached me to unleash my version of the story unedited, which of course played nicely into Tracy's take on things. This, in turn, allowed Nelson Scott to relax, sensing that he just might get out of this with his cummerbund unscathed.

The golden goose needed to sing as she laid the golden egg. The Feds were after the audit all along. And they were willing to give me a lot of rope to make it happen.

Which it did, that night on the beach.

I never told Sherlock that I'd recorded several of the meetings I'd had with him. Because we'd always met in hotels instead of a federal building, there were no metal detectors, no shakedowns, and, where he was concerned, no clue. Lucky for me, however, I never had to play that card. Sherlock and his boys made good on their end, and presumably the IRS was licking its chops for its cut.

Also lucky for me, Tracy had dished on the planting of the forensic evidence by the thugs who'd killed Boyd Gavin. Especially my gun as the murder weapon and strands of my hair taken from my condo in Portland. Even in our conspiracy, the Feds didn't like loose ends, and Tracy had done a good job of tying them off. With a little prompting from me, I must admit.

Turns out Tracy cut a deal, too. In return for her testimony against Scott, for turning over the audit data she'd taken from Wayne Rogers's computer, and for leading authorities to the charred bodies of the two foreign operatives, the charges against her were reduced to manslaughter and her sentence from possible life without parole to twenty years, out in nine with good behavior.

Hell, if the fish is big enough, you can barter your way out of just about anything. Bullshit in America, it seems, lives on.

I sort of liked it in Key West. Killer shrimp, lots of cruise ship ladies looking for someone to show them around—not much competition in that regard, to be honest—significant downtime to work on my book. They're asking me to change all the names, to fictionalize the company and some of the details to protect the guilty. By the time anyone reads this, the audit will have gone public and the stock of the *real* underlying company will have tanked like no stock before it. As for all the dead people involved, my guess is, that part will get buried and forgotten in all the hubbub surrounding the stock. Wouldn't surprise me at all if Nelson—not his real name, of course—gets off scot-free, if you'll pardon the bad pun.

The Feds said they liked the way I handled myself, and asked if I'd be interested in considering another assignment, something where a guy with my business experience and a nose that isn't quite perfect would fit right in. I said I'd think it over, and I just might. Better than advertising, but then again, so is custodial work. No need to rush into anything, though. I've got close to three million in a Cayman account that now bears my name. My accountant back in Portland—I'm nothing if not loyal—says he can't wait to rip into *that* tax return.

Life is good. It goes on, and when it does, you make the best of it or you die not trying. Bullshit comes, bullshit goes, but you've always got options. One of which is to burn the pages.

Like I've always said, shit happens.

But that's just me. Cynical as ever. Some things just don't change, even with a tan.